JESSE'S SMILE

by
Angelique Jurd

Cover: German Creative

* * *

DEDICATION

For Fiona,
who loved Jesse from the first page

* * *

1

Jesse knows he's not stupid. Not retarded, no matter what some people say about him. People who think they are normal. He doesn't understand things the way other people do and sometimes things sometimes get muddled, especially if he's under pressure, but that's not the same thing as stupid. Sometimes at work, if it's busy on a Saturday and he has to work the counter on his own, he gets flustered and makes mistakes. Regulars don't mind, they know him, they're patient. They wait and play with Sniffles, the rabbit that usually sits on the counter. It's the casual customers, the ones who have just dropped in because their regular store is out of their cat's favorite food, who are impatient. Who sometimes snap at him. Call him names. Like the couple in front of him right now. He keeps keying in the wrong product for them even though he knows it's the *Real Dog Organic Mix* for small dogs. It's the green button on the cash register, but it's not giving the right product. The husband keeps talking at him. At him, not to him; asking him if he's a retard or deaf or just stupid. Telling him they'll never be back. It's just been such a busy morning and Debbie didn't show up, so he's been on his own because Mr Greenwold, the store owner, has the flu and can't come in.

"I'm sorry," Jesse mumbles and glares at the cash register. Why won't it give the right price? In frustration, he keys in the price manually, tapping the blue key to code it to dog food.

"About fuckin' time," the man snaps at him and hands over his credit card. His wife is holding a small, shivery dog that is hairless except for long, wavy tufts sticking off its ears. Still glaring at Jesse, she sniffs and stalks off. "What the hell is wrong with the owner? Leavin' a fuckin' retard in charge ..."

"Buddy," the man waiting behind him says and the edge of disgust in his voice makes Jesse glance up. The man has a basket of cat food and litter. "Why don't you just pay for your food and move along. Kid's doing the best he can."

"Why don't you mind your own fuckin' business?"

Rude Guy snatches back his credit card, grabs the bag of food, and follows his wife out of the store, still throwing complaints over his shoulder. As he rounds the door, he knocks over a stand of bird food – Jesse is sure he did it on purpose – and just keeps walking. Jesse sighs and puts his hand out for the basket, eyes still on the register.

"What an asshole." At that, Jesse looks up and the man smiles as he hands him the basket. He's taller than Jesse, with long, sandy blonde hair that falls into chocolate brown eyes framed by wire-rimmed glasses.

Jesse shrugs and begins sorting the contents of the basket. Two boxes of kitten milk, some cans of food, a litter tray and litter, and a food dish.

"You have a kitten," he says.

"Seems that way," the guys replies but Jesse can't hear any mocking in his tone and when he looks up again, he can see amusement dancing in his eyes. "Got home from work last night and it was sitting on my doorstep. I came down, but you were closed so I just had to make do."

"Why don't you take it to a shelter?"

The guy smiles again. Jesse blinks; usually his directness is met with defensiveness.

"I live alone, be nice to have some company," he says. "Not that I know much about kittens."

Jesse nods. Not many people do, most just don't admit it. He looks away.

"You should probably get it some toys. They like these little catnip mice. And we have some wands over there with feathers on them." He points to the aisle of cat toys. "But if you scrunch up some paper they'll be happy with that. They'll chase a piece of string too."

The guy laughs.

"I don't think you're meant to talk me out of the sale, kid."

Jesse's face flushes red and he starts ringing up the items.

"I'm not a kid," he mutters.

"Huh?"

Jesse can hear the surprise in the man's voice.

"I'm not a kid," he says again, feeling defensive. "I'm twenty-six."

"Oh, sorry. I didn't mean anything by it."

"I know I look like a kid but I'm not. And I'm not stupid," he blurts out. Then because he's still annoyed by the couple with the dog food, adds, "or deaf."

The guy laughs again.

"Okay, I hear you. I'm as bad as the asshole ahead of me and I apologize," he says. Jesse frowns; that wasn't what he meant, but the guy is still talking. "You better add in one of those catnip mice while we're here."

Jesse adds the toy and reads the total out. He catches his breath when he sees the guy is paying in cash but lets it go when he has the exact change. Counting back change is Jesse's biggest nightmare because he's slow, has to think about each bill and each coin and people always get impatient. Even the regulars.

"Let me give you a hand to pick up the stuff he kicked over."

Jesse steps back from the register, startled.

"It's okay, I can do it. I'm going to shut for lunch and to tidy up. It won't take me long."

"You sure?'

He nods.

"Well, okay, then. Thanks for that."

"You're welcome," Jesse mumbles and follows him to the door, steps over the mess of bird food containers and closes the door behind the guy. Flips the OUT TO LUNCH sign over, gives a quick return of the wave the guy gives him, before picking up the fallen containers. He sighs, Saturday afternoons are usually a bit quieter so if he can survive until six, he can lock up and go home and spend the night watching Netflix. Maybe he'll pick up some beer and a pizza on his way home.

* * *

2

Jesse trudges up the stairs to his apartment on the third floor. It's small and compact –just one bedroom, a bathroom, and a minute kitchen off living room. But it's his. When his Grandpa died, he'd left Jesse some money and with a little help from his parents for the legal papers and to get a small mortgage, he'd bought this place. At first Mom hadn't liked the idea, but Dad thought it was great, and Jesse loves having his own place. It makes him feel normal. He knows where everything is and doesn't have to worry he's disturbing other people. He hates being a nuisance.

He unlocks the door and puts the beer and pizza on the table, edges lined up. Places the mail on his desk in the corner, by his computer; he spreads the envelopes out in a fan, so he can see where each one is from, running his finger under the words and saying each one out loud to himself. Later he'll open them and if he can't make sense of any, will put them aside to get Dad to help him with. He shouldn't need to do that though, there's only a mailer, the gas bill, and he thinks the other one is insurance but he's not sure. If it is he can pay them using his online account tomorrow. Turns back and locks the door, slides the chain over. Crosses the room and slides the curtains shut. Checks the cushions on the sofa are in the right order: green, white, green, white. Goes to his bedroom. Closes the curtains, checks the pillows on his bed are in the right spots: flat, openings toward the walls. On the dresser is a battered soft toy, Wicket, the Ewok from Star Wars; Jesse runs a hand over it as he passes. Once forward, once back, and relaxes.

Back in the kitchen, he opens a bottle of beer and the pizza box and counts the slices. Good, there are eight. He doesn't like it when there are ten – they're not the right size for chewing. Six is okay but eight is best. He can have four for dinner, two later if he gets hungry watching Netflix, and the last two tomorrow for breakfast. Jesse slides four slices on to a plate, puts it on the coffee table next to the beer and goes in search of the remote. He piles up the cushions, making sure they can't topple, and sits down.

The first slice is always the best in Jesse's opinion. It's still hot and the cheese is melted and gooey, so the texture is right; he likes it best like that. As he sips his beer he thinks over the day. Mr Greenwold would have come in but Jesse could hear how clogged up he was when he'd phoned to tell him Debbie had bailed. Even through the wet, sick sound of his voice though, Jesse had been able to hear the anger and knows Debbie might get fired. Jesse won't be sorry to see her go; she's lazy, she calls him stupid all the time, and he's sure she's mean to the animals when she thinks nobody is looking. Jesse is also sure she changed the register buttons too, so this will probably be it for Mr Greenwold. The only problem is it will mean Jesse has to do more of the counter work until they find someone to replace her and when they do, he'll have to get used to someone new all over again … he sighs. There's no point worrying about it now.

He turns the television on, brings up Netflix, and scrolls through looking for stills he recognizes so he doesn't have to try and read the words. Grins when he sees The Terminator and presses play. Dropping the remote back on the sofa, he picks up the second slice of pizza and lets his thoughts wander to the nice guy with the kitten. For a moment, he closes his eyes and sees the wide, open smile and big brown eyes in his mind. He said he lived alone so that meant he wasn't married; not that that means anything Jesse knows. There's probably a girlfriend who will end up taking care of the kitten and the floppy blonde hair. Jesse wonders what it would be like to have someone like that to care for you – someone kind, who speaks up for you, and then who comes home to you at night. Of course, there's mom and dad, they love him, they speak up for him if they hear anyone bullying him, and they always try to encourage him whenever he wants to do something. But it would be nice to have someone to watch a movie with or to curl up with in bed. And yes, even someone to have sex with.

In Jesse's experience – which is admittedly limited – your chances of finding someone for those things are limited if you aren't interested in girls and you're …. Not stupid. Not retarded. Jesse knows people think he's good looking. He has short dark hair, high cheekbones, and his mother insists he has beautiful eyes that change color. He's looked in the mirror for hours on end and all he ever sees is hazel. Whatever color they are, is immaterial because as soon as people figure out that he's not their idea of normal, they might stay long enough for sex but that's about all. Sometimes not even that. Nobody wants a relationship with a guy who works in a pet store and sometimes needs his Dad to help him read his bills, no matter how good looking he is.

Arnold appears from the future, crouched down and hulking, ready to begin hunting Sarah Connor and Jesse thinks again how nice it would be to have someone to watch with.

* * *

5

3

Drew Oliver shuts down his web browser and bends to scoop up the little bundle of black fur sitting at his feet. Holds it in the palm of his hand and smiles at the small face. He's never really had a pet of his own before, unless you count Bubbles, the goldfish he had when he was eight. Which he doesn't.

"Bubbles wasn't exactly big on cuddles," he tells the kitten. "What are we going to call you then?"

The kitten bats at his fingers with a tiny paw and makes a squeaky mewling sound.

"What about Scamp? You certainly are one," he says, pulling the small creature in closer. The kitten head-bumps his chin and purrs. Drew chuckles and pushes back his chair, takes the kitten to his bedroom and deposits it on a pillow, watches while it curls its tail around itself and dozes off. He goes back to the kitchen, picks up his plate of macaroni, pours himself a scotch, and retrieves the bundle of essays he needs to finish marking for his third period Monday, senior English class from his desk. Back in the bedroom, he sighs. Not really the way he wants to spend his Saturday evening but since he's kitty sitting he figures he may as well get it done and out of the way. Tomorrow he can see if Jody wants to go the movies or something.

Settling against the headboard, Drew finds the remote among the books on his bedside table and flicks on the screen hanging on the opposite wall. Finishes his macaroni as he scrolls through the Netflix menu. The Terminator has been added; he rolls his eyes and clicks play. If you're going to spend Saturday night looking after strays and marking essays, you may as well add Schwarzenegger. And besides, Arnie had been at his peak at the time so why not indulge in a little eye candy?

He puts his empty plate on top of the battered copy of Gatsby on his bedside table and picks up his glass; pushes his hair back out of his eyes, tucks the length under his collar. Drew knows that almost all the girls he teaches – and at least half a dozen boys – have crushes on him. Carol Anderson from the Art department has asked him out twice, the second time she'd had that ever hopeful 'maybe I can change him' look. Mademoiselle Jacqueline, the visiting French assistant had hit on him at the last staff function until Jody Lambert, the librarian, took her aside and whispered in her ear. From across the room where he was discussing curriculum funding cuts with Greg Taylor, he'd seen the young French woman's eyes widen before she shook her head and proceeded to argue with Jody. Jody had slung an arm around her shoulders, and directed her toward the bar, turning back to grin at him and give him a discreet thumbs-up. Drew and Jody hang out together a lot, setting each other up on dates with friends they think might suit. So far, they've all been disasters for both of them. Neither of them cares.

That thought leads him to this morning's encounter in the pet shop. The couple in front of him with the pampered pooch that looked as though it might provide his feline guest with a meal or two, had pissed him off. The way they treated the kid on the counter - the guy on the counter, he amends, recalling his scolding – was disgusting. It was clear to Drew, possibly because he's been teaching now for nearly ten years and can see signs other people can't, that the guy has some challenges. Whatever his challenges are though, at least he's not an ignorant asshat like the guy he was serving. Looking at him – after the scolding – Drew had seen a face that should be on magazine covers. His eyes alone would make him money, Drew thought. They were gold, more than hazel, and glimmered with intelligence but there was something else, something he couldn't quite name. Not fear. Wariness perhaps.

Sighing he puts the whiskey back on his bedside table and picks up his red pen. Okay, let's see just how badly this year's batch is going to mangle Shakespeare.

* * *

4

A light rain is falling when Drew leaves school on Tuesday afternoon. He glances at his watch, cursing; it's nearly five thirty. Auditions for the school production stretched later than he'd planned, he has a headache tapping at his left temple, and now he has to hurry to make it to the pet store.

He could, he supposes, get the kitten's food from the supermarket but he doesn't really spend his money on much, so he may as well spoil the furry little terrorist that has taken over his life. Besides, there are worse things than getting another glimpse of those unusual eyes.

Drew gives himself a mental slap. The last thing he needs to be doing is fantasizing about pretty boy shop assistants; he just needs to go get the cat food for Scamp and go home, finish today's marking, and sleep.

It's a five-minute drive to downtown, where the pet store is, but by the time he finds a park, it's nearly six and an older man is packing up the street displays.

"Are you still open? I'll be quick, I promise," Drew pants, ignoring the pang of disappointment that it's not the kid – guy – from Saturday.

"Of course, take your time," the old guy smiles, "I haven't closed the register yet."

"Thanks, I'll be as fast as I can."

Drew lopes down the aisle to the cat supplies. He selects a variety of cans, cradling them in his arms and looks at the accessories. The vet he took her to on Monday said he should get her a collar with a name tag and a cave and ... A basket appears under his nose and he looks up into golden eyes.

"You need a basket," the kid says, flicking those unusual eyes away. Is that laughter dancing in them? He thinks maybe it is.

"I didn't want to keep you guys waiting, I know you're closing," Drew says dropping the cans in the basket with a sigh of relief and taking it.

"Mr Greenwold stays open as long as there are customers."

Drew nods and goes back to looking at the accessories in confusion.

"Do you need some help?"

"Yeah," he admits and rubs his temple again. "The vet said I should get her a cave or a basket and a tree and I don't even know what the hell I'm looking for."

The younger man smiles, and it takes Drew by surprise; he thinks his heart might actually stop beating because that smile is honest-to-God beautiful. That thought is followed by a mental slap – heart might stop beating? Really? Drama queen much? He snorts at the pun. He realizes the smile is fading, which is a shame because it really is stunning. Drew shakes his head.

"Sorry, brain fart."

"Um okay." The smile is gone now, his eyes averted again, to Drew's disappointment, and he's chewing his lip – which, Drew is somewhat mortified to note, is almost as hot as the smile. "I can show you what we've got."

* * *

Drew selects a fuzzy, grey, two-tier cat tree with a cave at the top. Jesse – the old guy called him by name while they were looking at collars – assures him it will be easy to assemble but Drew looks doubtful. He adds a bright pink collar with a name disk he can get engraved over the weekend and a water fountain. Grins when he takes back his credit card.

"Thanks for your help Jesse. I'm obviously in way over my head."

"That's okay, it's kind of my job," Jesse replies fiddling with a box of puppy snacks on the counter in front of him. A black and white lop-eared rabbit that appears to have the run of the counter, nuzzles at his fingers. "What kind of cat is it?"

"A black, fluffy one," Drew says, deadpan. People keep asking him that question as though the creature came with some kind of label announcing its breed.

The vet said she was at least part Angora or Persian which as far as Drew can tell means he is going to be picking cat hair off his clothes for eternity. Jesse is grinning, the tip of his tongue caught between his teeth, which Drew finds makes it very hard to concentrate.

"I hope you've got one of those sticky roller things, then," Jesse says, echoing Drew's own thoughts. He's peering up from under long, thick lashes and Drew has more trouble thinking. "Do you need a hand to get this stuff out to the car?"

"I don't want to put you to any trouble..." Drew says and he doesn't, but he does want to keep talking to Jesse.

"It's okay, I'll just tell Mr Greenwold."

Drew puts the tray of cat food cans on top of the cat tree box. Jesse appears with his jacket, collects the water fountain and collar, and holds the door open.

"This is me," Drew says stopping next to his Honda and putting the box on the ground. He fumbles in his pocket for his keys. "Thanks, you've been a great help."

Jesse's face has closed again and he's zipping his jacket against the light, misty rain.

"Uh, you're welcome. I hope she likes her tree. Bye."

He turns and walks away, leaving Drew standing in the rain.

"What the hell?" he mutters to himself as he gets in the car. He peers through the windscreen, but Jesse has already disappeared into the crowd.

* * *

"Someone has a crush," Jody says topping up their glasses.

"Oh, do fuck off," Drew says, shaking his head. "I do not. Besides he's probably straight."

"So?" Jody retorts. "You're gay and the entire female student body has a crush on you."

Drew flips his middle finger in her direction and goes to the kitchen to get the lemon meringue pie she brought. Balances it on one hand and collects dishes and spoons with the other.

"You know who he reminds me of? His mannerisms I mean," Drew says as he serves them each some pie. "That Anderson kid, the way he avoids looking at you. Only this guy's not as withdrawn. Whatever he has, he's really high functioning."

"Maybe he doesn't have anything," Jody says. "Maybe he's just shy. Or anxious."

"No," Drew shakes his head, "there's more to it than that."

"Well, I only have two things to say on the subject," Jody says and Drew rolls his eyes.

"I somehow doubt that darlin'," he says.

"Bite me," she says around a mouthful of pie. "Why don't you just ask and find out? That way you'll know."

"And the other thing?"

"You do not want a repeat of David."

Drew sighs. He and David were together for close to two years. The first six months had been fun. Lots of laughter and sex and being a couple. The last ten months had been a nightmare as David spent more and more time and money getting stoned and drunk while Drew drove himself and his friends mad trying to save him.

Finally, it had fallen apart in a spectacular fashion and Jody had helped him find this apartment and put himself back together again over the past year.

"Drew," Jody's voice pulls him out of his thoughts. "You can't save them all."

"I know," he says and can tell by the look on Jody's face that she doesn't believe him, but she doesn't press it.

"In that case, I'll have more pie."

10

* * *

5

Max Greenwold doesn't consider himself to be an especially worldly man, but he believes he knows how to read people. And he thinks he has a fairly good idea what the tall drink of water with the ponytail and glasses, the guy from last night who is now standing in front of him, is interested in, and it sure as hell is not the kitten supplies he is clutching in one large hand.

"Is uh Jesse in today?" the guy is asking him.

"On his lunch break," Max says, not unkindly as he continues to size him up. "Can I help?"

"Oh, yeah probably. I bought a cat tree from here last night and Jesse said it would be really easy to assemble but um I can't figure the damned thing out ..."

The guy's voice trails off and if the red stain creeping up his cheeks is anything to go by he's not lying. Max doesn't revise his earlier observation though; he'd seen how the guy watched Jesse. A lot of their customers look at Jesse like that, but nearly all of them are female and Max knows the kid isn't interested. The fact that this guy asked for Jesse rather than just asking Max himself how to put the tree together makes Max think he's looking for more than just help on the tree. That's fine and dandy, and Jesse is his own man. Except, thinks Max, in many ways he isn't, and he doesn't want to see him hurt so he's just going to take his time and make sure this guy is on the level. He reaches for the bag of kitty litter the guy appears to have forgotten.

"Jesse could probably put it together for you if you bring it in," Max says as he rings up the sale.

"I'd pay him."

"Well that's up to Jesse." Max takes the credit card.

"I'm hopeless with anything like that," the guy continues. Blinks behind the glasses and licks his lips. "English teacher. Totally useless with a screwdriver. Unless it's the kind with vodka in it. I probably should have just bought one of the already assembled ones."

His voice trails off again and Max guesses he's realized he's babbling. In his book the babbling wins him some points. He could have hit on Jesse at the time, invited him home to put the tree together but he hadn't. Max takes pity on him.

"When can you bring it in?"

"I have it in the car."

Another point. Teach might have realized he has a way to see Jesse again but he isn't trying anything funny Max doesn't think.

"Okay, go get it and I'll get Jesse to take a look at it this afternoon," he says. "Call back in after school and hopefully it will be ready."

* * *

6

"Jesse, you almost finished?" Mr Greenwold asks.

Jesse nods without looking up from the screw he's twisting in place. Knows the guy with the kitten is standing in the doorway behind his boss but can't make himself to look up.

"Yeah, just two more screws."

"Oh man, you are a lifesaver." Jesse likes the sound of the guy's voice. "It looks great. Hope it'll fit in my car now."

Jesse frowns and tries to remember the car. Nods and says it should.

"It's not as big as you and you fit in your car."

Mr Greenwold and the guy both laugh. Jesse shrugs, he must have said something funny. People are weird he thinks, as he reaches for the final screw and begins fixing it in place. The buzzer sounds and Mr Greenwold excuses himself to go back out to the store.

"I'm Drew Oliver," the guy says, and a hand appears in Jesse's line of vision. Jesse eyes it for a moment, then puts the screwdriver down and shakes it. "I teach English over at Central High School."

Jesse nods and picks up the plastic cap that will cover the head of the screw. Taps it in place and stands the tree up.

"Wow, that's amazing," Drew says with a grin and reaches into his pocket. "How much do I owe you?"

Embarrassed Jesse shakes his head and mumbles that there's no charge. It took him less than half an hour. Silence surrounds them for a moment.

"Well can I buy you a beer?" Drew asks.

"Why?" Jesse asks, head jerking up.

"Because I'd like to say thanks."

Jesse hesitates.

"You really did me a favor and I'd like to say thanks, that's all."

Drew is smiling still, and Jesse bites his lip. Rubs the back of his neck and eventually nods.

"Okay."

* * *

Pepperjacks is a small bar, across the road from the pet store, specializing in craft beer and steak sandwiches. Jesse knows it well enough for the bartender to nod hello while Drew orders for them. They take the bottles and find a table by the window; Drew stands the cat tree next to the table and grins.

"I probably should have put that in the car," he says.

Feeling awkward, and unsure how to respond, Jesse rubs his thumb back in forth in the condensation forming on his beer bottle. Once he starts, he can't stop until the bottle has been wiped clear of moisture. Panic bubbles up in the back of his throat and when Drew asks him a question, he resists the urge to mumble a goodbye and run.

For a while they talk about his job at the pet store and then about why he likes working with animals – his answer that they're not people makes Drew laugh. Jesse likes how it sounds – a lot – and relaxes a little. Drew tells him about his work as a school teacher and when he asks if he'd like another beer, Jesse nods. It's nice to not be by himself for a change and he's wishes he didn't have to go home. While he's waiting for Drew to come back with the beer, Mr Greenwold walks past the window and looks in. He looks surprised and glances behind Jesse at the bar, nods, then smiles and keeps walking.

"Here you go," Drew says putting a beer in front of him. "I ordered us a couple of their steak sandwiches too, I'm starving."

"Oh," Jesse says. He's supposed to pay for his own things, Dad says, so that people don't think he owes them something. "I can pay for mine."

A foot taps his ankle and he jumps. Drew grins at him.

"Don't be a dork, you can pay next time."

Next time? What does he mean next time? Jesse frowns as he tries to make his brain process everything and get the words to line up with their meanings. It's not easy at the best of times and he's had a beer so it's even harder. What does he mean by next time?

"Do you have a girlfriend?" he blurts finally, cheeks bright red. The urge to flee is back and he fights it, sliding his finger along the edge of the table, glancing up now and then at Drew who shakes his head and smiles.

"No," Drew says with a smile. His eyes are serious, and Jesse knows he's being watched. "I, uh, don't date women."

Jesse sips his beer; okay he doesn't date women, but does that mean he's interested in Jesse? Jesse tells himself it's unlikely. The guy is just being nice. Or looking for a quick hook up. He realizes Drew is still speaking and asks him to repeat his last question.

"I asked, what about you?"

"What about me, what?" Jesse asks, confused.

"Women. Do you date women?" There's something about Drew's eyes that makes Jesse feel safe and he shakes his head. Then, because neither playing games nor being subtle are part of his skill range, he tells the truth.

"I'm gay."

Now Drew's smile reaches his eyes.

"Well, okay then," he says.

* * *

Drew slams the door on the cat tree – it did fit on the back seat without any problem –turns around and pushes his glasses up to the bridge of his nose. Jesse who has been watching with his hands shoved in his pockets, searches for something to say.

"Would you like to come and meet Scamp?" Drew asks, making him jump.

"What?"

"The kitten, would you like to come and meet her?"

"Um, when? Now?"

Drew laughs.

"Yeah, if you want, but if you're busy, maybe at the weekend?'

Jesse shakes his head.

"I'm not busy, I can come now."

Was that the right thing to say? Was it too forward? What if this is dangerous? What if he's wrong about this guy?

Drew unlocks the car and holds the door open for him.

"Cool, I'll probably need a hand getting this thing in my apartment anyway," he says.

* * *

7

Overflowing book cases fill the living room of Drew's apartment. There's no television screen in here, just his work desk and computer, two sofas, an armchair, and a lot of books. Even the big framed art prints on the wall have books in them. Everything is white and when Drew flicks the downlights on, Jesse's hiss of discomfort makes him aware for the first time of how blinding the glare is.

"You have lots of books and lots of white," Jesse says, squinting at Drew as if he's in pain.

Drew spins the dimmer dial, easing the light down.

"Better?" Drew asks, relieved when Jesse nods. "It's just kind of easy, you know, because everything goes with it."

"Like black cat hair?"

Drew snorts.

"Yeah, my cleaning lady is probably going to hate me even more than usual," he says. "You want something to drink? Beer? Wine? Coffee?"

"Um, no thanks." He points at the dishes by the kitchen counter. "You should change her water if it's been here all day. It needs to be fresh."

Before he can answer, Drew sees movement and turns as Scamp launches herself at the cat tree. She shimmies her way up the central pole, to the cave on top and pokes her head inside.

"I think we have a winner," Drew says and Jesse flashes that blinding smile again, reaching out to scratch her ears when the tiny face appears in the cave entrance. It's the first time he's really relaxed since they left the store and Drew is surprised how pleased it makes him feel.

"Hello, Scamp," he murmurs. "Aren't you a pretty girl?"

"I don't know if she needs to hear that," Drew says. "I think I'm turning her into a kitty Kardashian."

Jesse laughs and tells Scamp to ignore Drew, he's just jealous of how pretty she is.

"I'll have you know, my students all think I'm pretty," he protests.

"They just want good grades." Jesse continues stroking the small, black head.

"True," Drew agrees and looks at Jesse. "You have a great smile."

"Oh," Jesse drops his head. To Drew's disappointment, the smile has vanished –
again – and embarrassment is coming from the younger man in waves. Drew nudges
his foot with his own and Jesse looks back at him, eyes wary and defensive.

"I mean it," he says. "I was wondering, are you busy on Saturday night?"

"I work until six." Jesse stares at the floor.

"And after?"

"I go home and watch Netflix. Or play video games."

"I thought maybe we could see a movie and get dinner or something," Drew says.
"I could pick you up from work. Or from your place. If you wanted to, I mean."

He's surprised to see Jesse is staring at him, eyes still guarded.

"A movie?" Jesse asks.

"Yeah."

"And dinner?"

"Yeah, and dinner," Drew says with a smile.

"I don't know you," Jesse whispers.

"That's sort of why we need to go to a movie and dinner or something."

"Or something," Jesse echoes, eyes locking on Drew's.

Then, unable to stop himself, Drew leans down and covers Jesse's mouth with his
own. Feels Jesse catch his breath and draws back a little.

"Is that okay?" he asks.

Jesse nods.

"Can I do it again?"

Jesse nods again and this time a timid hand slides around Drew's waist as his
eyes shut and he leans into the kiss. Drew slides his tongue across the seam of
Jesse's mouth and is rewarded by him parting his lips and meeting it with his own.
Drew breaks the kiss and pulls back, breathing hard, and rests his forehead on
Jesse's.

"Do you have a cell phone?" Drew asks and leans forward to kiss him one more
time.

"Hmmmm?"

"Do you have a cell phone? So, I can get your number."

For a moment panic fills Jesse's face, and Drew is sure he's going to bolt for the
door. Instead, he fishes in his jacket pocket and takes out a small, battered smart-
phone. Drew waits and when Jesse doesn't offer a number begins to rattle off his
own. He stops when he realizes Jesse isn't moving.

"What's wrong?" he asks.

"Um," Jesse stutters. Blushes and chews his lip, looks uncomfortable. He fiddles
with the cell phone, then seems to decide and shoves the device in Drew's hand.
"Can you put your number in for me. It'll be quicker."

"Okay, yeah no problem. Is the screen locked?"

Jesse shakes his head and Drew can feel him trembling as he swipes his thumb across the screen. There are hardly any apps on the screen he notices as he taps the *Contacts* icon. When he opens it, he notices two things: the few entries in it all have photos by the names and the back screen is pale green. He enters his details and looks up. Jesse is looking at his feet again and even his ears are red.

"Jesse, are you dyslexic?" Drew asks, voice gentle.

"Yes." Jesse's extraordinary eyes glimmer with fear, but he lifts his chin and sets his shoulders; Drew leans forward to kiss him before speaking again.

"It's okay, I have several dyslexic students at school," he says when he breaks the kiss. "Can you send me a text, so I can get your number?"

Jesse nods and takes back the phone. He hesitates and then clears his throat.

"Can ... can I take a picture of you to put in the contacts book? Or of Scamp? It's just easier than the letters."

Drew reaches into the cat cave and scoops Scamp out. Holds her against his cheek, ignoring the tail flicking against his neck.

"How about both of us?" he says and is pleased when he gets a shy smile as Jesse clicks a photo. Waits, while Jesse taps on the screen, frowning in concentration, tip of his tongue in the corner of his mouth – mouth Drew, wants very much to kiss again but his own phone chiming stops him. Waves it at Jesse.

"Now we're good to go," he says.

"I should go home," Jesse says as if reading his mind. "It's getting late."

"Want me to drive you?"

"No. I get the nine-oh-six."

"You sure? I don't mind."

"Yeah, I'm sure," Jesse says.

Before Drew can do anything else, he's let himself out the door.

* * *

Drew is waiting for the kettle to boil while he rubs at his damp hair with a towel. After watching from the window until Jesse disappeared around the corner he'd all but dived into the shower, desperate to relieve some of the kiss induced tension. Feeling happy and sleepy, he's making tea to take to bed while he reads. On the counter his phone chimes. Jesse's name floats on the screen.

Other things too. I can tell you Satdy.

Puzzled, Drew taps back a reply.

Other things?

It's ten minutes before he gets an answer.

I have other things. Not just dislecsic.

Smiling at the typos, Drew fills his cup with hot water and jiggles the tea bag while he thinks. Obviously, whatever he has in addition to his dyslexia embarrasses Jesse and his self-esteem seems fragile. Not unusual or even that surprising, and Drew doesn't want to make things worse. His attraction is genuine, and he doesn't think he's trying to rescue him – though Jody will probably argue that point – he just doesn't want to say the wrong thing and make – oh screw it. The guy's not a kid, whatever issues he may have. Nobody's perfect, right? He picks his phone up, reminds himself to keep the phrases simple.

Drink on Friday night? Pepperjacks at 7. You can tell me about the other things, so we can relax on Saturday.

Five minutes later his phone chimes again. He grins at the smiley face, sends one back, collects his tea, and goes to see what horrors lay within tonight's marking.

* * *

8

Pepperjacks is already full, music and laughter spilling out around diners and drinkers when Jesse arrives on Friday night. He'd meant to find a table and wait inside but there are so many people and so much noise, he freezes at the doorway. There's a crazy flip-flop sensation in his gut when he sees Drew crossing the street, dressed in faded jeans and a plain black tee-shirt under a denim jacket. His long hair brushes against his shoulders as he jogs toward Jesse.

"Hi," he says with a grin, "am I late?"

Jesse shakes his head.

"No."

"Cool. Want to go in?"

Jesse hesitates. He really wants to do this but it's so noisy in there and he's not sure if he can take the stimulation. Drew's still waiting for an answer, one eyebrow raised.

"It's really noisy in there," Jesse says and scratches the back of his neck. Drew holds his hand up - wait – steps inside, looks around and comes back out.

"You're right, it's packed. I know a place a couple of blocks over that's usually pretty quiet if you don't mind the walk."

Grateful, Jesse nods and let's Drew steer him up the street. During the five-minute walk to *The Library Bar*, Drew asks Jesse about his day, nodding at his answers as if he's really interested, something Jesse isn't quite sure he believes yet. Eyes fixed on the footpath, Jesse has just plucked up the courage to ask Drew how his day was when they arrive in front of a small bar with heavily curtained windows. Drew pushes the door open and when he steps inside, Jesse is struck by how cool and quiet it is. Not like any bar he's ever known. The lighting is soft and muted and instead of leaner tables, there are low coffee tables and armchairs. The far wall is covered by a floor to ceiling bookcase full of books. His eyes widen, and he catches his breath.

"It's okay, they're just for decoration," Drew says in his ear. "You don't have to read them."

Jesse spins to look at him but sees no malice in Drew's face.

"We can read if you want to," Drew continues, a smile twitching his mouth up, "but I'd really rather talk to you."

Jesse follows him to table in the corner, head down, eyes darting from side to side as he tries to take in his surroundings. There's a couple seated over by the bar, foreheads brushing as they talk and occasionally kiss, fingers entwined; at one of the other tables, two women are curled up in armchairs, reading and sipping red wine. Behind the bar are more bookshelves but these ones only have a few wine books, the rest of the space is taken with bottles. An old-fashioned blackboard has a list of the kitchen's specials.

"What would you like to drink?" Drew asks.

Jesse blinks. He doesn't know what to answer, he's never been anywhere like this before.

"I don't know," he says, hoping he doesn't sound as lame as he thinks he does. "Um could you choose, and I'll just pay? It's my turn."

Drew looks surprised but nods. He raises his hand and a waiter seems to appear out of nowhere. He orders two glasses of wine and the cheese platter then turns to Jesse.

""That okay? Do you like cheese?"

"I love cheese. It's one of my favorites," Jesse says and is pleased when Drew agrees with him. "I don't know much about wine though. Or cheese either. Except I like it."

Drew laughs but Jesse, sure now he's not being laughed at, doesn't mind. The waiter appears and puts two glasses of red wine and a plate with wedges of cheese, a circle of wafer-thin crackers, and a small mound of fruit paste on the table between them. Jesse adjusts the square platter so its straight with a glass at each corner and is counting the wedges of cheese when he realizes Drew is watching him in silence. Embarrassed he sits back, fighting the urge to continue counting. It tugs at him like an insect bite he wants to scratch, leaving him feeling exposed and defensive.

"I'm not retarded," he says. The slight echo of his voice in the near-empty room makes the other patrons look up.

"I didn't think you were," Drew says, his tone mild. It's obvious even to Jesse that that isn't exactly true, that he knows something is different about Jesse, he's just not sure what. "I'm guessing a lot of people do though."

Jesse nods, misery etched on his face.

"Well," Drew says, "those people are dicks."

Jesse's mouth drops open in surprise, as Drew continues speaking. Usually, normal people find excuses for why people say stuff that is insulting or hurtful. They don't usually take Jesse's side.

"But you know how you don't like it when people make assumptions about you?" he says. Jesse nods. "Well, I don't like it either. So why don't you explain it to me, so I understand."

His voice is firm but not angry and Jesse wonders if that's how he speaks to his students. Biting his lip, he makes himself look Drew in the eye and nods again.

"I have to count things on plates. I can't help it, I have to make sure the numbers are even."

He holds his breath, rubbing his finger along the edge of the table, as he waits for the laughter or, worse, the pity. Instead Drew nods and picks his wine glass up, eyes flicking toward the platter.

"And? Is it?" he asks.

Astounded, Jesse blinks for a moment, then he looks back at the plate. His eyes dart from the cheese to the fruit paste to the crackers and back again.

"There's crackers, cheese, and paste. That's only three things. And there are eleven crackers, so that means there are thirteen things altogether. " He sighs. "It's okay."

Drew moves forward, examines the platter and picks up the cheese knife. Curious, Jesse watches as he separates out the cheese wedges into four groups.

"Look there are four different types of cheese," Drew says. "This is a brie, a soft white cheese. This one's Edam I think, which is a very hard, cooked cheese. This one's a blue cheese, so it's quite strong and smelly. And this is a sheep's cheese. So that's four types of cheese, crackers, and fruit paste. That makes six. And um sixteen I think if we count the crackers separately."

He looks up at Jesse, grinning.

"Does that help?" he asks. "Or we could ask the waiter to bring another plate and we can fix it that way."

Jesse laughs and that feels good. Really good.

"It's okay and if we get another plate one will probably be uneven again because of the number of crackers," he says reaching for his glass. He takes a small sip; when spicy cherry flavors coat his tongue, he takes another one. "That's really nice. I don't usually drink wine. It tastes weird, but this is nice."

Drew hands him a cracker with a slice of sheep's cheese on it. Sits back to watch while he nibbles at it.

"So, you're dyslexic and you need to count," Drew says. "Is it Obsessive Compulsive or is it part of some other syndrome?"

Jesse frowns, processing the question, and flapping his hand at Drew when it looks as though he's going to speak again.

"I'm dyslexic," he says, fixing his eyes on the wine in his glass, "and I have Mears-Irlen Syndrome which is sort of a stress thing for eyes that makes it really hard to read. Lots of ..."

"It's okay, I know what that is. It's why you have a colored screen on your phone, right?" Drew says, and Jesse flashes him a grateful smile and nods.

"I have some OCD things, like counting and I like things to be in certain orders or I start feeling weird."

"Okay. What kinds of things?"

"I have cushions on my sofa at home and they have to be in the right order. Green, white, green, white."

"Not white, green, white, green?" Drew asks over the top of his wine glass. Jesse looks at him trying to decide if he's joking or not.

"Are you trying to be funny?" he asks. The question is genuine.

"And failing at it obviously," Drew says. Jesse thinks about that for a moment.

"Don't be a dork," he says, unsure if that's okay.

"You first," Drew retorts and Jesse relaxes. "Is overstimulation an issue?"

Jesse supposes Drew must know some things, being a teacher, but it doesn't help. He still doesn't know how to answer without getting embarrassed.

"I don't like it when it's too noisy or when there are lots of people who might bump and touch me all the time, but I like to be touched and I like touching things. I like soft things – like Scamp's fur." He takes a breath, thinks about Wicket but doesn't mention him. "I like being kissed."

"I noticed," Drew says, tucking his hair behind his ear. He leans forward, and tips Jesse's chin up. "Can I kiss you now?"

Jesse nods, holding his breath and Drew brushes a light kiss over his mouth then settles back in his chair.

"Better?"

"Yeah," Jesse says and smiles.

"What else?"

Jesse takes a deep breath. This is where it's going to get hard.

"I was diagnosed on the Autistic Disorder Spectrum," he says, speaking as fast as he can to get the words out. "Disorder's a dumb word though. I'm not disordered. Or stupid. Or dumb. Or retarded."

He stops to catch his breath; notices Drew is watching him in silence and adds,

"And I'm not deaf. That man thought I was deaf but I'm not. That wasn't even my fault. Debbie changed the register keys and Mr Greenwold fired her. I just don't always ... understand."

"So," Drew says when Jesse finally stops speaking. He takes his glasses off to polish them, "let's see if I have this right: you're on the autistic spectrum, you're dyslexic, you're a bit OCD, your eyes get tired quickly, you like my kitten's fur, and you like kissing. That about sum it up?"

"It's more than a bit OCD," Jesse starts to protest but stops when Drew snorts. His glasses are back in place. Jesse thinks he's the most handsome man he's ever seen and that's strange because his Dad wears glasses for reading and he's not handsome. Then again, maybe his mom thinks he is.

"Dude, you have never seen my mother with housework, trust me you have a long way to go." Drew crunches on a cracker he's smeared with blue cheese. "Jesse, you know, you're not broken, you're just different. And I'd still like to take you out tomorrow night."

Sighing, Jesse sits back in his chair for a moment, unsure of what to do. Part of him wants to run home, lock the door behind him, grab Wicket, and rub his hand over him until his heart stops pounding. Part of him wants to go out tomorrow night and see what happens. And an entirely different part of him wants to climb in Drew's lap and kiss him again. He decides he should probably ignore that part. For now.

"Okay, what are we going to see?"

* * *

Jesse clicks his seatbelt in place and gives Drew his address. The rain has started again, and he likes the rhythmic sound of the window wipers swooshing across the windscreen. They're stopped at a red light when Drew clears his throat and Jesse glances at him.

"Can I ask you a personal question?" Drew says.

What now? Jesse wants to scream no but instead scrubs his palm down the length of his jeans and rests it on his knee, trying to stay calm.

"I guess so," he says finally.

"Okay so I don't want you to take this the wrong way, " Drew begins and Jesse starts to panic, trying to guess what he wants to know, "but do you date much?"

"Um, what?"

"You know, do you go out much? On dates."

Jesse frowns and tries to work out what he's being asked; people are always asking one thing when they really want to know something else. After a moment, he thinks he knows.

"Are you asking if I'm a virgin?"

"No! That's not what I'm asking." Drew snaps. "I was just wondering if you're always this nervous or if I'm doing something that's making you nervous. Jesus, Jesse, I'd just like to help you relax."

Embarrassed, Jesse rubs his eyes.

"Sorry, sometimes I don't always get what people mean."

"Yeah, no kidding."

"My mom says I have no filter," he offers, feeling small and silly. From the corner of his eye, he sees Drew nodding in agreement. He takes a deep breath. "I go out sometimes but usually people are put off by my ... stuff."

"The counting and things?"

Jesse nods.

"Yeah, or they call me a retard and they don't usually want to see me again after that," he says and can hear the bitterness in his voice. "I guess I'm surprised you do. But you're a teacher so maybe that's why you're different."

Drew is silent for a moment, then reaches across and takes Jesse's hand and smiles.

"I do want to see you again. I like you."

"Oh. I like you too," Jesse says, relief washing over him. "But, you're kind of gorgeous and that's scary."

Drew laughs as color creeps up his cheeks.

"Your mom's right, you have no filter," he says, "but it's not always a bad thing."

They pull up in front of Jesse's apartment building. Drew peers out the window at it.

"You live here with your folks?"

Jesse shakes his head and explains about buying his apartment two years ago. When Drew's eyes widen in admiration, the younger man grins.

"I keep telling you, I'm not a kid. Weird maybe, but not a kid." With that he leans forward and lays a firm kiss on Drew's mouth, wrapping a hand around his neck to pull him closer. He's pleased when he sees Drew's eyes widen then flutter shut before he closes his own.

When the kiss breaks, they sit for a moment, foreheads touching.

"Is that okay?" he asks, remembering Drew's words the other night.

"Uh yeah that is very okay," Drew says with a smile.

"Your glasses are steamed up," Jesse says.

"I wonder why. Should I pick you up from here or your work?"

"Here. I have to shower."

"Okay. Want me to walk you up?"

"You better not."

"Why?"

"I won't want you to come back down and I don't think that's a good idea and Scamp's home alone."

"True. She's probably destroyed the place by now."

Drew's mouth is warm when he kisses him again, flicking his tongue across Jesse's bottom lip. Jesse pulls away with a groan and opens the door.

"I have to go. I'll see you tomorrow?"

"You'll see me tomorrow," Drew says with a grin.

* * *

Inside, Jesse locks the door. Slides the chain over. Closes the curtains. Checks the cushions: green, white, green, white. Goes to his room. Closes the curtains, checks the pillows, runs his hand over Wicket, then picks him up and holds him tight, fingers rubbing back and forth over his head. His body and mind are a jumble of sensations and thoughts and he wishes Drew had come up with him.

Hugging Wicket, he goes back to the kitchen and pours himself some juice. Gets his cell phone out. Flirting is something he struggles with, it's too easy to trip himself up with all the multiple meanings of things and he never knows what the right thing is to say. But something tells him it will be okay with Drew, so he sits Wicket on the bench against his glass, and after stroking his head a couple of more times, taps at the screen, tongue clenched between his teeth. It takes several attempts to get the letters right and for it to say what he wants to say, then he hits send.

I like touching hard things too.

After a moment, his phone chimes and the photo of Drew and Scamp appears on his screen.

DUDE! FILTER!

He scrambles to make his fingers put the right letters in the right order and is starting to panic when his phone chimes again. He huffs in frustration and opens the text message.

But good to know

Relieved, he sends back a smile and buries his scarlet face in Wicket.

* * *

27

9

Drew is having trouble concentrating on his Black Forest Gateau. Across the table, Jesse is licking melted ice-cream off the handle of his spoon and Drew suspects it has replaced every porn image he ever had stored in his memory. Jesse stopped eating when Drew asked if he played sport, to explain that he swims every day and that he would love to learn to ride a horse. Fat droplets of melted vanilla ice-cream have trickled down the metal and when it dripped on to the base of this thumb, he looked startled and dipped his head to suck the skin clean before running his tongue up the length of the handle to catch the rest. Drew hopes he doesn't have to stand up in a hurry.

"Are you okay?" Jesse asks.

"Huh? What?" Drew says, dragging his eyes away from Jesse's mouth.

"Your face is all red. Are you okay?" Jesse repeats.

Drew nods and reaches for his wine glass. He knows enough about the autistic spectrum, he thinks, to not try and put Jesse in a box. All the same, he wonders how experienced he really is and keeps reminding himself that he's twenty-six, not a kid, and by his own admission does date. On the other hand, Drew's convinced Jesse has no idea of the attention he attracted when they walked in or of the effect he has. His black jeans and white shirt, sleeves rolled in neat folds to the elbow, are simple and unaffected, but almost every woman in the small restaurant has been stealing looks at him all evening. Looking at them now, Drew can tell by the number of glassy stares directed at their table that he's not the only one distracted by the spoon licking. Still, there's nothing calculated, coy, or deliberately seductive in what he's doing. Like everything else, he's just doing it. With no filter.

Drew reaches across the table and takes the spoon from Jesse and lays it in the almost empty sundae dish. Looks back at Jesse's confused face and smiles.

"I'm not going to be able to walk to the car if you keep doing that," he says, hoping he's not going to have to be more explicit. Jesse bites his lower lip and his forehead creases – already Drew thinks of this as his concentration face. Then his eyes widen just a little and he peeks up at Drew, a slight smile playing on his lips.

"Are you ha..." he starts, loud enough to attract attention, and Drew taps his foot against his ankle.

"Filter," he says, smiling in spite of himself.

"Oh, yeah, sorry," Jesse says but his grin widens, and he doesn't drop his eyes, clearly pleased. Damn this kid is going to be the death of him, Drew thinks, as he tries to will the blood away from his groin.

"Dork," Drew says. "Still want to go to a movie?"

They'd decided to eat first to try and avoid the big crowds at the movie theatre. Over steak, they've established that Jesse is an only child and Drew is the youngest of six with two brothers and three sisters. He has a Masters in English Literature and has written a book about modern poetry.

"It's not exactly going to make me a millionaire," he'd told an impressed Jesse but feels better about the book than he has in a long time.

Jesse did a year at community college before going to work for Mr Greenwold. When he's not working, he likes taking photographs and playing video games. Drew asks if he can see them some time and decides the look on Jesse's face – equal parts flustered and pleased - is almost as good as his smile.

A finger taps the back of his hand.

"Earth to Drew," Jesse says, "come in Drew."

"What?"

"I said I don't mind if you don't want to go to a movie. We can go some other time."

Nodding, Drew signals for the bill and finishes his wine. When the waiter returns with his credit card, he stands and holds his hand out to Jesse, who takes it without hesitation. Drew's aware of the eyes on them as they leave, some disapproving, others simply jealous, and doesn't care. As they approach the car, he slows down and pulls Jesse around so he's facing him when he leans against the door. Pulls him into the vee of his spread legs and slips his hands around his waist.

"So, since we're not going to a movie, what would you like to do now?"

Jesse balls his hands into fists against Drew's chest, eyes downcast.

"I don't know."

"I can take you home if you want me to," Drew says. Jesse shakes his head, no, and Drew breathes a sigh of relief.

"Well, we could get a drink at *The Library Bar*," he offers even though he really doesn't want to go there right now. "But it will probably be a bit more crowded than last night."

"If you like," Jesse says. He runs a finger around a button on Drew's shirt. "Maybe...maybe you could kiss me again."

Caught by surprise, Drew laughs.

"I think that can be arranged," he says and pulls Jesse forward, lays a soft kiss against his lips and leans back. "Like that?"

Jesse looks up. He narrows his eyes and Drew can see him trying to decide what to do next. He's never known anybody this transparent and there's something sweet, if a little unsettling, about it. He smiles when he sees Jesse's made up his mind.

"No," Jesse says, "not like that. Like this."

He locks his hands behind Drew's neck and stretches to kiss him. There's a fading hint of vanilla ice-cream on Jesse's lips and when he opens his mouth to meet Drew's tongue with his own, the faint warmth of red wine. He shivers and tightens his arms, pulling Jesse closer, bracing himself against the car.

"Get a room," a passerby calls, and Drew feels Jesse start to pull away. With one hand, he anchors him in place, deepens the kiss, and with the other flicks his middle finger at the intruder. They'll go when they're good and ready. Drew draws away from the kiss but doesn't let Jesse go.

"How about we go back to my place?" he says.

Jesse nods.

* * *

10

Letting Drew hold his hand is easy. Letting Drew kiss him in the lift is easy too; the citrusy scent of Drew's cologne on his skin and the spicy taste of wine in his mouth filling his senses. When Drew takes their jackets and hangs them on the coat rack, things stop being so easy.

Jesse has time to think now and anxiety is starting to wash away desire. He knows what he wants to do – everybody probably knows, he thinks as he adjusts himself in his jeans – but he doesn't know what Drew wants. What he expects. What will happen after? What if he's not good enough? What if he's too weird for Drew? What if Drew's like everybody else and just wants to get off and then get rid of him? Jesse doesn't *think* he's like that but he's not always very good at reading people and the questions just keep piling up in his mind. He wishes he'd brought Wicket with him even though he knows he can't.

"Hey," Drew says as he brushes past with two glasses of wine. "I can hear your brain whirring from here."

Jesse follows him to the sofa and sits down and Scamp wobbles her way across the cushions to his lap and when she curls up, he strokes her ears. Before he can take comfort from the soft fur, Drew laughs and picks her up; the backs of his fingers brush against Jesse's thigh and he catches his breath. When Drew has put her in her cat cave, he sits back next to Jesse. Takes his hand and laces their fingers together.

"Would it help if you tell me what you're so worried about?" he asks.

Jesse wants to, but he isn't sure how. Drew bumps their knees together.

"I won't laugh."

"I don't think I'm very good," Jesse says. He's trembling and feels a little queasy. Some of it's the wine, he's not used to drinking anything other than the occasional beer. Most if it is worry that Drew will laugh at him. Or get angry with him. "At sex, I mean."

"What makes you say that?" Drew asks, rubbing his thumb over Jesse's knuckles.

"Because that's what other people say. And they never call back."

If a hole opens in the ground in front of him, Jesse thinks, he'll happily crawl into it and disappear. Anything rather than sit here feeling paralyzed in front of this man.

"Well," Drew says taking his glasses off and laying them on the coffee table, "I told you yesterday, those people are dicks."

Jesse takes a breath and tries to nod. He knows he's not stupid, reminds himself of that over and over, but right now he feels that way and he hates it. Drew slips from the sofa to his knees in front of him and looks up into his face.

"Jesse, one-night stands aren't really my style," he says in a soft voice, taking his hands, "and I don't usually go around picking up random men in pet stores. We don't have to do anything you don't want to do. Hell, we don't have to do anything at all. We can just watch a DVD, or I can take you home if that's what you want, and tomorrow we can go out somewhere or something."

Jesse studies Drew's face for a moment then lets out a shaky sigh.

"I don't want you to take me home," he says. "I want to stay. I just ..."

* * *

Drew lifts up on his knees to reach Jesse's mouth and kisses him, cutting off the words. It's gentle at first; intended just to reassure. Then he feels a trembling hand on his neck and Drew leans into the kiss, opens Jesse's mouth with his tongue. Slides his own hand around his waist and tries to pull him closer. Frustrated he moves back on to the sofa pulling Jesse toward him so they can keep kissing. God, the kid – he has got to stop thinking of him like that - may not be experienced, but wow, can he kiss.

To Drew's astonishment, instead of breaking the embrace Jesse climbs in his lap, knees either side of Drew's hips, arms up around his neck. Damn, that feels good and Drew reminds himself to go slow. Slides his hands up the back of Jesse's thighs to cup both buttocks and is rewarded with a whimper that makes him buck. Just a little. Jesse whimpers again and Drew breaks the kiss, lets his head roll on to the back of the sofa, so he's looking up into those unusual golden eyes.

"You have no idea how stunning you are, have you?" he murmurs. Jesse blushes, ducking his head into the crook of Drew's neck. A ghost of warm breath on his skin makes Drew shudder. When it's followed by Jesse's lips, he groans. "Would you like to go to the bedroom?"

When Jesse nods against his shoulder, he nudges him off his lap, whining at the loss of pressure. In the bedroom, he remembers about the lights and guides Jesse to the bed where he fumbles for the bedside lamp which casts only a dim yellow glow over the pillow. He eases Jesse back on to the bed and crawls up beside him, smiling. Leans in and kisses him again. For a while they stay like this, kisses hot and desperate, breath coming in short, damp gasps. Drew pulls at Jesse's shirt until it comes free of his jeans and he's able to fan his fingers across the warm skin of his lower back, pleased when Jesse sighs into his mouth at the touch. Breaks the kiss so he can look into Jesse's eyes when he speaks.

"If you want me to stop," Drew whispers, pushing his leg forward, between Jesse's, "you just have to say."

"I don't want you to stop," Jesse says and rocks against Drew's thigh. He's shivering and if Drew couldn't feel how warm his skin is, feel the hardness being pressed against him, he'd think he was cold. "I really want to touch you. Your skin, I mean."

"Oh Jesus, Jesse," Drew groans and grinds back against him. That honesty is way too hot. His jeans are uncomfortable and he's desperate to take them off. Instead, he rolls Jesse onto his back, kneels between his legs. Pulls his shirt over his head and tosses it aside, takes Jesse's hands and places them on his chest; can't help grinning when Jesse catches his breath. He expects his touch to be either clumsy or timid and is surprised it's neither when gentle fingers sweep up his torso to rub circles over his nipples until he moans.

Murmuring encouragement, he unbuttons Jesse's shirt and lets it fall away, runs his hands up over skin the color of pale coffee and bends to kiss and nibble at the skin along one collarbone.

"Is this okay?" he asks, voice low and heavy, lips brushing against Jesse's skin.

Drew can feel Jesse's throat move as he swallows then nods.

"Yes," he whispers, "you don't have to worry, it's...it's not my first time."

"Okay," Drew says and kisses him again. "We're going to take our time anyway, okay?"

He takes Jesse's hands and places them on the pillow above his head. Smiles down at him. Nuzzles beneath Jesse's ear, biting down with firm pressure, then licks across the spot to soothe it, smiles when Jesse arches beneath him. Makes his way down, leaving a trail of wet kisses down his belly. Drew sits back on his heels and forces himself to take slow, even breaths for a moment; he's not sure why but he gets the feeling that whatever Jesse has done hasn't involved a lot of pleasure – not for the man himself at least – and he wants to make this good for him. When he's sure he has control, he tugs Jesse's belt buckle open and undoes his jeans, slides them down off his hips and lets them fall on the floor. Repeats the action with his boxers. Crawls back up and runs a hand over Jesse's thigh to his cock, and watching his face for reaction, wraps his fingers around the hard length and moves with firm strokes until he hears him moan. He shimmies down the bed a little and takes him in his mouth, licking around the head, and groaning when fingers twine in his hair, then drop away.

"Drew," Jesse whimpers, bucking up into Drew's mouth.

Hollowing his cheeks, Drew begins to bob his head, using one hand to stroke the velvety skin not covered by his mouth. When he looks up, Jesse is up on his elbows, teeth buried in his bottom lip, golden eyes filled with lust and something desperate that Drew can't quite name. He has to close his eyes or he's not going to last, not with the way Jesse is looking at him and moving beneath him. Runs his tongue across the cock head again, and this time Jesse cries out when he bucks up. Pleased with the reaction, Drew repeats the action a second and a third time.

"Drew, oh ... Drew... I ...I..."

Then Jesse is arching off the bed, his entire body twisting and shaking as he comes. Drew strokes and licks him through it then presses him back down on to the mattress. Trembling he undresses, straddles him, and begins to stroke his own cock, too worked up to wait for later and far too desperate to be gentle with Jesse right now. A hand closes over his, and he opens his eyes to see Jesse looking up at him. With a muffled curse, he gives in to his own orgasm and when it's over, gropes for his discarded shirt and wipes them both up before collapsing on the bed, pulling Jesse onto his chest.

"You okay?" he asks, stroking the back of his neck with his thumb.

"Mmhmm," Jesse says, voice muffled against Drew's skin.

"Next time will be better."

"Will there be a next time?"

Jesse's voice is small, stripped of any self-preservation and Drew's heart tightens a little.

"I hope so. Do you want there to be, Jesse?"

Silence fills the space around them until eventually Jesse nods and whispers yes.

"Good," Drew says pulls him up, so he can tuck Jesse's head beneath his chin and fights a yawn.

"I don't want to go home," Jesse says. Drew smiles against his hair and tightens his hold; thinks that lack of filter thing might take some getting used to but it's not always bad.

"Go to sleep," he murmurs.

* * *

11

"Mr Oliver?"

Drew blinks and sees Katie Lawrence standing in front of him.

"Sorry, Katie. Was away with the fairies," he says. Cole Davis, sitting in the front row, snickers, and Drew tells him to settle down. It's last period on Friday afternoon, a designated silent reading session for his senior class, but he suspects the only things being read, silently or otherwise, are the furtive text messages arranging weekend activities. "Is there a problem?"

Katie holds out a book and when Drew reads the cover, he sees it's his. He grins.

"Where did you find that?"

"My mom found it on Amazon and bought it for me. I was wondering if you'd autograph it."

Drew smiles and takes the book. Writes a greeting that can't be misconstrued by even the most suspicious of parents – or inventive of teenagers – and signs his name.

"It's good to know someone else's mom has bought a copy," he jokes. Katie squeaks something indecipherable and scuttles away, ponytail swinging.

Drew glances at his watch and sighs. Still half an hour left. There's no rehearsal for the production today so he has time to go home, feed Scamp and get changed before picking up Jesse. Tonight, he's meeting Jesse's parents for the first time and he's nervous; in truth, he's about to leave nervous behind and enter full-blown panic.

Jesse went home from their first night together and phoned his parents to tell them he'd met somebody. Drew knows this because Jesse phoned him immediately after to tell him what he'd done, voice hovering somewhere between matter of fact and terrified by the sound of it.

No filter, Drew has learned over the past four weeks, means that not only can Jesse be both disarming and brutally direct, but he is incapable of hiding his feelings or keeping a secret.

It hasn't taken long to realize that on some level Jesse understands his behavior unsettles other people, so he overcompensates with either more honesty or by withdrawing into himself. Drew's surprised reaction to the news that Jesse had told his parents about him had been met with a meek "it's okay isn't it?" and Drew had had to remind himself that Jesse might not be broken, but he *is* different. A week ago, realizing Jesse talks to people about them simply because that is how Jesse is, that there is no hidden agenda, Drew phoned his own parents to tell them he had met someone. Had even surprised himself by telling his father it was someone special.

Jody still thinks he's trying to be a knight in shining armor hoping to save Jesse from the big, bad, world. Which is why tonight they're having dinner with the Petersons and tomorrow they're having lunch with Jody. So he can prove to her she's wrong. Drew looks at his watch again. Still ten minutes to go. He stands up and clears his throat.

"Okay, guys, because I'm the best teacher you're ever going to get, let's call it day. I want your comparative essays on my desk on Monday, no extensions," he says and waits for the flurry of movement and noise to settle before continuing. "Do not, I repeat do not, make me regret treating you like human beings by making a noise in the hall and getting all our asses booted into detention on Monday."

They begin to file out, nodding and saluting as they do so. Some of the girls offer him shy smiles and a few of the boys high five him as they go past. When the door finally shuts behind them, leaving him in silence, he stuffs his own books and papers into his backpack and hefts it onto his shoulder, while pulling his phone out of his pocket.

Leaving school, going home to shower and change. See you at five thirty.

Taps send.

Makes his way to the library where he finds Jody shelving books. He leans against a shelf of neglected copies of Mark Twain and shoves his hands in his pockets.

"Any idea what I should wear to meet the parents?" he asks with a grin.

"Oh please," Jody rolls her eyes, "as if you need fashion advice from me."

"I'm not asking you for fashion advice," he retorts. "I just don't know whether to go formal or casual."

"What's Jesse say?"

"Not to wear my grey sweater because it makes me look old and boring."

"He's not wrong."

Drew narrows his eyes and lifts a finger but before he can speak, his phone vibrates in his pocket.

No grey swetr.

He flicks the phone around, so Jody can read it; she snorts and rolls her eyes.

"Jeans, button down, can't go wrong."

"Tie?"

"Did I say tie? Did you hear me say the word tie?" She shoves him along, so she can shelve the next set of books.

"Just checking. Hey, I have to go, or I'll be late and then it won't matter what I'm wearing. All good for tomorrow?

"Yes, I'm all good for tomorrow. Go on, get out of here."

He pecks her cheek, ducks away from the swat she aims at his butt and jogs toward his car. As he unlocks the door, his phone vibrates again.

Please. Not grey swetr.

* * *

Drew waits outside Jesse's building. In the four weeks, they've been together there are two things Drew has not done: he has not been inside Jesse and he has not been inside Jesse's apartment. Their time together is spent either out or at Drew's place; when Jesse stays over they explore each other with mouths and hands but have gone no further. It's not that Drew doesn't want to make love to Jesse or that he's not curious about where he lives, it's that he wants Jesse to feel confident enough to ask him, to invite him in. In every sense. Until then, Drew is happy to wait, any frustration he feels disappearing when Jesse curls in against his side to sleep, clinging to him throughout the night.

The more he gets to know Jesse, the more Drew wants to know. He surprises himself with how happy he is to take things slow. In the past, even before David, he's been impatient to jump as fast as possible. The fact that Jesse is ...unusual his mind supplies .... doesn't bother him either; it's not like he's lacking in understanding or intelligence. He simply processes things differently, Drew tells himself with what he likes to think is academic objectivity. The things that challenge Jesse daily, things that Drew doesn't even think about when he does them, make Jesse a source of surprise and, sometimes, frustration. When he's relaxed and happy, he's sweet and playful, enjoys teasing and being teased, and likes to learn new things. There is something almost childlike about him at times but nothing about him is infantile or immature. Just unusual.

When he's on edge or feeling anxious, Drew has discovered reading to him helps. They're half way through The Hobbit because Jesse has seen the movies a dozen times and has no trouble processing it. He often falls asleep listening to it, head in Drew's lap, fingers in Scamp's fur. Drew will then sit and read his own book until Jesse wakes, either wanting more or sometimes happy to be distracted with other activities.

The passenger door opens and Jesse slides into the car, looks Drew over twice, checking, Drew knows, for the dreaded grey sweater; satisfied, he offers his mouth for kissing. Amused, Drew complies, the first kiss soft and gentle, the second more intense. A hand lands against his chest, pushing him back.

"Mom's making meatloaf and if we're late it will be dry. It's gross when it's dry. I like kissing you, but I don't like dry meatloaf," Jesse says, straightening in his seat and casting side long glances at Drew. "That's a nice shirt."

Drew's wearing a navy button down with jeans and sneakers, his hair tied in the short ponytail he usually sports for school; it will pass Jesse's odd criteria of no grey, no green, no sweater vests, no polo shirts, nothing with polka dots, nothing with paw prints on it - that last one intrigues Drew but he's hesitant to ask why in case it's related to some memory best left forgotten. He's confident it will also pass parent muster – not so scruffy that they'll think he's a loser, not so formal he'll look like an ass.

"Let's go get meatloaf then," he says with a grin, "so I can get more kisses."

* * *

Mrs Peterson is a woman in her early fifties with the same refined features that on her son deliver his cover model looks; on her though they're sharper and, combined with an equally sharp haircut, make her look more severe than Drew hopes is accurate. The heavy rimmed black glasses don't help, nor does the red lipstick that is beginning to bleed into the fine lines around her mouth. Her eyes light up, softening her features, when she sees her son and she hugs him until he begins to squirm like a puppy and pulls free. Jesse turns from her to his father and this time the hug is less intense but no less sincere and when he's done, he steps back and takes Drew's hand.

"Mom, Dad," he says, and his voice is so solemn, Drew bites the inside of his cheek to keep from laughing. "I'd like you to meet Andrew Oliver, but everyone calls him Drew."

Drew takes a step forward, hand out, ready to shake, and Jesse speaks again.

"He's my boyfriend." Eyes skittering around the room.

Okay, that's new. That's the first time that word has been used. Drew doesn't mind it, likes it in fact, but his surprise must show on his face because he sees Mrs Peterson purse her lips.

"Mrs Peterson, it's really nice to meet you" he says, hand still offered. After a moment, she takes it and squeezes it. He offers her the bottle of wine he's brought.

"Thank you, Andrew, that's very kind of you, but you didn't need to bring anything."

"Nobody calls him Andrew, mom," Jesse says before Drew can answer, and he doesn't have to look to know he's rolling his eyes.

"Well my mom does, but only when I'm in trouble," Drew says hoping to lift the tension a little. Jesse's mom smiles but it doesn't touch her eyes.

38

"Jesse talks a lot about you Drew," Mr Peterson says shaking his hand with a firm, even grip. "It's nice to finally meet you."

"It's good to meet you both too, sir."

"Please, call me Ray."

Jesse disappears into the kitchen and comes back with a beer for all of them. He opens a bottle for his mother and offers it to her.

"We should get some glasses," she says.

"Why? We never use glasses any other time," Jesse says, sitting at the table.

"Drew might like to use one."

Jesse shakes his head.

"No, we never use glasses. Sometimes at night after we've …"

"Jess," Drew interrupts taking the chair opposite him, "filter."

He doubts Jesse's parents want mind pictures of the two of them in bed drinking beer – or doing anything else. To let Jesse know it's not a big deal, he taps his foot against his under the table and smiles until he gets a smile in return.

"Mom, is the meatloaf ready?" Jesse has an ability to switch tack with a speed that leaves Drew reeling at times. "It's gross when it's dry."

Drew shakes his head but says nothing; Mrs Peterson excuses herself to go to the kitchen.

"Drew, Jesse says you're a teacher," Ray says, opening the bottle of wine while they wait.

"Yes, I teach English at Central High."

"Drew's written a book," Jesse adds, peeking up at Drew with a grin. "A poetry book."

"A book about poetry, not a poetry book," Drew corrects.

"What kind of poems do you write?" Jesse's mom puts a tray with meatloaf, a tureen of mashed potatoes, one of green beans, and a large bowl of salad on the table.

"I don't really," Drew says, "I did my master's thesis on Modern American poetry and wrote a book about it. It's not very exciting. I think about sixty copies have been sold and I'm pretty sure my mom has about fifty of them."

Drew is relieved when Ray changes the subject by asking Jesse about his job. He asks if he needs any help with bills or invoices and Jesse brightens up.

"No, I'm good. I've paid everything and there was just one that I couldn't understand but Drew figured it out for me and now it's all sorted. I've even put extra in my savings account this week."

"Oh?" Mrs Peterson says. "Why didn't you phone your father?"

"Well because I asked Drew and he explained it, so I didn't have to bother Dad," Jesse says as he reaches for the dish of potatoes; his tone suggests this is the most obvious thing in the world, though Drew can see his mother doesn't see it that way.

He watches Jesse drop a small mountain of mashed potato on his plate next to his meatloaf, smooth it with the back of his spoon. No beans or salad yet, and Drew knows after only this short time together that if he can, Jesse will try to avoid them if he thinks he can get away with it.

"He'd overpaid the gas bill last month and there was a credit, that was all," Drew says hoping to reassure Mrs Peterson.

"Oh Jesse, you really must be more careful," she says and Drew notices the instant change in Jesse. The blinding smile fades and he begins to push his food around the plate. Stops looking around the table. "Perhaps Dad should check your bank account for you while you're here."

"No, it's fine," Jesse says but doesn't lift his eyes up. Drew presses his foot against his ankle.

"Jesse, I really think you should let Dad …"

"Erin, he said it's sorted, I'm sure it's fine," Ray interrupts. "If Jesse needs my help, he'll ask, won't you?"

Jesse nods.

"The meatloaf is great Mrs Peterson, thank you," Drew says hoping to steer them back on safer ground.

The rest of the meal passes with relative ease but Drew senses Mrs Peterson has retreated further into her mistrust of him. He supposes it's understandable but even so, he can't ignore the tickle of resentment in the back of his mind. All he did was help Jesse understand an invoice, going over what credit and debit meant until he saw it click in his eyes. How can she be mad at him for that?

"Drew's reading me *The Hobbit*, mom," Jesse is saying, finally looking up at Drew. "I fall asleep sometimes when he's reading it, but I really like it. There's lots of stuff the films left out. Drew says it's because they can't fit everything in, but I think it's because people are lazy and only want to watch the easy parts."

Drew is aware of Mrs Peterson's eyes on him; he smiles at her, hoping Jesse hasn't just made things worse.

"I suppose you must have students like Jesse at school," she says. She picks up her beer, leaving the glass of wine her husband has poured untouched.

"I have one with Mears–Irlen and I've had several with dyslexia over the years," he says, "I've had a couple of Aspergers kids and I did have a sophomore with Tourette's one year."

"That must have made teaching interesting," Ray says with a grin. Drew holds his thumb and finger together to indicate yes, a little. Having a student with no control over his brain's decision to spew profanity every few words had not been his easiest year.

"So, you're used to children with special needs then," Mrs Peterson says.

"I'm not a child," Jesse says, "and I don't have special needs."

"Jesse, don't be rude," his mother says but her eyes are still on Drew who thinks that if anyone is being rude it's her.

"I have had some students with different needs to most, yes," Drew says refusing to be painted as something he's not, "but Jesse's not one of my students. I'm reading him *The Hobbit* because I like reading out loud and he's a good audience."

"Except when he's snoring, I imagine," Ray says, and Jesse leans over to punch his shoulder.

"I don't snore," he protests.

Drew laughs and grins at Ray, grateful for yet another subject change even though he's certain he's not off the hook with Jesse's mom yet.

"Oh yeah you snore. You just ask Scamp," he says.

"Scamp loves me. In fact I'm going to sleep with Scamp when we get home and you can have the sofa," Jesse says and Drew chokes on his mouthful of potato, laughing with surprise.

* * *

When the meal is over and Mrs Peterson stands to clear the dishes, Drew decides to try and win back some points. He gathers up an armful of dirty dishes and follows her to the kitchen.

"You don't need to help," she says. Some of the coldness has left her voice but not her eyes.

"My mom would have my head if I didn't," he says with a smile and begins rinsing dishes for her to load into the dishwasher.

"How old are you Drew?" she asks after a moment.

Startled, Drew turns off the water, turns to face her, leans against the bench.

"I'm thirty-four."

She nods.

"Jesse's only twenty-six and he doesn't know much about the world."

"Oh, I think he does okay," Drew says trying to keep his tone light.

"Yes, all things considered he does, I suppose, but his challenges are much bigger than I think you realize."

"I understand he tested on the Autistic spectrum but very high functioning, that he is dyslexic and has Mears-Irlen, that he displays OCD tendencies especially when stressed and is sometimes socially anxious. I also think he's pretty special."

Mrs Peterson nods and reaches for the dishwasher powder.

"Do you know what the acronym I.D. stands for Drew?"

"Intellectual Disability Disorder?" Drew sighs. He has to admit this has been worrying him for the last couple of weeks – is he, in fact, taking advantage of someone who doesn't know what's happening? Certainly, he doesn't want to believe that about himself and if he's honest, he doesn't want to believe that Jesse might be ... he can't help thinking the word retarded. Logically he knows that Jesse is quite capable of reasoning and coping but...still...Drew takes his glasses off and pinches the bridge of his nose. "I don't know a lot about it beyond what I learned in a basic developmental ed course I took in college, but I know enough to know that Jesse must be very mild. I mean he's independent and employed and ..."

"Well that's all well and good," Mrs Peterson cuts him off, "but you must also realize that he doesn't know how to read people properly, so his judgement isn't always the best. My son may be a man physically, Drew, but he really is a child in very many ways."

Before Drew can protest that her son is no child, Jesse speaks from the doorway.

"I am not a child," he says and a lump forms in Drew's throat. "I'm not retarded."

"Jesse, honey, I didn't mean that you're retarded."

"Then why did you say I'm a child?"

"Hey Jess," Drew says and goes to him, winds his arms around him. "It's okay, your mom is just looking out for you..."

"What does Drew think of Wicket?" Mrs Peterson asks. Her voice is hard and cuts across Drew's words.

Jesse pales and withdraws from the embrace.

"Who's Wicket, Jess?" Drew asks, confused. He looks from mother to son but gets no answer. He repeats the question. "Jesse, who's Wicket?"

"Wicket is his teddy bear," Mrs Peterson says and Drew frowns at her tone. There's something in it that sets his teeth on edge.

"Wicket isn't a teddy bear, he's an Ewok."

"You mean like from *Return of the Jedi*? The furry, little be...guys?"

"Jesse has slept with him since he was four," Mrs Peterson says and this time the pity is obvious, but it isn't her Drew is worried about. Jesse's face is dark and closed, eyes fixed on the opposite wall, and Drew can see he's trembling. "He uses him for stimming."

"I want to go home," Jesse says.

"Jesse," Ray Peterson says from the doorway, but Jesse doesn't let him go any further.

"Drew, please take me home," Jesse looks at him and the desperation in his eyes is so raw Drew wants to gather him up and just hold him. He looks to Ray, who sighs and nods.

"It was really nice to meet you both," Drew says. "I – I'll take him home."

Erin Peterson pushes past him, her footsteps heavy on the stairs as she runs up them.

"I'm sorry," he says to Ray and hunts for his keys in his pocket.

"Jesse, wait for Drew in the living room for a moment," Ray says.

"Stop treating me like I'm a child, I'm not one," Jesse says again, his mouth set and stubborn. Glares at his father.

"No, you're not but you're behaving like one right now. Go and wait while I talk to Drew and then you can go home." Ray sounds tired and Drew supposes he can understand why that might be.

Jesse looks at him with wide, unhappy eyes, and Drew nods; he offers him a smile, heart aching when Jesse's shoulders slump and he turns away. When he's gone, Drew looks at Ray.

"I'm sorry Drew, and I'll apologize to Jesse too when he's ready to hear it. I appreciate that tonight can't have been fun for you, but I am going to ask you to try and spare a thought for Erin. He's our only child and it hasn't been easy. It was hard for her when he moved away, hard for her to accept he doesn't need her the way he used to. Now it looks like he's ready to make another transition – to having someone else help him with things we've always helped him with. It's not personal, it wouldn't matter who it was. And it wouldn't matter if you were a woman either so don't go thinking it's about that. She'll come around, but it will take time." He pauses and runs his hand through his greying hair. "But she's not entirely wrong either. I can see you care about him and I can see you do understand but I suspect you don't understand as much as you think you do and I'd just like to say that if you see Jesse as some sort of project then perhaps it would be better to let him down now. I don't want to see him hurt. Sorry if that's a little blunt but I have to say it."

Drew doesn't know what to say. He feels as though he's been caught in a revolving door. With an alligator.

"I don't see him as a project."

Ray Peterson nods and puts his hand out. Drew hesitates then shakes it.

"Well, take him home then and make sure he's okay. I'll give you my card and if you could let me know how he is tomorrow, I'd be grateful. I'll take care of his mother."

He digs into his pocket and takes his card out. Ray Peterson Plumbing it reads, then a phone number and his email address. Drew nods and they go to the living room. Jesse is slumped against the door waiting and when he hears them, he straightens up but refuses to look at either of them.

"Goodnight Dad, thank you for dinner," he says and Drew's heart sinks at the monotone. "I'm not a child."

"I know you're not. I'll talk to you tomorrow," Ray says and nods again at Drew before opening the door. "Drive safe guys."

* * *

They've been driving for ten minutes when Jesse speaks. His voice is quiet, and Drew strains to hear him.

"I'm not a child and I'm not retarded, and I can look after myself."

Drew tries to take his hand but Jesses snatches it away. Hurt, Drew hesitates, then stretches across until he can capture the hand and pull it toward him.

"No, Jess, you're not a child and you're not retarded, and you can look after yourself. I know that."

"My mom thinks I'm still a kid."

"Jess, my mom thinks I'm still a kid. You'll see when you meet her. She keeps asking me if I'm eating enough vegetables and getting enough sleep and she doesn't think I iron my shirts properly. Your mom's just being a mom."

"No, she's not." Jesse shakes his head. "She doesn't think I can do it. She thinks I'm stupid."

"Jesse that's enough," Drew says, using the voice he uses for especially unruly students near the end of the semester. "Your mom loves you and she worries about you, that's her job. She was just looking out for you is all. You *are* smart, and you *can* understand that."

That doesn't change the fact that he's actually pretty pissed at the woman right now. She might be worried about her son, but she didn't have to humiliate him like that. Drew supposes she thought the sting of humiliation now was better than the deeper pain of being abandoned later but that makes him even angrier. She's already decided he's just going to discard Jesse. He takes a deep breath, there's only one way to deal with this and it needs to be done tonight.

"Jess, what's stimming?"

Jesse lets go of Drew's hand and presses closer to the door.

"Come on, Jess, talk to me," Drew says. "Please."

Jesse sighs and from the corner of his eye, Drew sees him swipe at his face.

"It means self-stimulation," Jesse says, his voice low and heavy. "And it's something people like me, people who are autistic, do to calm down."

Drew licks his lips, trying to understand.

"Self-stimulation? How does that work?"

He's confused when Jesse snickers.

"It doesn't mean what you think it means, Drew. It's not a sex thing – that's different. I – I do that too, though," he says. Drew grins.

"Don't worry, so do I. Everyone does," he says. "Carry on, I'm listening."

"Stimming is like..." his voice trails off and Drew smiles to himself, knows he'd be looking at Jesse's concentration face if he could see him. Then there's a quiet 'ah' as Jesse's mind latches on to the words he's searching for. "I knew this girl who used to flap her hands when things got too much. And some people rock."

Drew nods, he's had a couple of students like that, he just didn't know it had a name.

"Some autistics hurt themselves too," Jesse says quietly, and then adds, in one of those flashes of Jesse insight that always take Drew a little by surprise, "but I don't think that's about being autistic. Lots of people hurt themselves like that."

"Yeah, they do Jess," Drew says thinking of David. There's movement beside him and Jesse take's his hand again. He gives it a gentle squeeze. "How do you stim, Jess?"

"Wicket's fur is soft," Jesse says. "It helps me when I stroke it."

"I didn't know that was called stimming, you taught me something," Drew says with a smile. "Is Wicket what they call a comfort object?"

Jesse nods.

"And you've had him for twenty-two years?"

Another nod.

"He must be pretty special," Drew says. "Pretty good at comforting."

Nod.

"Can I see him some time?"

There's a brief pause then Jesse nods again. Drew takes a deep breath; he knows he needs to be careful. The thin line between what he feels for Jesse simply because he's Jesse and wanting to protect or save him is all too obvious right now. Not to mention what it might mean to have a relationship with someone like Jesse.

"Could I come upstairs to your apartment and see him tonight?"

The pause is longer this time, then Jesse speaks.

"You won't make fun of me?"

"No Jess, I won't ever make fun of you. I promise."

After a moment, Drew feels a light squeeze on his fingers.

"Okay."

* * *

12

Jesse fumbles with his keys, catching them before they fall to the floor. He tries to calm down by taking a deep breath, holding it, then letting it out through his nose. Slow and gentle. Repeats it. This time he gets the key in the lock and the door swings open.

"Come in," he says without looking at Drew as he turns the light on, bathing the room in a yellow glow. Aware of Drew's eyes on him, he goes to the window and pulls the curtains closed, turns to the sofa and checks the cushions, lips moving in silence as he recites the colors. He looks up at Drew and bites his lip. "I have to check the bedroom."

Drew nods and follows him but stops in the doorway. Jesse can feel his eyes on him as he pulls the curtains, checks the pillows and moves to the dresser. Reaches toward the toy but stops, hand hovering in mid-air and drops his head. He wants to believe Drew will understand but what if Mom is right? What if he doesn't?

"Jess?" Drew's voice is quiet. "May I come in?"

He nods and counts Drew's steps as he approaches. Three. Drew has such long legs he only needs three steps to get to him from the doorway.

"Is this Wicket?" Drew asks.

"I don't sleep with him," he blurts out. "Not since I was a kid. I don't know why mom said that."

"It's okay," Drew says. "Jesse, please look at me."

Jesse shakes his head.

"I don't sleep with him," he insists. It's important he make Drew understand that. Drew picks Wicket up and hands him to Jesse.

"Jesse it wouldn't matter to me if you do," he says.

Jesse hugs Wicket to his chest and leans his head on Drew's shoulder.

"You really like Star Wars huh?" Drew asks.

He doesn't answer.

"Well I guess I know what we're doing on Sunday then," Drew says and Jesse steps back, finally looking at him.

"What?"

"Movie marathon of course," Drew says with a grin. "You do have all the movies, right?"

Jesse nods and smiles; his eyes glimmer with pleasure. Mom was wrong, and he was right. Excited by the idea, he grabs Drew's hand and takes him to the closet, opens the door and pulls a hanger out. Draped over it is a collection of cream and beige garments and a long cloak. Jesse can feel the heat in his cheeks when he looks back at Drew.

"This is my Luke Skywalker costume. I wear it when I go to the comic con."

"You cosplay?" Drew asks and for a moment Jesse worries. "That's really cool. I've never done anything like that."

"I have to go early before too many people get there. Maybe you could come with me next time," Jesse says, feeling shy and awkward.

"I won't have to dress as Princess Leia, will I? I don't think I could wear that bikini."

Laughter punches out of Jesse at the thought of Drew dressed as Leia and he feels shaky with relief as he says no. He thinks Drew would make a pretty good Han Solo though.

"Do you want something to drink?" he asks. "I haven't got any wine, but I've got beer and juice and coffee."

Drew asks for juice and follows Jesse out of the bedroom. While Jesse puts Wicket on the bench and pours juice, Drew takes his time to study the black and white photographs on the living room wall. Leaves, puddles, animals at the zoo, animals at the store. Some of Jesse's mom. Random animals asleep or resting. Drew asks if Jesse took them all and when Jesse nods shyly, gives a low, impressed whistle and comes to the kitchen. He leans against the bench, watching as Jesse piles up the cushions in the right order at the end of the sofa.

Jesse knows Drew is watching so he can get it right if he needs to do it and the thought makes Jesse feel warm inside. The only people who have ever done that have been his parents – not that he wants to think about them right now, he's still mad at them – usually, people either make fun of his tics and routines or, like Mr Greenwold, step back and let him do what he needs to do.

Drew always tries to understand what Jesse is doing; he always makes sure there are even numbers of food on Jesse's plates and knows where the glasses and napkins should sit on the table now. The cushions on his own sofa are always in the right order – black, blue, red – when Jesse is over and the pillows face in the right direction. It makes Jesse feel ... special.

When Jesse sits down, Drew tucks Wicket under his arm and picks up their glasses. Puts the glasses on the coffee table in front of them, sits down and rests Wicket on his knee, running his finger over the ageing fur.

"I really like your photos," he says.

"Thank you." Jesse stares at his fingers, embarrassed and nervous.

"Why didn't you tell me about Wicket, Jesse? I would never laugh at you."

He doesn't know what to do. He knows what he wants to say but he also knows he's not supposed to say that. People – normal people – don't say things like that when they've been dating someone for only a month. Mom would tell him he doesn't even know what he is talking about, but he does know.

"Jess?"

Drew is the only person who calls him Jess and it always gives Jesse a funny feeling inside, not unlike the feeling he gets when Drew runs his tongue over that spot on his neck where his pulse beats. Makes him catch his breath and curl his toes.

Mom was wrong about Drew and Wicket, maybe she's wrong about this too.

"Because I love you and I want you to love me, but I thought if you knew you wouldn't because I'm not normal," he says, the words rushing out before he can stop them.

Holding his breath, he waits for Drew to tell him to stop being ridiculous, he could never love someone like Jesse. Someone who needs a comfort toy and who isn't ...normal.

"You know you're a dork, right?" Drew says, putting his arm around Jesse's shoulder. Miserable, Jesse nods, his heart pounding so hard it hurts. "It's a good thing I don't mind loving a dork, isn't it?"

Jesse frowns, trying to make the words make sense. He repeats them to himself twice. He's a dork. Drew doesn't mind loving a dork. Does that mean.... he looks up and is surprised to see Drew is smiling.

"Really?" he says and when Drew reaches out to cup his cheek, he closes his eyes and leans into the touch.

"Really." Drew nods. Jesse flings his arms around Drew, pulling him close, shivering when Drew's hands rub his back; he likes that touch, knows what it usually means.

Before he can do anything about it, Drew pulls back and speaks.

"Would it be okay to stay here tonight?"

"What about Scamp?" Jesse hates the thought of the kitten being lonely; lonely is the worst feeling he thinks.

"She'll be okay for one night, tomorrow we can figure out what to do."

"I could get a litter box for here," Jesse says and his mind begins to jump around. "We could teach her to walk on a lead and go in the car. She's young enough. Lots of cats like going for car rides and walks. So, we could..."

Drew cuts him off by covering his mouth with his hand.

"Breathe. We'll worry about it tomorrow, okay?"

Jesse nods and Drew takes his hand away.

" I taught Sniffles, the bunny at work, to hop on a lead..."

"*Jess!* If you don't shut up so I can kiss you, I'm going to kiss Wicket instead."

Wait. What? Did Drew just threaten to kiss Wicket? Before he can think about that Drew is kissing him and it's so much better than thinking about anything at all.

* * *

Even though it's his apartment, Jesse lets Drew lead the way back to the bedroom. He puts Wicket back on the dresser and turns him to face the wall, feeling a little silly and is sure that Drew will laugh at him now, but he doesn't. Instead, he just opens his arms for Jesse to step into and rubs his cheek against Jesse's head. If lonely is the worst feeling in the world, Jesse thinks, then this is the best. Feeling loved. He tilts his head back and tiptoes, so he can kiss Drew, sliding his arms up and around his neck and pressing against him until he hears the taller man moan.

Jesse pulls at Drew's shirt until it's free from his jeans and fumbles for the buttons. He wants it gone, wants to feel Drew's skin beneath his fingers. Growls when he can't get them undone.

"Okay, okay." Drew chuckles and yanks the garment over his head and drops it on the floor. Tugs at the elastic until his hair drops against his shoulders.

Jesse watches, still and silent, as Drew takes off his sneakers and socks, then his jeans and finally his boxers, panting with the effort to not reach out and touch Drew's skin. Lets Drew undress him and guide him to the bed. Waits while Drew pulls the covers back before stepping back to let Jesse lay down. Finally Drew straddles him and leans forward, taking his weight on his elbows so they're close enough to breathe each other's air.

"You mean it right, Drew?" Jesse asks, eyes wide and searching. "You ... you didn't say it as a joke, you're not going to change your mind?"

Drew smiles and cards his fingers through Jesse's short hair.

"Not joking, not going to change my mind," he says. "I love you, Jess."

Jesse reaches up and takes Drew's glasses off, folds the earpieces with care and puts them on the nightstand, then lifts to kiss Drew, sighing into the kiss and trying to not drown in the sensations rushing at him from every direction. The wet heat of Drew's mouth and the tickling sensation of his long hair brushing against Jesse's skin. The hardness pressing against his thigh and then nudging against his own until he groans.

Drew's hands are everywhere, dragging fire across his skin. Jesse whimpers and rubs his thumbs back and forth across Drew's nipples, enjoying the sounds Drew makes in response. Long fingers glide down his belly and wrap around his cock, moving with slow, sure strokes until Jesse is gasping for air and straining for more friction.

"What do you want, Jess?" Drew asks and dips his head to suck Jesse's left nipple to a hard peak.

Want? What does he want? He wants ... he wants ... oh God...

"More," Jesse whispers, "I want more."

Flash of disappointment when Drew sits back, looking down at him without touching.

"We need..." Drew starts to say and Jesse cuts him off with a smile because this time he knows what he's talking about; he fumbles in the nightstand and finds a brand-new bottle of lube and a packet of condoms. Drew raises an eyebrow, amusement dancing in his eyes.

"I wanted to be ready," Jesse mumbles and presses his face against Drew's chest, embarrassed, "just in case, one day..."

"Just in case," Drew echoes.

The lube is cold and sticky when Drew dribbles it on him; not a sensation Jesse normally likes but right now he doesn't care. Propped up on the pillows, he looks down his body and watches as Drew caresses him with slow, easy movements, fingers dipping lower with each stroke. Then two fingers are touching him, there. Drawing firm circles that press into him. Every circle pushes a little deeper, a little harder until he's relaxed enough for the fingers to slide into him. Jesse catches his breath at the slight burn and tries to keep still.

"Relax," Drew whispers. "Just relax, Jess. I promise I won't hurt you."

Jesse knows that's a promise Drew can't keep.

It always hurts, always burns, but he wants Drew to keep going anyway. It doesn't matter that it's not something Jesse has ever really liked, Drew will do something later with his mouth or hands that he *will* like, so doing this for Drew now makes him happy. And that's enough. Knows that Drew will make it as good as he can – even if he can't stop it hurting. Then Drew twitches the fingers that are moving inside him, crooks one just a little and touches something inside Jesse that makes him arch high off the bed with a cry.

"There we go," Drew murmurs and Jesse has no idea what that means just that it feels as if fireworks are exploding under his skin.

"Again," he begs. Drew groans and moves his fingers, setting off another series of sparks throughout Jesse's body, and making him clutch at the sheets beneath him. While he's still trembling, Drew withdraws his fingers and Jesse is aware of movement over him. He opens his eyes to see Drew rolling the condom on then smoothing lube over it, before pressing forward, hands on Jesse's thighs.

"Relax," Drew repeats and leans down so their lips meet.

Jesse closes his eyes, trying to relax, running his fingers back and forth across Drew's chest, bracing himself for the intrusive, tearing burn he knows is coming. But Drew is gentle, pressing into him with care, taking his time. Jesse can hear

50

Drew's teeth grinding together as he forces himself to go slow, peppering kisses along Jesse's jaw.

"Jess," Drew's breath is warm on his skin, his voice is rough and deep, and Jesse shivers, "please, darlin', relax. Let me make you feel good."

Jesse wants to tell him he already feels good but when he tries to open his mouth, can only moan. Drew's movements are slow and measured and he alternates hard kisses with soft whispers of encouragement. Jesse feels a little dazed when the burning fades, becomes something that feels better – feels so much more than good – and he begins to lift his hips to meet Drew's thrusts. This is different to anything he's experienced before. Before, it's always been fast and unpleasant - at least blow jobs feel good and don't hurt, even if they're messy – but this is new. There's pressure and a sense of being filled, of being completed. A feeling that his whole body is going to explode with sensation. He digs his fingers into the meat of Drew's back and tries to pull him closer.

"Drew...oh ...Drew," he pleads.

Drew swivels his hips and the head of his cock presses against whatever it was his fingers had touched and Jesse can't help jerking his shoulders up off the bed, eyes blown wide with shock and need; Drew does it again, harder this time.

"Yes, yes, yes," Jesse pants. Everything Drew does feels good and Jesse can't think.

"That's it," Drew murmurs. "Come on Jess, let go."

He reaches between them, still murmuring, still swiveling his hips, still pressing with his cock. Jesse drops back against the pillow, his eyes closed tight, mouth open as he twitches and moves under Drew's touch, lost in the sensations. It only takes two firm strokes, and that feels too good, he can't help it, his hips snap up, making a cracking sound as pelvic bones hit pelvic bones, and even though he's trying hard not to, he comes. Hard.

Jesse is aware Drew is still moving, breath heavy and fast, still stroking him, but it's a vague awareness. Everything else is centered on the feeling that his entire body is shuddering into pieces; every inch of him is falling apart as come hits his skin.

"Jess ...oh fuck ... I'm going to ... oh yes," Drew pants against his neck and then his movements stop, his body rigid above Jesse. He makes a long, low whimpering sound and if Jesse didn't know what that meant, it would be easy to believe he was in pain.

They lay for a long time, the silence broken only by ragged panting, until Jesse wriggles out from beneath Drew, gets up and goes to the bathroom for a washcloth because that is what Drew does whenever they're at his apartment. Jesse looks at himself in the mirror. Nothing has changed but everything is different. He didn't know sex could be like that, could make him feel like he had been broken into millions of tiny fragments and put back together. Didn't know being loved could make him feel, for the first time ever, as though he's whole.

"Jess?" Drew calls. "Are you okay?"

He returns to the bed and takes his time cleaning them both up, then rinses the washcloth before throwing it in the laundry hamper, turns Wicket back around, and climbs back into bed. Drew is waiting and pulls him against his chest, strokes his hair when he's settled.

"We good?" Drew asks and Jesse hugs him tight; he thinks if he tries to speak he might cry and he really does not want to do that. "Jesse?"

"I didn't know," he says, trying to hide against Drew's body and drawing circles on the smooth skin of Drew's chest.

"Didn't know what?"

"That it could feel so good. Like even better than a blow job."

"The other times you've done that, haven't been good?" Drew kisses his head.

"No," Jesse whispers, tears close. "It always hurt, and it was always really quick and I never...you know..."

"Shhh, it's okay," Drew says. "It's meant to feel good and when you take care of each other it usually is."

"I didn't take care of you though."

Drew laughs again.

"Yeah you did, Jess. Don't worry, next time will be even better."

Jesse isn't sure he'll survive sex being even better and says so.

"I love you, Drew," he says when Drew stops laughing.

"I love you too Jess." Drew moves him so they're spooning, Drew's chest warm against Jesse's back. "You still mad at your mom?"

Jesse doesn't want to talk about his parents right now, but he supposes if he wants to be treated like he's an adult, he should try to act like one.

"A little bit. Not as much."

"You should call her."

"She'll be asleep," he says, not wanting to move. He's sleepy and just wants to close his eyes.

"Not now, you dork," Drew says. "In the morning."

Jesse can feel Drew's smile against his skin as sleep takes him.

* * *

13

"He's gorgeous," Jody says, handing Drew a Starbucks cup and unlocking the library. He sips his coffee. "And I don't just mean to look at. Though, I could look at him all day long. Wow – you sure kept that bit a secret."

"Yeah, I know," Drew says, grinning. He has half an hour before homeroom and is dying to know what Jody thought of Jesse. "Guess I didn't want to jinx it."

"Oh God, you're nauseating," she says. "Seriously, if you're going to be so vomit inducing happy, can you do it somewhere else?"

"Bite me. So apart from finding him hot, what else did you think of my boyfriend?"

"Ooooh, so it's official? We're using labels and shit?" Jody ignores the one-fingered salute Drew gives her, pushes some books to the corner of her desk, and sits down. She puts her feet on the desk, crossed at the ankle, and tips her chair back while she drinks her coffee. "I thought he was great."

"And?"

"And I don't think you're trying to rescue him."

Drew looks at her and narrows his eyes; she's staring at her shoes, a sure sign she's holding something back.

"But?" He nudges her foot. "Come on, spill it."

Jody sighs and sits up straight, letting her feet come to rest on the carpet.

"Drew, he's mildly retarded – sorry, intellectually challenged. He's very able and well adjusted, sure, but that doesn't change the fact that he is those things. Whatever the correct term is. Not to mention on the spectrum, dyslexia, and obsessive-compulsive. Any one of those is a big deal. But the combination?"

"I know," Drew says. He scuffs his toe along the carpet, feels his good humor evaporating.

"Do you?" Jody asks. "Look it's pretty clear how you feel about each other; hell, you'd have to be blind to not see it, and I'm not stupid enough to try and talk you out of whatever it is. But I do think you should talk to someone, get some help on how to deal with him."

"Deal with him?" Drew asks, anger flashing in his eyes.

"Okay bad choice of words, settle down. Tell me, honey, what are you going to do if something happens and he reacts in a way that's normal for him, but you don't know that? Or what if he starts doing something like pulling his hair out like the O'Brien girl did that time?"

"Stimming," Drew says. "It's called stimming. Self-stimulation. And he doesn't stim like that."

Jody just looks at him and he sighs. Knows she's right.

"I don't even know who to ask," he says letting a wave of misery crash over him.

Jody had come for lunch on Saturday and had been a big hit, in large part because she wore a Doctor Who tee-shirt, rainbow colored suspenders, and bright red sneakers. Tucked in the pocket of her baggy jeans was the sonic screwdriver Drew had given her for Christmas a few years back. Jesse had loved her immediately and had given her a long hug when she was ready to leave.

Now, Drew thinks, dragging himself back to the present, he has to face the real world. And Jody is right, he needs help. If he wants to have any real relationship with Jesse – and he does - he needs to understand what Jesse needs from him. He sighs.

"Casey would probably be able to help," Jody says. Casey is the school nurse and Drew nods. "Failing that, good old Google is your friend."

Drew glances at the clock; he still has twenty minutes until homeroom. Jody leans over to swat his arm and rolls her eyes.

"Oh, for God's sake, go. She'll be there already, so go on, go ask her." She accepts his hug with a grin. "And don't come back in here until you lose the puppy dog eyes."

* * *

Fifteen minutes later, Drew walks toward his room, backpack swinging from one hand, a piece of paper with a name and a phone number written on it in Casey's neat handwriting, clutched in the other.

* * *

14

"Drew Oliver?"

Doctor Sutton is tall, with silver hair, tortoiseshell hornrims and a beige cardigan. Drew shakes the hand he's holding out and follows him into his office.

"Thank you for agreeing to talk to me, I really appreciate it."

"Let's see if I can help before you thank me." He points to a chair in the corner by the window for Drew to sit in and sits back behind his desk. On the wall behind him are a series of bright colored finger paintings; beside them are two large, framed diplomas announcing the doctor's qualifications. "You said you wanted to talk to me about autism. Any particular reason?"

Drew studies his fingers for a moment while he collects his thoughts. Casey said this was the guy to talk to when he'd asked her, that he specializes in autism. Drew had brushed off her curiosity by saying he was asking for a friend whose teenage son he'd met, easing his guilt by telling himself that things were still too new with Jesse to be telling the world about him. Sitting here he feels guilty again, as though he's betraying Jesse's trust somehow.

"Mr Oliver?"

"Okay, so this is harder than I thought it would be," he admits, reminding himself this is for Jesse. "I am in a relationship, a fairly new relationship, with someone who has been diagnosed on the autism spectrum and I am just trying to figure out what sort of things I should be looking for or doing or – God that sounds so lame. I guess, I just want to understand Jesse better."

"I see," Doctor Sutton says. He taps his nose with an index finger. "And how long have you and Jesse been seeing each other."

"About five weeks."

"And when was she diagnosed?"

Drew takes a deep breath and runs his fingers through his hair. Clears his throat.

"Jesse was diagnosed, as far as I know, when he was quite young. He's twenty-six now."

"Oh, I see," the doctor says, and Drew prepares himself to be berated. Or thrown out. Or whatever. It's not like it would be the first time, but instead, Doctor Sutton simply nods, scribbles some notes on the legal pad in front of him, and asks him to continue.

"He's also dyslexic, quite severely I think, and has Mears-Irlen and some obsessive-compulsive traits. He's also mildly intellectually disabled or whatever the appropriate term is," Drew pushes his glasses up. "He struggles to process some things, especially socially, but most of the time he's just, you know, a normal guy. "

Sutton smiles.

"That's quite a bag of tricks," he says. "He is quite capable obviously though."

"He owns his own apartment," Drew says, unable to hide the awe in his voice; he's still impressed that Jesse, at twenty-six, actually owns his own apartment. "He has a job in a pet store, he's been there for about seven years. Likes to go to movies or out to dinner, if it's not too noisy or crowded. Plays video games. Takes incredible black and white photos. Like I said, just a normal guy."

"Okay. So, Drew, if he's just a normal guy, why are you here?"

Drew takes his glasses off and polishes them. Jody wasn't wrong; he's in love with Jesse but it's not going to be easy. He's a thirty-four-year-old high school English teacher and the man he loves is twenty-six, dyslexic, autistic, and at best has a mild intellectual disability. Forget how society is going to react to them being together as two men, how will society react to the differences in their minds? Before he can handle the rest of the world, Drew needs to figure out how he's going to handle their relationship.

"Because I know he's *not* just a normal guy. According to his mother, he's mildly intellectually disabled, though I should say it's more around social interaction as far as I can see. He doesn't strike me as impaired as such. But when he can't do things he thinks normal people do, he gets frustrated and he's easily flustered. In many ways, he can be quite childlike but he's not a child. Then there are things he does, he needs to do to feel okay, that I don't really understand, and I want to, like how he doesn't look at me especially if he's worried or scared. I just, I don't want to do something dumb and hurt him." He puts his glasses back on and looks across the desk. "I really care about him."

Doctor Sutton purses his lips and waits. Drew sighs.

"Look, I'm not trying to fix him and I'm not trying to take advantage him, I just - I don't want to screw this up."

"What about his family?"

"He's an only child and his parents seem very supportive, but his mom is a little wary of me. I guess she's worried I'll hurt him, which I understand, but it means she's kind of got me at arm's length."

"And his father?"

"Ray's a little more accepting but I think he's got his hands full trying to convince his wife to ease up a little on Jesse. He doesn't need to be trying to teach me."

"And what about Jesse himself? Have you asked him?"

"Well, that's kind of why I'm here." Drew gives the doctor a brief outline of what had happened the previous Friday. "I didn't even know what stimming was – I mean, I'd encountered it, but I didn't know it had a name, until he told me, and he'd never shown any signs of needing to do anything like that when he stayed at my place. So, I didn't know to even ask. Or to look for it. Or whatever. I feel like I'm walking on the proverbial damned eggshells."

"You say Jesse stays at your place regularly, but you've never seen signs of stimming? Or of needing it?"

Drew shakes his head.

"Not unless I'm missing it, which is why I'm here. Sometimes we go somewhere, and he might get tense, so we just go back to my place and I read to him."

"Read to him?"

"Yeah, he loves it. We're reading *The Hobbit*."

"And that helps him?"

Drew shrugs.

"I guess. Most of the time he falls asleep next to me and ..." Drew's voice trails off and he covers his eyes with one hand; he feels sure Doctor Sutton is going to think he's an idiot.

"Mr Oliver?"

"I have a kitten," Drew says. "That's how we met. I was buying stuff for her at the pet store he works in. When I read to him, he always has Scamp on his lap. Always. He strokes her head while I read. He's been using her as a substitute for Wicket, hasn't he? God, I feel stupid."

Doctor Sutton surprises him by roaring with laughter.

"Why? As you say you didn't know, and it's natural to assume the reading settled him down. After all, many of us fall asleep when reading for that very reason. But it does sound as though it's Scamp that's calming him and the story is incidental – which isn't to say he's not enjoying it. I'm actually more intrigued that he appears to have hidden his need to stim from you."

"When I asked him why he hadn't told me, he said it was because he thought I wouldn't love him if I knew. That I'd think it was too weird."

The doctor looks up from the notes he's writing.

"I take it, he was wrong."

Drew shrugs. He may as well admit it.

"I don't think there's much that could stop me loving him."

"I see. May I ask some personal questions?"

"If it will help Jesse, you can ask whatever you like. And if you're asking if we have sex, yes we do."

"And he's both willing and active?"

"Jesus, yes," Drew says, horrified at the suggestion he might force Jesse into something he didn't want. "I'd never, never ..."

"Mr Oliver, calm down. I didn't mean to suggest anything. Sometimes people do what they think will please the people they love; autistic people are no different and people with intellectual disabilities, even mild, can be very affectionate without really understanding what's happening."

Drew considers this, then shakes his head.

"He understands, that much I am sure of. We only had actual, you know, penetrative sex for the first time last week," he says trying to not look as embarrassed as he feels discussing this. "Before then it's always just been uh you know uh manual and oral and um stuff like that. But only ever anything Jesse was comfortable with and wanted. And he's always enjoyed it."

"Any history of abuse? Sexual or otherwise?"

"Not that I know of. Certainly not from his family. It wasn't his first time and he did say that his previous times hadn't been very enjoyable, but I don't think they were forced. And I don't think there's been any other kind of abuse either, except for people being typical assholes of course."

He tells Doctor Sutton about the first time he met Jesse, watching as he notes it down in his long, looping scrawl.

"Did you know, or did you suspect, he was autistic when you asked him out?"

"Not at all, I mean I could see he had some challenges. I've had some students who have had learning or social challenges, so I guessed he had something like that. When I found out he was dyslexic I figured it was that."

"How did you find out about his diagnosis?"

"After I'd asked him out he sent me a text saying he had things wrong with him. So, we met for a drink and he told me. Why?"

"I guess I'm a little intrigued. You said on the phone you're a high school teacher, and now you're saying you've met this young man who works in a pet store, who has a collection of challenges, to use your term, and you not only want to go out with him, you say you're in love with him. I'm sure you'll agree there's a bit of a difference between you, so I guess I'm wondering what the attraction is."

Drew picks a piece of lint off the edge of his cuff. The question isn't surprising or even unexpected and he supposes it's one he'll have to get used to, but it angers him anyway. He pulls his cellphone from his pocket and when he's sure he can speak without losing his temper, he chooses his words carefully as he presses the on switch.

"Look I get that it's probably not a very typical situation, quite aside from the gay component, but Jesse is not a very typical man. Even without his challenges, he wouldn't be. For a start, he's extraordinary looking." Drew hands the phone across to Doctor Sutton; the home screen is a photo of Jesse sitting under a tree at the local park. He's looking directly at the camera, smiling, head tilted to one side. "But that's not what attracts me to him, not that it hurts of course, but there's something about Jesse that I can't explain, you'd have to meet him to understand it. He's just, I don't know, Jesse —sweet and loving and kind and sometimes he comes out with this stuff that just blows you away. And okay he can't read very well but he owns his own apartment, manages his mortgage and his finances pretty much by himself with only a little help from his parents. All I know is I don't want to hurt him by doing something stupid out of ignorance."

Doctor Sutton looks at the phone for a moment then hands it back.

"You're right, he's extraordinary looking. Sometimes, life is a bitch that way," he says, making Drew blink in surprise. "I think the best thing to do, would, in fact, be for me to meet Jesse. Do you think that's possible?"

"I don't know about bringing him in here," Drew says. The sensation that he's betraying Jesse has returned.

"That's okay, Jesse's not a patient so we could meet somewhere neutral."

Drew thinks for a moment.

"He swims every morning and at the weekend I go with him. On Sunday, we usually go to the Library Bar for lunch after. Would that work?"

"Over on Collingwood? Yes, I could manage that this Sunday. About midday? Great. He swims every day? Even when you're together?"

"Pretty much, yeah. Why?"

"It's another form of controlling stimulation overload. Something for you to be aware of."

Doctor Sutton stands and walks Drew to the door.

"Well if we're having lunch together, I think we'd best be on a first name basis, Drew. I'm Martin and I have your contact details so if anything comes up I'll be in touch, otherwise I'm looking forward to meeting Jesse on Sunday," he says as Drew goes out to the reception area.

* * *

15

Jesse likes Wednesday nights. Wednesday is the one night of the week Drew has no rehearsals, meetings, or other school activities once the bell has rung, which means he leaves school earlier than usual. Sometimes they go to a movie or get pizza and watch Netflix at Drew's place. Tonight, though, Drew is coming to Jesse's apartment and they're going to have burgers and watch Alien. Drew said he might even be able to stay over. Jesse hopes he does. Drew had an appointment and said he'd pick up the food on his way over. Jesse hates pickle on his burger and just as he's getting ready to send Drew a text to remind him, the buzzer sounds.

When Jesse opens the door, all he can see are take-out bags and milkshake cups. Best of all is a carrier with two chocolate sundaes and Jesse grabs them before they can fall.

"Hey, burgers first Jess," Drew yells from behind the bags as he shuts the door with his foot.

"You're not my mother," Jesse retorts and helps him put the rest of the food on the coffee table. "I don't need your rules."

"Oh, is that so?" Drew says. He slips his arms around Jesse's waist and nuzzles his neck. "Well, I think we should have a rule that says you have to kiss me as soon as I appear in your doorway."

Jesse's hand is halfway to the bag of burgers and stops, frowning.

"But what if I'm really hungry?" he asks.

"What if I really need a kiss?"

"You always need a kiss," Jesse says, frown clearing as he realizes Drew is being silly and swivels in his arms.

"True," Drew says and dips his head to kiss Jesse's mouth. "And you're always hungry. So, the sooner you kiss me, the sooner you get to eat."

Jesse kisses him again, then steps out of his hold and starts piling up the cushions.

"I think it should be the other way around," he says. "I think it should be the sooner I eat, the sooner you get kissed."

Drew laughs and drops to the sofa. Jesse peers in one of the bags, checking for pickles.

"Yours is the other bag," Drew says, "The one with no pickle."

Jesse's eyes light up and he sits down with his burger.

"You remembered," he says around a mouthful of bun and meat.

"You sent me about a dozen text messages Jess, I could hardly forget. And gross, I really don't want to see what you're chewing darlin'."

Jesse swallows, pokes his tongue at Drew, and reaches for the fries. He examines them then chooses one and picks up one of the sundaes; flips the lid off and dips the fry in until his fingertips are almost touching the ice-cream. Pulls the fry out and eats it.

"Oh God, Jess, that's revolting," Drew says, screwing his face up in disgust.

Jesse looks at him in surprise.

"What?"

"French fries and chocolate sundae, that's what. Gross, dude."

"I like it," Jesse says with a shrug, unconcerned. He finds another fry and dips it in his dessert. Gives Drew a slow smile, shuts his eyes, closes his mouth around the fry and makes an obscene sound as he slurps ice-cream from it with as much enthusiasm as he can. When he finally swallows and opens his eyes, Drew is watching him, mouth open, burger in mid-air. His glasses have slid down his nose and his cheeks are red.

"What?" Jesse asks, worried he's done something wrong.

"Just hurry up and eat your burger," Drew says finally. "I'm going to need more kisses."

* * *

The alien is about to burst out of John Hurt's stomach on the screen, but Jesse doesn't care; he's seen it before. He's more interested in the sounds Drew's making as he kisses him; they're soft sounds that sort of remind him of Scamp and every time he rolls his hips forward against Drew's they get a little more urgent. It makes Jesse feel giddy, knowing he can make Drew sound that way just by moving. He snakes a hand up the back of Drew's shirt and wonders what other sounds he can get him to make. Just as he's deciding to try something, Drew breaks the kiss and, pulls away, panting. Annoyed, Jesse tries to pull him back down, but Drew resists.

"Let me catch my breath and calm down a second," he says. Jesse frowns, he doesn't want Drew to calm down. That's not the point of the exercise, he points out, and Drew gives a shaky laugh. "No, it's not, but I'd kind of like to make it to the bedroom and get undressed before I lose it and if we keep going, that's not going to be an option."

Oh well, if that's all he wants, Jesse thinks, that's easily solved and tries to stand up. Drew pulls him back on to the sofa.

"Just a moment, I also need to talk to you about something before I get completely distracted," Drew says. His voice sounds calmer and Jesse finds that annoying; he, Jesse, isn't calm and he doesn't think Drew should be either. He folds his arms and waits. Drew grins and shakes his head.

"Stop sulking, I promise this won't take long. On Sunday, after swimming, I thought we'd go to *The Library Bar* and meet a friend of mine for lunch. Would that be okay?"

"I thought we were going to your mom and dad's house?"

"No that's the weekend after. Remember?"

"Is it Jody?"

"No, it's not. His name is Martin Sutton, he's nice. Is that okay, Jess?"

Jesse shrugs; he doesn't care. He just wants to hear those sounds again.

"Jess?"

"Yes, yes, yes," Jesse says, throwing his hands up in frustration. "Can we stop talking now?"

Drew raises an eyebrow.

"Uh yeah, I guess. Are you okay?"

"No," Jesse snaps. "I don't want to talk about Sunday and weekends. I want to kiss you."

"Oh, okay." Drew laughs and reaches across the back of the sofa to run his fingers through Jesse's hair. "Shall we – woah!"

Out of patience, Jesse flings himself at Drew, pushing him down on the sofa and covering his mouth with his own. He grinds down against the older man until he hears the whimpering sound from earlier.

They never do make it to the bedroom.

* * *

16

The Library Bar is just starting to fill up when Drew sees Doctor Sutton arrive and raises his hand to wave him over. He introduces him to Jesse who stands up but won't look the doctor in the eye. Jesse has been in a funny mood all morning, withdrawn, almost sulky, and refuses to tell Drew what the problem is.

"I'm Jesse," he says and shakes the hand that is being offered without looking up.

"Hello Jesse, I'm Martin, it's nice to meet you."

Drew signals the waitress to bring another menu and asks Martin what he'd like to drink.

"What are you both drinking?" Martin asks.

"Drew's having shiz...shar...red wine with a funny name and I'm having apple juice because I feel fuzzy today," Jesse says. Drew explains he means Shiraz and frowns, that's the second time this morning Jesse has said he feels fuzzy. What does fuzzy mean? He has a growing lexicon of Jesse-isms and he supposes this is just one more addition.

"Then I'll join you in a Shiraz," Martin says. "What have you been doing this morning, Jesse?"

Jesse glances up, narrows his eyes and drops his head again. Drew bites his lip, fighting the urge to answer for him.

"We went swimming. I swim every morning."

"Swimming's good exercise. Do you like swimming?"

"Yes."

Something's wrong. Jesse's speaking with the same monotone he had when he was upset with his parents. Is he upset with Drew? Why? Drew frowns and rubs his eyes. The waitress arrives with his wine and Jesse's juice and takes Martin's order.

"Did you have fun swimming this morning?"

Jesse nods. He's still not looking at Martin but stealing glances at Drew and running his finger around the mouth of his glass. Drew frowns.

"Do you want your usual for lunch, Jess?" Drew asks. Jesse just shrugs. Confused, Drew looks to the doctor, who is watching Jesse, fingers forming a steeple beneath his chin.

"Jesse, do you mind me having lunch with you and Drew?"

Jesse runs his palms along his jeans and shrugs again.

"Jess," Drew leans toward him and laces their fingers together, "what's wrong?"

"Nothing." Jesse pulls his hand away from Drew's, lifts his head and shoots a look at Martin that is filled with such loathing, Drew's mouth drops open in shock. He's never seen him act like this before and racks his brain to try and pinpoint what he may have done. Martin leans forward.

"Jesse, did Drew tell you who I am?"

Jesse shakes his head. "You're his friend."

"My name is Martin Sutton and I'm a doctor," Martin tells him,

Jesse's head jerks up, eyes wide and suspicious; Drew's heart sinks. This was a bad idea; the whole thing is turning into a disaster. He takes a mouthful of wine to try and calm his nerves.

"What kind of doctor?" Jesse asks; his head is lowered but Drew can see that he's watching Martin all the same. He's more concerned by the tension he can feel in Jesse's body and his refusal to let Drew touch him.

"I'm a psychologist and I specialize in things like autism," Martin says.

Drew groans and closes his eyes. This could not get any worse, he thinks, and prepares himself for Jesse losing his cool. Not that he blames him, he should never have gone behind his back to Sutton. He should have just tried to figure it out with Jesse's parents and Google and maybe Jody to help. He slumps back in his chair.

"Drew, are you sick?" Jesse asks, voice high with panic. Fingers creep over the back of his hand and he opens his eyes. The suspicion is gone from Jesse's eyes, replaced by fear.

"What? No." Didn't he hear what kind of doctor Sutton said he is?

"You made a funny noise and you're all white and you look like my mom did just before she fainted when she was sick once."

Oh. Yeah, Drew bets he does. He's not entirely sure he isn't going to faint to be honest, if only from the shock that Jesse isn't having a meltdown about Martin.

"Uh no, Jess, I'm fine. I probably just need something to eat," he says and catches sight of Martin's amused face. What the hell is going on?

"Are you sure? Martin could give you a checkup if you feel sick."

Drew squeezes Jesse's hand, relieved to have it back in his own, and tries to smile.

"I'm okay, I promise. How about we order some lunch?" He signals the waitress.

Jesse nods and asks for his usual – the Chicken Parmigiana– and another glass of juice.

"That sounds pretty good, I think I'll have the same," Martin says. Drew orders the salmon fishcakes and a half bottle of wine to share with Martin.

"Jesse, why do you think I'm here?" Martin asks, and Drew holds his breath.

"Because of my stuff. Drew wants to know what he should do."

Red droplets spray over the table as Drew chokes on a mouthful of wine. Coughing and spluttering he gropes for a napkin to mop the mess up, while Jesse pounds him on the back. Eventually, he turns and stills Jesse's hand.

"Enough Jess," he croaks, "I'm good."

Jesse peers in his face and is obviously far from convinced by what he sees because although he stops pounding, he continues rubbing Drew's back.

"It's okay Drew," Jesse says. "I know it's not easy for a normie to understand and to put up with someone like me."

"Jess, don't say things like that. I don't put up with you," Drew says, horrified at the choice of words. "I love you."

Jesse nods.

"I know but that doesn't mean it's easy," he says.

"Why do you think that's why I'm here, Jesse?" Martin asks.

Jesse shrugs.

"You're a doctor for autistic people and I'm autistic."

"When I got here, Jesse, you weren't very happy to see me," Martin says and Jesse drops his eyes, color creeping up cheeks. "Were you worried I might take Drew away from you?"

Jesse nods, then looks up, eyes defiant, darting from Martin to Drew.

"I thought you wanted to break up with me," he says.

"Oh Jess," Drew whispers, "I'm so sorry. No, that's not what I want at all."

Before the conversation can go any further, their meals arrive, and they wait while Jesse rearranges the dishes into the right places. Checks his dish – one chicken breast and fries. He counts them and holds the extra fry out for Drew to eat. A small bowl with two lettuce leaves, two slices of tomato, and two mushrooms cut in quarters is on the side. The waitresses know his order. Happy he picks up his fork and begins eating.

"Jesse," Martin says, "I think Drew was worried he might upset you if he told you he had come to see me and that's why he didn't tell you. Do you know why he might have been frightened?"

Jesse frowns and Drew can't help but smile. There's the small crease between his eyebrows, the tip of his tongue just visible at the corner of his mouth. His hand wanders up to Drew's shoulders, fingers flipping strands of damp hair back and forth and in a flash of comprehension, Drew realizes Jesse is using him as a Wicket substitute. Jesse's face clears, and he looks up.

"Because people don't think it's right for normal people and people like me to be together. So, they think the normal person must be trying to fix the other person and Drew didn't want me to think he was trying to fix me because I got mad when my parents said that was what he was trying to do. People hate that we're gay, but they hate it more that Drew is normal and I'm not."

Drew is speechless. He'd had no idea Jesse had understood what his parents thought, had no idea Jesse even knew they thought that. Not only that, Jesse has a much wider understanding of how their relationship is likely to be seen than he's given him credit for. Shame floods him; the very thing he'd been reproaching Jesse's parents for doing, of not accepting Jesse as a whole person, he has been just as guilty of.

"That's a pretty good synopsis, Jesse," Martin says. His mouth quirks up in a smile when Jesse frowns again. "That means you explained it well. Do you think Drew is trying to fix you?'

Drew opens his mouth to protest but snaps it shut again when Jesse looks him in the eye and smiles.

"No, I think he just worries he's doing things wrong, but he's not. I think mostly he just loves me," Jesse says and Drew squeezes his hand. "I hope he does anyway."

Drew leans forward and bumps Jesse's forehead with his own and whispers that he does love him, happy when Jesse blushes and kisses him.

"So, what do you think he should do, Jesse?" Martin asks

Jesse shrugs.

"He's a teacher, they learn lots of things, so he could find out that way," Jesse says, slurping a French fry into his mouth. Drew taps his ankle with his toe and shakes his head. Jesse shrugs. "Or he could ask me. Just not when we're having sex."

Drew is very grateful that he doesn't have a mouthful of wine this time.

"*Jess! Filter.*"

" If I can wait until after sex to tell him stuff, he should be able to."

"*Jesse!*" Drew's face is scarlet, and he doesn't know what to say. Meanwhile, Martin is laughing so hard, tears are running down his face. Jesse sips his apple juice and looks up under his lashes and it dawns on Drew that he knows perfectly well what he is saying. His mouth drops open. Jesse leans forward and plants a loud kiss on his mouth.

"I keep telling you, I'm not stupid," he says, then smiles, "I love you."

* * *

"It was really nice to meet you, Jesse," Martin says as they leave the bar after lunch.

"I'm sorry I was rude when you got here," Jesse says, looking shamefaced.

"That's okay, Jesse, I understand why you were."

"Maybe Drew could come and see you some more," Jesse says, eyes darting from Martin's face to the ground and back again. "When he doesn't understand stuff or when it's hard for him. Because I don't think I'll be very good at helping him with that bit."

Drew is starting to feel like Jesse is far more qualified to help anyone than Drew will ever be and just shakes his head in stunned silence.

"I think that's a great idea." Martin turns to Drew with a grin. "Why don't you give me a call tomorrow? When you're over the shock of today."

Drew nods and they shake hands. He and Jesse watch the doctor walk away, then Jesse takes Drew's hand.

"I'm sorry I wasn't very nice this morning," he whispers.

"It's okay Jess, I think I deserved it," Drew says with a smile.

As they walk to the car, Drew pulls Jesse's hand and puts it on his waist, wraps his arm around his shoulder. The worst of winter is gone, and the first signs of spring are starting to show, but it's cool and he'll be glad to get back inside.

"Jesse," he says, "when you say you feel fuzzy, what do you mean?"

When Jesse doesn't answer immediately but rests his head on Drew's shoulder, Drew wonders if he hasn't heard him, but when he glances down at his face can see the familiar concentration mask. As they near the car, Jesse seems to come back to him and straightens up.

"When I get scared, it feels like I'm made of something fuzzy. Not soft like Wicket or Scamp or your hair," he says, and Drew is amused to see him bite his lip as he steals a glance at Drew's hair, "it's more like … you know when sweaters and blankets get old and covered in those little balls of gross stuff?"

Drew searches for what he means.

"Oh, when they pill, you mean?"

"Maybe," Jesse says, "when they get like that, they don't feel nice and that's how I feel when I get scared or angry."

"Were you scared this morning? You kept saying you felt fuzzy."

Jesse stops walking.

"I thought you wanted to break up with me."

"Jess I asked you if it was okay for Martin to have lunch with us, on Wednesday night. You can always say no if you don't want to do something."

Jesse's face wrinkles in concentration again.

"It didn't bother me on Wednesday, you were kissing me on Wednesday, but then I started thinking about it and then this morning I just wanted you to myself and when I saw him I just thought …" his voice trails off.

"You thought what?" Drew prompts but he has a feeling he knows what's coming.

"I thought maybe you were tired of someone like me and wanted someone normal."

Drew sighs and pulls Jesse against his chest. He supposes he needs to get used to this, that like the questions from other people about their relationship, Jesse's constant questioning of his feelings is something he needs to accept.

"I'm not tired of you and I don't want anyone else," he says. "Okay?"

Jesse nods as they continue walking.

"I'm sorry I frightened you Jesse but next time you're feeling fuzzy maybe you could tell me why," Drew suggests and is surprised when Jesse shakes his head and kicks at a can on the ground.

"Sometimes I can't. Sometimes I don't know why I feel fuzzy until after," he says, then adds, "but I'll try."

Drew smiles, he'll take it.

"Jesse," he says, "one other thing."

"Mmhmm?"

"Next time you want to make a point, could you leave our sex life out of it?"

"Okay," Jesse says, "next time you want to tell me something don't do it when you're kissing me."

Drew laughs and fishes in his pocket for his car keys.

"Deal."

* * *

17

Jesse scoops Scamp up in his arms as soon as they are in the door of Drew's apartment. The small black cat scrambles to his shoulder, bumping her head against his face and purring. He cradles her to him as he checks the cushions on the sofa and goes into Drew's bedroom to check the pillow slips.

"You know it's kind of insulting that she likes you so much more than she likes me." Drew throws his keys on the counter.

"She has good taste," Jesse says as he comes back. He bumps the kitten's head with his own before putting her in the cave on the top of the cat tree, stroking her head until she curls in a ball, eyes drooping. Drew pulls him back against his chest and he leans his head back on his shoulder, smiling up at him.

"Would you like to stay here tonight?"

Jesse blinks in confusion. It's Sunday, Drew has lesson plans and marking to do, and Jesse does laundry on Sunday nights, so they don't spend the night together even though Jesse would like to. He turns in his arms and runs his finger tip over the buttons on Drew's blue shirt, eyes fixed on the small pieces of blue plastic. It's his favorite shirt of Drew's.

"It's Sunday," he says.

"I know." Jesse can hear a smile in Drew's voice. "And I have to do some work for my classes, but you could watch a movie while I do that. You know, if you want to stay."

Jesse looks up and studies Drew's face. Frowns. Why does he look so worried? He doesn't think it's because of what he did at lunch – Jesse is still pleased with himself – so that means it's something else. Something not obvious that Drew isn't saying out loud.

"Do you want me to stay?" Jesse asks. He reaches his arms up and links his hands behind Drew's neck. His eyes shine in the mid-afternoon light streaming through the windows and he smiles. It's one of the rare times he thinks he knows how other people, how normal people, must feel; like everything makes sense. Nothing needs an order, nothing is confused, everything just fits. He wonders if maybe Drew is scared that Jesse won't want to stay which is silly.

"Yes, I want you to stay," Drew says and strokes Jesse's cheek. His shoulders relax, and Jesse knows he was right. But there's still a problem.

"I don't have any clean clothes for work tomorrow."

"We could go and get some from your place and bring them back here," Drew says. "Or we could go and buy you some new ones to leave here. That way you always have clothes when you stay."

Jesse considers this a moment and shakes his head. He has lots of clothes in his closet at home. Mom is always buying him stuff because she doesn't think he can do it himself. But he buys himself clothes all the time; the other day he bought a t-shirt with Darth Vader on it.

"No, I don't need any new clothes, but I could just leave some of mine here," he says, hoping he's understood what Drew is saying. "You could leave some of yours at my place too."

To Jesse's relief, Drew smiles and hugs him.

"Shall we do that now? When we get back, I can do my work and get it out of the way and then we can watch a movie."

Jesse snatches the keys from the counter and holds them out.

"Or maybe we might think of something better to do than watch a movie," he says and goes to the door. Yelps when his butt is slapped.

"Might we just?" Drew says in his ear. "I'm starting to think you're not anywhere near as innocent as you seem, you know."

Jess turns gold eyes on Drew and grins.

"It's not my fault you keep thinking things about me that aren't true." He holds the door open.

Jesse doesn't know what the word is for the opposite feeling to lonely, he doesn't even know if there is one. But, he thinks as they wait for the lift and Drew's hand is warm on the small of his back, he knows how 'not lonely' feels. He likes 'not lonely'.

* * *

Drew closes his laptop and rubs his eyes. Behind him, Jesse is curled up on the sofa with Scamp, watching a movie on Drew's iPad with headphones. Every now and then he laughs at something on the screen, surprising Drew with how much he enjoys the sound of it. He stretches and goes to the kitchen, trailing his fingers through Jesse's hair as he passes, where he pours a glass of scotch for himself and a glass of milk for Jesse. On a hunch, he grabs a bag of chocolate chip cookies from the pantry and goes to the sofa.

Jesse sits up when he sees him and accepts the glass of milk, eyes lighting up when he spots the cookies. Drew grins and holds them just out of reach until he takes the headphones off, making grabby hands and pouting.

"What are you watching?" he asks, dropping down on the sofa.

"*The Hangover*, but it's finished now," Jesse replies. "Open the cookies already."

"*The Hangover?* Really?" Drew starts to protest then reminds himself that even if some of the innuendo goes over his head, he probably understands more of it than the kids he teaches, and he knows they've all seen it. Maybe he does need to talk to Sutton a little more, he thinks.

"Mmmhmm, I like Bradley Cooper," Jesse says. He turns the iPad off and turns to face Drew. "Can I taste your drink?"

Drew blinks, caught off guard. He's never thought twice about the beer or wine Jesse has on occasion with dinner or in the evening, he's an adult after all, but he never drinks much, never more than one glass of wine or two beers and seems to prefer milk or apple juice. Somehow Drew has never even considered he might drink something stronger or that he might want to. As if reading his mind, Jesse reaches for the glass.

"I just want to taste it," he says and lifts the glass to his lips and takes a sip, then shudders and shakes his head. "It kind of burns. Like tea that's too hot but you don't know until you've swallowed it. Or chili sauce."

"You don't like chili sauce, what would you know?"

"I don't like chili sauce because it burns," Jesse says with perfect Jesse logic and reaches for the cookie bag. "Cookies. Now."

Drew hands the bag over in exchange for his glass and sits back with a sigh. Shuts his eyes. The day has been long and weird, he thinks, and it would be easy to just drift off and ... something heavy lands in his lap. He lifts an eyelid and is greeted by a wide, sunny smile. Oh lord, what did he do to deserve that smile in his life, he wonders.

"Can I help you?" he asks.

"Want a cookie?" Jesse holds one up to his mouth and he takes a bite, shaking his head when Jesse shoves the rest in his own mouth in a shower of crumbs. "Are you going to go see Martin tomorrow?"

"Doctor Sutton? Well, I'm going to call him tomorrow, but I probably won't be able to see him. Why?"

Jesse shrugs and finishes his cookie.

"I think you should talk to him if it makes you feel better. I think I should go and see my mom and dad and talk to them too. I don't like that mom only talks to you like you've done something wrong and that she won't treat me like I'm a grown-up," he says, reaching into the bag for another cookie. He nibbles around the edges of it as he speaks, covering Drew's shirt with even more crumbs. "I'm going to be twenty-seven soon and she needs to understand that I can look after myself."

"Jess," Drew brushes the crumbs away, then slides his hands up the back of Jesse's thighs, "try to be kind. It's hard on your mom, you're her only child and she's always taken care of you. Now you don't want her to. Be nice, darlin'."

"It's not like I don't love her anymore or anything," Jesse says but Drew sighs when he sees the way he sets his chin and shoulders, stubbornness pushing sweetness to one side. "But she can't be mean to my boyfriend and think I'll just be nice back."

Unable to hide his smile, Drew squeezes Jesse's ass.

"I think you just like calling me your boyfriend."

Something flickers in Jesse's eyes.

"I – I do like calling you my boyfriend," he says. The petulance is gone, replaced by uncertainty. "But I won't if you don't want me to."

"Dork," Drew says and slips his hands under Jesse's tee-shirt and down inside the back of his jeans. Rolls his hips against him, grins at the way Jesse's eyes flutter shut. "Of course I want you to call me that. I also want you to hand me the cookies. Come on, enough sugar for one night."

A sly smile surfaces on Jesse's face.

"If I give you the cookies, what will you give me?' he asks, holding the bag behind his back. Drew raises an eyebrow.

"What do you want me to give you?"

Jesse taps the tip of a chocolate-smeared finger against his lip, pretending to consider the question.

"I think I want you to give me a blow job."

Drew snorts and holds his hand out for the cookies.

"And..." Jesse continues as he relinquishes his prize.

"And? You have two demands? For one bag of cookies?" Drew peers in the bag, "Most of which you've eaten. Okay come on, give me your terms."

"I want a blow job and I want you to tell me you love me."

Drew stands up, pushing Jesse to his feet as he does so, and grins.

"God, I love you," he says.

* * *

18

Jesse finishes feeding the hamsters and stretches. His father will be here soon to pick him up for dinner and he needs to help Mr Greenwold bring in the stock that's outside on the pavement before he goes. He wipes his hands over the back of his jeans and double checks the cages are shut before going out back for the trolley to bring in the heavier items.

Mr Greenwold joins him and together they heft the large bags of dog food on to the trolley.

"How's your friend's cat?' Mr Greenwold asks as they lift the last bag. Jesse frowns then his face clears.

"He's my boyfriend now," he says, stealing a sideways glance at the old man and relaxing when he sees him smile.

"Is he just? Good for you Jesse," Mr Greenwold says. "He struck me as a nice feller."

Jesse nods, cheeks flaming.

"He's really nice," he says. "He loves me."

"And so he should." Mr Greenwold searches in his pocket for his handkerchief and when he finds it, mops his forehead with it. Jesse pushes trolley inside and parks it by the counter, then returns to pick up a rabbit hutch.

"His kitten's name is Scamp, she's getting really big now," Jesse says straightening up, with a hutch under each arm. "She's really cute. On Wednesday, we're taking her to the vet to get her fixed up."

"Excellent, we don't need any more unwanted kittens in here no matter how cute they are."

They take the hutches inside and set them down. Jesse reaches for the broom to do a final sweep out but Mr Greenwold shoos him away to find his jacket and backpack and takes up the broom himself.

"Drew doesn't have things to do after school on Wednesdays so that means we can do stuff together," Jesse says when he returns, twisting his arms into the straps of his pack. He sees his father through the window and waves to let him know he's coming. "Mr Greenwold, are you okay?"

"Hmmm? Of course, Jesse, just getting old and tired. Go on now, your Dad's here, you can tell me about Scamp tomorrow."

Jesse frowns, still troubled by how red Mr Greenwold's face is. He's reluctant to leave the old man alone. When his Grammie had a heart attack, she'd been raking the lawn and had died. It's always bothered Jesse that if someone had been there she might still be alive.

"The new guy starts tomorrow," he says, "that should help."

"Yes, he does," Mr Greenwold nods, "and yes, Jesse it will help. You and I might get to have our lunch again. Now go on before your Dad comes in here wanting a piece of my ass for making your both late for dinner and getting you in trouble with your mom."

Jesse grins.

"Yeah, she's scary. Okay, I'll see you tomorrow."

The door bangs behind him and he glances over his shoulder one last time as he joins his father by the car, chewing his lip. Mr Greenwold waves and Jesse returns the gesture, before getting in the car and pulling on his seatbelt.

* * *

Before letting him out of the car this morning in front of the store, Drew had put his hand on the back of Jesse's neck and pulled him close, enveloping him in a cloud of toothpaste and aftershave and reminded him to be nice to his mother. Jesse had nodded then given him a quick kiss for jumping out of the car to go and open the store. He reminds himself of the exchange as he goes inside from the garage; Dad has gone to water the roses.

His mother's voice floats out from the kitchen, she's singing along with the radio, and he pushes the door open. Swaying in time to the music, she's stirring something on the stove. When he puts his hand on her shoulder she shrieks, and he jumps away, worried he's made her burn herself.

"Oh, honey you gave me a fright," she says, fingers of one hand splayed over her heart. She holds the other arm out to him and after a slight hesitation he steps over, allows himself to be embraced.

"Sorry," he says and on impulse, he gives her a quick peck on the cheek before he pulls away and sees the surprise in her eyes as she raises her fingers to the spot he kissed. "I didn't mean to."

He watches as she turns the radio off and checks something in the oven. It smells like chicken; he hopes it is. He loves chicken.

"Can ... can I help?" he asks, a little unsure.

Growing up, although he was expected to set the table and clear it as well as do dishes and keep his room tidy, he was rarely allowed to help with cooking. She taught him simple things like how to make toast and heat cans of soup, but it hadn't been until he was in his late teens that his father had insisted he needed to know how to at least cook basics and his mother has never really been at ease with it.

"No, I'm okay," she says, "why don't you have a beer or a juice while I finish up?"

She's smiling but her tone of voice makes his skin tighten, makes that fuzzy feeling return, like yesterday when he thought Drew was going to break up with him. Jesse doesn't want to be angry with his mother, but she keeps doing this. He knows she's going to pretend it's about Drew but it's not, because she's been doing this ever since he got his apartment. In fact, she's been doing it since he got his job with Mr Greenwold. He clenches his fists and takes a deep breath.

"Mom, I could help you serve or I could carry dishes to the table," he says. "I cook my own meals at home."

For a moment, they stand, unblinking, then his mother sighs and hands him the salad and the bowl of mashed potatoes. Hardly a difficult job and he wants to protest that it's a child's job and doesn't count but knows Drew would shake his head and murmur 'filter Jess' so he takes the bowls and stomps through to the table, trying not to scowl. Dad is inside now, pulling his chair out to sit down and he raises an eyebrow in query when Jesse bangs the bowls down. He stands at the table, stares unseeing, while he concentrates, searching for something he can do.

"Sit down Jesse," Mom says sliding into her seat and putting a platter of rolls next to the chicken.

In the middle of the table is a platter with pieces of roasted chicken and next to it are bowls of green beans and carrots. Jesse sits and reaches for the platter of chicken, then stands and goes to his mother's side, mimicking what he'd seen Drew do when Jody was over for lunch, although they'd been eating Chinese from Drew's favorite takeout place.

"Can I serve you some chicken?" he asks and hopes he's said it right. When he sees the shock on his mother's face he thinks he must have and grabs a piece of meat with the tongs. The chicken skin makes it slippery and it slides on to his mom's place with an unceremonious 'splat' and the fuzzy feeling threatens to take over. He wants to show his mom just how capable he is and instead, he drops the meat; he breathes in and as he starts to count hears his mother's voice.

"Thank you, Jesse, that was very kind," she says and when he looks at her, he can see she means it, her smile is wide – Drew would recognize it as the same smile Jesse has – and her eyes are shining. "Could I have one more piece?"

Unable to speak, he nods, and this time makes sure he has a good grasp on the chicken before lifting the tongs up. Then he goes to the other end and serves his father, before finally serving himself. He adds carrots and beans – carefully counting them – and finally a mound of potatoes to his plate before picking up his apple juice and smiling. Serving a bit of chicken isn't that complicated, he thinks, but he's never served his parents before. On the rare occasions, they come to his apartment to eat they have pizza or his mom brings something. Even Jesse knows that this is a start.

When the chicken has been cleared away and his mom brings out ice-cream – chocolate, Jesse's favorite – Jesse sits up straight and waits for his parents to start eating.

"Is something wrong with your ice-cream?" his mom asks.

He shakes his head.

"Mom you haven't asked how Drew is."

"Oh," she says, "well, how is Drew?"

Jesse runs his finger along the handle of his spoon, aware of his father's silence and his mother's shift of mood.

"Why don't you like him?" he asks, his voice flat.

"Don't be silly," his mother says, spooning ice cream into her mouth. "You said I hadn't asked and now I have."

"Yes, but if you really wanted to know you would have asked yourself. Why don't you like him, mom?"

"Jesse, that's enough."

Jesse remembers this voice. This is the voice from when he was younger, and everything was too much. When he couldn't stay focused and he would walk in never ending circles sometimes before sitting and stroking Wicket for hours. He would hear his mother's voice – or his father's or his teacher's – in the distance, as though it was at the end of a long tunnel – but it was like he couldn't make out the words until he'd walked and sat and stroked enough. Sometimes he would come back to himself and his mother would be crying, pleading with him to stop and to answer her. Sometimes she'd be frustrated and cross and snap at him. As he got older, he got better at coping and at waiting until he was alone to try and unwind the snarled roll of emotions he was experiencing.

"Mom, I'm not a little kid anymore, you can't just tell me that's enough and expect me to behave. It's not like that now," he says, and his mother's sharp intake of breath tells him he's hit home.

"Jesse," his dad says, and Jesse can hear the warning in his voice, but ignores it.

"I'm sorry," he refuses to look at his father, "but I have to. Mom, I'm twenty-six, I own my own apartment. You helped me do that. I have a job. I'm a grown up."

"Jesse, I know you're an adult," his mother replies, her voice icy. "I wish you'd stop acting as though I treat you like a baby. I didn't stop you doing any of those things, did I? Yes, I was worried about how you'd cope but that's because I'm a mother and not because you have special needs."

Jesse nods.

"Yes, Drew says his mom worries about him too."

"Well good for Drew and Drew's mom," his mother snaps, then looks ashamed, though she offers no apology.

Jesse stirs his ice-cream with his spoon; it's starting to melt and get gloopy, which he hates.

"Mom, I don't want to make you angry because you're my mom and I love you but sometimes you don't listen to me -"

"Nonsense, I always listen to you," his mother says and stands up, reaching for his bowl but Dad interrupts.

"Erin sit down and let him speak."

Jesse wants to throw his arms around his neck and thank him but resists the urge. Instead, he waits for his mom to sit down before continuing.

"I really need you to listen to me, mom because sometimes I have stuff that's important to say. I have thoughts and ideas and opinions and ... and... feelings and sometimes it's really hard to make them come out right, even when I really want them to."

"Jesse, I am well aware ..."

Jesse slams his hand down on the table with all the force he can summon and feels a white-hot surge of satisfaction when the glasses jump.

"No, you're not. You're not aware. You don't know what it's like. You either think I understand and then get annoyed when I don't, or you think I can't understand and don't even give me a chance. I do understand I just don't ..." he stops, searching for the word he's heard Drew use, "I don't process things like you do. But that doesn't mean I don't understand them. I just understand them differently."

Jesse doesn't know the word sullen but if Drew was there he might not only point to his mother's face to explain it, but he might mention that he's seen that same look on Jesse's a few times too. He doesn't know the word sullen, but Jesse knows what his mother is feeling – she's feeling fuzzy and he tries to soften his voice.

"Mom I'm really lucky because I have you and Dad and you guys help me to do stuff, like get my job and learn how to take photos and get my apartment. You let me move out on my own even when you didn't want to."

Something in his mother's eyes flickers and he smiles at her.

"You're a good mom. Drew says it's hard for you because you only have one kid and that's me and I'm grown up now. I'm sorry you didn't have another kid who is normal, so you could do all the stuff parents do with normal kids."

"Oh Jesse," his mother whispers and presses her hand to her mouth.

"Mom I am a grown up. And I still love you and I still love Dad. And my job because I get to work with animals every day. And my apartment because I can have all the things I love and not worry that they mess up your house, but I like that I can come home, and my bedroom is still the same," he says, then stops and licks his lips. "But sometimes I used to get lonely. Even before I moved out, I got lonely. I want someone to love me. I know you and Dad love me, but I wanted someone to really love me, like you and Dad love each other. Like at Christmas when you're really happy and he kisses you under the mistletoe and dances with you and makes you laugh. And you hold his hand and look at him like he's really, really special. I want that."

Jesse takes a sip of apple juice and looks at his father from the corner of his eye. He hasn't moved, is sitting in silence, one hand on the table, the other on his thigh, listening. Mom still has her hand pressed to her mouth and Jesse can see she's going to cry soon. It makes him feel bad, but it won't stop him from finishing what he has to say. He reaches out and takes her hand.

"When I first moved out, sometimes I went out to places, so I could meet people like me," he says. He picks at the table cloth, unsure of how to continue. "Not autistic people. Men. Like me. Men who are gay. Sometimes I went home with them but when they found out I wasn't normal, they didn't want to be with me. Or be my friend. Or anything. Mostly they just wanted to have sex with me because they thought I was hot."

His mother is crying now and when he looks at his father, the hand that was resting on the table is clenched in a fist; Jesse takes a deep breath.

"None of them wanted to see me again, so I stopped going. They made me feel fuzzy all the time and I didn't like that, I don't like lonely, but I like it better than fuzzy."

Jesse's eyes dart from one end of the table to the other, checking to see if his parents understand and he's relieved when his father nods.

"Drew doesn't make me feel fuzzy." It's that simple and that complicated, and Jesse doesn't know how to make them see. "And I'm not lonely anymore. He loves me mom. I ... I know you find that hard to believe but he does. He doesn't want to fix me, he just wants me to be happy."

"Jesse, honey, I know you think you understand ..."

Jesse pushes his chair back from the table with a grunt and runs his fingers through his hair in frustration.

"Mom, I *do* understand. There are lots of things I don't understand but this is something I do. He loves me mom, like dad loves you. He found a doctor, Doctor Sutton, who works with people who are autistic but he's not for me, mom, he's for Drew. So he can learn and understand."

He can see the doubt in his mother's eyes and gropes in his mind for a way to make her understand.

"I used to get really scared that one day you and dad would die, and I would be all by myself," he says and now his own tears are spilling, "but Drew won't let that happen mom. Mom I have someone to love me and to hold me at night and he doesn't care that I can't read properly. He goes swimming with me and Mom, he doesn't care about Wicket. He really doesn't."

"Okay honey," his mother says, and he hears how tired she sounds. "Okay."

"I know you don't like him right now, mom, but maybe if you tried you might. Maybe one day you'll love him a little bit even. Can you try? Please can you try?"

Jesse's mom nods, reaches out to wipe away the tears on his cheeks.

"I'll try," she says.

"Good," Jesse replies, "because I love him a lot."

* * *

Jesse clutches a bowl of left over roast chicken on his lap as his father drives him home. Before he left his mother hugged him and kissed his cheek and asked him to say hi to Drew for her. He doesn't think she really meant that last bit, but he does think Drew would be proud of the way he'd said 'of course' and hugged her back.

"Jesse," his father says, breaking into his thoughts, "those people, those men, you met and went home with, did any of them hurt you?"

Jesse focuses on the road ahead of them, takes his time to answer.

"No, Dad. They didn't hurt me. I went because I wanted to. I … I wanted to have sex with them too, I just thought it would be different to what it was."

From the corner of his eye, he sees his father nod.

"And it's different with Drew?"

Jesse can't help grinning.

"Very different. It's good. Really, really …"

His father holds his hand up.

"Uh filter, buddy," he says, and Jesse feels like his eyes are going to pop out of his head he's so surprised.

"That's what Drew says," he tells his father.

"I know, I heard him when you came to dinner."

"I just forget sometimes but when he says that, it reminds me," he says, nodding, then remembers why they're having the conversation. "Sorry, I guess you don't want to hear about our sex life."

His father makes an odd, strangled sound.

"Not really, Jesse, no."

For a moment they drive in silence then Jesse sighs. He has a question and he doesn't know who else to ask but it will mean doing exactly what his father just asked him not to do – talk about his sex life with Drew.

"Dad," he says running his finger around the lid of the bowl, "can I ask you something?"

"Of course you can."

"About sex?" Jesse asks and there's that same odd strangled sound again.

"I suppose," his father says.

"Drew always takes care of me," Jesse says, "you know, makes sure I like what he's doing and that it's really good and that I uh ..."

"I get the picture," his father says.

"But I want to do that for him too. I want to sometimes be the one who takes care of him and makes sure it's good for him, but I can't because I don't know how to. I know he likes it when we have sex because he um you know but he's always ..." Jesse's voice trails off in frustration. He doesn't know how to explain what he means, that Drew is always in charge, or ask what he wants to know, how can he make it as good for Drew as Drew makes it for him, and he senses his father is embarrassed and he just wants to get home now so he can hold Wicket and call Drew.

"I think you're asking me how to please him," his father says in a strange, tight voice. "Um wow, I never thought I'd be having this conversation. I guess, buddy, the only thing you can do is ask him what he likes when you're, um, well, together like that."

Jesse mulls this over.

"Sometimes he asks me what I want," he says.

"Well, uh there you go, you just need to ask him."

They're approaching Jesse's building and his father begins looking for a place to park.

"Jesse, your mom loves you very much. Even when she's found things really hard, she's always loved you. I know she seems a little over protective at times but it's only because you're so important to her. You're smart enough to understand that."

Jesse nods.

"That's what Drew says too."

"Well Drew's right. Your mom and I are just looking out for you buddy, that's our job."

When he's parked the car, Jesse's dad turns to face him.

"Jesse, I know it can't be easy for you, but you never ever give up and that makes me really proud. If you say Drew is a good guy, I'll trust you and I'm happy you've found someone to love. Your mom will come around, you'll see. And I'm really pleased you thought you could ask me about you and Drew."

"There wasn't anyone else to ask Dad," Jesse says, "I didn't think I should ask mom."

"Uh no," his father says and hugs him. "I love you Jesse. You go on in now, I'll wait until I see your light come on."

"Thank you," Jesse says and smiles at his father.

"Say hi to Drew for me and to Mr Greenwold."

"I will."

"Good night, buddy."

"Good night Dad."

* * *

"Hey you."

"Hi. I just got home."

"How did it go?"

"It was okay, I was nice to her and I tried to explain but she cried, Drew."

"Oh Jess, I'm sorry she cried. Are you okay?"

"Uh huh. She said she would try to like you."

"Well that's good, because I like her. You sure you're okay darlin'?"

"I'm okay. I miss you though."

"I miss you too. So does Scamp."

"I wish you here now."

"Me too, Jess, me too."

* * *

19

"I'm just wearing jeans, Jess," Drew says from the doorway of the bedroom.

In front of him, Jesse finishes tucking his pale blue shirt into navy dress pants and reaches for a cream tie. Drew expects to be asked for help and is surprised when he sees the tip of Jesse's tongue poke from the corner of his mouth as he concentrates on knotting the tie. Just one more of those times Jesse has caught him off guard, he thinks.

"Yeah but they know you and you're normal, so you don't have to impress them," Jesse says as he pulls on his socks and shoes.

"Neither do you," Drew says and holds out the matching jacket he knows Jesse is going to insist on wearing. "They'll love you."

"You don't know that," Jesse say, pulling the jacket on. He picks Wicket up off the dressing table and runs his fingers over his head.

"I do know that," Drew says and wraps his arms around him. "They'll love you because I do."

He sees Jesse's mouth curve up in a smile and the fingers rub over the soft toy again.

"We have to put Wicket in the car too, for tonight," he says and pulls away from Drew. On the bed is a large bouquet of hot house roses and lilies in bright yellows and oranges that Jesse insisted on buying for Drew's mother.

Hand in hand they leave the apartment, Drew holding the flowers and Wicket as Jesse locks the door and carefully pockets his keys. Pats the pocket as if to reassure himself they're there They'll stay at Drew's tonight and tomorrow and Drew knows he worries about losing them. He presses the button for the lift and smiles. Jesse looks more like a model than ever in the linen suit and tie. As the thought occurs to him, Jesse turns to look at him and a crease appears between the large golden eyes.

"What?" he asks.

"I was just thinking how lucky I am," Drew says handing the bouquet back. The lift dings and the doors whoosh open.

"Why?"

Drew chuckles. The question isn't disingenuous or manipulative, Jesse really doesn't understand what Drew means. He's learned, partly from talking to Martin Sutton and partly from being with Jesse, that it isn't empathy that Jesse lacks, it's the ability to process social cues. He doesn't associate Drew's smile and comment with his feelings for Jesse, any more than he understands hyperbole or sarcasm.

"I'm lucky because you love me, and I get to take that suit off you tonight," he says at the doors shut and Jesse frowns as he tries to decipher the words.

They've just started driving when his face clears, and he turns to Drew and punches him on the shoulder.

"You better not say that to your mom, I'm trying to impress her."

Drew roars with laughter.

* * *

A small white dog hurtles toward Drew when he steps out of the car and leaps on him, yapping and snapping. When he picks it up, it proceeds to snuffle and lick at his face and hair, squirming and whining in his arms.

"Okay, okay brat, settle down," he says going around the car to Jesse who is frozen against his door, arms full of flowers, eyes like saucers.

"You have a dog?" he asks.

"Well my parents have a dog," Drew says. "Jess, this is Harry and he's a brat."

"Actually, he's a Bichon," Jesse says. His hand creeps out from beneath the bouquet to stroke Harry's ears. "Hi Harry. You're really hairy. Hairy Harry."

Drew deposits the squirming dog on the ground, cleans the smears left by Harry's tongue from his glasses and takes Jesse's hand. The front door is open, and his sister Sarah is leaning against it, arms folded, watching them. Sarah shares Drew's fair coloring, her blonde hair cut short to frame her face, and has the same wide chocolate eyes that are now studying the scene at the car with interest. He takes a deep breath and squares his shoulders. His parents had been thrilled to hear they were finally going to meet the mystery man who had been keeping him from visiting. Joy had turned to concern when Drew mentioned that Jesse might have some social challenges and that they should try to be open minded. Drew knows that's why Sarah is there; they're counting on her calm, logical, accountant's mind to see the truth behind what is obviously their overly romantic youngest son's latest folly.

"Hey sis," he says dropping a kiss on her cheek. "Bill and Mandy here too?"

"Yup," she says and hugs him. "Mack and Gloria too."

Oh great, they really are bringing out the big guns. Mack is Drew's oldest brother, a trust lawyer, and he has an even more black and white view of the world than their sister.

"Jess, this my sister Sarah," Drew says, pulling Jesse forward from behind him and noting with pleasure the widening of his sister's eyes. Even she, his most cynical and practical of siblings, can see Jesse's beauty. "Sarah, this is Jesse."

"Hi Jesse," Sarah says and holds her hand out to shake.

Jesse's eyes dart from Drew to the bouquet he's cradling, flick up to Sarah, and back down to the flowers. Drew shakes his head and she puts her hand in her jeans pocket and waits.

"Hello," he says staring into the flowers, "I didn't know you were coming so I didn't bring you any flowers. I'm sorry."

"She doesn't need flowers Jess," Drew says and kisses the side of his head. "She used to put bugs in my shoes and socks."

"Ew," Jesse says "Why?"

"Because he's a brat who deserved it," Sarah says. "Don't let that innocent look fool you. He's no angel."

Jesse mulls this over and then nods.

"Sometimes he eats the last cookies and leaves the bag in the cupboard." Jesse peers up at Sarah from under his lashes. Drew digs his fingers into Jesse's side and suggests he might like to go without cookies and kisses for the rest of the weekend. Jesse shakes his head and Drew sees a small smile.

"Yeah that sounds like him." Sarah steps aside, so they can go into the house, Harry trotting at their feet.

A tall woman with white hair pulled into a messy bun and a pair of bright red glasses perched on the end of her nose comes out of the kitchen to greet them and Drew pulls her into his arms.

"Hey ma, long time, no smooches," he says and kisses her cheek.

"Do I know you?" she says returning the kiss. "You sort of look like my youngest son, but I think he's run away and joined a circus."

Behind him, Jesse snorts. Drew grins. With his arm still around his mother's shoulders, he turns and beckons Jesse forward.

"Mom, I'd like you to meet Jesse," he says. "Jesse, this is my mom, Sue Oliver."

Jesse blushes and shoves the bouquet into her arms.

"It's really nice to meet you Mrs Oliver, these are for you, I really like Harry," Jesse says, eyes glued to the floor. "Sorry."

Drew lets his mother go and puts an arm around Jesse's waist and hugs him to him.

"It's okay Jess," he says, "there's nothing to be sorry for. Want me to get Wicket?"

Against his side, Jesse shakes his head, but his body is quivering, and one hand is sliding up down the back of Drew's thigh. Drew understands what Jesse is doing and why he doesn't want Drew to get Wicket, but he knows that if he keeps doing that with his fingers, things are going to get a whole lot more awkward for everyone, especially him. He steps aside and picks up Harry, places him in Jesse's arms. Tips Jesse's face up so he's looking in his eyes.

"Harry loves having his ears and belly scratched almost as much as Scamp does." He places Jesse's hand on the little dog's head, aware of his mother and sister watching them but he can't worry about them now. Jesse needs something to settle him. After a moment, he sees Jesse's fingers twitch against Harry's head, then his shoulders relax, and he does it again. Drew smiles and turns to his mother, one hand still on Jesse's waist. "Jesse was really nervous about meeting you and wanted to make a good impression so went out this morning and found you the biggest bouquet he could."

The concern in his mother's eyes recedes but doesn't disappear; she steps forward, cocking her head to one side so she's in Jesse's line of sight.

"Thank you, Jesse, they're beautiful. Let's put them in a vase."

"Great idea," Drew says, steering Jesse toward the kitchen.

* * *

By the time the flowers are in a vase, Drew has convinced Jesse to remove his jacket and loosen the tie. When Sarah compliments Jesse on his clothes and tells him he should give Drew a lesson in taste, Jesse lifts his head up and gives each woman a brief, shy smile before dropping his eyes again. Drew is about to respond to the insult when the door is flung open and a girl in her mid-teens, with blue streaks in her long blonde hair throws herself on him with a shriek.

"Uncle Drew, you're here," she says peppering his face with kisses. Dressed in baggy shorts, a tee-shirt that proclaims, "*Let's save time and assume I know everything*", and rainbow-colored tennis shoes, she's almost as tall as Drew and bears a striking resemblance to his mother.

"Hey squirt, I heard you were gracing us with your presence," he says, pleased to see his oldest niece. All his siblings have children, a fact that goes a long way to assuaging any mild guilt he occasionally feels about not wanting to have his own. The soft spot he has for Sarah's only daughter is mutual though and he smiles as he puts his hands on her shoulders and turns her to face Jesse. "Mandy, I want you to meet my boyfriend Jesse."

Jesse's face lights up at the introduction and Drew grins.

"Woah," Mandy says when she turns around. "How come you never said he was hot?"

"*Mandy!*" Sarah and her mother exclaim at the same time.

"Well he is," Mandy retorts, then turns her attention to Jesse. "Sorry I'm kind of a dork sometimes."

"That's okay, so am I," Jesse says, running his fingers through Harry's hair again and giving Mandy a shy smile. "I think Drew kind of likes dorks though."

"Good thing for us, huh?" Mandy says, then turns to her grandmother. "Grandma, Gramps says the grill is ready to go and that if we don't get out there now, they're starting without us."

"Okay we're coming," her grandmother says and opens the fridge. She hands a bowl of salad greens to the girl and one of potato salad to Sarah. "Drew, can you bring the beer? Oh, uh can Jesse have beer?"

"Why don't you ask him, Mom?" Drew says gently. "He can answer for himself."

"Oh," his mother says, hand flying to tug at a strand of hair that has escaped her bun. "um Jesse is beer okay? We have soda too."

"I can drink beer, Mrs Oliver, I'm twenty-six," Jesse says, looking at Drew. "I can help bring things out too, but I need to wash my hands because I've been holding Harry."

Drew shows him where to wash his hands and then gives him a tray with serviettes, seasonings, and dressings to carry out to the table. Together they go out to the garden where a large picnic table, covered in paper table cloths and surrounded by plastic chairs, waits. By the grill, three men and a small woman with bright red hair are laughing and talking. They look up as the group arrive and all look at Jesse with undisguised curiosity.

Drew's older brother is almost an exact carbon copy of their father. Both are tall with grey-blond hair and broad shoulders. Peter Oliver, wearing a plastic apron and wielding a spatula that he raises in greeting, has a greying beard and wire rimmed glasses like Drew's.

"Hey Dad," Drew says. When he's put the beer on the table, he goes to the older man and hugs him, before hugging the rest of the group, then holds his hand out to Jesse. When he finally moves forward and takes it, Drew clears his throat. "Uh Jess, this is my Dad, Peter, this is Bill, Sarah's husband, and this is my brother Mack and sister in law Gloria. Guys, this is Jesse."

Jesse bows his head and looks up from under his lashes and Drew tugs him a little closer. Mack moves forward with his hand out and before Drew can do anything, Sarah arrives and smacks the hand down with an exasperated snort.

"It's nice to meet you, Jesse," Peter Oliver says. "I hope you like grilled steak and chicken."

"Yes sir, I like chicken" Jesse says and throws a glance at Drew before stepping forward and holding out his hand. "It's nice to meet you."

"Excellent, that's what I like to hear. Let's eat."

* * *

At the table, Jesse pulls his chair as close to Drew's as he can get it and is relieved when he feels Drew's hand close over his, lacing their fingers together. For a moment, when they first arrived, and he met Sarah, everything had threatened to crash in around him and it had taken every ounce of willpower to not turn around and run. It was only the thought of letting Drew down that held him in place. His need for Wicket is so strong it's making him lightheaded and he's grateful Drew offered him Harry. Harry isn't quite right but he doesn't want to embarrass Drew by getting a toy from the car.

"Jesse would you like some salad?" Drew's mom asks. He shakes his head.

"No thanks. I already have four things on my plate," he says and counts again. Two pieces of grilled chicken, potato salad – six chunks of potato - and, a bread roll cut in two. Drew passes him a bottle of beer and squeezes his hand.

"What do you uh do, Jesse?" Mack asks dishing himself some salad.

"I work in a pet store," Jesse says. In a faltering voice, he talks about his job and the pet store. When he starts to describe the animals, his voice grows stronger and Drew squeezes his thigh under the table. He lifts his head and looks around the table. "Sometimes, we get Bichons like Harry and they always sell really fast because they're so cute. And they're really friendly and happy so they're really good for people who are lonely or who are ... like ...me."

Embarrassed he counts the things on his plate and picks up his fork.

"Does your store sell rats, Jesse?" Mandy asks. "I really want a rat."

"You are not having a rodent," Sarah says around a mouthful of steak.

"Rats are really smart," Jesse says. "And they're really friendly and lots of fun. But they smell if you don't clean their cage out."

"You're not having a rodent," Sarah repeats.

"You could come see the rats at the store. They're really tame and they like being held. We have a rabbit too, called Sniffles," Jesse says. Sarah makes an exasperated sound and he ducks his head again, cheeks coloring. Did he say the wrong thing? Is Drew's sister mad at him? She's sort of scary.

"Mandy Walters you are not having a rat or a rabbit," Sarah says.

"I'll just come visit," Mandy says, ignoring her mother and grinning at Jesse. He relaxes. Nods when Drew offers him some salad, keeping a close watch on the serving. When Drew puts the bowl down, he takes a slice of tomato from Jesse's plate and eats it with a grin.

"Now you've got the right amount."

Jesse is happier when the family starts asking Drew about his job and what he thinks about the new Congress. When Drew sits back and winds an arm around his shoulders, he rests his head against him, feeling self-conscious and unsure until he catches Mandy smiling in his direction.

"Want to come play with Harry with me for a while?" she asks. "You can tell me about the rats."

He looks at Drew who grins and nods, then grabs Jesse's shirt.

"Give me a kiss first," he says and pulls him forward. Scarlet, Jesse brushes his lips over Drew's.

"Uncle Drew," Mandy says behind them, "please, keep it seemly, impressionable teenage mind and all that."

"Yeah, whatever," Drew says and strokes Jesse's cheek. "Don't you break him, squirt or you'll be sorry."

* * *

Drew turns his chair so he can watch Jesse and Mandy throwing the ball for Harry but still talk to his family; braces himself for the barrage of questions he knows is coming.

An awkward silence settles over the group, interrupted only by the sounds of Harry barking and Mandy's laughter.

"Is he autistic?" Mack asks handing him another beer. Drew takes a deep breath and nods.

"Yes, he's on the spectrum and he's dyslexic and has a thing that makes it hard for him to read printed material. He ... uh... also has a mild intellectual disability," he says looking at each of them in turn. "A *very* mild disability."

"He's retarded?" Gloria asks and Drew resists the urge to snap at her.

"No, he's not retarded. He struggles to process some things, he particularly struggles with social situations and complex reasoning but most of the time, for most things, he's fine."

"Most of the time, for most things?" Drew's mother says. "What does that even mean?"

"It means exactly that. Most of the time he's just fine. He has a job, he has an apartment, pays his bills on time, votes. Most of the time for most things, he's just fine."

"Except he counts the things on his plate, can't look anyone in the eye, and doesn't understand social interaction," Mack says.

"I never said he doesn't understand social interaction," Drew says, "I said he struggles with social situations. When things are new or there's too much stimulation, he gets flustered or if it's really bad, he can get really tense and we might go home."

He's not sure he's up to explaining Wicket to his family just yet and hopes they'll move on. His mother looks upset.

"Drew, he's very sweet," she says watching Jesse chase Harry for a moment, "and he's very beautiful but ..."

"But what, Ma?"

"Don't take that tone, Drew. You know perfectly well how mismatched the two of you are. I can see you're besotted with him, but I don't think it's unreasonable to ask if you have thought this through?"

"Oh, for God's sake." Drew throws his hands in the air. "What's to think through? He's sweet and he's funny and he's got more compassion in his little finger than most people have in their entire bodies."

"Settle down." Drew's father looks at him over the top of his glasses. "Drew, those things may all be true – don't give me that look, I've just met the kid, I'm still taking your word for it – but he does have problems. Problems you can't ignore."

"I'm not ignoring them," Drew protests. "I've found a doctor who specializes in the type of things that Jess has ..."

"So, he's treatable?"

Drew closes his eyes and when he opens them, makes himself watch Jesse and Mandy for a moment, ignoring his mother's prodding. When he's sure he can give a calm answer, he faces his mother.

"Doctor Sutton isn't for Jess, he's teaching me how to understand him. Jess doesn't need treating. He's fine how he is."

Mack snorts and Drew raises an eyebrow.

'Nothing," Mack says.

"What about the differences in your intellectual abilities?" Drew's mother asks.

"Mom, I teach high school English. I wrote a book about modern poets that has sold fewer than a hundred copies. I'm hardly Einstein. So, he can't read very well and he's not going to win a Nobel prize anytime soon, who cares?"

"Besides, I don't think it's Jesse's intellect that has Drew's attention, Ma," Mack says shoving a piece of garlic bread in his mouth. Drew glares at his brother.

"You know what Mack? Why don't you just fuck the hell off?"

Mack sits back, holding both hands up in surrender and rolling his eyes at his wife.

"Don't use that language at the table please," their mother says, "Mack don't be vulgar."

"Drew," his father leans forward, arms on his thighs as he chooses his words, "you are a very caring man. It's an admirable trait but it's also one that gets you in strife far too often. Look at that mess with David."

Drew reminds himself that his family is just looking out for him. That their intentions are the best and that getting pissed at them will help nothing. Of course, that might be easier to believe if Mack and Sarah weren't here to sing chorus on the "Drew doesn't know what he's doing" song.

"Jesse is nothing like David, Dad. Look I get it – it's not a typical situation. And I get that everyone just wants us to be happy - Jesse's parents, you guys, everyone. But that doesn't change the fact that we love each other. Don't ask me why it happened. I don't know why any more than I know why I prefer men to women. It's just how it is, okay? And, Mack since you're so damned interested, yeah, we have a great sex life." Drew runs his fingers through his hair and looks around the table, willing them to understand. "You know, he woke up this morning and all he could talk about was coming here. He wanted to bring you flowers mom and he chose his best suit because he wanted to impress you, wanted you to like him. Didn't want you to think of him as retarded or not normal. So, do you think maybe you could give him a chance?"

Panting he takes his glasses off and tosses them on the table in front of him, hoping Jesse doesn't come back to the table until he's had a chance to calm down.

The wind picks up and his mother excuses herself to get a jacket. Drew looks over at Mandy and Jesse; their heads are bowed, almost touching, as they examine something in the grass. It will be an insect of some sort he imagines; Mandy has always been fascinated by bugs and Jesse, well, he's Jesse.

"Does he have sensory overload issues?" Bill asks and Drew turns to him in surprise. His brother-in-law smiles and scratches his balding head. "We have a guy at work who's autistic and he rocks when things get too much for him."

Drew nods.

"Jesse's more tactile. He has a soft toy he strokes," he glares at his brother, daring him to comment, but Mack remains silent. "If he doesn't have Wicket he strokes Scamp, my kitten. Or a piece of fabric if that's all there is. Last week he used my hair."

He chuckles at the memory then realizes nobody else finds it funny and sighs, admits you probably had to be there.

"Is that what you were doing with Harry earlier?" Sarah asks, loading more potato salad on her plate. It's the first time she's spoken, and everyone turns to look at her. Drew nods. She smiles at him then looks at her daughter and Jesse who are now sitting on the grass talking while Harry rolls on his back between them. "I like him, Drew. I agree with Mom and Dad that you need to think this through very carefully. It would be a terrible thing to hurt him; I know you wouldn't mean to, but it could happen so if you think you can't handle this long term, you need to call a halt to it sooner not later."

Drew shakes his head, blinks hard at the thought, and puts his glasses back on.

"I know it won't be easy," he whispers.

"Then I think," Sarah looks around the table, "you should go ahead and try to make it work. If you make each other happy who are we to question that? And why should Jesse miss out on something that might be the one part of his life that is normal just because it makes the rest of us uncomfortable?"

Astounded, Drew gawps at his sister. She was the last person he'd expected to come to his defense but he's grateful. Sarah nods toward the lawn.

"They're coming over, so I suggest we all get ourselves together," she says. "He certainly is beautiful."

* * *

Dark clouds are gathering, and the wind has gone from a moderate breeze to strong gusts as Drew and Jesse say goodbye. Drew hugs Mandy and kisses her stripy hair, he knows she took Jesse to play with Harry, so he could talk to the family.

"Thanks squirt."

"For being awesome? You're welcome," Mandy says. She leans forward and whispers in his ear. "I think he's totally a keeper."

He gives her a hug and turns to Sarah.

"Thank you," he says unable to find anything else to say.

"Yeah well if we end up with a rodent in our house, I'm blaming you. Not him, you. Got it?"

"Got it."

"Man, I'm sorry I was a dick before," Mack says, clapping a hand on Drew's shoulder.

"Whatever," Drew says. He's not quite ready to forgive him yet but knows that Mack's apology is sincere. He pulls away and says goodbye to Bill and Gloria, then takes Jesse's hand and approaches his parents. His mother smiles at Jesse.

"Jesse, it was really nice to meet you. Thank you very much for the flowers."

Jesse lets her hug him and even gives her a light hug in return, to Drew's surprise.

"It was nice to meet you too," he says and manages to keep his head up and look her in the eye. Drew's father holds out his hand and Jesse shakes it, then steps back for Drew to move in.

"Thanks Dad," Drew says when he's finished hugging him. "Food was great."

His father nods and he turns to look at his mother.

"It would be good if you two weren't such strangers please, it's not that much of a drive" his mother says holding her arms open. He tightens his arms, so she knows he's heard her trying. "I love you Drew."

"I love you too, Ma."

"You boys should get going, there's going to be rain I think," Drew's father says.

As they pull away from the driveway, Drew reaches behind Jess to the backseat and grabs Wicket. Jesse takes him and hugs him close, smiling.

"I like your family," he says, "your sister is sort of scary, but I like Mandy lots. And your mom is nice."

Drew swallows and tries to not roll his eyes; reminds himself that his family had good intentions even if the delivery was a little rough.

* * *

20

They are two blocks from Drew's apartment when the storm hits with a deafening clap of thunder. Jesse, who has been dozing for the last twenty minutes, sits bolt upright, eyes wide in terror.

"Holy shit," Drew mutters as a heavy curtain of rain makes it impossible to see much further than the end of the hood. Rain was in the forecast, but he remembers nothing about storms. Just as he's about to say something more there's a silver flash of lightening. Beside him, Jesse moans. Drew glances at him and is shocked to see Jesse scrambling up against the back of his seat, pulling his legs up and struggling with his seatbelt.

"Jess, what are you doing?" He tries to reach out, but Jesse slaps his hand away.

There's a drawn-out moan when another clap of thunder sounds overhead, and Jesse squeezes his eyes shut, pressing himself back against the seat. Drew is torn between stopping the car, so he can comfort the obviously terrified man beside him and just getting him home and indoors. He opts for home and puts a hand out to try and reassure Jesse.

"We're nearly home, okay?" He sends up a silent prayer that they'll have a clear run for the last block. A feverish, sweaty hand grabs his and is squeezing it tight when there's another flash of lightning ahead of them. Jesse shrieks.

Drew turns into the parking space in front his building and stops the car. The rain is getting heavier and the next boom of thunder suggests the storm is moving closer. He eases his hand out of Jesse's grasp, wincing at the distressed whimper it causes. How the hell is he going to get him from the car to the building? He waits for the next flash of lightning and as soon as the thunder has sounded, gets out and runs to Jesse's door and opens it. Jesse cowers away from him, arms wrapped around his head muffling his pitiful crying.

"Jess come on you have to get out, so we can go inside," Drew yells over the rain. Jesse shakes his head. "Jesse, please get out of the car."

There's a crack as lightning flashes again and the deep growl of thunder following close behind pulls a terrified keen of fear from Jesse. Desperate, Drew reaches over him and unlocks the seatbelt and gathers him in his arms. As soon as the next flash has been, he pulls Jesse with all his might, hooking Wicket with the fingers of his left hand, ignoring the sobbing as best he can, and gets him on to the sidewalk. He slams the car door and thumbs the remote lock, shoves Wicket into

Jesse's arms, then wrapping both arms around him, so his head is down against Drew's chest, propels him toward the building. While he's keying in the door code there's more lightning and thunder and Jesse screams against his shoulder.

Once inside, Drew puts himself between the door and Jesse, slapping at the lift button. Pushes him inside when the doors open. He leans against the lift wall, murmuring words against Jesse's hair, not caring what he's saying just wishing the lift would go faster. When they're finally in the apartment he moves Jesse to the sofa and presses him down.

Shivering, Jesse curls into a ball, still crying and moaning while Drew runs from window to window closing drapes. Finally, he turns on the sound system hoping some music will help mask the sounds coming from outside. He grabs a towel and returns to Jesse.

"Hey Jess," he says softly, "let me get you and Wicket dry."

He tries to rub at Jesse's shoulder with the towel but gives up when Jesse insists on pressing against him, hiding his hot, wet face in Drew's shoulder. Thunder sounds again making Jesse jump and tighten his grip, but Drew thinks it might have passed over them now, might be moving away.

"It's okay Jess, I've got you. It's just a storm, you're okay, I'm here."

Jesse shakes his head. The sobs have eased off to a low, sustained crying now and just as Drew is trying to decide what he should do next, Jesse's cell phone chimes from his pocket. When he doesn't move, Drew pats his pockets and pulls the phone out. A picture of Erin Peterson fills the screen and Drew taps the ACCEPT button and holds the phone to his ear.

"Jesse? It's mom, are you okay? Are ..."

"Mrs Peterson," Drew interrupts, "it's Drew."

"Is Jesse okay?"

"Uh not really," he says, "I mean, he's safe, we're at my place, but he's really frightened."

"Oh God, he's terrified of storms," Erin's voice sounds tinny and distant over the line and he fights the impulse to snap that yes, he has figured that bit out thank you. "There was nothing about storms in the forecast damn it. What's he doing?"

Drew looks down at Jesse; he's still trembling and crying, one arm strangling Wicket the other clinging to Drew.

"Crying," he says, hating how the word sounds, "and I can't get him to talk to me. He's shivering like he's in shock."

"What's your address, I'll come and get him."

Drew has had enough of well-meaning parents who think he can't, or shouldn't, cope with Jesse.

"Mrs Peterson please can you just tell me what to do. You shouldn't be driving in this weather and I don't think he can wait for you to get here," he says trying to pick his words with care. "I want to help him."

"Drew, I don't think this ..."

"Mrs Peterson I promise I will call you if I need more help," he says. "Please."

He can hear sounds from the other end of the phone and it occurs to him that Ray is arguing with her. Eventually she speaks again.

"You need to close all the curtains and put some music or the television on, something that will cover the sound of the thunder," she says. Her voice is unsteady, and he knows she doesn't want to tell him this and is able for just a second to feel sorry for her. "If he's really upset already, you could try getting him in a bath. The water needs to be warm but not too hot. And quite deep, so he can be under the water. And he'll need Wicket."

"We have Wicket, he's got him, and I've done the curtains and music," he tells her. "I have a tub, I can give him a bath. I'll call you as soon as he's in it, okay?"

"Drew, I ..."

"Mrs Peterson I promise I'll call you if I need to. Please let me do this for him."

A long, trembling sigh sounds then she says goodbye and hangs up.

"Jess," Drew says, easing Jesse to his feet, "Jess, we're going to have a bath okay?"

Jesse doesn't answer but allows Drew to take him to the bathroom. The rain is still pounding the windows and the thunder, though not as loud, is still regular. Drew lets go of him, ignoring the scared whine Jesse makes, and puts the plug in the tub, turns the water on.

It takes him a moment to pry Wicket from Jesse's grip and put him on the sink, then he begins to undress him, dropping the wet clothes in the hamper to worry about later. When Jesse's naked, he nudges him toward the toilet, tells him to pee, and checks the bath water. It's warm and just over half full; he turns the faucet off as Jesse lays his head against his back, still trembling and snuffling.

"Okay, all done? Let's get you in some warm water, shall we?" he tries to keep his voice even and bright, hoping it will reassure them both.

Jesse hunches over in the water and Drew frowns. Mrs Peterson said he needed to be under the water. He reaches for a washcloth, swirls it in the water and begins to wash Jesse's back in slow, even movements.

"When you're nice and warm, we can have some soup and get into bed and I'll read to you," he says, not knowing if Jesse is hearing him or not. After a minute or so he thinks the trembling has lessened a little and he puts a little pressure on Jesse's shoulder until he's laying back in the water. "Are you okay if I go and heat some soup and get you some dry clothes?"

Jesse nods, eyes filling with tears again and Drew cups his face with one hand.

"I won't be long, I promise. I love you."

He hurries to the bedroom, turns down the covers on the bed, then finds some sweat pants, a tee-shirt, some socks, and one of his old hoodies to wrap Jesse in when he gets out of the water. In the kitchen, he empties some soup into a pot and puts it on the stove, on low to heat. Then he copies Erin's number from Jesse's phone to his own and sends her a quick text.

Mrs Peterson this is Drew. He's in the bath and seems to be calming down. I'm going to give him some soup and see if I can get him to sleep a little bit. I'll let you know how he's doing. Promise.

Back in the bathroom, Jesse has slid under the water and for a moment Drew catches his breath, then gold eyes open and stare up at him. He smiles down, puts the dry clothes on the sink, and kneels next to the tub.

Jesse sits up and allows Drew wash his hair and help him from the tub. Stands, motionless as Drew dries him off and dresses him. As soon as the hoodie is on, he reaches for Wicket and when he has him, leans in against Drew again. Sighing, Drew puts his arm around his shoulder and takes him to the bedroom, helps him climb into bed.

"I'm going to go and get the soup and our book, and I'll be right back."

Jesse says nothing, simply looks up wide eyed and pale from the pillow. Drew goes to the kitchen and pours the soup into mugs. His phone chimes and when he looks, sees it's Erin.

He sometimes withdraws after things like this and shouldn't be alone. I can come and get him.

Drew thinks for a moment then replies.

He's in bed and I've made soup. We're going to read The Hobbit. I promise I won't leave him alone.

He picks up the tray, finds *The Hobbit* in the living room on his way, and returns to the bedroom. Scamp has found her way to the bed and is curled up next to Jesse who hasn't moved. Drew coaxes him to sit up and holds the mug while Jesse sips, insisting he drink half of it. Then he strips out of his own damp clothes, pulls on some old pants and a baseball shirt and gets into bed next to Jesse. He puts his arm around him and pulls him closer.

In the distance, there's another roll of thunder and Jesse flinches but is quiet. Drew picks up the book, finds their last page, and begins reading. After half a dozen pages Drew realizes Jesse's breathing has evened out and when he looks, dark lashes lay against his pale cheeks, one arm is curled around Wicket, the fingers of the other hand beneath Scamp, curled in a ball, tail over her nose; they're both sound asleep. Smiling, Drew puts the book down and picks up his phone. Snaps a photo and sends it to Jesse's mom.

I think the worst is over Mrs Peterson.

He's sipping the last of his own soup when his phone chimes and he glances at the screen.

Thank you. I think perhaps you should call me Erin.

* * *

21

Any sense of pride Drew feels in his ability to cope is destroyed without ceremony at three in the morning when the second storm bursts overhead. The simultaneous thunder clap and downpour are so loud and sudden that Drew at first thinks there has been an explosion of some kind. Jesse sits straight up in bed with an anguished wail, all but flattening Scamp in the process. The little cat lashes out a paw full of needle sharp claws in self-defense and fear before fleeing in a hissing streak of black spiky fur.

Scrambling to get his arms around a howling Jesse, Drew can see tiny bubbles of blood welling in the four short scratches and tries to soothe him, find Wicket, and wrap his still confused mind around what is happening. More thunder booms overhead and Jesse cries out, yanking his hand away, arms pin wheeling as his body tips back off the bed.

"*For fuck's sake, Jess!*" Drew yells as he lunges, hooks his fingers in Jesse's tee-shirt and drags him back to the middle of the bed. A pounding on the wall and a muffled shout to 'shut the hell up' reminds Drew it's the middle of the night and he lowers his voice as he continues. "Jesus, sit still and let me look at your damned hand. You're safe, I'm right here."

Jesse hunches over, sniffling, his scratched hand outstretched for examination. Head and heart pounding from adrenaline, Drew gropes for his glasses and puts them on so he can at least see what he's doing. Yanks some tissues from the night table, dips them in his glass of water, and dabs at the scratches. They're shallow, will probably be gone in a day or so, Jesse must get worse working with the animals in the store. Drew suspects that had he not woken the way he had and been so frightened, Jesse wouldn't even have reacted. There's yet another roll of thunder – Drew curses under his breath at the weather - and Jesse cringes into the pillow, chewing his lip and making a pathetic, broken sound in his throat. Guilt floods through Drew as he realizes he yelled at Jesse for something over which he has no control. That he didn't mean to - he had been in a deep sleep when all hell had broken loose himself- doesn't make him feel any better. He winds his arms around Jesse and pulls him against his chest. At first, he resists but when Drew doesn't let go, gives in.

"Jess, shhhhhh," Drew whispers against his head, rubbing his arms "I didn't mean to yell. It's okay. Shhh. I'm sorry."

Jesse snuffles against his chest, trembling as the storm continues to rage. Wicket has fallen off the bed and Drew leans over to snag him with one hand, reluctant to let go.

"Here you are, darlin'" he says, tucking the soft toy between them. "It's okay."

He pulls them both up against the headboard, bringing the covers up to their chests, still murmuring apologies and reassurances. Jesse, his face wet with tears, trembles against him but doesn't speak and this troubles Drew more than the panic attack itself. Has he triggered some sort of withdrawal by yelling? Is Jesse scared of him? Worried, he keeps rubbing Jesse's arm as he listens to the storm abate and move into the distance.

"Jess?" he says when the thunder sounds distant enough to no longer be a threat. "Do you want to have another bath?"

Jesse shakes his head. Drew's at a loss, he doesn't know what else to offer and makes a mental note to make sure he tells Erin how sorry he is for his arrogance. This is going to be so much harder than he had imagined.

"What about some tea?"

Jesse shakes his head again and mumbles something that Drew doesn't catch.

"Jess? I didn't hear that; can you say it again?"

Leaning back, Jesse keeps his eyes downcast and Drew's feels another pang of shame - it's been a source of pride that Jesse rarely avoids eye contact with him now.

"Did I hurt her?"

"Who? Scamp?"

Jesse nods and lifts his head as a large tear rolls down his cheek.

"She's so little and I didn't mean to squash her, but it was so loud, and I got a fright and forgot she was there. She's so little, Drew and I didn't mean to." Panic makes his voice thin and reedy and spots of color are forming high in his cheeks. Drew feels a disconcerting sense of relief at the hysteria - this is something he can deal with. Hysterical teenagers are a regular occurrence in his job. He takes Jesse by the shoulders and keeps his voice firm.

"Jesse, look at me," he says and waits until red rimmed eyes are peering at him from beneath wet lashes before continuing, "she's okay. You didn't hurt her, she just got a fright, we all did. That's why I yelled, I was half asleep and got a fright when I thought you were going to fall. I'm sorry sweetheart. Scamp's fine, I promise. Does your hand sting?

"No."

"How about if I make us some hot chocolate and then we can go back to sleep? You okay here until I get back?"

Jesse scrubs at his face with his sleeve and nods. When Drew is at the door he hears Jesse mumble his name.

"Yeah Jess?"

"I love you," Jesse says in a small voice taut with exhaustion.

"I love you too, Jess. I'll be right back."

He makes the hot chocolate and is making his way back across the living room when he spots a pair of indignant yellow eyes glaring at him from the cave on top of the cat tree. Grinning he puts down his mug, picks her up and, then hooks a finger in the handle of his mug, trying not to spill anything. In the bedroom, Jesse is all but hidden beneath the duvet and Drew puts the mugs on the bedside table before attempting to get back in bed.

"Look who I found sulking in the cat cave," he says putting Scamp on the pillow next to Jesse. A finger appears from beneath the covers and strokes the kitten's head; as if nothing has happened she closes her eyes and curls into the gesture, purring. Drew rolls his eyes. "Okay, I'm starting to think I'm excess to requirements here."

"I don't know what that means." Jesse's voice is still hesitant.

"It means I think you two only keep me around to feed you."

"Oh."

Jesse sits up and reaches for his mug, still clutching Wicket with his free hand. When Scamp stands on the toy and bumps it with her head, Drew is relieved to see Jesse smile. Drew is putting his empty mug on the night table when Jesse speaks again.

"And the sex."

"What?" Drew has no idea what Jesse means.

"I don't just keep you around to feed me," Jesse says. He's looking up under his lashes again, eyes timid and pleading. "It's for the sex, too."

Drew laughs.

"Is that so?" he says, taking Jesse's mug. Takes his glasses off and puts them on the table. "Let's try and go back to sleep and maybe in the morning we'll see if I'm worth keeping."

Drew turns the lamp off and slides down under the covers, pulling Jesse against him as he does. He can hear Scamp's squeaky purr from her usual spot on the other side of Jesse's pillow and feel the weight of Wicket between them; he strokes Jesse's hair and reminds himself to call Erin when they wake up.

"Drew?" Jesse says against his chest.

"Mmmmmm?"

"I don't like storms."

The level of understatement is so ludicrous Drew snorts out a sharp, hard laugh.

"Yeah, I noticed."

"I'm sorry."

"Well I don't like snakes and I'm not apologizing for that, so don't worry about it Jess. I'm sorry I yelled at you."

"That's okay. Mom sometimes yells when I get scared too. Sometimes I can't hear you until you yell."

Drew thinks this over as sleep creeps over him and he's almost under when Jesse speaks again.

"Drew?"

"Mmmmmm?" If he doesn't use actual words, maybe Jesse will stop talking.

"We have snakes at the store sometimes. They're not scary."

Oh, God.

"Go to sleep you dork."

"I love you."

"I love you too, Jess, but if you don't stop talking I'm going to make you go sleep on the sofa."

The last thing Drew is aware of as he finally slips back into sleep is a soft ghosting of lips against his chin.

* * *

When Jesse opens his eyes, he tenses, waiting for the sound of thunder and torrential rain; when all he hears is soft snores coming from Drew's side of the bed, he lifts his head and is relieved to see sunlight through the gaps in the curtains. Scamp has disappeared, and Wicket is once again on the floor. He leans over the edge to pick him up and set him on the night table. Behind him Drew stirs and snuffles in his sleep, then resumes snoring.

Jesse turns over and tucks one hand under his pillow. On his back with one arm flung over his head, Drew has a strand of hair across his face and each puff of breath makes it flutter above his mouth. For a while, Jesse is happy to lay there and just watch him sleeping; he looks so pretty - Jesse knows that isn't the word he wants but it's close - and peaceful, he doesn't want to wake him. The problem is, all that pretty makes him want to touch Drew's skin. He wonders what would happen if he did. Would Drew wake up or keep sleeping? Would he make little noises in his sleep? The ones that make Jesse's skin feel hot and his toes curl, making him want to buck and squirm. Just the thought of those noises is making him hard and the desire to touch is a growing itch he can't ignore.

Jesse shimmies out of his tee-shirt and drops it on the floor; runs his hand over his own skin, over the light scatter of dark hair that stretches up from under his sweat pants over his belly and chest. Holding his breath, he slips his hand under Drew's sleep shirt, watches to see if he'll wake up and when he doesn't, spreads his fingers over the soft silky skin of Drew's belly. He loves everything about Drew's skin, loves how different to his own it is, how smooth it feels beneath his fingers, how pale it looks next to his own tan skin. Once, he asked Drew why he was so white, and Drew explained it was because his great, great grandparents came from Ireland while Jesse's came from somewhere with more sun and less rain. Jesse isn't sure he understands what any of that means, just that he loves Drew's skin. Still trying not to disturb him, Jesse inches closer, withdraws his hand from beneath the shirt and lifts the strand of hair away from Drew's mouth, leans forward and brushes it with his own. Drew makes a low humming sound and wriggles down in the bed.

"Are you awake?" Jesse whispers.

"Nope," Drew says without opening his eyes. Jesse sniggers.

"Yeah, you are." He presses closer.

"Nu-uh," Drew says, still not opening his eyes but smiling now. Jesse leans over and kisses him again, applying more pressure this time and lifts the hem of the sleep shirt again so he can trace the fine line of pale, blonde hair he knows runs down from Drew's navel to his groin.

"You're clearly feeling better this morning," Drew says finally opening his eyes and rolling to his side.

"Uh huh."

"Not feeling scared?"

Jesse shakes his head and kisses him again, tongue flicking over Drew's lower lip.

"Not feeling fuzzy?" Drew asks.

Jesse shakes his head and tugs at the sleep shirt. Why is Drew still wearing it? Drew grins and pulls the offending garment over his head. Jesse murmurs his approval and runs his hand over the expanse of skin on offer, thrilling when the muscles quiver beneath his touch. He wants to follow his father's advice and ask Drew how to please him but he's nervous he'll say it wrong and spoil the moment. Drew pulls him into another kiss and when he breaks it, keeps his hand on Jesse's neck.

"I can hear you thinking, Jess," he says.

Jesse follows the line of soft hair down to the waistband of Drew's pants and inches his fingers beneath the elastic until he encounters Drew's cock which is anything but soft. The sound Drew makes when Jesse strokes him helps him make up his mind.

"Tell me how to take care of you," he says, nosing Drew's chin up and nipping at the soft skin beneath.

"Huh?"

Licking at the hollow at the base of Drew's throat results in a soft moan and Drew's hips nudging against him. Jesse searches for the right way to ask what he wants to know.

"I want to know what you like."

"I like what you're doing now," Drew says, and his voice has a soft, breathy quality to it that fills Jesse with heated want.

"I want to know where you want me to touch you. What you want me to...do... to you so it makes you feel good, the way you make me feel good,"

"You always make me feel good, Jess." Drew murmurs.

Jesse growls in frustration and although he's not looking at Drew's face now - he's flicking the tip of his tongue over Drew's nipples instead - he can tell by the huff of noise that Drew just laughed. He squeezes Drew's erection and the laughter transforms into a moan and when his own cock twitches in response, he presses against Drew, panting.

"Tell me what you like," he says and lifts his head, so he can see Drew's eyes. "I want to know."

"Oh God, Jess..." Drew drops back on the pillow with a moan. "I like everything you do."

Jesse shakes his head.

"I need you to tell me."

Drew's body is trembling and there's a light gloss of sweat forming on his chest; Jesse can see the pulse beating in Drew's throat and dips his head to suck at it.

"I need to get these off," Drew mutters, wriggling out of his pants and reaching to pull at Jesse's until they too are gone. Thrusts into Jesse's fist with a moan. "I like when you touch me like this, and I like it when you use your mouth and tongue."

That is one thing Jesse already knows. Whenever he uses his mouth on Drew, Drew never lasts long, but it feels good to hear it. Drew pulls Jesse's head forward and kisses him; the kiss slow and torturous, Drew biting and sucking at Jesse's lips and tongue. Jesse groans but when Drew tries to push him on to his back, he resists and shakes his head, breaking the kiss.

"No," he whispers, "I want to know what else."

"Jesus, Jess, I ...uh...I don't know...you're making it really hard to think."

Encouraged, Jesse rubs the pad of his thumb back and forth over the tip of Drew's cock swirling the dampness he finds there and bites down on his shoulder.

"Oh God Jess if you keep doing that you'll make me come," Drew pants.

"Good." Jesse only smirks a little when Drew whines.

"I ... I ... don't know darlin'. I guess if something feels good to you, you should try doing it to me. Oh Jesus ... Jess..."

Without letting go of him, Jesse nudges Drew onto his back and straddles his hips. He reaches for Drew's hand and places it behind him.

"I like it when you touch me here," he says, watching Drew's face and whimpering when Drew traces the cleft between his cheeks. If Drew doesn't touch him soon, he's going to have to, just to get some relief from the pressure and Jesse's not sure if he can do that with Drew watching. Drew does that sometimes and it gets Jesse all kinds of hot and bothered but he doesn't know if Drew would like him to do it. "Do you like that?"

Drew bucks his hips up, lifting Jesse from the bed, and Jesse takes it as a yes. Lust and curiosity replace shyness and he lets his free hand drift between Drew's legs, stroking the warm, velvety spot behind Drew's balls and is rewarded with a sharp, whine from the man beneath him.

"Jess...." Drew moans. Jesse reaches further down and presses his fingertips against the warm muscle and draws circles, pleased when Drew whimpers and squeezes his eyes shut.

"I like it when you're inside me," Jesse whispers. Drew grunts in agreement and rolls his hips up again, begging without words, and for a moment Jesse thinks about giving in, they can talk about this later. But he knows he won't be able to find the words later and right now, he likes the way Drew looks. Likes the desperate pleas for him to stop teasing and the frustrated moans each time Drew thrusts up. Jesse tightens his grip and increases the speed of his strokes.

"Jess ... please ..." Drew's fingers dig into the flesh of Jesse's thighs.

"Do you want me to do that to you?" Jesse asks. His heart is pounding, and he doesn't know if he can take much more of this, but the sounds Drew is making, the way his eyelids are fluttering, and his mouth is twisting, are just too good to abandon yet. Knowing he is the cause of those things makes Jesse feel powerful. Thunder might frighten him, but he can make Drew pant and plead and that feels good. Drew groans when Jesse repeats the question.

"Oh ... Jess... I.... I'm ... coming," Drew stutters, "*Jess!*"

Jesse watches, fascinated, as Drew's shoulders lift from the bed, his eyes shut tight, body jerking in time with the pulsations his cock makes in Jesse's hand. He keeps stroking until Drew hisses and pushes his hand away then lays back chest heaving, arms out at his side. Jesse doesn't think he's ever seen anything so beautiful and leans forward to kiss him, but his own neglected erection brushes against Drew's damp skin and he sits back up, moaning. Drew reaches up to run a trembling finger down Jesse's chest.

"Do you want to take care of that, darlin', or do you want me to?"

"You," he whispers. Drew smiles and begins to stroke him with slow, gentle strokes, making the younger man whine in frustration. Jesse covers Drew's hand with his own, tightening his grip and forcing Drew to move his hand faster.

"Yes," he breathes and runs his fingers along the skin of Drew's belly, losing himself in the sensory stimulation. Drops his head forward, breathing in short, sharp gasps as his body tightens and he comes, spots of color dancing behind his closed eyelids.

When he opens his eyes, Drew is looking up at him with a sleepy smile.

"Better?" he asks.

Jesse nods and stretches out beside him, warm in the crook of Drew's arm.

* * *

"Hey, we really should get up and take a shower," Drew says, nudging Jesse who is dozing against him. There have been two text messages from Erin asking if everything is okay and according to his phone it's nearly lunch time. As much as he'd be happy to stay in bed with Jesse all day, they really should get up.

"Don't want to," Jesse mumbles.

"Yeah, you say that now but, in an hour, when this mess is all dry and itchy you'll be sorry." He pulls his arm out from beneath a still protesting Jesse and pushes the covers back. "Besides I thought we might ask your mom and dad if they want to come over later."

Jesse lifts his head and frowns.

"Why?"

"Because your mom was really worried about you and it would be nice for her to see you're fine." Drew shrugs. "Or we can go see them if you like. You want to call them, or shall I?"

"You can," Jesse says and stands up.

Shaking his head, Drew reaches for his phone and calls Erin. Once he's reassured her that Jesse is fine, he asks if she and Ray would like to come over later in the afternoon. Jesse would love to see them, and they could see where Drew lives. She can also see, he thinks but doesn't say, for herself that Jesse is alright. They fix a time and Drew hangs up. He goes in search of Jesse and finds him at the cat tree playing with Scamp, still naked.

"You know, you might want to get some clothes on before you play with her. If you thought a scratch on the hand stung, imagine what it would be like elsewhere," he says with a grin and scratches Scamps ears as he passes. "Come on, we need to shower. Your mom and dad will be here at two."

The towels from the night before are still on the floor and he gathers them up, drops them in the hamper, and gets fresh ones from the cupboard. Turns the shower on and steps under the water with a sigh.

"Can we get a chocolate cake?" Jesse asks, joining him. "I feel like chocolate cake."

Drew reaches for the soap and starts rubbing it over Jesse's chest.

"Sure. Why not? It's Sunday."

"I love you," Jesse says.

"Because I said we can get chocolate cake?"

"Uh huh," Jesse's smile is so bright that for a moment Drew struggles to catch his breath.

"That's what I thought."

* * *

By the time Erin and Ray arrive, Drew wonders if he'll survive the aftermath of Jesse's fear of storms. It took another half hour and a blow job that left Drew's ears ringing to convince Jesse to get out of the shower. Together they'd made the bed and Jesse had promptly pulled him down for a heated make out session until breathless, Drew had pointed out that not only did they need milk and apple juice but there would be no chocolate cake if they didn't go out now. Every time he let go of Jesse's hand it would creep under his tee-shirt or into the pocket of his jeans and he's been ambushed with so many kisses he's worried his lips might go numb. Just as he switches the coffee maker on, Jesse winds his arms around his waist, and begins nuzzling the back of his neck, which while pleasant – okay more than pleasant he amends adjusting himself in his jeans before opening the door – is bad timing because that is when the door buzzer sounds.

Erin's smile is notably warmer this afternoon, but her hug is brief and distracted; all things considered Drew supposes he understands why. While she rushes to hug Jesse, Drew shakes hands with Ray, then takes their jackets to the bedroom and lays them on the bed. When he returns, Jesse has them both at the cat tree and is chattering about Scamp.

"He can be a little hyper after a meltdown," Erin says, stroking Scamp's head. "A swim usually helps with the excess energy."

"I noticed, maybe we'll go to the pool later," Drew says with a grin, though if Jesse's behavior the supermarket was any indication, he's not sure being near naked with Jesse in his current mood would be such a good idea.

"We've got chocolate cake," Jesse says, making a beeline for the kitchen counter. Drew intercepts him with an arm across his chest and turns him back to the living room – Jesse has been trying to get at the cake since they got home. "Why don't you help your mom and dad get comfortable, while I get the coffee. Do you want apple juice?"

Although Jesse likes beer and some red wine, he doesn't drink coffee or soda, claiming they make him feel fuzzy, which Drew assumes is the caffeine. Jesse shakes his head and asks for milk, giving Drew a look that suggests anyone who thinks anything else should be drunk with chocolate cake is of questionable sanity. When Erin asks if she can help, Drew passes her the cake and a knife.

"Your mission is to keep him from devouring this," he says. He smiles at her. "I'm not silly enough to think I know nearly enough to be able to achieve that yet."

Erin looks at him, unblinking and for a second he sees Jesse when he's confused.

"Last night was hard," he says softly. "But thank you for letting me care for him. Also, I think I may have been a bit of jerk."

Erin reaches over the counter and squeezes his hand.

"I think I may be having trouble letting go."

"I do love him, if that helps," he says putting the coffee and Jesse's milk on a tray.

"It does."

"Mom," Jesse calls from the living room, "yesterday we went to Drew's mom's house and they have a Bichon called Harry. He's really cute. Oh, and Drew's niece Mandy was there. Her hair is blue and she's a dork like me. Well, she's not like me, she's normal but she's still a dork."

"Jesse, that's not very nice," Erin says putting the cake on the coffee table and smacking Jesse's hand when he reaches for it.

"It's okay, Erin, Mandy is a self-proclaimed dork and a law unto herself. Luckily, she's adorable," Drew says grinning at Jesse who is glaring at his mother and rubbing his hand.

He passes cups of coffee to Ray and Erin and pushes the creamer and sugar toward them. Sits down with his own cup; Jesse sits at his feet, back straight against his legs, head resting against his knee, and Drew notes both parent's look of surprise.

"Can I have my cake now?" Jesse asks. Erin scolds him again but Drew can tell she doesn't mean it; there's no real heat to her words. She cuts the cake, hands a plate to Drew and then to Ray. Finally, she hands one to a pouting Jesse who tips his head back to look up at Drew. "You're getting really spoiled today. First you get se..."

His words are cut off when Drew puts his hand over his mouth and leans forward.

"Jess, filter," he says, cheeks burning. Ray snickers and gives Drew an amused look that makes his cheeks burn even hotter. "Why don't you tell your mom and dad what happened to the new guy at the store?"

For the next fifteen minutes, Jesse recounts the tale of Marcus and how he dropped his phone in the bearded dragon terrarium and Wally, the bearded dragon had sat on it. Marcus had been too scared to try and move him and every now and then his phone would chime, and it sounded like Wally was chiming. Eventually Jesse had reached in and pushed Wally off and retrieved the phone. Jesse finds the story just as hilarious now as when he recounted it to Drew the first time. It's not the idea of the bearded dragon chiming that amuses him, but that Marcus who is, according to Jesse, about the size of Chewbacca and has a million tattoos, is scared of a bearded dragon.

"Wally doesn't bite or anything," he says, making it clear what he thinks of the new guy at work. "Bearded dragons aren't poisonous to humans. And they only bite if you give them a fright."

"Well in fairness, you've known Wally since he was an egg," Ray says, "Marcus doesn't know he's not dangerous."

Jesse mutters something about whether Marcus should work in a pet store or not if he doesn't know something as basic as how to pick up a lizard and curls his arm around Drew's calf. The conversation turns to Ray's work and then Erin's, drifts to the previous night's storms and whether the coming season is going to be a bad one for storms. This hadn't occurred to Drew but for the first time in his life finds himself wishing for snow.

During all this Jesse stays pressed against Drew, stroking his calf and from time to time pulling his hand around to kiss it. He yawns, smothering it by hiding his face against Drew's leg and rubbing his cheek against the denim of his jeans. The closest he comes to letting go of Drew is when he leans forward to accept a second piece of cake from his mother.

"You're very calm for a day after two storms, Jesse," Erin says. "Did you go for a walk this morning?"

Jesse shakes his head.

"No, we just ..."

"We just took it slow, slept late, showered, went to the supermarket," Drew interjects, ignoring the look he gets from Jesse.

"Well you're remarkably calm, considering," Erin says, "but maybe you should still go to the pool later."

Jesse shrugs and excuses himself to go to the bathroom. As soon as he's left the room, Ray's shoulders begin to heave with laughter.

"What on earth are you laughing at?" Erin asks.

Drew knows and blushes a deep red again, wishing the floor would open up and swallow him.

"I think Jesse has found a new outlet for post storm hyperactivity," Ray finally manages to say. He nudges the cake toward Drew. "I suggest you have another slice or two, son, because if I know Jesse, you're probably going to need the strength."

"Thanks," Drew says trying to will the blood away from his cheeks. Erin still looks confused, but Jesse is back, and she can't ask either of them to clarify.

When it's time for them to leave, Erin folds Jesse into a hug and Ray pulls Drew to one side. Eyes dancing, he keeps his voice low.

"I'm sorry for teasing you before, that was a little childish," he says, unable to hide his grin, "but I want you to know that I'm grateful to you for giving Jesse that. You know, the opportunity to know at least that as a man."

Drew hugs him and tells him not to mention it. Really, please, please don't mention it again. Ever.

As they wait for the lift to open, Ray turns back to Drew and Jesse waiting in the doorway and calls.

"Vitamin B, Drew. And protein. Plenty of protein."

Oh. God.

* * *

22

Drew smiles when he sees Jesse filling the sink with hot water and detergent to wash the cups and dishes. While Drew doesn't consider himself a slob, he's learned that Jesse likes order and order means not leaving dishes stacked and waiting on the bench. Evidently it doesn't mean rinsing them and stacking them in the dishwasher, Drew's usual habit, either.

"I have school work to do," he says. Jesse stops washing up and his head drops down.

"Should I go home?" he asks in a small voice. "I can finish the washing up and catch the nine-oh-six."

Drew turns him by his shoulders and tips his head up so they're looking at each other.

"You're a dork sometimes, you know that?" he says. "That wasn't what I meant. I just meant it's Sunday night and I need to sort out lesson plans, so maybe you'd like to watch a movie."

A relieved smile replaces Jesse's disappointment and he nods.

"Good," Drew says. "You know, maybe I should get a games console. You could come with me and tell me which one to get."

"I could just bring mine over," Jesse says turning back to the sink. "Then you wouldn't have to buy one."

"What if I want to buy one?"

"You don't play video games," Jesse points out.

"You could teach me," Drew says. Jesse looks skeptical. "What? You could. Besides I've played Mario Karts before, with Mandy and my nephews."

Jesse's face suggests he has doubts about Drew's Mario Kart talents.

"You know if you're going to be so rude about my gaming ability," Drew says picking up a plate to dry, "maybe I won't give you your present."

Jesse jerks his head up, eyes shining.

"Present?"

Drew laughs and points to the sink. Dishes first, presents after. Jesse pesters him to tell him what the present is, but Drew refuses to give in. He'd picked it up on Friday and would have given it to Jesse last night had they not been interrupted by the sudden introduction to how to manage Jesse in full melt down.

When the dishes are done, Drew pours two glasses of milk and cuts two pieces of cake, ignoring Jesse's protest that they've just finished the darned dishes, why is he messing them up again. He puts what remains of the cake away in the fridge and steers Jesse to the sofa and puts the snack on the table.

"Don't touch," he says pointing to Jesse's plate. "I'll be right back."

When he returns, he's amused to see Jesse is sitting bolt upright on the sofa, Scamp on his knee and his cake is untouched. He sits next to him and hands him the bag. A part of him thinks it's not normal to enjoy Jesse's childlike qualities the way he does – what does it say about him that he gets a kick out of Jesse's reactions to kittens or chocolate cake or presents? But he finds he just can't find a way to believe it's wrong. Jesse isn't a child and he generally doesn't behave like one, but Drew finds his transparency and his innocence endearing. More than once he's thought the world could use a few more people like Jesse.

"It's not my birthday yet," Jesse says, hand hovering just inside the bag.

"I know," Drew says. "Come on, open it, I have essays to grade."

Jesse plunges his hand in the bag and pulls out a rectangular box with a picture of a device that looks like his computer only smaller and with no keyboard. He runs his finger under the letters above the picture.

"P ... por.... table..." he stammers, frowning and Drew has to resist the urge to tell him. "Por Table bl ... blur.... BLURAY PLAYER."

He shouts the last two words in triumph and looks to Drew for confirmation, smiles when he nods.

"Portable, not Por Table, it means ..."

"I know what it means," Jesse says. "I just didn't know what it looks like. Blue looks funny too."

Drew decides now is not the time to explain the nuances of brand names. He nudges Jesse.

"There's something else in there."

Surprised, Jesse puts his hand back in the bag and pulls out a boxed set of the first season of *Torchwood*.

"Captain Jack," he says, eyes shining. Drew rolls his eyes; Jesse and Jody had bonded over *Doctor Who*, *Torchwood* and Captain Jack, on whom both have a huge crush. When Jody told Jesse that John Barrowman, the actor playing Captain Jack, was gay, Jesse's infatuation had magnified. Drew can't see the attraction himself. What does the guy in the overcoat have that a bespectacled English teacher doesn't?

"There's one more in there," Drew prompts. He'd thought Jesse would be like his nieces and nephews, tearing the bag open and pouncing on the contents but Jesse seems to assume that each thing he withdraws is the only one. He pulls out another movie, holds it up and shrieks. *Guardians of the Galaxy* is the one movie that comes close to *Star Wars* in Jesse's estimation and to Drew's surprise it isn't because of Rocket, the raccoon but because of...

"I am Groot," Jesse says clutching the box to his chest, eyes shining. Drew knows Jesse has a copy of the DVD at his apartment but that it has a scratch caused by dropping it down the back of the television cabinet one evening. He suspects Jesse has been punishing himself for being clumsy by not buying a new copy.

"Now you don't have to go to the bedroom to watch movies or use the iPad," Drew says. "And you can bring it in the car if we go on a trip somewhere."

"I am Groot," Jesse repeats and puts his arms around Drew's neck and kisses him, "and I love you."

"Okay Groot, well I'm going to go mark essays. You find the headphones, the guy in the shop said they'll work just fine with the player," Drew says and reaches for his cake and milk and stops, mouth open in surprise. In the middle of the frosting on his cake, there's a long, deep furrow and he turns an unbelieving face to Jesse. "Hey, what happened to my cake?"

"You said I couldn't touch mine," Jesse says with a smirk. He goes to retrieve the headphones from the sound system and says over his shoulder. "I am Groot."

* * *

When the movie finishes, Jesse sits up and rubs his eyes. He's watched the director's cut and the special scenes and now his eyes are sore from watching the small screen for so long. He looks over at Drew who is still hunched over his desk, writing things with a red pen, head resting on his hand, his hair a curtain that hides his face. Jesse considers what to do for a minute, then gets up.

"You okay?" Drew calls, looking over his shoulder. Jesse grins and nods.

"Too much milk, need to pee," he says and goes into the bathroom.

He's washing his hands when the overflowing laundry hamper catches his eye and he stands for a moment, staring at it as water flows over his fingers. If he was at home, he would do his laundry. Sort the whites first, then the colors. Clothes, then towels and sheets. At home, there's a laundry room in the basement with washers and dryers but Drew has a washer-dryer like Jesse's mom has in the kitchen next to the dishwasher. Jesse is so used to washing dishes at home he's forgets about the dishwasher, but he doesn't really mind; he likes keeping things tidy.

"Jess?" Drew calls from the living room, snapping Jesse back to reality. He turns the water off, grabs the laundry basket, and goes to the kitchen. After a moment's hesitation, he dumps everything on the floor.

"What are you doing?" Drew asks from right behind him, making him jump.

"The laundry," he says sorting the mess into colors, clothes, and towels, then bundling a load into the washer.

"Why?"

Jesse looks at Drew as if he's gone mad and pushes past him to the bedroom. Strips the bed and gathers up the sheets and their sleep wear from last night. Drew is still in the kitchen looking confused.

"It's laundry night," Jesse explains.

"But ..."

"It's okay, Mom has the same washer as you, I know how to use it," he says and starts opening cupboard doors and prodding at their content.

"Now what are you doing?"

"Looking for a pan."

"Why do you need a pan?"

"So I can make dinner."

Drew blinks at him for a moment, then runs a hand through his hair, looking bewildered.

"Go finish doing your work, I'm making dinner." Jesse finds a pan he approves of and puts it on the stove top.

"I can order something ..." Drew starts to say, it's what he usually does on a Sunday, and Jesse blows an exasperated breath out his nose and turns on him, hands on his hips, and narrows his eyes.

"I cook when I'm at home," he says, "I know how."

"Well, do you need me to help?" Drew asks.

"Nope," Jesse says, then adds as he peers in the fridge, "I am Groot."

"You are a dork," Drew says and backs out of the kitchen.

Smiling, Jesse lines up bread, butter, and cheese on the counter next to the stove before looking to see what else is in the pantry. He finds a tin of tomato soup and puts it on to heat while he makes grilled cheese sandwiches. When everything is ready he gets two bottles of beer out of the fridge, adds them to the tray, and goes to Drew.

"Wow." Drew drops his pen and pushes some of the papers on his desk to one side so Jesse can put the tray down. Takes his glasses off and rubs his eyes.

Jesse takes his plate of sandwiches, sits at Drew's feet, and admits he doesn't know how to cook anything fancy or how to grill things like Drew's dad but he can make simple things like grilled cheese, scrambled eggs, and even macaroni cheese. Telling Drew that makes him feel embarrassed; he knows most people can cook those things and stuff that's much harder. Drew finishes chewing a mouthful of sandwich and grins.

"Well I can't cook anything that doesn't come in a can or a box and I have all the local take-out places on speed dial, so you're ahead of me darlin'. Also, I usually wait

until I'm out of clean underwear or for the cleaning lady to come, to do the laundry."
He rubs his foot along Jesse's thigh with a grin.

Glowing from the praise, Jesse sits up straighter and reaches for his soup. He looks up at the piles of paper on Drew's desk and shudders. All that writing and reading and words and numbers. Looking after animals is so much better and he says as much.

"Well, each of us is good at something Jess," Drew says. "I don't find any of this hard, but I couldn't do your job. For a start, I don't even like cleaning out Scamp's litter box, I sure wouldn't like cleaning out rats and mice and lizards as well."

"Also, we sometimes have snakes," Jesse says.

"Oh, you remember that do you?"

"Mmmhmmm," Jesse leans forward and rests his forehead on Drew's knees. When he feels Drew's hand on the back of his neck, he sighs and closes his eyes. Drew asks if he's sleepy and he nods.

"Little bit," he says.

"I still have a few of these to finish, I'm afraid," Drew says pointing at the essays and putting his glasses back on.

"That's okay, I'm going to do the dishes and then watch Captain Jack."

Jesse unfolds his legs and pulls himself upright. He gathers up the dishes and takes them to the kitchen. When he's satisfied the kitchen is clean enough and the first load of laundry is drying, he feeds Scamp and curls back up on the sofa with his movies. He does feel sleepy, but it's a good sleepy. Not like last night when he was scared because of the thunder and lightning. Tonight, sleepy is a warm feeling. It's nice not being alone. Knowing that there'll be someone warm to curl up next to in bed. He thinks that's the very best thing about having someone – it's not having someone to do things with, although that's nice, and it's not the sex, although that's really nice. No, it's the feeling of being warm and loved in bed at night. Jesse smiles to himself, he doesn't think he'll ever get tired of that feeling.

* * *

23

Drew throws his satchel in the back of the car, waves to Jody, and pulls out of the staff parking lot. Slams his brakes on when Jayden Wilcox from his sophomore English class zips in front of him on a skateboard and winds down the window to tell the kid not to ride it in the parking lot or he'll forget he's a good guy and put him on bin duty for a month. What the hell is the kid doing on a board in this weather at this time of night anyway? It's after six and spring or not it's damned cold out there – God he sounds like his mother. Or worse, his sister Glynnis, who Drew is convinced was born aged ninety. His phone chimes and he doesn't need to look at it to know it's Jesse asking how long he'll be. Glancing in his rear vision to make sure he's not holding anyone up behind him, he stops in the exit and sends a quick message to say he's on the way.

Over the past months, the two of them have fallen into an easy routine. Tuesday, Wednesday, and Thursday they stay at Jesse's apartment, the rest of the week at Drew's. Each has copies of the other's keys. Scamp has a litter box and a cat cave at Jesse's; there's a new Play Station at Drew's. Drew's laptop and Jesse's camera travel back and forth. Jesse still takes the bus to and from work – he's proud to have found the route and bus he has to catch without Drew or his Dad's help – and Drew still has after school activities he has to attend. They always start the day by going for a swim together and they always end it curled around one another, Scamp in a ball on the edge of Jesse's pillow, Wicket on his night table. Drew has a new weather app on his phone, so he knows of storms before they hit so last week was able to have the curtains pulled and the music ready before the first clap of thunder. He'd pulled Jesse into bed, holding him against his chest and read him the first Harry Potter book until the weather had transformed from terrifying to just wet and windy.

Drew is surprised by how much he enjoys the regular rhythm of life with Jesse. Sundays, Jesse cooks grilled cheese sandwiches or omelets and does laundry, with one eye on his Blu-ray player, while Drew creates lesson plans and marks assignments. Tuesdays are faculty meetings, so Jesse collects Scamp and takes her to his apartment; when Drew gets home they have frozen dinners and play video games. Drew still gets beaten by Jesse every time. Wednesdays and Thursdays, Drew always bring pizza or burgers and they start out watching a movie but always end up making out on the sofa. On Friday's Jesse puts Scamp in her carrier and takes her to

Drew's, feeds her and wait for Drew to get home so they can go to the Library Bar for the cheese platter and wine.

But this Friday is different. It's Jesse's birthday and he's waiting for Drew at his parent's home; Ray picked him up from work an hour ago. Jesse has been excited about today for the past ten days, trying to find out what Drew has got him by any means possible from buying him his favorite candy to threatening to abandon him for Captain Jack to last night a prolonged and intense blow job that had almost succeeded in getting him the information he needed. Luckily for Drew, Jesse had needed something else more urgently than information by the time he'd shimmied back up Drew's side and had been easy to distract. Drew hopes after all this that Jesse won't be disappointed – although he'd run his gifts by Ray and had been reassured they would be a hit.

As soon as he pulls into Ray and Erin's driveway, their front door is flung open and Jesse is running down the steps to meet him. Drew grins, gathers up the wine he's brought and the wrapped presents, and gets out. Jesse throws his arms around him, covering his face in kisses.

"I didn't think you were ever going to get here. Why were you so late? What took so long? Did the rehearsal go bad? Was there traffic? What took so long? Is that my present? Can I open it?"

Wrapping his arm around Jesse's waist, Drew steers him back in the house. Although it's too warm for the fire to be lit, Ray has still turned on the central heating enough to take the chill off the air. Jesse's immune system isn't as robust as most and nobody likes the idea of a spring cold. Ray gives him a hug and takes the wine while Jesse flattens himself against Drew, and gives him a firm, warm kiss on the mouth, the lays his cheek against Drew's shoulder.

"Happy birthday, Jess," Drew says against his forehead. "I love you."

"I love you too," Jesse says and hugs him closer. "You're the best part of today. You and my cake."

The kitchen door swings open as Erin backs into the room carrying a large roasting pan containing a leg of lamb, still sizzling from the oven.

"Hi Erin," Drew says. He holds the door while she turns and puts the pan on the table, then kisses her cheek. "Has he been driving you mad?"

"Not really," she says, casting a fond look over her son who refuses to let go of Drew, "he helped prepare the beans and the brownie. He's been really helpful."

"We're having chocolate brownie for dessert," Jesse tells him. "And birthday cake."

"Oh wow, you'll be a bundle of fun with all that sugar," Drew says, surprised when Erin snorts and suggests with a sly grin that she's sure he'll figure out some way of dealing with the excess energy.

Jesse pulls on Drew's shirt; he looks into wide, shining golden eyes and a dazzling smile and shakes his head. He knows what Jesse wants.

"What do you think, guys, shall we give him his presents?" Drew asks Ray and Erin.

"Oh, I think we should eat first," Erin says but Drew can see she's teasing. There are no vegetables on the table so she's not ready to carve the meat yet.

"Or perhaps we should have a drink to celebrate first?" Ray adds, eyes twinkling.

"No," Jesse protests and Drew half expects him to stomp his foot. "It's my birthday, I want my presents."

Ruffling his hair, Drew pushes him toward the sofa and sits down. Jesse presses in as close as he can get and turns his face toward his mother.

"Yours and Dad's first," he says and when Drew prods him in the ribs, adds, "please Mom."

Ray disappears into his small office off the side of the living room and comes back with a red box wrapped with gold ribbon and a large gold bow. Eye shining, Jesse tugs at the ribbon and when it falls away, places it with care on the back of the sofa before folding down the paper. Inside is a camera, and Jesse's eyes widen, and his mouth falls open.

"Wow, this is a Canon Power Shot," he says. "Wow."

Drew doesn't know much about cameras, but he can tell by Jesse's reaction this is a big deal. He waits while Jesse carefully unpacks the contents of the box, exclaiming over each lens and charger piece, and the fold up tripod. When he's done, he goes from his father to his mother, first hugging them, then kissing their cheeks, and finally telling them how much he loves them. Erin strokes his cheek and Drew pretends he doesn't see Ray dabbing at his eyes with a rumpled handkerchief pulled from his pocket.

Jesse sits back by Drew and puts the camera on the coffee table, and turns to look at him, face filled with expectation. More nervous than ever that he'll be disappointed, Drew offers Jesse the larger of the three gifts he has next to him.

"This is from Scamp," he says and pushes his glasses back up with trembling finger. Jesse peels back each piece of tape with care until Drew is almost ready to just shred the paper himself. When the paper falls away he gives an excited squeak and holds the box up for his parents to see.

"It's the Lego Death Star," he says, then throws himself on Drew. "Thank you, thank you, thank you."

"Don't thank me, thank Scamp," Drew says hugging him, pleased with the reaction. "I thought we could make it together."

Jesse gives him an enthusiastic nod and stars examining the pictures on the box.

"Jody sent you this," Drew says and hands him the next parcel. This one turns out to be a tee-shirt with the Tardis on it and Jesse immediately starts humming the

Doctor Who theme and chanting 'exterminate'. Drew rolls his eyes and waits. When Jesse has settled down again he hands him the last present, a small flat envelope but doesn't let go, instead he holds Jesse's hand in his and makes him look at him.

"This is from me and it's not a present for right now," he says. Jesse frowns and the tip of his tongue appears at the corner of his mouth. "Mr Greenwold is giving you next Friday and Saturday off work and I've taken a leave day on Friday. On Thursday, we're going to go away for the weekend."

"Go away?"

"Mmhmm. We're going to drive to Alberton and stay in a hotel there for three nights. And on Friday and Saturday we are going to go to the place that's in this envelope, okay?"

"O-okay," Jesse says, his voice unsure.

"Why don't you open it and see where we're going?"

Jesse fumbles the envelope open and pulls out a glossy brochure that shows farm animals and children. When he looks up at Drew in confusion, Drew takes his finger and runs it under the words.

"You can do this Jess, take your time."

"J – Joh – Johstn," he stumbles, and Drew gives him the right syllable, "Johnst – ons. Johnst-ons. Johnstons. F-farm? Farm."

Drew encourages him with a smile and rubs his back.

"You know part of the next word," he says and points to it.

"Pet – ting, petting and r -rid -ridding," he stops and frowns. Drew grins when he sees the point of pink tongue again. "No that's not right. Rid -ing. Ri – riding. Johnston's Farm, Petting and Riding. Open Monday to Saturday. P-pr-private s-s-sessy, no, when you see two esses they make a sh sound, sesh-ion, sessions by a-ar – arrang-arrangement. Private sessions by arrangement."

Drew nods and he continues. The next words form a list and he knows most of them from work.

"Rabbits, cows, goats, ch-chickens, pigs, l-l-la ..." he points to the word and looks again at Drew, who just nods at him to continue, "l-l-la-ma, llamas, horses."

He stares at the brochure for a moment.

"Horses?"

"Yeah Jess," Drew cups his face, "horses."

"Can – can I ride one?" Jesse asks. Drew nods.

"That's what the riding part means. It's a special farm where you can go and pet the animals and feed them and ride the horses. And you can take all the photos you want too, I asked. They're expecting us at nine o'clock sharp next Friday morning."

"Mom," Jesse says, his eyes shining, holding the brochure up for his mother to see, "I'm going to ride a horse."

Erin nods and smiles but says nothing and Drew leans forward to touch her hand.

"Are you okay?"

"Yes," she whispers. "He read the brochure."

"Mom, you know I can read." Jesse turns the brochure over in his hands and Drew is tempted to nudge him and remind him to filter, but his next words stop him. "It just takes me longer because I have to keep figuring out what the things are all the time. And it hurts my eyes. Drew says I just have to take my time and never mind what other people say. It's hard though."

It's the first time Drew has heard him speak of being different without using the words normal or abnormal and when he looks at Ray and Erin he can tell they've noticed it too. He hugs Jesse and kisses his temple.

"I'm going to ride a horse," Jesse says looking down at the brochure with a smile.

"Jess?" Drew waits until Jesse is looking up at him. "I have one more thing for you."

He reaches into his pocket and brings out something small, takes Jesse's hand and drops it in. When uncovers Jesse's palm there is a key chain on the end of which is a plush, miniature Wicket in perfect proportion. Jesse gasps and strokes a finger over the head of the miniature. Looks up with a grin.

"We'll put your keys on him after dinner, okay?" Drew says, smiling at the delight in Jesse's eyes. "But I think for now we better get to that roast your mom has made."

* * *

As far as Jesse is concerned his mother's roast lamb is perfect. Always has been, always will be. There are lots of things she cooks that are okay – like her meatloaf – and some that are ... well ... not okay. He tries not to think about her hamburger casserole because... ew...gross. But her roast lamb is perfect, so he has two helpings and is reaching for a third when he remembers the brownie and birthday cake. For a moment he hesitates, hand hovering over the serving dish then he catches sight of Drew grinning and pokes his tongue at him.

"You forgot your cake, didn't you?" Drew says.

"No, I just like Mom's lamb," he retorts, reaching for his glass. Drew brought champagne tonight. He says it's not real champagne but it's close enough; Jesse doesn't care if it's real or not, he likes it. It's just the right amount of sweet, the bubbles tickle his nose, and he feels all floaty and happy.

"Quite rightly," Drew says, kissing his cheek. "But you still forgot your cake."

His mom starts to clear the table and when Jesse tries to help her, Drew, already on his feet and helping, presses him back down into his seat.

119

"You don't have to help, it's your birthday. You sit there and try to remember there is birthday cake coming."

"I didn't forget," Jesse calls after him. He puts his hand in his pocket and strokes the mini-Wicket keychain, not because he needs to but because he can. Being able to do that, whenever he wants, and nobody will know, makes mini-Wicket the best birthday present ever and he wonders how Drew knew. Drew knows he likes Lego and Jody knows he likes Doctor Who, so those gifts were easy. Jesse has mentioned wanting to learn to ride a horse several times since they met, so that's easy too. But how did Drew know to get mini -Wicket?

The kitchen door swings open and Drew and Mom come back out with the cake. It's chocolate and has Jesse's name on the frosting. He waits while they sing to him then blows the candles out.

"This is the best birthday ever," he says, not taking his eyes off Drew.

* * *

Jesse waits while Drew turns the lights on in the apartment, then follows him in. Scamp pops out of her cave as soon as she hears them, and Jesse drops his bag of gifts to scoop her out and dances around the room with her.

"Thank you for my Lego, Scamp, even though I know Drew really bought it. Best. Birthday. Ever."

"I think you may have had enough champagne," Drew says and Jesse spins around with Scamp until they are leaning against his chest.

"Maybe," he says and kisses the top of Scamp's head. "Or maybe I'm just really happy tonight."

Drew smiles and kisses his forehead. If this is what champagne does, Jesse decides he likes champagne. Scamp squeaks and wriggles out of his arms, jumping to the kitchen counter in a neat arc and landing on all fours at Drew's elbow.

"Hey you, nu-uh, no way. Off the counter," he says and takes her over to her dish and puts her down.

Jesse slips his arms around his waist and leans his cheek on Drew's back, breathing in the warm, spicy scent of him. Drew's hands settle over his and he smiles.

"What do you want to do now?" Drew asks, and Jesse can hear the smile. Can hear that Drew already knows.

"Thank you," he says, kissing Drew through his pale blue button down.

Drew turns in his arms and rests back against the kitchen cupboards; Jesse leans in, molding himself to Drew and stealing a kiss.

"You're welcome," Drew says.

* * *

24

"Are you sure?" Jesse asks him for what Drew is sure must be the fiftieth time since they left home and possibly the millionth – as a conservative estimate – since last Friday.

"Jess, I'm sure," he says with a sigh, listening for the GPS to tell him, in Arnold Schwarzenegger's voice installed at Jesse's insistence, when to turn. "I'm also sure you're driving me crazy asking."

"Sorry," Jesse says and peers out at the night.

Drew grins and reaches for his hand, squeezes it. All week Jesse has been worried that they'll be turned away from the hotel, or even worse Johnston's Farm, when people realize they are a couple. It's the first time since Drew has known him that he's expressed any self-consciousness about his sexuality; Drew isn't quite sure what to make of it.

"Turn left at the next intersection," Arnie drones from the GPS unit making Jesse jump. Drew takes the turn and just as Arnie informs them the destination is on their right and that he will be back – garnering a giggle from Jesse – he spots the sign for the hotel. When he'd booked the room, Drew had warned them they would be a late check in, making sure they would still be able to get room service, and had made sure that no it wasn't Mr and Mrs, Ms, or Miss but that yes, they are a couple. The reservations clerk had not appeared to care one way or the other once she had a valid credit card number entered in the system.

There's no car valet system – the hotel is too small – but there's ample parking and Drew finds a spot near the door without problem. Jesse slings his back pack, containing Wicket and his Blu-ray player and some movies on his shoulders and gets his camera bag from the back while Drew gets out the bigger bag from the trunk. Drew locks the car and holds out his free hand to Jesse, who after a moment's hesitation takes it, goggling at their surroundings as they go in.

A young blonde woman with perfect teeth smiles at them from the reception desk and gives Drew an approving once over. It's a look he's seen before from both men and women: nice facial structure, tall, long hair, big brown eyes behind glasses that make him look a little serious and studious, yes that all works. He sees the moment when her eyes slide from him to Jesse and she does a double take, unable to hide her reaction. Not as tall as Drew, with a lithe, swimmer's build, short hair, high cheek bones under smooth skin, and of course, those spectacular, golden eyes. When her gaze drops to their entwined hands, Drew can see the disappointment in her eyes and bites the inside of his cheek to keep from laughing. He stops at the desk and smiles as he reads her name tag.

"Hello Donna, we have a room booked for Oliver."

She taps on the keyboard in front of her. Jesse is looking around the lobby at the advertising cabinets and displays. From the end of the hallway comes the distinctive sounds of a restaurant and Drew wonders if Jesse would like to eat there rather than have room service.

"Of course, Mr Oliver and uh Mr Peterson. I just need to take a hard copy imprint of your credit card and we'll be good to go. Our restaurant is still seating if you'd like to have dinner," Donna says in a sing-song voice, flashing them a blinding a smile.

"Jess? Do you want to have dinner in the restaurant?" Drew asks. Jesse shakes his head and Drew squeezes his hand. "No, that's okay thank you Donna, room service will be fine."

She finishes printing out their details, then hands them a key card, a room service menu, and a map of the hotel. With her pen, she points to where they are in the lobby and how to find their way to the room from there.

"We're going to Johnston's Farm tomorrow for the day," Drew says. "Could we order a wake-up call and breakfast?"

"I can book your wake-up right now and there's a form in your room to fill in for breakfast. If you give it to the room service waiter he'll make sure it's lodged for you."

Drew books the alarm service, thanks Donna for her help, and tugs Jesse's hand. They find the correct lift at the end of the hallway and when the door shuts, he presses the button for the third floor. Their room is four doors down from the lift. Drew slides the key card in the slot and as the door swings open the light comes on, obviously wired to the locking system. Jesse seems hesitant so Drew tugs him in and pushes the suit case to one side.

This is no five-star room but it's large and comfortable looking with an oversized couch, a small desk beneath a TV screen, and a very inviting queen size bed. After a moment, Jesse goes to the bed and checks the pillow slips, changes the pillows so they're all facing in the right direction, and corrects the threadbare cushions on the couch. Drew watches all this leaning against the wall, smiling.

"Hungry?" he asks when everything has been put in its rightful place. Jesse nods and Drew takes him the room service menu. Jesse runs his finger under each item, saying the words out loud - complete with description and price – as he goes. Finally, to Drew's relief he seems to decide and points to a chicken burger and fries. Drew phones and orders two, no pickle for Jesse, along with soda for him and apple juice for Jesse.

"You want to call your folks and let them know we got here okay or take a shower?"

"I sent them a text when you were talking to the lady downstairs," Jesse says, "so I'll take a shower."

He drops his eyes and doesn't move; Drew frowns.

"Jess, is everything okay?"

Jesse doesn't answer. Instead he continues to stare at the ground for a moment, hand in his pocket and Drew knows he has mini-Wicket beneath his fingers.

"Jess?"

Jesse hasn't been able to stop talking about the trip since last Friday and has had his bag ready since Tuesday. The brochure that Drew gave him has been folded and unfolded so many time it's falling apart. He wonders if this is still about them being a couple and wonders why this is suddenly bothering Jesse so much. Worried, he pulls him into his arms.

"Jess, what's wrong?"

"Drew what if they ..." Jesse's voice trails off.

"What if they what, darlin'?"

"What if they laugh at me because petting farms are for kids and I'm not a kid?"

Drew breathes a sigh of relief. If all Jesse is worried about is being laughed at, Drew can handle that. He sits on the bed and pulls Jesse down next to him, wraps his arm around him until Jesse rests his head on his shoulder.

"Jess, listen they're not going to laugh at you. Lots of adults come to places like Johnston's farm to learn to ride and even to pet the animals," he says. Jesse looks doubtful and Drew continues. "You know a lot of people in cities never get to see farm animals or even animals like rabbits, so they come to places like Johnston's. Sure, lots of them bring their kids or grandkids, but lots of them come because they want to see the animals themselves."

"I bet they don't come for their birthday though."

"Well that's because they don't have an awesome boyfriend who thinks of it," Drew says. "Jesse, I promise, nobody will laugh. Now why don't you go shower before dinner gets here, you're a bit stinky."

"Am not," Jesse retorts.

"Well, I'm not kissing you again until you've been in the shower, so it's up to you."

Grumbling Jesse goes to the bathroom. At the door, he stops and looks back. Drew is touched to see his smile is almost shy when he speaks.

"You are awesome," he says, then goes into the bathroom and shuts the door.

* * *

Jesse is awake before the courtesy call in the morning. Over Drew's shoulder he can see the red blinking numbers of the digital clock on the night table. It's six-thirty, the time he usually wakes in the morning for work. The courtesy call is for seven-thirty so there's no need to panic. He curls in against Drew, listening to the sounds he makes sleeping and thinks about what it will be like to ride a horse. He hopes it will be as good as it looks in the videos he's seen. On the website for Johnston's Farm there had been videos too; some showed Mr Johnston and his employees helping put saddles on horses and go for rides, others showed Mrs Johnston showing children how to pet baby animals. There had been a lot of children in the videos and the adults had all been parents. Everyone had been … normal. Watching the videos was exciting – oh how he hopes the horses will be as nice as they look – but they made him feel anxious and fuzzy too. Nobody in the videos was like Jesse and there were no couples like him and Drew. What if people laughed at him? Or were horrible to him and Drew because they're a couple? Sometimes when he and Drew go out, someone will stare at them holding hands or comment if Jesse reaches up to kiss Drew. Even if it's just on his cheek. Sometimes the comments are just rude but once or twice they were mean, and Drew had taken his hand and they'd had to leave. Jesse doesn't want that to happen today. He doesn't want to miss out on the animals and horses, but he also doesn't want Drew's present to be spoiled by people being mean.

Sighing, he rests his head on Drew's chest.

"You know, the whole point of ordering a later alarm is so you can sleep late," Drew murmurs without opening his eyes, running his fingers through Jesse's hair. Jesse smiles against the steady thump of Drew's heart.

"I can't help it if my brain knows what time to wake up," he says. He thinks for a moment. "Does it make me weird? That my brain does that, I mean, when it can't remember how to read a book properly, but it knows when to wake up without an alarm. Is that weird?"

"Oh darlin', that doesn't make you weird, that just makes you Jesse and I love Jesse." Drew rolls to face him. "What makes you weird is that thing you do with fries and ice-cream. Now *that* is weird."

Jesse grins.

"You haven't even tried it."

"Not going to happen." Drew runs his hands up Jesse's back. It feels warm.

"You should," Jesse says, "it tastes good."

"Know what else tastes good?" Drew asks and nuzzles the skin under Jesse's ear. "You."

Drew's hands are back down at Jesse's waist, fingers tracing figures of eight on the soft skin of his belly, and Jesse decides he doesn't want to talk about food or alarms or being weird anymore. He pulls Drew closer, pressing against him. Drew wriggles down in the bed, disappearing beneath the covers, and when he flicks his tongue over Jesse's nipple, Jesse sighs. Drew closes his lips around the bud of flesh, grazing it with his teeth before sucking it to a tight, erect point, making Jesse moan and bury his fingers in Drew's hair. He rocks his hips forward, wanting more.

Drew slides further down the bed and Jesse squeezes his eyes shut as gentle kisses are trailed from his navel to his hipbone, then down to the top of his thigh. Lips and tongue cover every inch of skin, except where Jesse wants him to go.

"Ohhhhh ..." he groans and can feel the upturn of Drew's mouth against his skin, knows he's smiling. Trembling, he tilts his hips a little further forward and pushes the covers back, just as Drew takes him in his mouth. A shudder ripples through him and he moans again. Drew moves on to his back, pulling Jesse after him so he's straddling Drew's chest; Drew's hands on his hips coax him to move and he grabs the headboard, so he can steady himself.

Jesse's panting fills the room. Everything feels good: the wet warmth of Drew's mouth, being able to thrust into it, being able to watch. Then Drew slides his hand beneath him, finds the patch of skin just behind his balls, and rubs it with the pad of his thumb.

"Drew," Jesse gasps, "Drew...don't stop."

Drew doesn't stop, instead he increases the pressure of his thumb and hollows his cheeks, sucking harder.

"Yes ...yes...yes...." Jesse pants. Sensation crashes over him like a wave and his back arches into the feeling as he comes. "Drew ... Drew... now, now, NOW."

Eyes closed, his head drops forward and he kneels for a moment, still gripping the headboard, breathless. His body feels electric, almost the way it does after the storms that terrify him, as though some switch beneath his skin has been flicked on and he thinks he should ask Drew why he feels like that. Does Drew feel that electric sensation? Drew. Jesse opens his eyes; Drew is smiling up at him, rich chocolate colored eyes filled with love and want. This is a social cue Jesse has learned to recognize since meeting Drew and one he can't get enough of seeing. Knowing that Drew wants him is better than the sensation still buzzing under his skin and knowing Drew loves him is the best feeling of all.

Jesse lets go of the headboard and eases himself back, so he's resting on Drew, skin pressed against skin and smiles at Drew's low groan when he grinds against him. Still sensitive from his own orgasm, Jesse hisses, but repeats the action and is pleased when Drew growls and digs his fingers into the flesh of his thighs. When he rubs himself against him for a third time, Drew whimpers and grabs Jesse's hand, pushes it between them.

"Jess, please," he begs.

Jesse wraps his fingers around the hard length of Drew's cock and strokes in time with the light rocking movement he's still making with his own body. Drew buries his head against the side of Jesse's neck, kissing and nipping the skin; the sounds he's making in his throat growing in urgency and Jesse smiles. He understands what that means now too and beams at having learned something this important – being able to understand what someone means from their sounds and expressions is so hard except when the someone is Drew. Tightening his grip just enough to make Drew groan louder than he has been, he grinds down and strokes harder, twisting his hand the way Drew has showed him. Drew's arms wrap around his waist and tighten, as though he wants to lock Jesse there, breath coming in short, hard bursts.

"Going to come," Drew groans against Jesse's throat and a flood of heat covers Jesse's hand. Jesse dips his head, strokes now light and feathery, and covers Drew's face with kisses.

"I love you," he repeats over and over in between kisses before rolling away, searching for a towel to wipe them up with.

Eyes still closed, Drew gropes for his hand and squeezes it.

"I love you too."

* * *

25

Drew squeezes Jesse's hand and smiles; the younger man is trembling, eyes darting from side to side as they wait for Mr Johnston to cross the yard. An older man whose bulging belly strains against his overalls, he takes his time, no doubt sizing them up; Drew wonders if the farmer's look is deliberate, for the paying customers, or authentic. When the man approaches, nods at Drew, then waits until Jesse's skittering gaze briefly settles on him before speaking, he decides he doesn't care - he already likes Mr Johnston.

"You must be Jesse," the farmer says. "I hear you want to learn to ride a horse."

With what Drew knows is a supreme effort, Jesse looks Mr Johnston in the eye and nods. Johnston grins and holds his hand out.

"Well we'd best shake hands, so I know which horse will like you," he says.

Oh yes, Drew likes Mr Johnston. He'd given him a brief explanation of Jesse's challenges, hoping it would forestall any misunderstandings, but he's obviously underestimated how important this man finds his customers. Jesse's eyes are round as he takes the offered hand.

"How do you know which horse just by shaking my hand?" he asks, then blushes and ducks his head to look at his feet. Drew rubs his back.

"Well now, it's all in the grip. Nice firm grip like yours, Jesse, means you'll probably be just fine with our chestnut mare, Hazel." Johnston holds his hand toward Drew, who accepts it with a rueful smile. "Drew? Nice to meet you."

"Which horse will Drew get?" Jesse asks, excitement flooding back into his face.

"Uh no, I'm not ..."

"Oh well now, I think he's going to need old Dallas." He leans toward Jesse and in a stage whisper adds, "we usually keep her for grannies."

"Hey," Drew protests but the burst of laughter from Jesse is worth the teasing. Not that he intends riding anyway – this is Jesse's present, he's just here to enjoy the sight of him having fun.

Mr Johnston leads them across the yard, running through health and safety regulations as they go. He glances at Jesse from time to time to ensure he understands, nodding when he sees he does. A white wooden gate at the end of the yard swings into an area with a large oak in a corner, a grill in another, and dotted with picnic tables. They must have set up the picnic area around the tree, Drew thinks, and wonders how old it is. Before he can ask, Mr Johnston tells them the tree was planted by his father when he was born and is seventy-five years old. Jesse nods but says nothing, he's too busy scanning the surrounding fields for animals. The farm used to be two hundred acres, Johnston is saying, but he has sold most of it and now only has forty. He runs some livestock still but most of their income comes from the petting farm. As he speaks they pass from the picnic area and move around the corner of a small building to an open space. On the far side, a woman is scattering food for a large mass of squabbling chickens and ducks that are scratching in the dirt and gobbling grain as it hits the ground.

"There's enough for everyone, just stop your fighting. We have guests coming, you could try to behave," she scolds the birds. When she sees the men, she smiles and approaches.

"Hello." Dressed in similar overalls to her husband, her grey hair pulled back in a low ponytail, she offers her hand to Drew.

"Brenda, this is Jesse and Drew," her husband says. Jesse looks up at her from beneath his lashes and gives her a timid smile. When Drew nudges him, he holds out a trembling hand.

"Hello, I'm Jesse, it's nice to meet you," he says and drops his eyes again.

"It's nice to meet you too Jesse," Brenda says, shakes his hand then lifts the bucket of grain she's holding. "Would you like to help finish feeding the ducks and chickens?"

Jesse hesitates, and Mr Johnston leans forward.

"Got plenty of time Jesse, you can go ahead if you want. Drew and I will wait here in the sun."

Drew watches as Jesse trails behind her, smiles when he hears him tell her he works in a pet store. The old man clears his throat.

"Don't take this the wrong way but he's not at all what I expected."

Drew chuckles.

"Yeah, he's kind of unique," he says.

"Certainly a good-looking kid, isn't he?"

"Yes, he is but I'd really appreciate it if you didn't call him kid when he's around. He's a bit sensitive about it."

"Drew, at my age, everyone's a kid," Johnston says, "but I'll take that on board."

"I understand but a lot of people think he's a child, or has the mind of a child, and it really upsets him," he rubs the back of his neck, watching Jesse in the distance scatter grain, surrounded by chickens and ducks.

"I understand. Do you mind if I ask how bad he is, well I know retarded isn't exactly politically correct but it's the word I know. You explained about his bein' autistic and we get a few kids like that through here and I can see how he's like some of them. The way he doesn't like to look people in the face – now don't go gettin' all protective, I've been doin' this job long enough to know when it's because someone is rude or when someone is not so sure of themselves – but there's somethin' a little different about him."

Drew nods to show he understands. He's spoken to Martin Sutton about this several times and the doctor is at as much of a loss as anybody else as to why Jesse's particular mélange of disorders has resulted in the sweet, even tempered man he is. Some of it is certainly nurture Sutton thinks, Jesse's parents love him unconditionally and have encouraged him to be independent without trying to fix him. He'd then gone on to suggest that Drew needs to accept that he's having a positive influence on Jesse too, for similar reasons, waving away his protest. Most of it, Sutton says, is just that Jesse has simply been lucky enough to have the right levels of everything – "so to speak" he'd snorted – for it all to work. Drew's explanation is much simpler: Jesse is just Jesse. Maybe if he'd been like everyone else he would have still been this way or maybe he would have let life knock the sweetness out of him, the way most people do. As far as Drew is concerned none of it matters anyway, all that matters is Jesse's smile.

"Well he's lucky he found you," Mr Johnston says when Drew finishes explaining. "Lot of creeps out there lookin' to make a meal of someone like Jesse. Here they come, now let's go introduce him to Hazel."

Jesse's eyes are shining and his smile wide when he and Mrs Johnston approach with the now empty bucket.

"There are ducklings, Drew," he says, "they're so cute and fluffy. I wish we could take one home, but Scamp would eat it."

Quietly thankful for the carnivorous habits of cats, Drew hugs Jesse to him and tells him Mr Johnston says they're going to meet the horses. Unless of course he'd rather stay here and play with ducklings.

"You go and meet Hazel, Jesse, and I'll see you at lunchtime," Mrs Johnston says, waving them away.

* * *

The barn is cool and airy and smells of straw and animals reminding Jesse of the store in the mornings when they first open the doors. Behind wooden doors, at the far end of the barn, comes a soft snicker of sound and the shuffling of hooves. Jesse steps closer to Drew and takes his hand; he's a little bit scared but doesn't want to say so. Drew looks down and gives it a squeeze which makes him feel better. Mr Johnston is ahead of them talking to the horses as they approach. A big marmalade colored cat glares at them from an overhead beam.

"That's Pumpkin," Mr Johnston says. "Best ratter in the county but never met a meaner creature in my life. He's in a permanently bad mood that cat."

"Well if you only ate rats and someone called you Pumpkin you'd be grumpy too," Jesse says, looking at the cat over his shoulder. When he turns back, Drew is giving him an odd look as though he's said something smart, but he doesn't know why. "What?"

Drew just shakes his head and Jesse is about to ask him to explain what he's done – he hates not understanding – when Mr Johnston stops walking. When they've caught up with him, he addresses Jesse.

"Jesse, can I take your hand?"

Jesse swallows and let's go of Drew's hand and offers it to Mr Johnston, forcing himself to stay calm. Drew rubs small circles over his back and he bites his lip as Mr Johnston places his hand on the soft muzzle of the glossy, brown horse in the stall next to them. Jesse stretches his fingers over the hair that is both sleek and coarse at the same time, smiles when Hazel presses back against the palm of his hand.

"Hazel, this is Jesse. Jesse, this is Hazel. She's a mare, do you know what a mare is?" Good. Now Hazel likes people and she'll take good care of you but only if you take good of her, okay?"

Jesse frowns, trying to decide what that means.

"If I'm nice to her, she'll be nice to me?" he asks.

"Yes, Jesse. But also, you need to be lookin' around once we get you up on her back. You need to pay attention for things that she might not see. You and Hazel need to be a team, okay? Can you do that?"

Jesse looks back at Hazel and rubs his hand down her nose to her soft velvety muzzle; she snickers against his hand and his eyes widen at the rush of hot breath and the feel of her mouth on his skin. He nods, smiling and turns to look at Drew.

"Isn't she beautiful?"

"Yeah, Jess, she is," Drew says and there's something strange about his voice that makes Jesse frown. Drew kisses his temple and nudges him to pay attention to Mr Johnston who is still talking.

"We're going to get her gear and I'm going to teach you how to saddle her up and then we'll go for a ride. How strong are you, Jesse?"

"I lift all the crates and pet food bags at the store," Jesse says. "And I can pick up the big dog kennel by myself if I have to."

"You'll be fine lifting a saddle then," Mr Johnston says. "What about our school teacher pal here – think he'll manage his saddle by himself?"

Jesse's face falls when Drew steps back, hands raised.

"No, I'm not riding. I'm just watching. Just here for the show."

"But you have to come too Drew," Jesse pleads, disappointed at the thought of riding without him.

"Jess, I can barely handle a nine-month-old kitten let al..."

"Please, Drew, please." Jesse turns to Mr Johnston who looks like he's trying not to laugh but Jesse doesn't see anything funny in the situation. Drew has to come with them. "He can have the granny horse can't he Mr Johnston? She'll be really nice to him, won't she? Drew, *please*."

"Oh, Dallas will take good care of him," Mr Johnston says and to Jesse's delight, Drew lowers his hands and rolls his eyes.

"Fine. But she better be nice," he points at Jesse, eyes narrowed, "or you are so going to owe me."

"Anything," Jesse says, throwing his arms around Drew's neck, then remembers Mr Johnston is with them and pulls away. "When we get back to the hotel, we can ..."

"*Jess! Filter!*" Drew interrupts and it's Jesse's turn to roll his eyes. He was just going to say they could stay in and watch movies in bed instead of going downstairs to dinner like Drew had suggested this morning but fine, if Drew wants to have a dirty mind, let him. They can do that too. When Jesse turns back to Hazel, Mr Johnston is mopping his eyes with a large blue handkerchief and he's grinning at Drew over Jesse's head. Honestly, sometimes he thinks it's Drew who needs a filter.

* * *

Mr Johnston shows Jesse where to leave his backpack, then opens the stall door and slips a bridle over Hazel's nose.

"Does that hurt her?" Jesse asks as he watches the farmer settle it in place.

"Not if we don't buckle it too tight," Mr Johnston says and steps aside, so Jesse can do just that, showing him which hole is the right one, before attaching a rope to a metal loop on the bridle. "Now, Jesse we're going to walk with Hazel down to find Dallas for Drew here, so if you take this rope and don't go too fast, Hazel will show you where to go. Think you can handle that?"

Jesse takes the rope, frowning in concentration, both scared and proud to be trusted with the horse and gives a gentle tug. Hazel begins walking forward and Jesse has to jump to catch up with her. When Mr Johnston tells them to stop, at Dallas' stall, Jesse turns and rests his head against her muscular neck and breathes in the strong, musky scent of her. He smooths a hand over her side and in a low murmur tells her how beautiful she is. Behind him Mr Johnston is putting a bridle on Dallas, an older white mare that stands patiently while he places the bridle on her and, still sniggering, hands the rope to Drew.

When they get outside a large grey horse is waiting already saddled up in the corner, nibbling at a bale of hay.

"This is Duke," Mr Johnston says. "We've already been out this morning, so he's ready to go. We just need to get his girls saddled up and we'll be sorted."

Jesse approaches when Mr Johnston nods and strokes Duke's nose, then follows him to the table where two saddles are ready. He runs his hand over the buttery leather then hefts the saddle up when Mr Johnston tells him to bring it to Hazel. It's not as heavy as he expected – lighter than the big dog house at the store, but heavier than a bag of dog food – but he still needs the old farmer to help him get it on the horse's back because he's afraid he'll hurt her. Mr Johnston passes the belt below her belly and Jesse attaches it, then turns to Drew with a smile.

"I did it," he says and Drew laughs.

"Yeah you did, Jess. Now you can help me with Dallas, since you got me in this."

Jesse doesn't need encouraging; he's already lifting the saddle and moving toward Dallas. When she's saddled, and waiting, Jesse turns an expectant face toward Mr Johnston.

"Ready to go, Jesse?" Mr Johnston asks.

"Ready to go," Jesse says, then looks at Drew. He doesn't look ready at all and Jesse slips his arms around his waist and hugs him tight. "We're going to ride horses, Drew."

"Mmmhmm, yes we are," Drew says and pushes his glasses up with a sigh.

* * *

Drew is relieved to be finally back on solid ground again and one of the farm employees is leading Dallas and Hazel away. If it hadn't been for the look on Jesse's face as they had started moving, he would have refused to leave the barn yard and gone to feed chickens. Feeding chickens, he thinks, is much more his style. Jesse on the other hand had been a natural; within seconds he had been confident enough to lean forward on Hazel's neck as she plodded along and whisper in her ear. He didn't appear uncomfortable or frightened and if Drew is certain he is going to have a reminder of every pebble and bump on the trail in the form of a very sore back - not to mention butt - he's equally certain that Jesse won't. Or if he does he won't notice it.

Tomorrow when they come to the farm when it's open to the public, they'll bring a picnic Drew has already ordered from the hotel but part of the private package he has bought for today includes a barbeque lunch with Mr and Mrs Johnson. They make their way to the picnic area where smoke is already rising from the grill and Brenda Johnson is bustling around one of the tables. Jesse has laced his fingers through Drew's, no longer concerned by being with relative strangers, and is asking Mr Johnston questions non-stop about the horses. How much do they eat? Do they have to be ridden every day? What kind of shoes do they have? Does Mr Johnston put their shoes on or does someone come and do that? Asks Drew what you call the person who does that.

"A farrier. Or a blacksmith," Drew says.

As they open the gate to the picnic area, what Drew took for a bundle of hay from a distance, stands, shakes and makes its way toward him. He freezes, fingers tightening over Jesse's who unfortunately has also seen the beast approaching them.

"Oh my God," Jesse breathes and turns excited eyes to Mr Johnston. "He's a Lion burger, isn't he? Can I pet him?"

A what? Did he say lion? Can he what? No, he most certainly cannot, Drew thinks in a panic. He doesn't know what that animal is, but a lion wouldn't surprise him. It's the right color. And size.

"You mean a Leonberger," Mr Johnston says not unkindly. "And yes of course you can."

Before Drew can react, Jesse lets go of his hand, approaches what Drew has now decided is a small bear and drops to his knees. The animal sits in front of Jesse and puts a paw up.

"You know," Mr Johnston says in his ear, "we can't have a dog here that might eat the kids. Be real bad for business."

"That's a dog? What the hell do you feed it?"

"School teachers," Johnston says with a smirk.

"Very funny. It's huge, how much does it weigh?"

"Right now, about a hundred and ten pounds but he's only a little over a year old so he's still got some growth left. Some of them make it all the way up to a hundred and seventy."

"Jesus, that's more than Jesse weighs. Hell, that's more than I weigh."

"They're from Germany, original lines were Newfoundlands crossed over Saint Bernards. They need a lot of attention and exercise, which they get here, and as guard dogs go, they're pretty impressive. All he has to do is stand up and the battle is over."

Drew doesn't doubt it. The dog and Jesse are currently eye to eye and if Jesse still has a few pounds on the animal, Drew isn't sure it would do him much good.

"What's his name?" Jesse asks over his shoulder. He's still kneeling, hands on his thighs; the massive dog is seated opposite, long ropes of drool falling from his lolling tongue.

"George," Mr Johnston says, and the dog thumps his tail.

"You're kidding right?" Drew can't help laughing. "His name is George?"

"Granddaughter named him, what can I say?"

Drew turns his attention back to Jesse who has stretched a loose, closed fist out toward George.

"Hi George," he's saying softly, "I'm Jesse. You're really big."

His hand disappears into the dense coat under George's chin and George inches forward.

"What a good dog, George. What a good dog. Yes, you're such a good dog."

Drew is mesmerized watching him. There's no fear, no hesitation, none of Jesse's usual reticence. His shoulders are relaxed, face open and calm. George inches closer still and slurps his long tongue up Jesse's face, making him laugh. Drew's stomach churns and he makes a mental note to make sure Jesse showers before he even thinks about kissing him later.

"Let's go over to the shed and wash up, then you boys can help me grill the meat. You a chicken or a steak man, Jesse?" He orders George to stay and the dog drops down, panting, in the grass. Mr Johnston leads them to the utility shed.

Jesse's smile disappears, and his eyes drop.

"It's okay," Mr Johnston directs them toward a sink where towels are waiting for them, "you didn't meet the chicken this morning, I promise."

"Oh okay," Jesse says reaching for the soap, "then I like chicken. Drew likes steak."

"Good thing we have both isn't it?"

Drew has to admit the idea of freshly grilled steak is appealing – who knew horse riding could make you so hungry? Jesse turns and leans against the sink while Drew washes his hands.

"George is like a real-life Wicket," Jesse says.

"Yeah?" Drew wipes his hands on the towel Jesse holds out.

"Yeah. This is the best day ever, Drew. Thank you."

"Jess, you are so welcome," Drew murmurs and leans down to brush his lips over Jesses, remembering too late that the bear masquerading as a dog has just licked them. Oh well...

"If you two are done romancin', I'm ready for my lunch," Mr Johnston says from the doorway. He steps aside, a large grin on his ruddy face, as they go in search of lunch.

* * *

"How do you know about Leonbergers, Jesse?" Mr Johnston asks as he drops the meat on the heated grill. He points with the grilling fork to a dish of corn cobs wrapped in tin foil and Drew passes them to him. "They're not very common. Most people are like Drew, convinced they're a bear or a lion."

"We had some puppies in the store once," Jesse says, "and I looked them up online."

He can feel Drew's eyes on him and for the first time in a long time feels self-conscious in front of him.

"I …I can't read very well," he explains to Mr Johnston, "because the words kind of get mixed up and the pages hurt my eyes, so I watch videos on YouTube and sometimes on the websites. And I have a screen that fits on my computer that is supposed to help. It sort of does but not really. I like videos best, they're easy."

Both Mr Johnston and Drew are nodding. Mr Johnston asks if he'd like to do some of the grilling, but Jesse shakes his head.

"Well in that case, you'd best get the beers out of the cooler," Mr Johnston says. "Think you can manage that?"

Jesse goes to the picnic table and fishes in the cooler; there's beer, lemonade, and to Jesse's delight, apple juice. He decides to have beer for now, since Drew and Mr Johnston are having one, but he doesn't think anyone will laugh at him if he has apple juice later. Twisting the cap off the first bottle, he sets it on the bench next to the barbecue for Mr Johnston, who thanks him and flips the chicken over. Jesse offers Drew his beer before opening his own and leaning against Drew's back, his chin resting on his shoulder.

"Will George get much bigger?" Jesse asks. "We have a client, Mrs Hughes, she has a Newfie and he's pretty big, but I think George is bigger."

"A Newfie?" Drew asks him.

"A Newfoundland. They look a bit like George but they're black. Only Mrs Hughes' isn't as big as George, I don't think. His name is Beorn," Jesse says. "You know, like in *The Hobbit*."

Jesse likes Beorn; Mrs Hughes brings him at least twice a month and he's like a big, black bear. He never barks or pees on the stock and Jesse has taught him to sit and wait and he'll give him a chew stick.

"The lady who had the Li …" he stops, catching himself before he repeats the error, "Leonbergers, she already had three and she couldn't keep the puppies. I really wanted to have one, but it wouldn't be fair in an apartment."

Drew rubs his cheek against Jesse's and Mr Johnston nods.

"No, it wouldn't Jesse, you made a wise decision," he says.

Jesse wishes he could have a dog like George. He loves Scamp, but he thinks people can love lots of things all at once, and that Scamp would understand. But, he says finally, he can't. It's not fair in an apartment because there's no room for them to move. And Jesse has to work too. Drew reaches up and strokes his cheek.

"You never know, Jesse, maybe one day we'll get a Lion Burger," he says.

"Leonberger," Jesse murmurs, dropping his eyes.

* * *

Over lunch Mr Johnston asks Jesse if he knows how Leonbergers got their names and Jesse's eyes light up as he tells them it is for the place they were first bred. Leonberg - he kicks Drew's ankle when he asks if Jesse isn't sure it's not Lion Burg – in Germany. When Brenda asks him if he would like to see the other farm animals after lunch, he bites his lip.

"Will I be able to ride Hazel again before we go?"

"You can ride her to see the other animals if you like." Brenda gathers up the plates.

"Yes please," he grins at Drew, "but I think Drew wants to walk."

"That's right, laugh at the city boy," Drew says, bumping their shoulders together.

"Well I'm a city boy too," Jesse points out.

"I'm not so sure about that, Jesse," Brenda says as she lifts an enormous pie out of the cooler. "I think you could just about come and work for us if you ever decided to leave the pet store."

Jesse's cheeks flame and he ducks his head. His hand creeps into his pocket and he runs a finger over mini-Wicket and inches closer to Drew. For a moment, he's confused; he doesn't like the idea of not being at the pet store or not being a city boy like Drew, of not being where Drew is.

"Jess? You okay?" Drew's asking and when Jesse looks up, Brenda is holding a plate of apple pie to him.

"Thank you," he says as he takes it and waits for Drew to get his before picking up his fork. Brenda offers him some cream, but he shakes his head, he's fine.

"Maybe you boys could give me a hand to milk Lizzie, after we've seen the other animals," Mr Johnston says.

"What exactly is a Lizzie?" Drew asks, and Jesse can't help it, he has to smile because Drew sounds worried, like maybe milking Lizzie would be worse than horse riding.

"Is Lizzie a cow?" he asks.

"Yes," Mr Johnston says digging into his pie.

"You could do that Drew," Jesse says, grin wide, confusion forgotten, "you're really good at pu..."

Drew's hand is over his mouth, silencing him before he can finish, and his face is bright red. From the corner of his eye, Jesse see's Brenda splutter bits of pie crust over the table cloth and the sound of Mr Johnston's laughter makes George sit up and bark.

"Filter, Jess," Drew says, narrowing his eyes, "filter."

* * *

Drew watches Jesse throw sticks for George while he helps Mr Johnston clean up the grill. What had that little blank out been about? That's the second or third time he's done that. He'd been relieved when Mr Johnston had mentioned Lizzie and Jesse's smile had broken through the zombie-like set to his face, but he's still bothered. Something's going on with Jesse and he wishes he understood.

"How long have you two boys been together?" Brenda asks behind him, breaking him out of his own reverie.

"Hmmm? Oh, almost six months," Drew says.

"Really? I would have put it at much longer," she says and flaps her hand at her husband's muttering. "I am not being nosey. You don't often see anybody as in love as these two are, and it's nice."

Drew blushes and smiles a little, remembering how worried Jesse had been. Thankfully that had been unfounded. Jesse drops the stick he's been throwing and asks Mr Johnston if he has time to take some photos of George and when the farmer nods, goes to get his backpack.

"What was it that you noticed about him first? Oh, hush yourself Frank."

"His eyes," Drew says, not as embarrassed as he thinks he normally would be. "And then he smiled and that was pretty much me, gone."

"I can understand that," Brenda says and pats his arm. "He's got a lovely smile."

"Yeah," Drew says watching as Jesse, in true Jesse fashion, lays on his back and takes a photo upside down of George. His photos are either so unusual nobody can tell what they are or so unusual they're beautiful. Something tells Drew there will be at least one or two of the latter variety in today's selection. He watches for a moment or two then wanders over to where Jesse is now sitting, taking photos of the oak tree in the corner, and drops down on to the grass next to him. When Jesse turns to smile at him, Drew kisses him; a small, chaste kiss on the lips, which is not what he wants to do but he's too conscious of their hosts still standing at the grill, watching them.

"I love you Jess," he says.

"I love you too," Jesse replies and snaps his photograph. "Is it time to milk the cow yet?"

"Yeah, you dork, it's time to milk the cow."

* * *

26

When it's time to go, Brenda Johnston hands Jesse a box with half a pie, some homemade jam, and a dozen fresh eggs in a brown paper bag. Drew raises an eyebrow and grins at her.

"You know we're coming back tomorrow, right?"

"I do and I'm looking forward to it," she says and holds her arms out to Jesse who steps into them with a grin. Drew accepts his hug and they shake hands with Mr Johnston.

"I can't wait for tomorrow," Jesse says as they turn on to the main road.

"You understand there will be other people there tomorrow too, don't you Jess?"

"Yeah I know. I can only ride Hazel tomorrow once because other people will want to ride her too. But I still can't wait, Mr Johnston said if we get there early I can help get the animals ready."

Jesse shifts in the seat next to him and pulls his keychain out of his pocket and runs his finger back and forth over Wicket's head.

"I had a really good day, Drew," he says in a soft voice.

"Good, I'm glad."

"I've always wanted to ride a horse because I always thought I would like them and now I know I really do," Jesse continues. "And George is really cool. And I liked the baby goats and the chickens and the ducklings. And the pigs. And Lizzie."

"What about the sheep and the alpacas?"

"Llamas."

"What?" Drew's confused.

"They were llamas not alpacas. Llamas have different ears. And they do different things. Llamas carry stuff and alpacas are for their wool."

Wow, Drew knew Jesse loved animals, but he hadn't realized just how much. He's about to say as much when Jesse clears his throat to speak.

"Drew, can I ask you something?"

"Yeah, of course, what's up?"

For a moment, Jesse doesn't answer him and Drew flicks his eyes right to see what's wrong. Jesse is biting his lip and clutching mini-Wicket.

"Jess?"

"At lunchtime when I said I wished I could have a dog like George, you said maybe one day we could have one," Jesse says, "what did you mean?"

"I don't understand Jess, what are you asking me?"

Jesse's looking straight ahead now, and Drew can see the color in his cheeks and the way his fingers are twisting the key chain.

"Well, I know you like me ..."

"I more than like you, Jess," Drew interrupts. Jesse nods.

"I know but like I said before people can love lots of people or things and in lots of different ways," Jesse says. Suddenly sure he knows where this is going, Drew glances in the rear vision mirror and when he sees it's clear, pulls over to the side of the road and turns toward Jesse.

"Jesse ..."

Jesse shakes his head.

"No, you have to let me finish. I'm not normal, Drew. I know I'm not. And it's not like having a cold, I'm not going to wake up tomorrow and be normal," he says. Then in a voice that breaks Drew's heart he continues, "I wish I was going to. I wish I could wake up in the morning and just be like everyone else. Like you. But I can't. Ever. And I know that. And even though I know that, I kind of don't mind so much anymore. Not like before. Because you make me feel happy."

Swallowing what feels like a boulder in his throat, Drew pushes a strand of hair off Jesse's forehead and waits for him to go on.

"I think we have lots of fun together," Jesse says.

"We do."

"And I think we have good sex together." Jesse peers up at Drew and smiles when he nods that yes, that's true too. "But I'm a bit scared."

"What are you scared of Jess?" Drew asks but he thinks he knows what Jesse is going to say.

"I don't think you're always going to want me. I get scared it will be too hard for you to be with me because I'm not normal." A tear slips down his cheek and Drew brushes it away. "But dogs are for a long time, so I want to know if that means you think you want to be with me for a long time too."

Not caring they're in the car on the side of the road, Drew leans over and pulls Jesse into his arms. Cards his fingers through the short hair that still has bits of grass in it from when Jesse wrestled with George. Kisses the side of Jesse's head and pulls back.

"Jesse, you're right. You're not like other people, you're not what other people call normal. But so what? The first time I met you, I liked you. That's why I asked you out. Even when you told me about being autistic and ..."

"And ID," Jesse says and Drew leans forward again until their foreheads touch.

"And ID. It didn't matter because I liked you. Then I got to know you and I fell in love with you. You're not like anyone I have ever met Jess but not because of those things. You're sweet and funny and kind and that's what makes you special, that's what I love," Drew says and kisses him, laying gentle pressure on his quivering mouth. "I'm not going to get tired of you, I don't want anyone else. We do have fun, we do have good sex and I do love you. You're right, dogs are for a long time but Jesse, you're forever. Okay?"

Jesse buries his face in Drew's shoulder, clinging to him as they sit, letting cars rush past.

* * *

Even though he knows Drew is hungry and tired, Jesse asks if they can stop at a mall before going back to the hotel. When pressed, he admits he wants a pair of overalls like the ones Mr Johnston was wearing and he wants to wear them tomorrow when they return to the farm.

"Jess, you sure it can't wait? I could really use a shower and a drink. Not all of us are natural horsemen, you know. My butt hurts."

Jesse sniggers and when Drew flicks his hand in his direction, catches it and holds it tight.

"You can wait in the car while I go in," he says, grinning, "I've been buying clothes without you for years. I might even bring you a present if you're really good."

"A present? Well in that case, I suppose we can, but only if I can stay in the car."

When they pull into the mall carpark, Jesse takes a deep breath, pulls his wallet and phone from his backpack, and checks his keychain is in his pocket. Satisfied he has everything, he kisses Drew and tells him he'll be right back. The truth is Jesse doesn't like going to unknown places by himself, but he really wants to get some overalls today and now that he's thought of it, wants to buy Drew a present. If something goes wrong, he can find somewhere to sit and call Drew; but he hopes he doesn't have to.

After what Drew said before, about forever, Jesse wants to do something, he's just not sure what yet. Surely, a mall in Alberton can't be too different from the mall at home, right?

Thankfully *Alberton Central Shopping Center* is only two floors and it doesn't take long for Jesse to find a store on the ground floor that carries jeans and, tucked away at the back, overalls. With the help of a girl whose long blonde hair reminds him of Mandy and whose disappointment when he says no he doesn't need to try them is evident to everyone but Jesse, he finds a pair that look like Mr Johnsons. On the way to the register he spots a tee-shirt with a galloping horse and adds that to his purchase. When she returns his debit card, Jesse gives her a brief smile, thanks her, and hurries out.

Checking his phone for messages from Drew, he takes the escalator up to the second floor. Halfway along he finds a store with what looks like a stone dragon in the window and the distinctive smell of incense wafting through the door. Inside, Jesse decides this must be what a Hobbit hole would look like – every surface is overflowing with treasure: books, jewelry, knick-knacks, and statues are everywhere. Dishes of small crystals surround a huge purple one; Jesse knows it's called an ammysomething but can't remember what exactly.

He's looking around with wide eyes when a girl with purple hair and a nose ring, dressed in khaki shorts and tee-shirt and combat boots grins at him.

"How you doing? Anything I can help you with?" she asks with a look that suggests she'd be happy to help with absolutely anything.

"I'm looking for something special," Jesse says. "But I'm not sure what."

"Special huh? For yourself or is it a gift?"

"A gift," Jesse says, looking everywhere but at the girl. "For my boyfriend."

If he sees her eyes widen just a little, Jesse doesn't register it as disappointment, but when he sees her smile, he relaxes a bit.

"Good deal, dude. So, what's your boyfriend into?"

"Huh?"

"You know, does he want to do tarot, does he like crystals, statues? What does he like?"

Jesse doesn't know what most of that is. He thinks for a moment then grins.

"We read *The Hobbit* and we're nearly finished reading the *Harry Potter* books. He doesn't really like *Doctor Who* or *Torchwood* but that's okay, that means I get Captain Jack to myself."

"I hear you, man," the girl leads him to a glass cabinet in the corner, "oh boy, do I hear you. Captain Jack rules."

"He's a teacher, he wrote a book about poems."

"Cool. I think I know exactly what you need."

The cabinet is full of jewelry, most of it has crystals and looks like something his mom or maybe Jody would wear. It doesn't really look like something Drew would wear.

"Silver or gold?"

"Well, his glasses are silver."

"Silver it is," she says and reaches into the back of the cabinet. When she withdraws her hand, she's holding a small box. In it is an odd shaped, silver key on the end of a silver chain. "The key to Erebor."

"Thorin's key?" Jesse asks, reaching out to run a finger over the pendant.

"Uh huh," the girl says and looks over her shoulder, then back to Jesse. "It's the last one we have in stock, so if you want it, I can give you a discount."

Jesse asks her what the cost is because he has to be sensible, but he already knows that if he needs to, he'll go to the internet café he saw on the ground floor, log into his bank account and transfer some money out of his savings account. He's very careful with his savings because Dad taught him to be prepared for things to go wrong, but he's sure this would be okay. And he wants to give Drew the necklace.

"It's normally eighty-five but I could do it for seventy. Boss will bitch regardless so may as well give him a reason."

Jesse hands over his debit card and asks her if she can wrap it for him. The girl nods and tells him not to worry, she'll take good care of him – and gives him another look that says she'd love to do just that – and his boyfriend will love him forever.

"I think he already does," Jesse says, shoving his hand in his pocket to touch Wicket. "I'm very lucky."

The girl hands him the small gift bag containing the necklace and grins.

"You're not the only one, trust me," she says.

Jesse gives her a shy smile, mumbles thanks, and picks his way through the clutter to the entrance.

He glances in the window as he passes and the girl waves to him; Jesse nods and hurries to the escalator hoping Drew will like the gift.

Back at the car, Drew has put his seat back and closed his eyes. His glasses are pushed up on his forehead, arms over his chest, and he doesn't stir when Jesse opens the door until he leans over and kisses him. Drew gives a start and his glasses fall back into place.

"Must have dozed off," he mumbles, adjusting his seat and starting the car.

"You were snoring," Jesse says.

"Was not."

"Were too." Jesse puts his shopping on the floor of the car and clicks his seatbelt in place. "I bet they could hear you in the next car."

If he keeps that up, Drew informs him, he'll be sleeping on the couch. Jesse shifts in his seat, so he can see Drew's face and grins.

"No, I won't," he says.

"Want to bet?"

"I bought you a present," Jesse says.

"And you think that will save you from the couch?"

"Well that and if I do that thing with my tongue that you like."

To Jesse's delight, Drew goes bright red and takes his eyes off the road to look at him. By accident one night, Jesse found that if he licks and nibbles at one spot, just behind Drew's knees, Drew becomes pretty much boneless. If he does it while he strokes Drew...things get explosive really fast. It amuses Jesse that the spot is behind

Drew's knees, although he supposes it is a bit like the curve where his shoulder meets his neck.

Jesse isn't sure, but he thinks Drew drives faster back to the hotel.

* * *

27

Drew leans back in his chair and sips his scotch. By the time they'd showered and changed, Jesse's stomach was growling loud enough to make them both do a double take and Drew had to admit he was feeling peckish himself. The lunchtime barbecue feels like it was a year ago.

The restaurant was already busy but there will be a table in about ten minutes the waitress assured them as she took them to the bar. Jesse is perched on a barstool, sipping a beer, his eyes on Drew's face and his feet resting between Drew's. He insisted on buying the drinks, managing to maintain eye contact with the bar man for most of the transaction; Drew smiles at the display of independence. Jesse is strict about paying his share of expenses and picks up tabs when he can. Drew's salary is hardly impressive, and book royalties are not about to push him into another tax bracket, but it's still better than a pet store assistant's; that said they're both careful enough with money and simple enough in tastes that the luxuries they permit themselves are hardly hardships. One of Drew's pleasures, he admits, is good scotch and it is made better by the look on Jesse's face whenever he pays for it.

"You've caught the sun," he says, smiling over the top of his glass. "We'd better pick up some sun block tomorrow."

"Is your butt still sore?" Jesse asks. He's grinning but Drew can see genuine worry beneath it; the bartender sniggers and Drew gives him the look he usually reserves for Cole Davis on slow Friday afternoons.

"Hey, not all of us can be natural horsemen like you Jess." Then seeing the concern in Jesse's eyes grow, adds, "it's fine."

He doesn't add that his back, in the other hand, hates him with a vengeance and if he never rides a horse again he won't be sorry.

* * *

The waitress eventually leads them to a table by the window, hands them menus and a wine list, and retreats.

"Want me to tell you what they have?" Drew asks, keeping his voice low. Normally Jesse would at least try with the menu, asking when he needs help but Drew suspects he's tired and close to overstimulation point; he's certainly tired himself. Jesse nods and Drew reads out the dishes he knows Jesse will like: chicken cutlets, lasagna, and glazed ribs. When Jesse asks for ribs, Drew signals the waitress, orders ribs for two and another round of drinks.

When she's gone, Jesse leans forward and smiles. Winces when the sunburn stings.

"Do you want your present?" he asks.

"You didn't have to get me a present, darlin'," Drew says. "This is meant to be your birthday treat."

Without answering, Jesse withdraws his hand from his pocket and puts a small gift bag on the table. Pushes it toward Drew with one finger. Drew quirks an eyebrow.

"Open it," Jesse says.

Drew opens the bag and takes out a small blue box. Sets it on the table between them and sips his scotch again. At Jesse's prodding, he lifts the lid off the box to reveal a small silver, key shaped pendant on the end of a silver chain. A scrap of paper covered in what looks like Tolkien's elvish flutters out of the lid and Drew guesses what the gift is.

"Is that the key to Erebor?" He looks back at Jesse. The younger man is biting his lip, rubbing the condensation off his beer bottle with one finger; he nods yes.

"It opens the secret door to Lonely Mountain," Jesse says. The shyness in his voice reminds Drew of the first time they met. He wonders if the metaphor Jesse has created is deliberate or unconscious; decides it doesn't matters. Lifts the chain from the box and lets it drape over his fingers so he can see the key glimmer in the overhead lights.

"Jesse, thank you, it's beautiful." He clasps it around his neck and the key settles at the base of his throat. Not caring if the bar-tender – or anyone else – sees them he reaches for Jesse's hand. "I love you, Jess."

"I love you too," Jesse replies.

* * *

Drew wraps his arm around Jesse's shoulders as they leave the restaurant, ignoring the disgruntled huff from a woman coming through the door. She can huff all she likes, nothing will spoil his mood this evening. He's had two glasses of scotch, a plate of the best ribs he's tasted in a long time, and he even let Jesse talk him into a slice of butterscotch pie. In between mouthfuls and licking glaze from his fingers in a way Drew had found very distracting, Jesse recapped the day, face lighting up each time he mentioned riding Hazel or playing with George. Finally, the chatter trailed off and he told Drew he looked tired.

"I am," Drew agreed. "I don't remember the last time I spent the entire day outside in the fresh air and sun. I teach literature remember? Come on, let's go upstairs and find a movie."

In the lift, Jesse leans against his chest, fingers playing over the pendant and Drew smothers a yawn against his hair. Smiles when Jesse calls him an old man. The doors open, and he fumbles in his pocket for the key card to their room. Inside, he tosses the card on the desk and heads for the bathroom. Jesse can find a movie, he tells him, while he takes a pee and cleans his teeth.

As he brushes his teeth, he fingers the key and thinks about how easy it is to love Jesse. How different this is to what he has had before. Thinks of David and how hard that had been, even before the drugs and the booze. How he had always felt as though he had to be switched on and performing for David, as though nothing he did or said would be enough. Jesse's occasional insecurities are minor in comparison to David's jealous rages or his sulks that sometimes lasted several days. He rinses his mouth out and wipes it on a towel, pulls the elastic out of his hair so it falls over his collar. By now, he would normally have had a trim, keeping it just on his shoulders, but Jesse seems to like it, so he hasn't bothered. They're planning on calling in to see his sister Glynnis on the way home on Sunday and he has no doubt she'll have a comment about the length. Tucking a strand behind his ear, he opens the door and stops in his tracks, mouth hanging open.

Jesse has decided to try on his overalls, the clothes he'd been wearing discarded in a pile on the floor by the bed. One strap of the overalls is attached over a bare shoulder and he's turning in circles trying to trap the one that is hanging behind him, but it keeps swinging out of reach. The tip of his tongue is caught between his teeth, high cheekbones glowing from sunburn, short spiky hair tousled from pulling his tee-shirt over his head. The unattached portion of the bib hangs down, revealing the light scattering of hair over the coffee-colored skin of his chest.

"Damn it, come here," he mutters as he twists again, giving Drew a view of the back of the overalls and more importantly a glimpse of the clear, smooth skin on his back. For a moment, Drew isn't sure he remembers how to breathe. Jesse looks like all of Drew's teenage fantasies come to life. His eyes drift, with some reluctance, from Jesse who is now turning in the other direction still trying to capture the errant buckle to the pile of clothes on the floor. Recognizes the navy blue of the boxers Jesse put on after his earlier shower. Swallows with difficulty as he realizes Jesse is naked beneath the denim.

"Drew, I can't do it up," Jesse grumbles and Drew returns his gaze to the vision that appears to have walked straight out of almost every wet dream he's ever had.

"Jesus, Jess," he breathes. No longer tired, he crosses to the bed in two long strides and lays his hands on Jesse's denim clad hips, slides them up the length of his torso, breath catching at the feel of bare skin beneath his fingers tips. Licks his lips. Finally, he raises his eyes to look into Jesse's and lets out a long, shuddering breath.

"Jesus," he repeats in a low voice.

"Do you like them?" Jesse asks. His face is still and serious and for a moment Drew sees how Jesse would be if the autism and the dyslexia and the ID didn't conspire to keep him from being what the world considers normal. Knows in that moment that the weird combination of synapses and chemicals that make Jesse the way he is are a gift, not a handicap, and that gift is his.

He dips his head and covers Jesse's mouth with his own; forces himself to keep his eyes open until he sees Jesse's close and feels his hands creep around his waist. The fog that had settled over him lifts and he just wants to touch, taste, feel every part of Jesse he possibly can. He flicks his tongue over Jesse's bottom lip and is rewarded by the younger man meeting it with his own.

Drew's hand slides up Jesse's side and he rubs his thumb over the exposed nipple until the younger man whimpers and presses against him, fingers tightening in the small of his back. Breaking the kiss to drag in a breath, Drew moves his hand to Jesse's back, slips it down the back of the overalls, and groans at the feel of warm skin beneath his palm. He sinks to the bed and Jesse places his knees either side of his hips, settling on his lap with a sigh and leaning down to press their mouths together again. Drew falls back against the mattress with a groan, pulling Jesse with him. Jesse grinds against him and for a brief, agonizing second Drew thinks he might come in his jeans, making his return to adolescence complete. Groaning he pushes Jesse back enough so he can fumble with the buttons on his shirt until it falls open at his side.

Golden eyes locked on his, Jesse tugs at Drew's belt buckle then slides back until he's kneeling between his thighs. Drew lifts his hips off the bed and helps Jesse ease his jeans and shorts down, hissing at the cool air on his aching erection. Jesse moves back, pulling the clothes with him, until he's standing. Drops Drew's pants to the ground and reaches to unbuckle the attached strap but instead of undressing, crawls back up Drew's body to kiss him again, pressing against him.

"Jess," Drew whines when he feels the drag of denim against his cock.

"What?" Jesse whispers and when he looks up, Drew knows Jesse understands, he simply wants Drew to tell him what he wants.

"Take them off, please, take them off."

Jesse wriggles out of the overalls, drops them over the side of the bed, and straddles Drew again. Drew let's his hands run over the expanse of skin on offer, up Jesse's belly, across his chest, brushes a nipple, then frames his face and pulls him back down so he can kiss him again. The first kiss on Jesse's mouth is hard and demanding, then he moves along his jaw line with soft, gentle kisses, until he reaches his ear. Moves his lips back to Jesse's throat with short, sharp nips, and kitten licks.

"God, you're so beautiful," he says against the pulse he can feel under the warm skin.

Jesse moans and lifts his head away from the teasing, rolls over and stands up.

"Jess," Drew complains reaching for him. Oh god, he's so hard it hurts, why the hell is Jesse moving away? "What are you doing?"

Jesse rummages in one of the bags until he finds what he's looking for and holds it up with a triumphant smile and Drew can't help laughing. A bottle of lube. The irony that it's Jesse who remembered it is not lost on him.

"Good idea, now get back here," he says.

Reaching for Jesse as he returns, Drew begins to roll to his side, to pull Jesse beneath him but finds himself pushed back. Eyes widening a little, he settles back against the pillow as Jesse flicks the lid off the bottle in his hand and squirts some of the thick liquid over Drew's cock. Wraps his fingers around him and with feather light strokes – enough to frustrate but not enough to push him over the edge – begins to slick his length. Drew closes his eyes, enjoying the feel of Jesse's hands on him, the warmth of his skin, the weight of him against his thighs and it occurs to him that this too feels different to before. There's no aggression, no display of domination; Jesse just wants to please and be pleased, and Drew feels a spark of pride that he's been able to give this to him. He reaches for the bottle and Jesse, instead of giving it to him, covers his fingers with lube and drops it to the pillow before moving his hips forward just enough so Drew can reach beneath him.

Drew circles the ring of muscle gently, waiting for the change in Jesse's breathing and tension that will tell him he's ready. When it comes, he presses one finger into him, taking his time and searching for the small bundle of nerves that will make Jesse spark with pleasure. After a moment, he eases in a second finger, stilling when Jesse moans until he's sure everything is okay; he scissors his fingers, stretching and easing the muscle and finally finding that spot again. Rubs his fingers over it until Jesse jerks his hips forward with a ragged moan.

"Drew, please," Jesse pleads. "I'm ready, please."

He moves back and Drew grips his hips, rolling his own up until he's pushing against him, gritting his teeth trying to take his time. Jesse, however, appears to have other ideas and steadies himself by placing his hands on Drew's chest and lowering on to him in one swift movement.

"Fuck, Jess," Drew gasps, struggling for control. He holds Jesse still while he tries to calm himself down.

"Yes, please," Jesse whispers and begins to move.

Drew rolls his hips up, trying to match the rhythm Jesse is setting; he digs his fingers into Jesse's hips, trying to give him some balance. Jesse leans forward to kiss him again and Drew's arms slide up around his back, desperate to pull him as close as possible. Skin slides against skin as they breath each other in through the heat of the kiss. Finally, Jesse sits back drawing a figure eight with his hips, moaning each time Drew's cock rubs against his prostate.

"Feels good," Jesse murmurs, drags his hands over Drew's chest, scraping his nails over the tender skin of his nipples until he hisses and bucks beneath him. Biting his lip, Jesse lets one hand continue down Drew's skin, over his belly, until he reaches the point where their bodies meet. Drew watches, breath held, as Jesse begins to stroke himself.

"Oh God, Jess," he moans, trying to lift his chest up, wanting to kiss anywhere he can capture – lips, skin, nipple, anything. He cups Jesse's ass, loving the way the firm muscle clenches beneath smooth skin; slides his fingers forward and up the rippling muscles of his thighs to quivering abdominals. "Won't last much longer, darlin'."

Everything feels as though it's too hot, too tight, too hard; as though his body will burst apart. Jesse tips his head back, eyes closed, throat exposed, and grinds down hard against Drew, lifting up into his hand, grinds back down again. Then he's looking into Drew's eyes and Drew moans as pressure begins to wind through his body.

"Drew," Jesse murmurs and Drew reaches up to stroke the pad of his thumb over Jesse's cheek. When Jesse turns his face and flicks the point of his tongue over Drew's palm it's too much.

"Jess ... coming ...Jess...Jesse."

Gripping Jesse's hips with both hands, he pulls him down hard as his shoulders curl up and his body pulses and thrums through his orgasm. When he opens his eyes, body still shuddering, Jesse's eyes are closed tight, teeth sunk into his swollen, lower lip; his face contorts with pleasure as he comes over Drew's belly, stroking until he's finished, hips jerking forward and eliciting a groan of pleasure-pain from Drew.

Panting, Drew pulls him down onto his chest, not caring about the stickiness between them, driven by the still overwhelming need to have as much of Jesse against his body as possible. He can feel Jesse's heart thundering in his chest and places his hand over it. Finds Jesse's mouth with his and kisses him, hands trying to cover every inch of skin he can reach before he has to let go.

Finally, he helps Jesse lift off him and lie down; goes to the bathroom, returns with a washcloth and cleans up the worst of the mess, then folds back the covers, nudging Jesse beneath them, and crawls in beside him. With a soft murmur, half asleep already, Jesse curls against his chest, arm over his waist. Smiling, Drew works his arm under him, so Jesse's head is on his shoulder.

"Does that mean you like my overalls?" Jesse asks, voice heavy with sleep.

"Yeah I like your overalls."

"Is it okay if I wear them tomorrow? Or will that ... you know ... bother you?"

"Well, I think if you make sure you're wearing boxers and a tee-shirt under them tomorrow, I should be able to control myself," Drew presses a kiss against Jesse's head.

"Okay," the words are swallowed by a loud yawn, "I'm sleepy now. I love you, Drew."

"Go to sleep. I love you too."

* * *

28

Jesse waves when he sees Mr Johnston at the barn, but Drew's back is sore from yesterday's riding and Jesse doesn't want to embarrass him by leaving him behind. He waits while Drew locks the car and joins him at the gate, taking his hand. Jesse squeezes it; he's pleased Mr and Mrs Johnston don't mind about them, but he knows that when other people arrive they might not be able to hold hands or kiss, so he wants to enjoy it while he can.

He dressed in the bathroom this morning, calling out his progress through the door, and finally asking if he could come out without Drew trying to undress him again. Peeking through the crack of the door he'd seen Drew rolling his eyes and laughing and had gone to join him; throughout the ride Drew kept reaching across to play with the buckles on the straps of the overalls. Jesse knows he's being silly, but it doesn't matter; it feels good to have something that unsettles Drew.

"I like your overalls Jesse," Mr Johnston says as they approach.

"So does Drew," Jesse says with a smirk as he dodges away from the cuff Drew aims at him. "I had a good day yesterday, thank you."

"I'm pleased to hear it. How about you come and help me get Hazel's stall cleaned out, then we can take her for a ride. Not too sore after yesterday?"

Jesse shoots a sidelong glance at Drew, grinning when Drew mutters 'behave' under his breath.

"No, I'm okay. I swim a lot so maybe that helps. Drew's back hurts though," he says, and rests his head on Drew's shoulder. "Maybe he could help Brenda feed the chickens."

On the way to the yard, Jesse lets go of Drew's hand to pull his camera out of his backpack. When he looks up Brenda is coming toward them, bucket of grain in one hand, the other stretched out to be hugged. Jesse wraps his arms around her with a grin, then asks if he can take her photograph. He takes two of her hugging Drew and one of her leading him to the flock of poultry waiting to be fed, then follows Mr Johnston to the barn.

When Mr Johnston offers him a shovel to clean out Hazel's stall, he doesn't hesitate. It's like cleaning the pet cages at the store, he explains, and he's been doing that almost every day for seven years.

"Only there's more poop here," Jesse says and for the next half hour works alongside Mr Johnston, cleaning stalls and preparing the animals for the gates to open. When they're done, they saddle the horses and do a round of the riding track to make sure it's clear for anyone riding today. Over by the outbuilding where they washed their hands yesterday, Drew and Brenda are washing out feed buckets, George at their feet. For a moment, Jesse wants to go over and see the huge dog, then remembers they'll be here for the day again. He waves to Drew and rubs Hazel's neck as they follow Mr Johnston through the gate.

"You're a good worker, Jesse, that's good to see. Rare these days too," Mr Johnston says as they cross the first paddock. "And you're very good with animals."

Jesse sits up straighter in Hazel's saddle, face glowing from the praise.

"I like animals, they're nicer than people," he says, then amends "they're nicer than most people."

"You got that right," Mr Johnston agrees. "You're a natural on Hazel and I can see from how you are with George and the small animals, like the rabbits, that you know what you're doing with them."

"Drew said I was a natural," Jesse says. "I don't really understand what that means but I like Hazel. She's the first horse I've ever met, and I like riding her."

"I think she likes you too," Mr Johnston says. "You'll have to come back and see here again some time."

Jesse ponders this as they go up a small hill. Maybe they could bring Jody or Mandy. Or Drew has some nephews who are younger than Mandy, they could bring them. He wonders if Drew would mind if they came back sometime, just the two of them; somehow, he thinks Drew would be okay with that if he didn't have to ride a horse. The thought makes Jesse smile and he shares it with Mr Johnston.

"Well, I'm sure we can arrange that," the farmer says. They've stopped moving and are looking out over the farm.

"This is the most beautiful place ever," Jesse whispers.

***

Drew watches Jesse stretch out on the ground next to George and smiles. The hotel picnic basket is open on the table, the remains of lunch scattered beside it. Around the picnic area are several families, eating lunch, stretching out in the sun and dozing, some simply sitting and looking around at the animals. Brenda had brought George over and asked Jesse would he mind making sure he behaved while she went to get something from the house. Drew is sure she would normally just take the oversized puppy with her, but he appreciates the gesture, especially seeing how happy Jesse is. The Johnstons have been wonderful and Jesse loves the place so much, Drew is beginning to worry about what will happen when they return home tomorrow. Deciding to deal with it when and if it happens, he's distracted by a small boy racing past him toward George and Jesse and straightens up in readiness. Watches as Jesse sits up in the grass, one hand on George's back.

"My name is Jesse," Drew hears him say, "and this is George. What's your name?"

The little boy stares at his feet without answering, then darts forward and Drew sees Jesse tense and lean to form a shield between the child and the dog, fingers tightening in the George's coat.

"Tommy, leave the dog alone," a young woman calls, running toward him. She's out of breath, red faced, and Drew can hear the worry in her voice. He stands and goes to her, still watching the scene unfolding before them. Jesse reaches his hand out to Tommy, who after a moment's hesitation, takes it, eyes fixed on the ground between them. In a quiet, calm voice Jesse explains how to form a loose fist and hold it out for George to sniff, doing the same thing with his own.

"If you're gentle, he'll be friends," Jesse says and places the boy's hand on George's chest. "See?"

Drew hears the young woman catch her breath and he can't blame her. He'd thought George was going to eat Jesse yesterday and her son – he assumes it's her son – is much, much smaller.

"Jesse will look after him, don't worry," he says, and she jumps, aware of him for the first time. "He works in a pet store and I'm starting to think he's part canine himself."

"Sometimes when Tommy gets a bee in his bonnet, he doesn't listen to other people."

"Why don't you come sit down?" Drew says, smiling. "I promise you, Jesse won't let anything happen to him. Besides, George looks impressive, but I think he's actually a marshmallow with a stomach."

"George?"

"The dog." Drew takes her elbow and leads her to the table. There's a container of brownie in the picnic basket and he offers it to her; after a moment's hesitation, she accepts and takes a piece.

"That's kind of a weird name for a dog like that. I was expecting something a little more dramatic like Hercules or something."

Drew laughs and agrees with her. Tommy is now kneeling beside Jesse, one arm slung around George's neck as he leans toward the drooling mouth with a grin. Without warning he swipes his tongue up the side of the dog's face and George returns the favor making the small boy squeal with delight.

"Oh my God," Tommy's mother groans and starts rummaging in her bag, no doubt for hand wipes or something. Drew puts his hand out to stop her.

"Don't worry about it. I'm pretty sure Jesse French kissed him yesterday and he's survived. Trust me, he's fine." He smiles and extends his hand. "I'm Drew."

"Laura," she replies shaking his hand. "I should probably ..."

"Sit. Have some more brownie. Honestly, he's at more risk from the chickens here than he is from George. And I can promise you Jesse is perfectly safe."

Laura runs her hand through her hair and accepts another piece of brownie, watching her son bury his face in George's neck. He hasn't made eye contact with Jesse yet, Drew has noticed and it's enough to make him wonder about the child, though he doesn't ask. It would be awful if he was wrong and her kid was a just a little shy.

"It's hard to find places to take him where he can cope. Where we can both cope," Laura says, as if she's read Drew's mind. "Tommy's autistic."

"So is Jesse, among other things."

Laura's eyes drift over to Jesse and Drew's mouth twitches up in a smile. She's trying to marry his appearance with what she knows of autism, Drew knows; he's been there, and he's used to seeing other people there now.

"Are you his care-giver?" she asks and Drew watches Jesse and Tommy a second before answering.

"Actually no," he says. His hand wanders to the key at the base of his throat. "Jesse's my boyfriend."

Laura's mouth drops open and she mouths 'boyfriend' a couple of times as she looks from Drew to Jesse and back again. Defenses triggered, Drew holds her eye and prepares for her to snatch Tommy up and stalk away.

"Wow," she says eventually. "Really?"

"Really," he says in an even tone.

"So he must be really mild then?" Laura asks, eyes back on Jesse and Tommy, who is trying to clamber over George.

"Not especially," Drew says. "He's also dyslexic and has a very minor intellectual disability. He struggles with social cues and his reading isn't great, but he has a full-time job and an apartment."

"And you," she says softly, and Drew can feel the heat rush to his cheeks.

"Well yes and me," he says.

"And you have a normal relationship?"

Drew resists the urge to roll his eyes.

"Yes," he says, the words sharper than he intended, "quite normal in every possible way."

"Wow," she says again. "It never occurred to me that he might ..."

Annoyed, Drew reaches up and pulls his pony tail loose then reforms it while he speaks.

"I wouldn't worry, I'm pretty sure being autistic does not automatically guarantee being gay."

Laura turns back to face him, eyes clouded in confusion.

"I didn't mean that," she says frowning. "It's just I'd never considered that Tommy might be able to have a regular relationship. I wouldn't care who he was with if it meant he got to do that. You know meet someone, go out, fall in love, have se ..."

Her voice trails off and Drew feels a little ashamed of himself.

"Well I think you have some time ahead of you before you have to worry," he says. "But yes, it's possible. I don't know if what Jesse and I have is ordinary but for most things it's pretty regular. We go out, we argue, we annoy each other, and yeah everything else as well, including sex."

Drew supposes he understands why most people's thought's turn to sex when they find out he and Jesse are a couple, is even amused by the fact that for most people once they know, it's not about them both being men. Everyone assumes either that Jesse won't understand or want sex, or that Drew doesn't want sex. Jody pointed out once that a few people probably suspected him of a wide variety of deviances, but he'd dismissed that, refusing to entertain the thought that anyone he knew would be so ridiculous. So yes, he supposes he understands it, but that doesn't make it any easier. He's neither shy nor especially introverted by nature, but he does get tired of their sex life being under constant scrutiny. He realizes Laura is still speaking.

"Are you sure the dog, George, is safe?" she asks, and Drew looks over to see Tommy all but has his head in George's mouth. He goes over and crouches down by Jesse, sliding his arm around his shoulders.

"Hey Tommy, my name is Drew," he says, taking care to keep his voice low and his eyes on George rather than Tommy. "Do you want to come and have some brownie with your mom and me? George can come too."

"He can't have brownie though," Jesse says, "chocolate is bad for dogs."

Drew chuckles and pulls him against his chest.

"Okay, no brownie for George," he says and turns his head so he's speaking only to Jesse. "Tommy's mom is a little worried, so how about we go over by the table, so she can see everything's okay?"

Jesse frowns.

"Why is she worried?"

"Because Tommy is autistic and he's little and George is the size of a Wookie," Drew says, rubbing Jesse's shoulder to reassure him he's done nothing wrong. He stands up, pulling Jesse with him. Jesse loops his fingers in George's collar, nudging him toward the table and after a brief moment of hesitation Tommy follows. George's tail sweeps across his face and Drew has a moment of sympathy for Laura, no wonder she was nervous.

"Jesse, this is Tommy's mom, Laura," Drew says as he takes his place at the table. Jesse sits on the end of the seat and George rests his chin on his thigh.

"Hi Jesse, it's nice to meet you," Laura says with a smile.

"Hello. This is George. He's a Leonberger but you don't have to worry about him, he's really safe. He won't hurt Tommy." Jesse presses himself against Drew's side but holds her eye. "He's not even full grown yet but he likes people."

Tommy sits next to his mother, one finger in his mouth, body swaying back and forth. His eyes dart from George to Jesse but Drew notices he doesn't touch his mother or look at her.

"Would you like some brownie, Tommy?" he asks but the only reaction is an increase in Tommy's swaying.

"Tommy, Drew is offering you some brownie," Laura says, trying without success to get him to look at her. She sighs. "Sorry. He was totally non-verbal until he was four and even now at six he doesn't speak a lot."

"Maybe he just doesn't have anything to say," Jesse says.

"Jess."

"Well when you don't talk, it's just because you have nothing to say. It's the same for us. Just because we're autistic and not talking, it doesn't mean we're stupid, sometimes we just don't have anything to say."

Drew glances at Laura to see how she's coping with Jesse's candor, but she's too busy with her son to seem bothered. Head still on Drew's shoulder, Jesse reaches out and takes a piece of brownie.

"It's really good brownie," he says to Tommy as he takes a bite. "It's got chocolate chunks in it. Not those little pieces, big pieces."

To Drew's surprise, Tommy stops sucking his finger and takes a piece of brownie. Judging by the look on Laura's face, Drew isn't the only one surprised.

"Big pieces," Tommy says through a mouthful of chocolate, showering the table cloth with crumbs.

"Told you," Jesse says. He turns to face Drew. "Mr Johnston said I can take Hazel for one more ride since nobody has booked her. Do we have enough time?'

"I don't have to come do I?" Drew asks, and Jesse shakes his head. Drew kisses his cheek. "Then yeah, we have plenty of time."

"Not a horse rider?" Laura asks.

"Drew's got a sore butt and back from yesterday," Jesse says with a snigger. Drew shoulder bumps him and shakes his head.

"Alright you, settle down," Drew says, blushing. He starts gathering up the left overs.

"Why are all the decent guys taken or gay? Or in your case, both." Laura says, wiping Tommy's mouth with a napkin. Drew laughs and she looks embarrassed, as if she's just realized what she said. "God, I'm sorry I shouldn't have said that."

"It's all good," Drew says, taking the brownie container from Jesse. "It can't be easy on your own. Do you have anyone to help?"

Even he can see Tommy is an entirely different case to Jesse and reminds himself he is in no position to judge anybody. Jesse is showing a little girl and her father how to approach George; he has one hand on George's back and the other stretched out, showing them how to do it. The little girl smiles, and Jesse smiles back before turning his face up to Drew; Drew catches his breath at the rush of emotion that rushes through him and resists the urge to lean down and kiss him. A disgruntled father is not going to improve anyone's day. A scuffling sound distracts him and when he turns back, Laura is trying to stop Tommy climbing over the table.

"I think I'm going to keep him moving, see if I can't tire him out a little," she says, clutching the back of the boy's hoodie. "It was nice to meet you and Jesse."

"It was nice to meet you too, Laura," he says. Tommy wriggles loose from his mother's grasp and is off running. "Good luck."

"Thanks for the brownie," she calls over her shoulder, racing to catch her son. "Tommy, come back here."

* * *

Jesse tugs his shoes off and sits on the bed, back up against the padded headboard. After a moment he reaches for Wicket and wraps his arms around him, stroking back and forth over the soft fur with the fingers of his left hand. He wonders what Scamp is doing and if Jody played with her.

There's a sound from the other side of the room and he looks up. Drew is leaning against the wall, arms folded, watching him with a small smile. Jesse rests his cheek on Wicket's head and smiles at him. After two days of horse riding and romping with George and the animals, Jesse's tired and when he's tired it gets harder to understand what's happening around him and even harder to explain how he's feeling. He doesn't know why but he thinks Drew's smile means he knows that. Drew pushes off from the wall and crosses to the bed, grabbing the room service menu as he comes.

Settling next to Jesse, he puts his arm around him. "How about we order room service and watch a movie tonight?"

"Have they got pizza?" Jesse feels like something familiar tonight, maybe that will help his fuzzy feeling.

"If they haven't we'll get one delivered," Drew says. "In fact, why don't we just do that. We'll get one delivered. Give me a second."

Jesse leans against him, still stroking Wicket, as Drew orders the pizza then tosses his phone on the night table. Tomorrow they have to go home. He'll be pleased to see Scamp and have their things around him, but he feels sad about not seeing Hazel or George again. Mr Johnston and Brenda too, but mostly Hazel and George.

"Hey," Drew tips his face up, "you sad to be going home?"

Jesse shrugs. He doesn't want Drew to feel bad, but he is sad.

"You know, we can come back any time you like. It's only a couple of hours' drive, we can come after work on a Friday."

Jesse grins and presses in a little closer. He would like that, a lot.

Drew strokes his hair and Jesse, who is still stroking Wicket, can't help pointing out that Drew is sort of stimming. With a laugh, Drew agrees.

* * *

29

Jesse's mom greets them at the door with a wide smile, flings her arms around her son and then turns to embrace Drew. He kisses her cheek and they follow her into the living room where Ray waits.

"Did you have a good time Jesse?" Ray asks when he's shook hands with Drew.

"It was awesome," Jesse says, eyes sparkling with excitement. Drew accepts a beer from Ray and settles back against the couch cushions while Jesse recounts the weekend.

"Mom, Hazel was so beautiful, she really was," Jesse tells Erin as she serves a plate of grilled cheese sandwiches. "I got to ride her lots and she smelled really good. Drew had to ride the grandma's horse."

"Yeah well, I'm still feeling it," Drew adds, rolling his eyes. Ray chuckles and tells him he's glad it was Drew riding the horse and not him.

"I'm so glad you had a good time, boys," Erin says. She reaches over and squeezes Jesse's hands. "And I'm glad you liked the horses. You must be tired though."

Jesse nods and Drew rubs his shoulder; Jesse slept most of the way home and there are high spots of red beneath his eyes. He's exhausted.

"I'm not even going to watch Guardians tonight," Jesse says. Viewing Guardians while Drew marks essays or plans the week has become a regular habit and Drew now makes him wear head phones. Not that it stops the regular calls of "I am Groot" from the couch.

"So, you're going straight back to your place, Drew? I've made you some soup and sandwiches to take home. You can just heat them up tonight or tomorrow as you like."

Jesse hugs her with a yawn and excuses himself to use the bathroom. When he's left the room, Drew leans forward and leans his elbows on his knees.

"Actually, there was something I wanted to talk to you about," he says clearing his throat, "I've been thinking about this for a while and this weekend really sort of made me consider it seriously and I just wanted to have a chat with you before I do anything more. You know, Jesse and I spend pretty much every night together ..." his voice trails off and he can feel the blush creeping up his cheeks. "I was thinking maybe instead of us keeping two apartments, maybe he should just move in permanently with me."

"Oh," Erin says, raising her hand to rest at the base of her throat. "Oh, you mean live together? Officially?"

"Yes," Drew says. "I love him Erin and it makes no sense to have two sets of utilities and tenants' association payments."

"Oh," she says again. Drew follows her gaze to Ray.

"Look, I know this is an unusual situation, but I want you to know I would take good care of him," Drew says. "I ..."

"I want to go home," Jesse says from the doorway. Drew spins around, startled.

"Jess?" he starts to say but Jesse crosses the room to the front door.

"I want to go home," he repeats.

"Jess," Drew is behind him in two long strides, reaching for his elbow, but Jesse jerks it away, "what's wrong?"

"Nothing, I'm just tired. Can we go home now?" He turns his back on Drew.

"Jesse, you're being very rude," Erin says, moving in front of him to see his face better. "Drew just took you away for a lovely weekend."

"I know," Jesse says, "and I'm tired. I want to go home."

Erin looks to Drew and he shrugs; he has no idea what is going on. They both look at Ray who remains seated, impassive.

"I'll get the soup and sandwiches," Erin says with a sigh. She hurries to the kitchen and returns soon after with a box containing a thermos of soup and a Tupperware container of sandwiches. When she holds them out to Jesse, he ignores her and finally she gives them to Drew, who shrugs again.

"I guess we're going home," he says, opening the door. Erin holds a hand to her head, miming holding a telephone and Drew nods. Yes, he'll call her when he's figured out what the hell is going on.

* * *

The trip home is quiet. Drew tries several times to get Jesse to speak but he's sitting as close to the door as he can get and refuses to answer his questions. As they approach the end of town Jesse's apartment is in, he clears his throat.

"I want to go to my home," he says.

"What?"

"I want to go to my apartment."

"Jess, Jody is expecting us ..."

"You can go to your apartment. Just drop me at mine."

Drew's mouth drops open. What the hell? How has this gone so wrong? He understands the saying 'hit by a truck' with sudden clarity. Two days ago, they were talking about getting a dog. Talking about forever.

"Jesse, please tell me what's wrong?"

"Nothing, I'm just tired. I just want to be by myself tonight."

A lump forms in Drew's throat. He doesn't want to take Jesse home and leave him. Not like this. Not knowing what's wrong. He tries again to coax a response from Jesse and again is refused. Finally, he admits defeat and turns toward Jesse's apartment.

When they pull up in front of the building he turns the key off and turns toward the younger man.

"Jess? Please darlin', what's wrong? We had a good weekend, why are you upset?"

"I'm just tired." Jesse opens the door and gets out. Drew scrambles to undo his seat belt and open the car door. Runs to catch up with Jesse. At the building door, when he's keyed in the security code and holding the door open, Jesse turns to face him.

"You don't need to come up, I can take care of myself."

"Jess ..."

"Goodnight."

Jesse pushes the door open and enters; before Drew can react, the door has swung shut in his face and clicked. Desperate he pounds on the thick glass, calling Jesse's name, watching, helpless, as he gets in the lift and disappears.

* * *

30

At six thirty, Drew is dressed and drinking coffee. Not one of the text messages he has sent Jess has been answered. Jody had stayed for a while the night before and had tried calling him too to no avail. When he'd gone to bed Ray and Erin still hadn't heard from him either. He sends another text and tries to call. No reply. Head in his hands, he fights tears, wishes he knew what to do. He has to be at school in an hour and a half and hasn't had more than two hours' sleep, if that. Jesse starts work around eight thirty; Drew considers going back to his apartment and letting himself in but can't bring himself to intrude that way. Not when he has no idea what has triggered this whole mess.

Scamp winds through his ankles, meowing and he bends to pick her up.

"What did I do wrong, little one? I wish I knew, I really do."

She nuzzles against him before meowing again; he knows he's not who she wants. From the moment Jesse and Scamp met, they bonded – he was just the conduit.

"I'll get him back, I promise."

* * *

Drew decides against going to Jesse's building or the pet store and making a scene, though Jody disagrees with him.

"Go fight for your man, dammit," she says, punching him hard enough to make him spill his coffee down his shirt.

"No, I don't want to make things worse."

"How do you know not going won't make them worse?" she asks. Great. Now he can worry about that as well. This isn't about pride, Drew groveled for David often enough. It's that he doesn't know what happened and until he does, he has a feeling he isn't going to be able to fix it.

"And are you going to find out what it is, moping around here?"

"I don't fucking know," he snaps. He takes his glasses off to polish them. "I'm sorry. I don't know what to do, Jody. I love him and … I don't know."

Jody puts an arm around his shoulder and pulls him to her. Kisses his head.

"I know kiddo."

Drew is walking to the staff room at lunchtime when his phone rings. He fumbles it out of his pocket praying it's Jesse. His heart sinks when he sees Ray's name on the screen and thumbs it open.

"Ray?"

"Hi Drew." Ray's voice sounds tired and broken. "How are you?"

"Crap," Drew says and leans against the wall. "Have you heard from Jesse? He won't answer my calls."

There's silence from the other end.

"He's here Drew," Ray says finally. "He asked me to pick him up last night around eleven thirty."

"What? Why? Is he okay? Ray? Why didn't you tell me?"

"Calm down. He's fine. Physically."

Drew closes his eyes and breathes a long slow sigh of relief.

"Drew, um he says he doesn't want to see you."

"W – what?"

"He says he doesn't want to see you."

All the air rushes from his lungs, his knees give way, and he slides down the wall.

"I don't understand."

"I don't imagine you do. After your last text message, he asked me to call you, and tell you he *says* he doesn't want to see you." Ray emphasizes the word says. Repeats the phrase. The second time, his voice is lowered as if someone has come into the room with him and something in Drew's brain finally clicks.

"I'll be right there."

Ray hangs up.

Drew hauls himself up the wall and runs to the carpark, thumbing through his phone for Jody's number as he goes. Breathless he explains and asks her to tell the admin staff and the principal he's had to go home with vomiting. Hopefully it will be a twenty-four-hour bug and he'll be back tomorrow or the next day. Everyone who has seen him today has remarked on how pale and unwell he looks so he doesn't think there'll be any trouble with them accepting it. It's not a complete lie, he's fairly sure if he tries to eat anything he'll throw it up.

"Go," Jody yells into the phone. "Just go."

* * *

31

Erin answers the door again. Her eyes are red and swollen; she looks surprised to see him.

"Drew, what are you doing here? I'm sorry honey, he doesn't want to see you."

"Let him in," Ray says from behind her.

"But ..."

"Let him in." Ray drags the words out and Drew steps inside. "Sit down, Drew. I'll get him."

Still protesting, Erin trails behind him toward the kitchen and Drew thinks Jesse must be in the back yard, surely not the kitchen if this is as cloak and dagger as Ray is making it out to be. When they return, Ray has his arm around Jesse's shoulder and is all but forcing him into the room. Drew's chest tightens; Jesse looks worse than he, Drew, feels. His eyes are red and swollen, lashes wet and spiky – he's been crying. Blotches of scarlet have spread from his cheeks down to his throat and Drew can see his hand in his pocket, the compulsive movement of a finger over the Wicket key chain.

"Hey Jess," he says softly. "I missed you last night."

Jesse looks at his feet.

"Can you tell me what I did wrong, darlin'?"

The shake of Jesse's head is so slight, Drew almost misses it.

"Jesse, he deserves to know," Ray says.

"Jesse, please? Whatever I did, I'm so sorry, please just tell me so I can fix it."

Jesse jerks his head up and glares at Drew, tears in his eyes.

"Why didn't you ask *me*?" he demands.

Confused, Drew doesn't know how to answer.

"I thought you loved me," Jesse yells.

"Jesse, shhh, calm down," Erin says but Ray pulls her back.

"Jess, I do love you. I love you more than I've ever loved anyone or anything, you must know th ..."

"Then why didn't you ask *me*?"

"Ask you what, Jesse?"

Jesse looks at his feet again, body swaying just enough for Drew to think of Tommy on Saturday. His breath is coming in short pants and Drew can smell the sharp tang of sweat.

"I thought you were different but you're like everyone else," Jesse says still not looking up and it's that more than anything that pierces Drew's heart. "You don't think I can make my own decisions. You didn't even *ask* me if I wanted to come and live with you."

"Jess ..."

"*No!* If you thought I was a man you would have asked me, not my parents. But you only think I'm a man when you're fucking me." A broken sob bursts from him and he runs from the room.

"*Jesse!*" Erin yells, horror shining in her eyes. She moves to follow him, and Ray holds her back, lips pursed.

Drew is frozen in place. Despite his lack of filter, Jesse never curses, ever. It doesn't seem to bother him when Drew does, not even in bed, but he's never heard him say anything stronger than damn. Astounded and struggling to get his thoughts under control, Drew listens to the sound of Jesse's feet pounding up the stairs. He looks at Ray.

"I think you better sit," Ray says. He waits while Drew sinks onto the couch.

"Does he hate me?" Drew asks eventually, and Ray huffs out a laugh.

"He's hurt Drew, and he's disappointed, but he doesn't hate you. He loves you, he just doesn't know what to do with this. If you want to save this, it's going to be up to you."

"Ray ..." Erin begins but Ray holds his hand up and shakes his head.

"No Erin, you need to hear me out too," he settles back in his arm chair and folds his arms. "Drew, we knew very early that something wasn't quite right with Jesse. We just didn't know just how not right it was. As it turned out, it was bad enough, but it wasn't so bad that he couldn't turn into who he is. Does that make sense?"

Drew tells him it does; he understands that. Jesse has problems, sure, but they don't stop him from being everything Drew loves about him.

"When we figured out he liked boys and not girls," Ray continues, "and yes, we figured it out before he really did, God help me, my heart broke. And not for all the reasons you think. But because God damn, doesn't my boy have enough to deal with? His eyes and brain don't work the way they should and that's more than enough for one person to handle. And now, he's going to have to face the ignorance and stupidity of a world that can't see further than its own fucking navel because he doesn't fit the mold? That's a lot to ask of one person, and like I say, God help me I wished he could have just one thing easy."

"I think I can understand that," Drew says softly.

"Thank you, I appreciate that. You came along, and it was easy to see from the get go that you didn't discount his challenges, but they didn't stop you either. I don't think you understand how unusual that is. Or how hard it is to accept. When you are the parent of a child like Jesse, you get used to trying to make sure they don't get hurt."

Drew nods and murmurs something that Ray asks him to repeat.

"I said he's not a child anymore."

"No, you're right, he's not a child," Ray says. "But you treated him like one last night. For six months, you've treated him like any other man, any other lover, but when it came to something this important, you asked us if you could take care of him, instead of asking him."

Drew closes his eyes and tries to swallow the tears that threaten to swamp him.

"That wasn't what I meant at all," he says. "I wanted to make sure you were both okay with it, that you understood that I wouldn't take advantage of him."

"That may be the case, Drew, but that isn't what Jesse heard."

Drew runs his hands through his hair, tugs the hair elastic free from his hair and shoves it in his pocket. Looks from Erin to Ray.

"Have..." he stumbles, "have I ruined it? Will he let me try again?"

"One thing you should know about Jesse is that he doesn't suffer fools easily," Ray says, then stands up. "However, he's not easily put off. The problem here is he's hurt, and he doesn't know what to do. He's misunderstood something yes, but you need to decide if you want to try and make him understand. Because if you don't, if this is too hard, now is the time to go Drew. He's already hurting but it's on his terms. If you try again and this keeps happening, it will be so much worse for him."

Emotion clogs Drew's nose and eyes and throat. He knows how that feels, has been there in the past and he would rather take his own life than inflict that on Jesse. But the thought of a life without Jesse, he realizes, is not something he wants to consider anymore.

"Please, Ray, I want to make it work. Tell me what to do."

"Well," Ray says and pushes the door open. "First of all, we're going upstairs, and I am going in and you are going to stand outside and wait. Oh, and Drew," he waits for Drew to show he's listening, "if he says no, can you accept that?"

Drew wants to scream no, he can never accept it, but instead bows his head and agrees as he follows Ray up the stairs.

* * *

Jesse is curled on his bed, arms wrapped around Wicket. This was his room growing up and it's still his room now whenever he comes home. Star Wars posters decorate the walls and the bedspread is faded green and white, the one he's had since he was twelve. When he phoned Dad last night he just wanted to be surrounded by things that were comforting because more than anything he wanted to phone

Drew and couldn't. He was so angry with Drew it hurt – deep down in his stomach and his chest. After Drew said they were going to have a dog and that Jesse was forever, Jesse thought he really loved him. Then he'd acted like Jesse was stupid, like he was a little kid. Like he wasn't a man who could make his own choices. Drew didn't love him like a normal person after all. A tear drops from the end of his nose to Wicket's fur and he buries his face in the back of the toy.

There's a tap on the door and he stiffens.

"Jesse?" Dad comes in. "Are you awake?"

"Uh huh," Jesse says and draws his knees up to his chest, trying to make himself small and invisible, hoping it will stop everything hurting.

"Jesse, I want to talk to you," Dad says and sits on the edge of the bed. "Can you turn over please."

After a moment and with great reluctance, Jesse, still gripping Wicket tight in his arms, turns over.

"Jesse, do I treat you like a child?" Dad asks.

"What?" Jesse's eyes widen in surprise – this is not what he was expecting.

"Do I treat you like a child?"

Jesse shakes his head. Mom still does, quite a lot. It's because she's a mom, according to Dre...not he doesn't want to think about Drew. That hurts the most. No, Dad doesn't treat him like a child; sometimes he gets cross with him and scolds him but it's usually for things that Jesse thinks he might get scolded for anyway, even if he wasn't ... the way he is. Like when he left the lawnmower out in the rain once.

"Okay, so I want you to listen to me. I understand you're hurt and you're angry with Drew at the moment. And to some extent you have a right to be ..."

"*He* treated me like a child," Jesse says, petulant and cold.

"He didn't mean to; he thought he was doing things the right way."

"Well he wasn't. He's supposed to be smart."

"He made a mistake Jesse."

Jesse glares at his father.

"We all make mistakes. That's part of being an adult."

"But ..."

"No, Jesse, there's no but. People make mistakes, even people we love, people who love us. And when you're an adult and you love someone who made a mistake, you give them a second chance."

Jesse sits up, swinging his feet around so they're on the floor. His father is speaking in slow, easy words so he can understand but he's still not sure what he's trying to tell him.

"Do you remember when you really wanted to learn to drive? And I didn't think it was a good idea?"

"Uh huh." Jesse nods. Jesse had had a meltdown during the first lesson trying to cope with all the controls in the car. He'd backed the car into the garage door, denting both door and car.

"That was a mistake. And what did we do the next day?"

"We had another lesson."

"That's right. I gave you a second chance."

"We didn't have any more lessons after that though, because it didn't work."

"No Jesse, it didn't, but we had to try and see. And it might have."

A sound across the room makes Jesse look up, Drew is in the doorway. Jesse can't help it, he begins to cry when he sees him. Biting his lip, he turns his face away. Drew crosses the room and sinks to his knees in front of them but doesn't try to touch him, his hands rest on the top of his thighs.

"I'm so sorry, Jess," he says. "Truly I am, I didn't mean to hurt you. I just wanted to make sure your folks didn't worry, that they understood how much I love you, before I asked you."

"You should have asked me first," Jesse sobs.

"Yes, you're right I should have and I'm so sorry," Drew says. There are tears on his cheeks.

"You said I was forever and that we would get a Leonberger one day."

"Yes, and I meant it."

"But that means you love me like I'm a normal man. Not ..."

Dad's hand is rubbing his back and he tries to catch his breath and calm his thoughts down.

"Jess, I know I screwed up and I'm *really* sorry. I don't just think you're a man when we're... making love. I think of you as a man all the time. I've never, ever thought of you as a child. I promise."

Jesse lifts a tear streaked face to look at Drew. Searches the chocolate brown eyes and recognizes the truth in them. Reaches out a trembling hand to wipe the tears away from Drew's face. He doesn't want him to cry.

"I don't want us to break up," he whispers.

"I don't either," Drew says. "Jesse, I want you to come and live with me more than anything but if you don't want to, if you still want to carry on the way we are that's fine too. We'll do what you want to do. If you want, we can live in your apartment. It's up to you."

"My apartment is too little, your books won't fit," Jesse says, and Dad makes an odd strangled sound. Jesse ignores it. "If...if I come and live in your apartment what will we do with mine?"

"We can figure that out Jesse," Dad says. "There's no rush."

"I want to help pay the bills and rent and things. It has to be real, not .... Not you taking care of the retarded boy you fuck."

He feels his father's body jerk and Drew's face pales.

"Okay, darlin', I promise we can sort that out," Drew leans his head on Jesse lap. Jesse can feel the heat from his face through the denim of his jeans.

"If we do that, will it be my apartment too?"

To Jesse's horror Drew sobs against his thigh but when he lifts his face up he's smiling, and he thinks maybe the sob was about Drew feeling better. Maybe.

"Of course it will be, it will be ours."

* * *

32

Drew pours himself a glass of scotch, piles the cushions in the right order, and sinks to the couch. Erin had insisted on not just making them dinner but in giving them a large Tupperware container of leftovers to bring home. Her farewell kiss was brief and cool however, and Ray had clapped him on the shoulder, assuring him she would be fine, it had been a rough day for everyone.

Jesse is in the shower, Scamp is asleep in her cave, and Drew has just hung up from his own mother. He sips his drink and replays the conversation in his mind.

"Mom, we're just making it official, and tidying up loose ends, you must know that."

"Drew, I know you care about Jesse, but have you thought this through?"

"Not at all. Decided it on a whim. No clue what's involved here."

He leaned against the bathroom door, listening to Jesse list off the things he needed to do as he prepared for his shower and smiled.

"Drew, there's no need to be like that."

He sighed.

"I know, I'm sorry, but you're acting as though we're horny teenagers with no idea what we're doing."

"Well perhaps not teenagers," his mother said, and he could hear the smile in her voice, knew she was trying to placate him, "but Drew, whether you like this or not, Jesse is the way he is. And that will have repercussions. Is it fair to him? Or you?"

"Mom he's autistic and mildly retarded," Drew said, hating himself for using the word, "so let's not tiptoe around it. And I get it - you're worried. Erin and Ray are worried. It's not a normal situation, but I can't help that. I can't help how I feel about him, how I believe he feels about me. Oh, and I'm thirty-four not seventeen."

"How do you know he does feel that about you? How do you know he's able to actually feel that?"

Drew pushed his glasses up and pinched the bridge of his nose.

"You know what's interesting, mom? What's interesting is that when David, stoned and drunk, not only cheated on me but took a swing at me when I found out, you believed he still loved me."

"Drew that's not fair ..."

"Neither is everybody discounting us before we even have a chance to try, Mom. I hear your concern, I do. I even understand where it's coming from, but Jesse loves me, he doesn't need rehab to show it, and I love him. So, please can we just move on?"

He closes his eyes and listens to Jesse singing off key in the shower and fights another wave of emotion. The day has been hard enough without having to yet again explain their relationship. Especially to someone he was sure understood. Constantly having to defend his feelings, defend Jesse's ability to feel, is exhausting. If only he could convince them all that it's not loving Jesse that's difficult – it's explaining how and why. Everyone, except possibly Martin Sutton and Ray, thinks he ignores Jesse's differences. As if that were possible, as if it were possible to not see how open and blunt he is, how transparent he is with his feelings, how every little flicker of emotion from joy to anger to confusion is broadcast loud and clear. These are the differences that Drew loves. The other things, no longer bother Drew. So what if Jesse searches the images on packaging for the right brand of cereal or pasta at the supermarket instead of reading the names? Or if he frowns and bites his tongue when someone asks him a question he can't quite decipher, taking his time, determined to get it right? Or if he just hands restaurant menus to Drew for translation? As far as Drew is concerned, it's no different to his own need for glasses or his inability to make head or tail of his tax return without his accountant sister's help. So what? Who cares? Loving Jesse is the easiest thing he's ever done. The thought he had come close to destroying it makes him feel sick to his stomach.

The bathroom door opens, and Drew drops his head back on the couch and opens his eyes. Smiles at Jesse who is standing in the doorway in his pajama pants and scrubbing at his hair with a towel.

"Was your mom mad?" Jesse asks. "I think my mom is a little bit."

Drew sighs, he'd hoped Jesse hadn't heard any of the conversation, should have known better. Jesse might not always know how to respond but he rarely misses much. He sits up, turning to nestle into the corner of the couch and pats the seat in front of him.

"Come here," he says. Jesse hangs the towel up, then comes to sit between Drew's legs, his bare back against his chest. "They're not mad, not really, darlin', they're just being moms."

"You always say that," Jesse nudges the hand holding the scotch up toward his mouth. Takes a sip and shudders. "Is it because I'm a guy?"

Drew laughs against Jesse's hair.

"Dork. Of course not. My parents gave up on me bringing a girl home years ago and I don't think it would matter if you were a girl, your mom would still be worried."

"So, it's because I'm not ..." his voice trails off and Drew squeezes his eyes shut against a rush of emotion.

"Jess, I lo ..." he starts to say.

"I know, and I love you too. And they'll just have to get used to it." Jesse turns his face up, resting his head against Drew's shoulder, and smiles. Drew wishes everyone could see that smile the way he does and just ... understand. "I don't want to talk about our moms."

"Good, neither do I," Drew says and finishes his drink. He nuzzles Jesse's neck. "Jess, I'm so sorry."

Jesse's body stiffens in his arms. Drew waits.

"It's okay." His voice is small and quiet, fingers rubbing strands of Drew's hair together between his fingers.

"No, it's not," Drew says. "Not really."

* * *

Jesse wants Wicket, but he doesn't want to move away from Drew; he senses that this is important, that they need to talk. So, he uses Drew's hair and runs his finger along the soft linen of Drew's slacks. Scamp is asleep in her cave, but he hopes she'll wake and come over.

He's feeling better than he has since he walked through the door to hear Drew telling his parents that he would take care of him. Tired but not so fuzzy, not so much like something large was sitting on his chest. Something like a hippo or an elephant.

Jesse had been feeling good as he returned to his parents' living room; he was going to tell them what Drew had said about getting a Leonberger. When he'd heard Drew talking to his parents, he'd stopped to hear what he was saying. Mom always says that's rude, but he thought Drew might be talking about their weekend. When he'd said he would take good care of Jesse, Jesse had a laser sharp moment of understanding. When you love someone, you ask them not their parents. At least when you're thirty-four and your boyfriend is twenty-seven. Drew wasn't doing that; Drew was asking Jesse's parents. Which meant, he didn't think of Jesse as a man. The pain, pressing in from all sides, had been suffocating, and he hadn't known what to do to stop it.

When he finishes speaking, he turns his head to look at Drew. He's crying again.

"I'm really sorry. That wasn't what I meant Jess, I promise."

Jesse shrugs. He understands – now – that it wasn't what Drew meant but that doesn't change how it had felt hearing it.

"Jess, listen to me," Drew says, tipping Jesse's head back with one a finger. "You were right the other day in the car. You're not like other people. You're not ordinary and you're not what everyone else calls normal. But I don't care. I love you anyway. Those things – your autism, your ID, your dyslexia and every other fucking little thing you have going on, are a part of what makes you who you are. And I love who you are. You're right I should have asked you, so I'm asking you now. Jesse would you like to move in here permanently?"

Jesse hesitates. More than anything he wants to say yes, but he's still not sure if Drew really understands how hard it had been hearing that. Drew rubs his back.

"Jesse, I swear to you I just wanted your folks to be okay about it before I asked you and I know I screwed up. I am really sorry."

Jesse makes a decision. He settles his head back against Drew's shoulder.

"Everyone makes mistakes."

* * *

Drew lets out a shaky sigh.

"Thank you, darlin'. I didn't like not having you here last night. I didn't like not talking to you. It made me really sad."

"It made me sad too," Jesse breath hitches and Drew hugs him tighter to his chest.

"I might make more mistakes though Jess," Drew says against his head, swallowing tears, "so can you make me a promise?" When he gets no answer, he continues. "Can you promise to talk to me?"

There's a long silence before Jesse whispers his promise.

Relief surges through Drew and he rests his face on Jesse's head. Jesse reaches up and takes his glasses off, places them on his own nose and crosses his eyes.

"Your eyes are really bad," he says. "I like your glasses though, they're cute."

Drew smiles despite himself, a little disconcerted by the change of subject, and takes them back.

"Not as cute as you are," he says.

Jesse seems to consider this, then shrugs and turns around to face him. Drew dips his head and brushes their lips together, sweeps his tongue over the seam of Jesse's mouth until his lips part to let him in. Tightens his arms around him again, pulling him closer to him until they're both fighting for breath.

"Your scotch burns when it's in a glass but not when it's on your tongue," Jesse whispers against Drew's cheek. "On your tongue it's just sort of warm and spicy. Why?"

Oh god, when he says things like that he has no idea of the effect he's having. Drew shakes his head.

"I don't know, Jess."

"I like it," Jesse says and leans forward for another kiss.

"Good," Drew says into the kiss, unsure if he's responding to the declaration or the kiss itself. He doesn't really care.

* * *

33

Drew balances the tests he's marking on his lap while he sips his coffee, feet resting on Jody's desk. The librarian, wearing Jesse's favorite rainbow suspenders is loading new titles in the computer data base, holding a cookie between her teeth as she types.

"So, then what happened?" she says around the cookie, showering the keyboard with crumbs.

"Well Jesse is letting me try to not fuck up, his mom is currently sulking, and mine is probably enlisting my siblings to help show me the error of my ways," Drew says with a sigh. "For all the good it will do them." He stretches, laying the pile of tests to one side. "You would think they'd be pleased I'm happy after that mess with David."

Jody stops typing but doesn't answer.

"What?" Drew asks.

"Nothing."

"Bullshit, nothing. I know you. What?"

"Look it's none of my business."

Drew scrubs his hand down the side of his face and leans forward.

"Just say it, okay?"

Jody spins her chair around to face him, looking apologetic.

"Okay, you have to see why this bothers everyone, right?"

"Oh Christ, not you too?" Drew glares at her.

"Hey, you know I love Jesse. I see the attraction – he's hot, he's got that whole mostly innocent but not really thing going on, and he adores you. And he has great taste in men," she says, knocking his foot with her own. "You, Captain Jack, Lord Elrod, Chris Pratt – some of my favorites right there. But you can't blame them – Jesse's parents are probably worried you're going to get bored and then they'll have to put the pieces of their son back together and yours are worried you're avoiding reality by picking someone as removed from David as you find. Especially after what just happened."

White hot fury threatens to bubble over and Drew fights the urge to slam his fist on to the desk in front of him. Trembling and gritting his teeth against the things he wants to say, he begins packing up the papers. Jody puts her hand on his shoulder.

"Drew, come on, you know I don't think that. I've seen you two together, I've seen how happy you are since you met him. But I also understand where they're coming from."

"Where they're coming from, Jody? They're coming from the conviction that neither of us know what we're doing. Jess because they're convinced he's a child in an adult's body and me because well we all know I'm emotionally incompetent, right? Jesus, I am so fucking sick of this."

Jody pulls herself up to her full height – a full five foot four in heels – and pokes him in the chest with her index finger, forcing him to sit back down.

"Listen up, this is exactly what I'm talking about. If you are as serious about Jesse as I think you are, you need to get over yourself – this is going to be your life if you stay with him. His parents, your parents, friends – they're nothing. They'll all get used to it when they see how serious you are, just like I did, but the rest of the world is never going to be okay with this. There is always going to be someone who won't understand. And they won't always be assholes either – some of them will just be people who see two men with a canyon of intellectual difference between them. No, don't even say it. I know, okay? But the world doesn't and if you want to make this work, you need to accept that and find a way to deal with it because if you flip the fuck out all the time when you're faced with those reactions, what are you going to do with real assholes?"

She's panting when she sits back down and reaches for her bottle of water. Drew swallows and shrugs.

"I don't know. I ... it just doesn't seem fair. All they seem to see is what Jess isn't and ..."

"And you see everything he is. I get it, I've seen you look at him. It's nauseating."

A grin surfaces and Drew feels the anger recede a little.

"Yeah I've noticed how nauseated you get whenever you catch us kissing."

"I'm conflicted – it's equal parts sweet and vomit inducing watching you, you're so in love, what can I say? The point remains, most of the world is always going to have a problem with this so you need to not have a problem with that or you guys aren't going to survive it."

Drew sighs; he knows she's right. It might not be fair but then what is, right? If it wasn't him in the relationship, would he be any different?

"Speaking of assholes," Jody continues, "did you hear David is coming on Friday night?"

Paling, Drew jerks to his feet. There's an end of year faculty barbeque on Friday night and it's the first time he's bringing Jesse to a school event. David is coming?

"You're fucking kidding?"

"Nope, evidently Chisolm invited him, God knows why. Something about wanting to show a sign of good faith. Typical Chisolm happy crappy."

Nigel Chisolm is the school's deputy principal and is as known for his new age ideals as he is for his lack of taste in clothes. He believes everyone on faculty and in the student body loves him, a fact that Drew has on good authority – and now experience – is far from true.

"Jesse knows about David, right Drew?"

Drew pulls at his ponytail and shrugs.

"Well he knows I have an ex named David and that it didn't end so well, yeah."

"Didn't end so well? Drew, the man put you in hospital. What are you going to do? You can't bring Jesse in blind, dude. Maybe you should just give it a mi ..."

"No. I'm not going to be pushed around by him anymore, I'll just have to prepare Jesse and try and keep us out of his way."

* * *

34

Drew drapes his arm over Jesse's shoulder and rests his cheek on his head while they wait to order their burgers. He knows he's avoiding going home so he doesn't have to talk to Jesse about Friday night, but he just needs some breathing space. Some time just to relax before tackling what lays ahead.

"Mr Oliver?" a girl's voice says beside him, and Jesse digs his fingers into his side. He glances over to the next queue of people and sees Katie from his Friday Senior Lit class.

"Hey Katie, how are you?" he says, tightening his grip on Jesse's shoulder. Watches the girl's eyes flit from him to Jesse and back again and smiles. Katie's had a crush on him all year but she's a good kid. "You like *JJ's Burgers* too?"

"I'm good, thanks." She bites her lip, obviously unsure of herself. "Yeah, they're good."

Before either of them can say anything further, Jesse speaks.

"I'm Jesse," he says, holding his free hand out. Katie shakes it and lets go.

"Hi," she says, "I'm Katie."

Jesse pulls his arm free from Drew and turns to him.

"I have to use the bathroom. Juice, not soda."

"Yeah, yeah, I know."

As Jesse disappears toward the bathrooms, Drew turns back toward Katie who is now second in line in front of her register.

"Nearly finished your final project, Katie?"

"Yes. I really liked Wordsworth. I think I'm going to major in English at college."

"Great, you'll be really good at it, you do good work."

He's genuinely pleased with the news and a little flattered because he knows she's probably looking at English in part because of him. Katie flushes a deep red and turns to the counter to give her order. When she turns back with her tray, Drew is only one person from the counter himself.

"Your uh boyfriend is really cute," Katie says in a rush, "you guys look really good together."

After the previous evening and hearing about David, Drew is grateful to the teenager for her timid compliment.

"Thanks Katie. Enjoy your dinner, I'll see you in class."

Tucking a long ringlet behind her ear, she nods and scuttles into the main dining room just as Jesse returns.

"Was she one of your students?" he asks.

"Yes. Katie, and she thinks you're cute." Drew smiles. "Ready to order?"

"I am cute," Jesse says without any embarrassment. "Yes, chicken burger, no pickle. Apple juice."

* * *

Jesse rubs his face over Scamp's head and puts her in the cat cave, before glancing over at Drew who is working at his desk. For the past hour, he's been marking school work while Jesse tidied the bedroom and played with Scamp, but the pile is nearly finished and now Jesse can find out why he's been acting so weird all evening. There's only one paper left on the desk and Drew is already dotting it with red marks. Biting his lip, Jesse goes into the kitchen, gets a tumbler, and pours some scotch in it. It doesn't look as much as Drew usually puts in the glass, but Jesse thinks that will be okay. When he looks back, Drew is shuffling the papers into his bag for tomorrow, red pen capped and discarded next to his laptop.

Jesse crosses the room, grips the back of Drew's chair, and swivels it around to face him, then drops onto his lap, glass of whiskey between their chests. Drew smiles and runs his hands up Jesse's back.

"Did you want something, Jess?" he asks.

"Uh huh," Jesse says holding up the glass for him to take. "You."

"Good deal," Drew replies and moves forward to kiss him. Jesse leans back, avoiding the kiss even though he really wants it. "What's wrong?"

"That's *my* question," Jesse says. "You're weird."

"Uh, thanks?"

Jesse wriggles, trying to find a comfortable position.

"You didn't want to bring the burgers home, you kept hugging me at JJ's, and you didn't even tell me off for dipping my fries."

"I was hungry, I like hugging you, and I'm used to you doing that now, you know."

"You hate eating at JJ's because you say it's cold, you don't usually hug me that much except when you want to have sex, and it was your sundae."

Drew chokes on his mouthful of whiskey and Jesse grins; he likes it when he can make that happen.

"Well, I was too hungry to wait, I always want sex with you, and uh that's gross darlin'," Drew says finally, wiping his mouth with the back of his hand.

"I want to know what's wrong. Tell me."

"Nothing's wrong, Jess."

"Yes, there is," he insists. "I can tell, and you're supposed to tell me, that's what people do when they love someone, remember? You made me promise to tell you, so you should tell me."

Drew sighs and leans his head on Jesse's shoulder. Jesse pulls the elastic from Drew's ponytail and untangles the hair with his fingers.

"Tell me," he says.

Drew pushes him off and stands up, leads him to the couch and pulls him back down on his lap. Jesse slides an arm around Drew's neck and rests the other hand on Drew's chest, focusing on his face as he starts to speak.

"You remember I told you about David?" Drew asks.

"Your boyfriend before me?"

"Yeah, him," Drew says with a nod. "So, do you remember what I told you about him?"

Jesse scrunches his face up as he concentrates; searching for the memory.

"Um, you said he was your boyfriend, that you broke up because he drank too much whiskey and took drugs, and that you thought you loved him," Jesse says. He frowns at the end because he doesn't like that bit, it makes him feel fuzzy. He knows it's silly because even though he didn't really have a boyfriend before Drew, he had been with other men, and his dad told him that it doesn't matter if Drew had other boyfriends. What matters is now. Jesse still doesn't like it. He realizes Drew is speaking again.

"Yeah, I thought I did, but that was before. Now I know that I didn't really, I was just too scared to let go. It wasn't like it is with you, Jess."

Jesse doesn't really know what that means so waits for him to continue.

"I kind of didn't tell you the whole story though," Drew says. "At the end when David was getting drunk and stoned all the time, he uh cheated on me. Do you understand what that means?"

Jesse rolls his eyes and nods; sometimes even Drew forgets he's not stupid.

"He had sex with someone else." He's starting to feel sleepy and closes his eyes while he listens.

"Yeah. Well with a lot of someone elses actually and one day I got home and found him with one of them."

Jesse's eyelids snap open and he looks around the room, heart pounding.

"Not here," Drew adds hastily, rubbing his back. "I moved here after we broke up. Remember? I told you that."

"Okay, yeah" Jesse says, relief that David hasn't been in his new home rushing through him. He nestles his head back into the crook of Drew's neck.

"I was pretty pissed off when I found them and there was a big argument," Drew's hand tightens on Jesse's side. "David was really stoned and got mad and he hit me."

"What?" Jesse draws back to look in Drew's face, eyes wide and shocked. He can't imagine anyone hitting Drew, he's tall and strong and he's kind to everyone. "He hit you? What about your glasses?"

Drew makes a funny sound that Jesse thinks was supposed to be a laugh but can't think what he said that was funny. You can't hit someone with glasses.

"He broke my glasses, Jess. And my cheekbone. And one of my ribs."

Jesse covers his mouth with his hand, eyes filling with tears.

"He beat you up?"

"Well he tried, bu ..."

"But he was the one who was wrong," Jesse protests. He brushes his fingertips over Drew's cheekbone, trying not to cry at the thought of Drew being hurt. "He was wrong."

"Shhhh, it's okay. Yeah, he was wrong, and he hurt me, but it could have been worse and I'm alright now. I have you now and I know I love you."

"I would never do that to you," Jesse says, framing Drew's face with his hands. "Never."

"I know that Jesse, it's okay. That's how I know what we have is real and what I had with David wasn't. That's why it was so scary when ... when you wouldn't answer my calls and you went to your mom and dads. I thought I'd lost you."

Jesse nods and wraps both arms around Drew's neck wanting to take the sad look away from Drew's eyes. Drew's hands settle on his hips and he licks his lips.

"Jesse, David worked at the high school with me. He was a history teacher and when that all happened I pressed charges. You know what that means?"

"Yeah, it means you went to the police and they put him in jail."

Drew purses his lips and explains that it doesn't always mean that.

"He didn't go to jail?"

"No, he went to rehab, a hospital where they help people stop drinking and taking drugs."

"Okay," Jesse says and sets his mouth, unaware how much he resembles his mother in that moment, "but I think he should have gone to jail. He hurt you."

Drew kisses his cheek and smiles.

"Yeah, well it didn't quite work that way darlin' but that's not important. The thing is David has been invited to the barbeque on Friday night and he's said yes, so he's going to be there."

A line forms between Jesse's eyes and his tongue appears between his teeth as he tries to understand what Drew is saying.

"He's coming on Friday?"

"Yeah."

"What if he tries to hurt you again?"

"That won't happen, but he might not be very polite," Drew leans his forehead against Jesse's. "Especially to you."

Jesse considers this a moment.

"Because we're together?"

Drew nods, eyes closed.

"And because I'm ..." Jesse swallows and takes a breath, "because of the ID? Because I'm retarded?"

"Oh Jess," Drew pulls him in, "don't say that."

"It's okay. Just because it's an ugly word doesn't mean it's not true."

"Jess," Drew breathes against his neck.

"What do you want to do?" Jesse asks. Drew raises his head and quirks an eyebrow. "On Friday night? What do you want to do?"

"I don't want him to be able to say anything to you or to be able to touch you. Fuck I don't even want him near you Jess," Drew says, "but I don't want to be afraid of him either."

Jesse thinks about this for a moment.

"It's your high school, Drew. Even if he used to be a teacher there, he isn't now. It's your school so if you want to go, we should go. And you won't have to worry about him hurting me."

"Why is that?"

"Because I know you and Jody won't let anything happen to me."

"That's true, darlin'," Drew says with a smile.

"But what if he tries to hurt you?"

Drew shakes his head.

"He won't."

"If he does, I'm going to do the pressing charges thing and I'm going to make sure he goes to jail," Jesse says and lifts his chin in defiance. He leans forward and kisses Drew on the mouth. "I love you."

"I love you too Jesse," Drew says.

"Okay then," Jesse says, stroking Drew's hair and resting his head on his shoulder.

* * *

35

Jesse steps out of the bedroom, still rolling back the sleeves on his shirt, and glances toward the bathroom. Scamp is perched on top of her cat tree, tail flicking in annoyance at the sound of the hairdryer coming from behind the closed door. He goes to her, lifts her down and lets her snuggle in under his chin; her tail sweeps back and forth across his chest.

"Scamp doesn't like your hairdryer," he calls to Drew.

"Scamp will have to get over it." Despite the reply, the noise of the dryer stops, and the bathroom door opens. "Oh Jesus, Jess. Are you trying to kill me?"

"What?" Jesse asks looking around, eyes wide in false innocence.

"You know what," Drew says, stepping closer and running a finger over the metal fastener on the strap over Jesse's left shoulder. Jesse bites his lip and smiles, looking up through his lashes. Drew's not wrong, he does know. He knows Drew likes his overalls as much as he does – and that is exactly what Jesse wants tonight. If Drew's ex-boyfriend is going to be at the barbeque and if there are going to be lots of other people wanting Drew's attention, he wants to be sure Drew isn't sorry he's taking Jesse with him. He also wants Drew to know he has forgiven him for what happened. In one of his flashes of clarity he thinks of his overalls as insurance.

"We don't have to go you know," Drew says and runs his hands down Jesse's back. When they come to rest on the curve of Jesse's butt, he presses in against Drew and smiles. "No seriously, we could order in and watch Guardians and I could ...uh... find out what you have on under those things."

Jesse's giggles, tipping his head back, eyes dancing with pleasure.

"I want to see Jody and meet the other teachers."

"Jody's coming to help us pack up your apartment, you'll see her tomorrow."

Drew strokes his thumb over Jesse's bottom lip. Jesse shivers a little at the sensation then breaks away to return Scamp to the cat cave.

"I want barbeque chicken."

"I want to take your overalls off," Drew says.

"We have to go, we said we'd go."

"You really know how to stop a guy having fun, you know that?" Drew grumbles, hunting for his keys. Jesse smiles as he watches him; Drew's hair is loose, the way Jesse likes it, covering the collar of his grey Henley. On impulse Jesse leans over and steals a kiss.

"You can take my overalls off when we get home and then you can find out what's underneath."

Drew catches his breath.

"W... what's underneath?"

"I don't know," Jesse says with a shrug, "I think I forgot something when I was dressing, maybe it was my shorts."

Drew lunges for him but Jesse steps out of reach with ease and holds his hand out. Sometimes even Drew forgets he's not stupid.

* * *

The barbeque is being held at Joe Adams', the head coach, house and when Drew pulls up in the street, the sound of music and laughter already fills the evening air. He scans the cars for David's old Toyota but sees no sign of it. Not that that means anything, he could well be driving something else by now. Or, more likely, he came with one of the other teachers. Not all of them had taken Drew's side after the split; something Drew has long since made peace with.

Taking Jesse's hand, cooler containing a six pack and some marinated chicken in the other, he leads the way. Jesse is carrying a cake box with chocolate cake for the dessert table and it's taken all of Drew's ingenuity to keep him from tasting the frosting on the way over. Jesse's sweet tooth, he's decided, is going to be the death of him. Well, that and trying to figure out if Jesse is commando or not. Surely not. This is Jesse and they're going somewhere with people he doesn't know. No. Of course he's not. Right?

With a shake of his head, Drew forces his thoughts away from Jesse's underwear, or lack thereof, and smiles as he knocks on the front door. Joe's wife, Penny, opens it mid knock and welcomes them in.

"Thank you," she says, taking the cake as Drew introduces Jesse. "Nice to meet you Jesse. Go on through, everyone's out the back."

They go through a large set of French doors to the back garden. Fairy lights are strung everywhere, casting a glittery glow over the crowd and Jesse's eyes light up and dart from tree to tree, strand to strand, as they cross the lawn. Jody calls from beside the inground swimming pool where she's talking to an older woman with spiky white hair, dressed in bright purple. When they approach, Jody throws her arms around Jesse with a squeal.

"Hey Jesse, you still hanging out with this loser?" she says with a grin.

"Drew's not a loser," Jesse says but Drew's relieved to see he's smiling, he gets the joke. Drew's still not sure about being here, about what could happen if – when – they encounter David.

185

"Ah, true love. I tell you Bronny, these two will make you puke, they're so sweet."

Drew kisses her cheek.

"You'll be first if you keep knocking back the vodka at that speed," he says, then leans forward, so his lips are against her ear. "He here yet?"

Jody nods toward the oversized grill in the opposite corner of the garden.

"Over there somewhere. Came with Chisholm." She turns to Jesse again. "Hey Jesse, this is Bronny Lord, she teaches English with Drew. More importantly she likes *Doctor Who*."

Drews nods when Jesse glances at him; smiles when Jesse offers the older woman his hand.

"Hello," he says, eyes doing their usual dance back and forth from his feet to the face of the person he's speaking to. There are only a few people he can easily keep eye contact with – his parents, Mr Greenwold, and now Drew. Even with Jody he struggles, and it says a lot about the Johnstons last weekend that he had been as relaxed with them as Drew has seen him. Bronny is a seasoned teacher though who started out teaching in tough New York public schools. Drew often thinks there isn't much she hasn't seen – and to be honest if she hasn't seen it, it probably isn't worth worrying about. She smiles and shakes Jesse's hand, not bothering to try and force eye contact on him.

"Who's your favorite Doctor?" she asks and Drew groans.

"Oh God, you're not going to talk Time Lords all night, are you?" he asks.

"Number ten," Jesse says, ignoring his protest. "David Ten ...Tenn...." He frowns as he tries to get the name right.

"Tennant," Bronny supplies, "good choice. I like him too. Though of course I was always a Tom Baker fan before but Ten has his ... qualities."

"Does he ever," Jody says waggling her eyebrows.

Jesse looks confused and Drew hugs him, explaining they think the actor is sexy.

"Oh," Jesse says, looking at his feet. "Well, that's good, I suppose. That means I can keep Captain Jack to myself."

Drew glares at Jody who has exploded into giggles. Muttering about how overrated the character and the actor in question are, he leans down to get some beer from the cooler. There's some apple juice as well for Jesse but he shakes his head and takes the beer. As he straightens, there's a burst of laughter from beside the grill and Drew recognizes the voice that booms out, delivering the follow up to whatever joke he just told. Drew's breath catches in his throat, he hasn't seen or heard from David since the day he was given a suspended sentence and sent to rehab. That was nearly two years ago, and the sound of his voice still fills Drew with fear, but it's tinged with anger now, most of it directed at himself. How could he have been so stupid? Let himself be so manipulated.

The beating had been more intense than he'd been prepared to admit to Jesse, not after seeing the distress in his eyes. A broken cheekbone, a broken rib, four broken fingers, two chipped teeth, and a mild concussion. Still it wasn't as bad as the humiliation and the pain of betrayal. It wasn't lost on Drew that David had never tried to contact him to apologize or ask forgiveness despite it being part of every rehab program Drew had researched. It is Drew's considered opinion that sober or not, David isn't sorry for any of it.

He realizes Jesse has his hand on his arm and is looking at him with worried eyes; Bronny and Jody are silent, watching.

"Sorry, away with the fairies," he says and is pleased when Jody snorts. He lifts Jesse's hand and kisses the palm. "What did you say?"

Jesse just shakes his head and sips his beer.

* * *

Jesse knows Drew is worried about what will happen when he meets his ex-boyfriend. He's not though, because he's used to people being rude to him. That happens every day, people call him names or ignore him or try to take advantage of him in all kinds of ways, so what will make him any different? What does he care if Drew's ex-boyfriend is rude to him too?

What does worry Jesse is that he might try to do something to Drew and then what should he do? He knows he should protect Drew, that's what boyfriend's do, he knows that, but he doesn't know how. It's not like he's Captain Jack or Doctor Who or Star Lord; what can he, Jesse, do? He's never hit anyone, ever. Maybe Jody could help, Jesse thinks. She's fiery and stroppy and she could take him. Jesse thinks Jody could take on an entire Star Fleet by herself. The thought makes him smile, and he feels better. Maybe he should ask Dad about learning self-defense or something; he doesn't want to fight but he wants to be able to stand up for Drew the way he knows Drew would stand up for him.

Drew's arm is warm over his shoulder and he leans into it, looking around the garden from beneath his lashes. Jody and Bronny are arguing over which is better: Classic Doctor Who or Modern Doctor Who. Jesse tunes the conversation out, some of the early Doctor Who episodes are scary, and he doesn't want to think about them. Not tonight.

A short, plump man in baggy shorts and a Hawaiian shirt, with heavy horn-rimmed glasses and a grey goatee is approaching; he reminds Jesse of Colonel Sanders. Drew withdraws his arm and puts his hand out.

"Barry," Drew says as the two men shake hands. "How are you?"

"I'm good thanks, Drew. Are you feeling better?"

Jesse frowns. Feeling better? What does that mean? And why is Drew blushing?

"Uh yeah, sorry about that, it was just something I ate. All sorted. I'd like you to meet my boyfriend, Jesse Peterson." He turns toward Jesse. "Jesse this is Barry Reynolds, our principal."

Principal? This is Drew's boss? Anxiety shudders through Jesse. He wants to make a good impression on Drew's boss and so forces himself to keep his eyes lifted as he takes the man's hand in his own. Hopes the principal won't notice he's shaking.

"H–Hello," he says, "it's nice to meet you. Drew's a good teacher, he likes Central High School."

Barry Reynolds leans back and guffaws; when he has his laughter under control, he claps him on the shoulder and Jesse resists the urge to flinch away from him. The warmth of Drew's hand is comforting on the small of his back.

"He is indeed a good teacher and Central High likes him too," Reynolds says. "You boys staying to eat, I hope."

"Yup, marinated chicken in the cooler," Drew says.

"Good man. I've barely had a chance to catch up with you this week, so I need you to make a time to come by my office some time, Drew, so we can talk about next year's rostering." As Drew replies, Reynolds spots someone on the porch behind them and excuses himself.

Jesse sighs in relief and sags against Drew. This garden is nice, he likes the lights, and Bronny is nice – he supposes Mr Reynolds is too – but all these people he doesn't know, and worrying about what could happen, is exhausting. He wishes he'd agreed to staying home and he slips his hand in his pocket to stroke his Wicket keychain.

"Oh kid, I think he's got his eye on you for department head," Bronny says topping up Jody's vodka then her own.

"Pffft, whatever. You'd be the obvious choice, Bron."

"Too old, too grouchy, too unpopular with the kids," she says, "and besides he's offered it to me three times and I've turned it down. I'm happy where I am."

Jesse knows the person who is the leader of Drew's department is leaving and that they need to replace him. Drew said it was kind of like being put in charge of all the lizards or all the fish and when Jesse asked if it was like the way he is sort of in charge of Marcus for Mr Greenwold, Drew had blinked, kissed him, and murmured "yeah, exactly like that".

"So, are you going to be the new lizard leader?" he asks and Jody sputters vodka down her shirt.

"Never a truer word," she manages between coughs.

"I don't have the job yet," Drew says and presses his lips to Jesse's temple, "but yeah something like that."

At that point, Jesse's stomach makes a loud gurgle and he slaps his hand over it, cheeks flushing bright red.

"Sorry," he says looking at his feet. "I'm hungry."

Drew laughs and picks up the cooler.

"How about we get this chicken on the grill then?" he asks.

Jesse's hesitates, chewing his lip. If they go over there, they might meet ...him.

"It'll be okay Jesse," Jody says in his ear and he jumps. "If there's any problem, you come back and get me and Bronny okay?"

He nods and takes Drew's outstretched hand.

* * *

36

They'll have some chicken and maybe say hi to one or two more people and then they'll leave, Drew decides. If it's too early for dessert, they'll stop at the *Cheesecake Shoppe* and get some of the salted caramel cheesecake he knows Jesse loves. Whatever it takes to get out of here without a scene. Though that pisses him off too. He likes the faculty parties usually; he gets on with most of his colleagues and it's nice to be able to relax without the students around every corner.

He likes having Jesse with him. Jody and Bronny know the truth about Jesse and so does Barry Reynolds; Drew had been to see him as soon as he realized things were getting serious. The last thing he needs is someone tattling and trying to cause a scandal; forewarned, forearmed, all that jazz. He snorts laughter when Carol from the Art Department gives Jesse a very thorough once over before giving Drew a double thumbs up and he laces his fingers through Jesse's, pulling him closer to his side.

"You're a huge hit with the people I work with," he tells Jesse, "they think you're cute."

"I am cute," Jesse replies and Drew bumps with his shoulder.

"You're a dork. But you're my dork."

"Mmmhmmm." Jesse smiles at him sending shiver of happiness down Drew's spine.

"We won't stay late, darlin', I promise," he says as they step around a group of teachers strumming guitars.

"Go ..." Jesse is cut off by a thundering voice from the left.

"Well, well, well, what do we have here? Andy Pandy found himself a real pretty little thing by the looks of it."

Drew stiffens and tightens his grasp on Jesse's hand.

"Hello David."

David O'Henry is a big man in every sense; he's tall and broad shouldered and, when he and Drew were first together, was a lean two hundred and twenty-five pounds. Everyone said he was the fittest history teacher they'd ever met. Drew would always joke "or the geekiest body builder, depends on your outlook". Even when the alcohol and drugs started to take over he'd not lost a lot of form. Now though, he's soft and carrying much of his weight in his belly which hides his belt buckle. His face is pudgy and covered in a fine sheen of sweat; large circles are forming under his arms too. A cloud of alcohol fumes surrounds him, and Drew takes a step back. Out of arm's reach.

"Long time no speak Andy Pandy," David growls as he approaches, eyes wandering up and down Jesse. Drew tries to put himself between the two but David steps to the side so he's once again sizing Jesse up like a slab of meat. "Hear you moved over to the West side."

"Yes."

A hush has settled over the garden and all eyes are on the three of them. Drew has a split second to wonder what game Nigel Chisolm thinks he's playing bringing David here tonight, then to regret coming then David speaks again.

"And I see you found someone to replace me." He reaches out as if to touch Jesse, who leans out of reach with an audible gasp. Drew smacks the hand away.

"Don't touch him."

"Aw, you never were one for sharing your play things, Andy Pandy."

"His name is Drew, not Andy Pandy." Jesse's voice is loud and clear, gives no sign of the trembling Drew can feel beside him. David stares, astonished, then laughs.

"Oh, she has a pretty voice to go with that pretty mouth," David taunts.

"Ignore him," Drew mutters to Jesse and attempts to lead Jesse around him toward the grill.

"I see you're still queen of the bitch face." David moves to block their path.

"And I smell that you're still drinking, so much for rehab." Drew pushes past, counting on his combined weight with that of Jesse's to give them some momentum. "Come on Jess, let's go."

David's face darkens, and his arm shoots out, holding them back.

"Oh, she even has a pretty name. Jess. Isn't that sweet?"

A couple of teachers are muttering to one another but most of the staff are waiting to see how the standoff is going to play out. Drew knows at least some of it is self-preservation – they had all seen the mess David had made of his face – and he doesn't blame them.

"David why don't you leave?" Jody says from behind Drew and he wants to kiss her, just for being there.

"Jody why don't you shut the fuck up?" David's voice is loud enough for those who are close to hear but not loud enough to carry. Turns back toward Drew and Jesse. "Does that pretty little mouth suck as well as it speaks?"

A gasp ripples through the gathered group and Drew sees someone running up the steps to the house, no doubt in search of Reynolds and Chisolm and it occurs to Drew that this would be amusing for the kids to see. The teachers having a typical school yard brawl. He drags his hand through his hair and takes a deep breath.

191

"Look I don't want any trouble, so Jesse and I'll just go," he says and turns, tugging Jesse with him.

"So, what's it like, fucking a retard?" David asks behind him and Drew freezes, lets the cooler drop to the ground with a thud. The remaining beer bottles clink and clatter together. He lets go of Jesse's hand and has a vague notion that Jody steps forward as he steps closer to David.

"What did you say?"

"Oh yeah I've heard all about your dummy. Finally get the balls to top did you Andy Pandy? Or did you teach pretty boy how to take good care of you?"

Blood pounds in Drew's ears and behind his eyes like some ridiculous drum beat from a horror movie. He can feel it making his cheeks blaze scarlet and his fists curl.

"Let me spend an hour with your pretty boy, I'll really teach him what he needs to know. Bet you're ..."

David doesn't get to finish his sentence. Tall and broad shouldered or not, Drew's anger makes up for the difference in size – and he is angry. Angrier than he's ever been. Angry about the disdain with which David had always treated him, even before things got ugly. Angry about the beating and the pain of waiting for his rib and cheekbone to heal. Angry about the cost of having two teeth capped and having to buy new glasses. But most of all he's angry about the way David's speaking about Jesse.

There's a very satisfying crunch as David's nose disintegrates beneath Drew's fist; loud and with a stomach-churning liquid sound and feel to it. It reminds Drew of chicken bones being twisted and pulled apart and more than makes up for the fiery blaze of pain that works his way from Drew's wrist to his elbow. Blood cascades down David's shirt as he howls in agony.

"By dose, you fugging asshole, you broge by dose. I'm going do fugging gill you."

Drew leans forward, ignoring Jesse's pleas behind him. Makes sure everyone can hear him.

"If you come near me again I'll have your ass thrown in jail, not rehab." He takes a deep breath. "And if you come near Jesse I won't break your nose, I'll break your fucking balls."

Jesse is tugging his arm, trying to pull him away, and when Jody begins pushing him, he lets him. Barry Reynolds arrives, cheeks red, Hawaiian shirt flapping around him, demanding an explanation. Bronny gives him a breathless and expletive filled explanation before assuring him she and Jody will make sure Drew and Jesse get home.

Reynolds nods and flaps at them to go, go. He'll clean this mess up. As they cross the foyer toward the front door, Drew hears him begin to yell.

"What the blue fuck is going on here?"

* * *

193

37

The glaring light in the emergency room hurts Jesse's eyes and he wriggles on the hard, plastic seat trying to find a comfortable spot. They said the x-rays wouldn't take long but they've been gone for ages. Jody, insisting she had only just started her second drink when the fight broke out, drove them here in Drew's car, with Bronny following behind in her own. Jesse had huddled in against Drew in the back seat and when he reached for his hand, Drew hissed and pulled it out of reach. Pulling over to see what was wrong, Jody swore loudly and announced they were going to the hospital, ignoring Drew's protests. After an hour in the stuffy waiting room some nurse has taken Drew away in a wheelchair to x-ray his wrist.

Jesse takes mini-Wicket out of his pocket and closes both hands around it, so nobody can see it. He leans to the side to look down the corridor, hopeful he'll see Drew coming toward him but there's only an old lady pushing a tea-trolley. Jesse slumps back in his seat with a sigh, jumps when Jody touches his shoulder.

"He'll be back soon, Jesse, and he'll be fine," she says with a smile.

"Do you think he broke his hand?" Jesse asks.

"His wrist probably, but yeah I think so."

Jesse looks up at her. Shock and fatigue have left smudges under his eyes and his usually coffee colored skin pale.

"Because he was protecting me."

Jody's face falls and she slides an arm around him. He stiffens for a moment, then his shoulders fall, and he leans against her.

"Oh honey, it's not your fault," she says. Bronny slides over to the seat on the other side of Jesse and rests a hand on his elbow. "This is all on that piece of shit, David."

"Jody's right, Jesse, David was bad news before and he's bad news now," she says in a quiet voice. "And I for one will be finding out what the hell that idiot Chisolm thought he was doing inviting him. God, that man's a little creep."

Jesse isn't sure what she means but he understands both women are trying to comfort him and he's grateful for that. He just wishes they would bring Drew back, so he can see that he's okay. They sit in silence, listening to the Emergency department continue around them.

Another hour has slipped past when Jody, standing to stretch her back, touches his shoulder with a smile and points to the corridor. A nurse is pushing Drew toward them in a wheelchair. He's clutching a large envelope stamped with the word X-RAY and a sheaf of papers; his right hand and forearm are encased in a white plaster cast and Jesse squeezes Wicket when he sees it. When they're close enough to speak to, Drew lifts his head and smiles at Jesse. He looks tired and his eyes have a glassy sheen to them.

"They give you the good stuff?" Bronny asks.

"Oh yeah," Drew replies, and holds his injured hand out to Jesse who takes it gingerly. "Hey cutie, how are you doing?"

"Does it hurt?" Jesse asks in a small voice.

"Not one teeny, tiny bit. No sir, not at all." Drew hiccups a laugh.

"Oh yeah, they gave him the good stuff," Jody says and sniggers.

"Mr Oliver has all his paperwork, there's nothing left to sign, so if you would like to get your car, I can bring him out to the pickup bay," the nurse interrupts, not unkindly.

Jody darts off, keys jangling in her pocket, to get the car. The papers and envelope begin to slide out of Drew's grip and Bronny grabs them before they can hit the ground; Drew pats his knee and gives Jesse a drunken smile.

"Want to sit on my lap while we wait?" he asks. Jesse shakes his head with a shy smile. It took him a moment to figure out what Bronny and Jody meant by The Good Stuff then he remembered the day he had his wisdom teeth out. The dentist had given him a shot of something that had made him feel loopy and say silly things to his dad all the way home. He figures The Good Stuff must be something similar. Drew pouts but tugs him close enough so he can slip his free arm around Jesse's waist and leans his head against him.

"I love you Jesse," he says.

Jesse blushes, his eyes dart from the nurse to Bronny and sees both are smiling. He crouches so he can be on the same level as Drew.

"I love you too."

Drew looks as though he might say something but Bronny's phone buzzes and she stops him.

"Jody's ready. How about we go home?"

* * *

Drew smiles at Jesse's refusal to let him do anything. He watches from the couch while Jesse locks up and turns off the kitchen lights. As soon as they walked in, Jesse had picked up Scamp and explained in a very serious tone that she had to be a good girl tonight and stay in her cave because Drew was hurt. The little cat has taken that under advisement and chosen to proceed exactly as she pleases Drew notes with amusement as she chases a cat nip mouse around his feet.

"I need to go to the bathroom and clean my teeth," Drew says, fighting a yawn. Jesse bites his lip, uncertainty in his eyes.

"Do you need any help?"

"I'm all good Jess," Drew reassures him, "but maybe you could get me a glass of water for by the bed? In case I need to take another pill."

Jesse nods and takes Scamp with him to the bedroom while Drew makes his way to the bathroom. After using the toilet and flushing it, he leans against the sink and stares at his reflection. This was not how he had intended to finish this evening and there's a dull spark of anger first at David then at himself for being naïve. Had he really thought he would get away with nothing more than a frigid exchange, maybe a bit of rudeness? That had never been David's style, even before things got bad. His arrogance, the sense of danger that surrounded him, had been part of the attraction in the very early days; he was everything Drew wasn't – reckless, confident, physically superior. Then when things began to go wrong, Drew wanted to save him, save his talent – David's knowledge of history had been profound and passionate, and Drew hated seeing that destroyed. Now though, even through his own stoned haze – they really did give him the good stuff and ladies and gentlemen isn't that ironic – he can see that David is simply a bully interested in nobody but himself.

Drew sighs and closes his eyes. When David tried to touch Jesse, Drew had felt something like a bow string begin to tighten within him. When he'd called him a retard the string stretched as far as it would go. When he'd suggested being alone with Jesse it had snapped. While the technician had taken x-ray after x-ray of the shattered bones in his wrist and the crack running up the main bone to his index finger, one of the ones David had broken last time, he'd been able to think of nothing but Jesse. Was Jesse okay? Was he scared? Did he blame himself? Did he understand what's happening? Drew knows there are people who get pleasure from loving someone sick or disabled, that they're enamored with the illness or the disability, not the person. For some time, he worried about being that way himself. Was he simply in love with being able to take care of Jesse? When David had suggested he could ... spend time with him ... Drew had been enraged and it wasn't entirely a protective rage. Most of it he realized, as they gave him a shot and prepared to wrap him in plaster, was jealousy. He'd nodded, not paying attention, as they told him they would need to x-ray it again in a week and there was a chance he might need surgery, as he turned over the idea in his head that his anger was fueled by the thought of losing Jesse in any way.

A tap on the door brings him back to the bathroom and he washes his good hand and the tips of his fingers peeking out through the plaster; everything is still blissfully numb thanks to the shot the nurse had given him. It won't last though, and he hopes she gave him at least enough to get through most of the night before scrambling for the pill bottle. Tucking his hair behind his ear, he opens the door and smiles at the worried face that greets him.

"Let's go to bed, darlin'," he says, "before I fall over and break the other wrist."

"Not funny," Jesse says tucking his arm through Drew's.

"Little bit funny."

"No. Not funny at all. Not even a little bit," Jesse says.

Drew sinks on to the bed and sighs.

"I might need a hand to get undressed," he says, and Jesse is on his knees in an instant, pulling at Drew's shoe laces. When he gets to his belt buckle, Drew runs a hand through Jesse's hair and tips his head back so he's able to see his eyes. "This is not how I pictured this evening ending," he considers a moment then continues, "okay well it was sort of like this, but I was going to be doing the undressing."

"It's okay, Drew," Jesse says and pulls him to his feet, so he can step out of his jeans. He snags Drew's sleep pants from the hook behind the bedroom door and crouches, so he can step into them, pulls them up his legs, and reaches for the tee-shirt. Drew raises an eyebrow; the sleeve is not going to stretch over the cast. Jesse frowns for a moment, tongue in the corner of his mouth, then his face clears, and he whirls on his heel and runs from the room. When he returns he has one of the kitchen knives and Drew pales.

"Uh Jess, that's a really sharp knife."

"Well duh," Jesse retorts and lays it on the bed. He tugs on the shirt until Drew's good arm and head are free and the shirt is hanging inside out over the cast. Drew catches his breath when Jesse picks the knife up again, folds the tee-shirt sleeve in half, and with one sharp movement rips through it with the knife blade. The shirt falls to the ground and Jesse kicks it to one side before disappearing to return the knife to the kitchen. Letting out a shaky breath, Drew lays down, broken hand resting on his belly, good arm across his eyes.

"Do you want a shirt?" Jesse asks, and Drew looks out from beneath his arm; he didn't hear him come back.

"No. I just want you to come to bed."

Jesse undresses – Drew notes with not a little disappointment that he had been commando and vows to make sure he feels that confident again - and pulls on his own sleep pants. Climbs into bed and turns the lamp out. Drew shifts so he can be as close to him as possible without jostling his hand or braining Jesse with his plaster. There's a rustle of movement as Scamp lands on the bed and curls up in her usual spot, then another which Drew knows is Jesse reaching for Wicket.

"Jess? Do something for me?"

"Okay."

"Do you think you can come around this side to sleep for a while, so I can hold you?" Drew knows he's asking a lot, routine and familiarity are key for Jesse, change like this induces anxiety but he really needs to feel him in his arms and he suspects he might not be the only one. The sheets rustle, he can hear the pad of Jesse's feet as he walks around the end of the bed, and the mattress dips as he slides in on Drew's side. With his uninjured arm, Drew pulls him close, so his head rests on his chest – smiles when he feels the cool softness of Wicket's fur against him. Kisses Jesse's head and runs his hand up and down the length of his arm.

"Jess, I'm sorry."

Jesse lifts his head and Drew knows he's looking at him in confusion.

"Why? You didn't do anything."

"I'm sorry he said those things. That he called you a retard. That he said you were a girl."

"He's not a nice person so he says not nice things. There are lots of people like him," Jesse says, and Drew feels him shrug. "But I don't mind him calling me a girl. I like girls, they're cool. I don't know why people think it's bad to call someone a girl."

Oh God, he's too tired and too stoned to even consider a discussion on gender politics, so he rubs his cheek over Jesse's head to let him know he understands.

"I'm sorry you got hurt because of me," Jesse says.

Drew thinks for a moment, choosing his words with care. Jody told him what Jesse thought and he knows the longer Jesse dwells on it, the worse it's going to be.

"Don't be sorry, Jess," he says hugging him tighter. "Yes, I punched David because of you but I didn't get hurt because of you..."

"But ..."

"Jess, listen to me. You *can* understand this," Drew tries to make his voice firm through the analgesic haze that is settling over him now he's in bed, "David's not nice, you're right about that, but I didn't punch him because he called you a retard or a girl. You don't need me to protect you like that. I punched him because he said he wanted to ..."

"He wanted to fuck me," Jesse says in a low voice and Drew's stomach does a slow somersault making him gag. He vows never to curse in bed again. Of all the things Jesse understood tonight, why is he not surprised it was that one?

"Yeah, I didn't like that. It made me jealous and angry and I wanted to hurt him. I got hurt because I got jealous and wasn't thinking. And because I'm an English teacher who has no place throwing a punch at anyone, let alone at him. My hands are not designed for that."

Silence settles over the room and Drew has just decided Jesse has fallen asleep when he speaks.

"No, they're not. Your hands are designed for being kind. And for making me feel good."

He smiles in the darkness.

"Yeah they are."

"Drew, can I ask you something? But don't get mad, okay?"

"Why would I get mad?" When Jesse doesn't answer, Drew sighs. "Okay I won't get mad, ask me."

"What did he mean when he said you finally got the balls to top?"

Drew isn't sure whether he wants to laugh or cry; it's nearly midnight, he has a shattered wrist and Jesse wants a lesson in gay sex? In time it occurs to him that Jesse has probably been worrying about this all evening, for some reason that Drew has yet to even consider, and is able to stop the laughter before it takes over.

"Um okay, so you know what topping and bottoming is, right?" Jesse's silence is all the answer he needs and Drew curses himself for being as self-absorbed and lacking insight as David. It's been nearly seven months and he's never even considered this conversation with Jesse. He's just been happy to continue with things as they are because he, Drew, is happy. Even knowing Jesse hadn't had much experience. "Okay, wow I'm glad the lights are off or you'd see just how much I'm blushing," he traps Jesse's hand against the sheet as he feels it move toward the lamp, "nope, you get an answer, or you get to see my red cheeks, not both. Not tonight."

"Answer," Jesse says.

"Right. Okay so when we have sex, uh, make love and I'm inside you that's called topping, you're the bottom."

"Even if I'm like on top of you?"

"Even then." Drew tries to not squirm in embarrassment. "When I was with David, I was um always the bottom."

"Oh."

"Jess, he was just trying to find a way to provoke me into doing exactly what I'd..."

"Did you like being the bottom?"

"What?"

"Did you like being the bottom?"

Drew blinks.

"Well I guess I did. But Jess I like what we do, I like what we do a l..."

"Which do you like more?"

"I uh – oh God Jess, it's way too late for this conversation – I guess I like both."

There's more silence as Jesse considers this, then Drew feels the weight of Wicket being rested on his belly just above his plastered wrist and Jesse's head on his chest.

"I'm tired," Jesse says. "I love you."

Drew smiles, he loves how Jesse does that, just shuts a subject down. He slurs his answer against Jesse's hair as he gives in and lets his body sleep.

* * *

38

Drew leans back in the armchair and sips his soda; Jesse is at his feet, one hand curled around his calf, head leaning against Drew's knees. This is one of Jesse's favorite places to sit, sometimes when he's watching You Tube videos while Drew is working, he'll sit under the desk, arm around Drew's calves, body resting against them like a cat. It was disconcerting at first, but Drew's used to it now and finds it comforting. The pain in his hand has dropped to a dull, persistent hum he feels instead of hearing; it feels like an entire hive of bees has taken up residence in his wrist. The pills the hospital gave him aren't quite The Good Stuff, but they keep the hive under control. He puts his drink down and runs his hand through Jesse's hair, smiling.

Ray and Erin came as soon as Jesse told them what had happened and their concern, now they are sure that Jesse was indeed fine, is genuine. Erin was doing an inventory of the fridge to see what she could make and leave for them to heat later when Drew's parents arrived. Drew's mother had hung up on him mid-sentence telling him she was on the way. Now all four parents are seated around the room, sipping coffee and eating the cake Sue and Peter had stopped to pick up on the way. Jesse has a slice in front of him but hasn't touched it. Drew nudges him with his knee.

"Eat your cake, it's double fudge," he says.

"Yeah, I will," Jesse says and presses closer.

"If you don't, I will." Drew pretends to reach for the dish and Jesse moves it out of the way; Drew relaxes, maybe he just isn't hungry yet if he's still territorial about his treat.

"Will you be going to the police?" Peter asks.

"Dad, I threw the punch, not him."

"Even so, Drew, there's history and he clearly provoked you, tried to make you react," his mother protests.

Drew shakes his head.

"There's not much I can do but if he so much as looks this way, I'll take out a restraining order." Jesse's fingers tighten around Drew's calf; Drew made sure he explained what a restraining order was this morning and he knows Jesse understands it even if he finds it frightening.

"Are you okay, honey?" Erin asks, leaning toward her son. Jesse nods and gives her a tired smile.

"You know, Erin, Jess was fantastic last night when we got to the hospital. He remembered what my blood type is and that I'm allergic to penicillin and was able to tell the nurses."

"Really?" Erin asks, surprise turning her cheeks pink. Jesse shrugs when she pats his shoulder as though it's not important.

"Hey, that's a big deal Jess," Drew nudges him again, "because if they'd decided to operate last night, they probably would have given me penicillin and it might have killed me. Would have made me very sick at least. You being able to tell them is a very big deal, trust me."

"Operate?" Sue asks, fingers tented over her mouth. "Oh my god, you didn't break it in the same place as ..."

"As last time, yes, well fractured, not really broken, but I doubt it will come to surgery." He flicks his eyes toward Jesse, praying his mother gets the hint and when she does, relaxes.

For the next half hour, they talk about packing up Jesse's apartment, currently on hold thanks to Drew's wrist, Scamp's naughtiness, and who will win the election. At least, Drew thinks, they all agree about who they don't want in the White House, even if he does have a hunch they're going to be disappointed. When he yawns for the third time in ten minutes, both mothers stand and announce it's time to go. As much as he appreciates the visit, Drew is grateful, he'd really just like to take a nap with Jesse now.

* * *

When they finally leave, he goes to the bedroom and lets himself fall back on the bed, groaning when a bolt of pain shoots up his arm.

"Bees are awake," he thinks, waiting for the discomfort to pass. The mattress dips and he opens one eye. Jesse is stretched out beside him, head propped up on one hand. "Hey, you."

"Hey," Jesse says and reaches out to brush Drew's hair out of his eyes.

"Our folks finally met and looks like our moms like each other," Drew says.

"They don't think it's a mistake us living together anymore either."

"Very true. If I'd only known all I had to do was break my wrist ..."

"Not funny."

"Really? Not even a little?"

Jesse shakes his head, no not even a little, and Drew pretends to sulk. Jesse smiles and Drew reaches up to pull his face closer, lifts his head and kisses him. Jesse settles against him with a soft sigh, and Drew deepens the kiss, coaxing Jesse with this tongue to open his mouth. Presses himself against Jesse, rocking in smooth, easy movements until Jesse pushes him back.

"What about your hand?"

Drew thinks about this for a second, then rolls his hips forward so Jesse can feel how hard he is.

"Well you might have to do most of the work," he says.

Jesse's hand trails down Drew's chest and he trembles at the touch.

"Jess..."

Jesse leans down and kisses him again. Drew makes a low soft sound in the back of his throat that he will deny if anyone asks and tries to pull Jesse closer, but Jesse leans away. Drew frowns, then Jesse is stretched out alongside him, hardness pressed against Drew's hip and his hand is inching down Drew's belly to the waistband of his sweats.

"Jess, please," Drew pleads when his hand dips beneath the fabric and brushes against his aching cock. Wraps his fingers around Drew's length, begins to move his hand in slow steady strokes.

"It's okay, Drew, I'm going to take care of you," Jesse says and rubs the pad of his thumb over the damp head and oh God that feels good; better than anything that happened in the past twenty fours. Drew moans and thrusts up into Jesse's fist. When he opens his eyes, Jesse is watching him, and he licks his lips.

"Feels really good, darlin'," he manages to whisper.

Jesse tightens his grip and speeds up, eyes still locked on Drew's face. Drew whimpers; he wants more, needs more and tries to push his sweatpants away so Jesse has better access. Jesse stops what he's doing to push him back against the mattress, making him groan.

"I love you," Jesse says resuming his tortuous stroking and rubbing. Drew swallows a small moan, rocks up and back, looking for friction. His cock is diamond hard and the teasing is just the wrong side of enough.

"Jesse," he moans, unable to think. Must be a combination of The Good Stuff and the stroking.

Jesse increases his speed and Drew can't help the sound that escapes. He's very close to the edge and doesn't know if he wants it to last or be over. Runs his plaster clad fingers over the back of Jesse's hand. Jesse squeezes, just enough for Drew to feel and leans forward, hand still moving. Drew groans, feels everything begin to tighten. When he feels Jesse's lips against his ear and feels his warm breath on his skin, he almost sobs with frustration and desire.

"Jess," he warns.

"I want to take care of you properly," Jesse whispers in his ear. "I want to top sometimes."

That's all it takes; just the thought of what Jesse is suggesting sends Drew over the edge.

"Jesse ... oh god......" he cries out as his back bows and he comes, hot, wet, and sticky across his belly. For a moment the bees in his hand are forgotten as he rocks into Jesse's fist.

Finally, Jesse lets go and reaches for tissues, cleans them both up, and lays down against Drew, knees drawn up against his chest. His breath is warm again on Drew's skin when he speaks.

"Would that be okay?" he asks and Drew smiles at the shyness he can hear.

"It would be more than okay, if you're sure you want to do that."

"I'm sure."

Drew smiles and closes his eyes. They can talk about this later, when he's had a nap.

* * *

Pain wakes Drew wakes around eight, he takes a pill and goes to the bathroom. Stopping in the kitchen on the way back he pours two glasses of milk and puts them on a tray with some cookies– hardly a balanced meal but he's not sure either of them cares tonight. Jesse is still dozing when he sets the tray next to the bed, so he coaxes him under the covers and climbs in, pulling him closer so Jesse's back is against his chest. Smiles when Jesse's hand brushes the plaster cast and wriggles under it so he's not putting any pressure on the injury. Within minutes he's asleep again.

* * *

Jesse stirs at two and gets out of bed. Scratching his head, he pads to the bathroom. When he returns, rubbing his eyes and yawning, Drew is awake. They sit against the headboard and drink their milk; Drew takes another pill and they slide down under the covers again. As his eyes slip closed, Jesse feels Scamp land on the bed next to him and scratches her ear. He falls asleep like that, warm and calm.

* * *

39

Drew opens his eyes and lifts his head to glance at the clock over Jesse's shoulder; he's surprised to see it's after nine. It's rare for Jesse to sleep this late even on a Sunday and it occurs to him he must be exhausted after the past forty-eight hours. He stretches and winces at the bite of pain in his hand.

Deciding he may as well get up since he's going to have to take a painkiller anyway, Drew edges out of Jesse's side of the bed taking care to not wake him. Wicket is still on the bedside table. He collects the tray of glasses and uneaten cookies, smiling at the still sleeping Jesse; Scamp is tucked as usual under his chin, tail over her nose.

Leaving the tray in the kitchen, he finds a plastic bag, wraps it around his plaster and ties a firm knot. He's having a shower, he's decided. It's bad enough he won't be able to swim for the next month or so, he's showering. This turns out to be more difficult that he'd envisioned and when he finally gets out his eyes are red from shampoo and there's condensation forming on the inside of the bag. Discarding it in the wastepaper basket, he wraps a towel around his hips and returns to the bedroom.

Jesse is still sound asleep, and Drew does his best to not make any noise as he finds clothes and dresses. As he collects his glasses, Jesse turns, snuffling and smacking his lips but doesn't wake so Drew slips out, pulling the door behind him. Scamp is waiting in the kitchen and meows when she sees him.

"Okay, okay, don't go waking your boy up. Just give me a minute and I'll feed you, your majesty."

Drew tosses the towel in the laundry basket, flicks the coffee maker on, and feeds Scamp. Collects his coffee and considers sitting at his desk to grade papers but the throbbing in his wrist convinces him to leave it and to stretch out on the couch with a book instead. He has just poured his second cup of coffee when a panicked cry comes from the bedroom.

"I'm out here, Jess," he calls and seconds later Jesse appears, hair sticking out in spikes, pajama pants drooping, and eyes still bleary from sleep. "Hello sleepy head."

"I didn't know where you were," Jesse mumbles and frowns, makes his way to the kitchen and pours some apple juice.

Drew chuckles.

"Where did you think I'd be?"

Jesse shrugs and comes back, and pushes Drew's knees apart, crawls up between them and snuggles against him, eyes drooping again. Drew runs a hand over the bare skin of his back.

"You'll catch cold like this," he says. Jesse shakes his head.

"Nope. You're warm."

"Whatever. Don't complain to me when you've got a runny nose. Hungry?"

Jesse shakes his head again and Drew frowns. Normally on a Sunday morning – well any morning really – Jesse is a like a puppy, full of energy and enthusiasm. They go through a box of his favorite cereal every couple of days and after swimming they ... Drew stops mid thought and decides. He taps Jesse's bare shoulder.

"Come on you, time to go swimming."

"No," Jesse says. "Don't want to."

Drew blinks.

"What do you mean, you don't want to? You love swimming."

Jesse pouts and rubs his nose against Drew's shoulder.

"It won't be fun if you can't swim too."

"Jess, I'll be right there by the pool with my book"

Jesse burrows his head deeper against Drew's neck. Drew sighs and rubs Jesse's neck.

"You swam for years without me, this is only going to be a few weeks," he says. Taps his hand against Jesse's thigh. "Jess, come on, you need to swim. Go get dressed and I'll get the swimming bag."

Jesse doesn't move; his face is sullen and drawn. Drew puts his arm around him, turning him so he can look him in the eye.

"Listen to me Jess, I'm fine. You're fine. And I know you don't want to swim without me, but you have to. You need to swim, you know that." Jesse lowers his eyes but Drew tips his face up, forcing him to look at him. "Come on, this is important. You said you want to take care of me and part of that means you go swimming or I'm going to worry about you. Is that what you want? No, I didn't think so. Now come on, go clean your teeth and get ready."

Jesse takes a step toward the bathroom, shoulders slumped, then turns around.

"Can we go to *The Library Bar* after? For lunch?"

Drew smiles.

"Well, you need to hurry up then or I'll go without you."

Jesse returns the smile, opens his mouth to say something, stops, and turns back to the bathroom.

Drew sighs. Something is going on and he really needs to figure out what it is. It would be so much easier if the damned beehive would shut up.

He finishes his coffee and goes in search of the swimming bag.

* * *

After reading the same page for the third time, Drew puts a marker in his book and watches Jesse do laps of the pool. Although not fast, Jesse's stroke is steady and even, he lifts his head on every third stroke, and he stops at the end of each length to stand and look toward Drew. After twenty lengths, Drew gets a towel out of the bag and approaches the side, waiting for Jesse to pull himself up the ladder. Despite the heavy smell of chlorine signaling the pools have been tested that morning, Drew wishes he could have gone in; swimming is part of their routine.

"Want me to come and talk to you while you get dressed?" he asks, draping the towel around Jesse's shoulders. Jesse hesitates then nods. Drew goes back to the bench, picks up the bag and his book, and follows Jesse into the changing room. They have one end to themselves and Drew leans against the concrete block wall, flexing the fingers of his injured hand, wincing at the small flares of pain.

"Does it hurt?" Jesse tucks his shirt into his jeans, but his eyes are on Drew's fingers.

"A little. Not as bad as yesterday though," Drew lies. "Come on, darlin', I'm starving, I'm ready for chicken pajamas."

Jesse grins at the joke. He'd been trying to sound out the word parmigiana one day, took a guess at it, and the name had stuck.

"Me too. I'm having chicken pajamas too." He bends to lace his sneakers. "And I'm buying lunch. Out of my account."

On Wednesday, they had opened a joint account, but Drew insisted they keep separate accounts as well and he knows this is what Jesse is referring to. Something in the tone of Jesse's voice seems a little off to Drew but maybe it's just fatigue.

"But I thought I was taking you to lunch for going swimming?"

Jesse shakes his head and stows his goggles and swim shirts in a plastic bag, rolls the bag in his towel and tucks it into the swimming bag before slinging it over his shoulder.

"No, I'm taking care of you," he says in a quiet, firm voice. Standing like that, head tilted to one side, hair damp, sport bag over one shoulder he looks like a model ready to be photographed. He gasps and claps his hand to his pocket, feeling with fingers, then his face clears, and he sighs in relief. Drew knows he's found mini-Wicket and leans over to kiss his cheek.

"Okay, Jess, but I warn you I could get used to being looked after. Now, come on, I'm starving."

* * *

The walk from the swimming pool complex to *The Library Bar* isn't long and most Sunday's they follow the same routine: bus to the pool, swim, walk to *The Library Bar*, then either walk or bus home. If it's raining or they're meeting someone for lunch, Drew drives. Today they took the bus, in part because Drew doesn't relish the thought of driving yet.

When they arrive at the bar, Jesse holds the door open and as soon as Drew is inside darts in front of him to speak to the waitress. A short girl with a wide, open smile and bright red hair approaches.

"Hi Jesse, how are you today?" she asks. "Your usual table is free if you want it."

Before Drew can say yes and thank her Jesse shakes his head.

"No. Can we have one of the ones over by the books?"

"Sure, no problem," she replies doing a remarkable, in Drew's opinion at least, job of maintaining her composure. She leads them to a corner table, places the menus and wine list on the table and reassures them she'll be back in soon.

It's rare for them to miss a Sunday brunch here and they know all the waitresses. If any member of staff at the bar is bothered by Drew and Jesse's relationship, they've never been rostered on when they've been there.

"Do you want wine?" Jesse asks. He knows the menu by heart and hasn't bothered to look at it. Drew considers the question, then shrugs, he's not driving.

"Maybe one glass."

"Can you choose it, I want one too."

Drew looks over the menu and selects a Merlot that he knows has a soft peppery flavor to it and Jesse will like. When the waitress returns he orders two glasses and two orders of chicken parmigiana with side salads; he doesn't bother specifying how to do Jesse's anymore, they all know.

"What have you been up to Drew?" she asks, nodding at his hand.

"Nothing much, broke it by trying to knock down something with my bare hands when I should have used a mallet," he says, eyes on Jesse. "Thought I was Superman, turns out I'm just a teacher after all."

She makes a sympathetic noise, gathers up their menus and leaves. Drew reaches over the table and takes Jesse's hand, rubs his thumb over the knuckles.

"What's wrong Jess?" he asks but Jesse just shakes his head.

"I'm okay."

"Are you sure?"

"Yeah, it was just really scary and that made me tired."

Drew murmurs an apology just as the waitress returns with the wine. Shortly after she brings their meals and Drew is amused to see that Jesse's earlier disinterest in food has gone. He's barely finished counting and arranging his vegetables before he begins shoveling food into his mouth and after watching for several seconds, Drew reaches out to catch the hand holding his fork and tells him to slow down.

"You're going to choke, you dork."

"Hungry," Jesse mumbles but puts his fork down.

Drew sips his wine, still watching Jesse. He's not convinced by the answer Jesse has given him about just being tired; it's not that he doesn't believe him, it's that something is telling them there is more going on than simple reaction to Friday night. Picking up his knife and fork he examines his own plate and it occurs to him that a dish with lots of sauce and pasta noodles might not have been the best choice for someone with only one hand in the game.

"I got scared when I saw the blood." Jesse takes a careful sip of wine then smiles at the flavor and takes a larger mouthful. "And you were gone for a long time at the hospital."

Drew has finally managed to cut his chicken into several small pieces, an activity he's in no hurry to repeat since the wine means he'll have to wait several hours to take a painkiller. He stabs a chunk with his fork and chews while he searches for the right thing to say. In the end, he decides there is no right thing to say.

"I know it was scary for you Jesse and I'm really sorry. I wish it hadn't happened at all. I was scared too."

Jesse looks up, concern in his golden eyes.

"You were?"

"Of course I was Jess. David is bigger than me and he…"

"He beat you up before," Jesse interrupts, twisting noodles with his fork.

"Yes. And I was scared he might do something to you. Not just what he said but that he might try to hurt you."

Drew takes his glasses off and tries to wipe them with his napkin but the cast – and the wine – make him clumsy. Without a word, Jesse reaches over and takes them, uses his own napkin to clean them and hands them back.

"Thank you," Drew whispers, touched by the simple gesture. "Also, I suppose I didn't want you to see how weak I am."

Jesse shakes his head and pushes his now empty plate away, reaches for his salad. He must really be hungry, Drew thinks.

"You're not weak. You're strong. You're like … like…," Jesse's hand holding a forkful of lettuce hovers in the air while he searches for a comparison, squinting in concentration, "you're like Captain Jack. You're smart and strong."

Drew laughs. That is high praise indeed.

"You're my hero," Jesse adds, cutting through Drew's laughter.

"I'm no hero, darlin', but thank you." Drew fumbles his fork as he blinks back emotion. The fork slips from his grip and hits the floor with a clatter. Jesse leans down and picks it up for him. "And I'm a pretty useless hero at the moment."

"Well, I'm going to look after you." Jesse looks down at his salad bowl, seems surprised it's empty. That's the second or third time this morning Jesse has mentioned looking after him and Drew turns the phrase over in his mind while he eats. Is that what the problem is, he wonders. Has this triggered some protective instinct in Jesse? A far more important question, he thinks, is should he worry about it? Jesse is still speaking and it's almost his normal stream of chatter.

"I can carry your books and things to the car. I can make you dinner. I could even wash your hair."

The last is offered in a shy voice. Drew knows Jesse loves it when he washes his hair for him; he knows he loves playing with Drew's hair too. Swallowing the last chunk of chicken takes an effort; he's distracted by the thought.

"That's not all I could wash," Jesse says with a sly smile. "I could also ..."

"Filter, Jess." He's rewarded with laughter from the other side of the table and smiles. He's noticed he needs to remind Jess to filter less than when they first met and on more than one occasion he's suspected Jesse has been teasing him. Jesse is still blunt and transparent and Drew hopes that never changes, but he's much better at reading simple social situations than he was, and Drew thinks he might have a part to play in that. It's an idea that makes him happy; he knows there is no space for the word cure in Jesse's world but if Drew has helped him navigate one social minefield, even in a small way, he'll take it.

The waitress arrives to take their plates and asks if they would like dessert.

"Not for me but I think someone else might be good for some brownie," Drew says and Jesse nods. When she leaves, Drew settles back with a sigh.

"So, after your brownie what do you want to do?" he asks and sips his wine.

"You."

Drew chokes, spitting red wine down his shirt and over the table cloth. Eyes watering, he gropes for a napkin to clean up the mess as Jesse comes around and pounds on his back. He nods to show he's okay and Jesse returns to his seat. Of all the things Drew thought Jesse might answer, that was not one. Across the table, Jesse is watching him in silence; eyes dark and guarded. The waitress appears and sets Jesse's brownie in front of him, but he doesn't move.

"Drew?" his voice is quiet and concerned, his hands are under the table and Drew forces himself to resist the urge to look and see if he is holding his keychain. Instead, he reaches out his good hand, waits, and after a moment Jesse places his own in it.

"Will you take care of me, Jess?" he asks, somehow sure that Jesse will understand the double entendre. Jesse nods, a faint pink blush staining his cheeks. "Eat your brownie and let's go home."

* * *

40

Jesse pays the bill and waits while Drew asks the waitress if she would mind calling them a cab. Drew smiles as he guides Jesse out to wait in the sun. Resting back against him, Jesse traces a gentle line from the tips of Drew's fingers to the edge of the plaster, just below the middle joints. When Drew wraps his good arm around Jesse's waist, he closes his eyes and enjoys the sun on his face comforted by the solid feel of Drew's chest against his back.

Sunday streets are quiet, and it only takes ten minutes for the cab to find their building. Jesse watches Drew pay the driver, then takes the hand held out to him with a shaky smile. Looks at his feet as they walk, too shy for the first time in a long time to look at Drew. Some of it is fear – what if he can't do this? What if he's bad at it and Drew doesn't enjoy it and stops loving him? What if he does it wrong and hurts Drew? That idea makes his stomach turn in on itself. Not all that feeling is fear though, some of it is excitement. Jesse likes the idea of being able to make Drew feels how he feels, of being able to take care of Drew the way he takes care of Jesse. Not just the sex – although thinking of that sends a frisson down Jesse's back – but the way Drew makes him feel when he holds him and talks to him with gentle whispers. The way he makes him feel loved and protected.

Drew taps the door code into the keypad and the doors make a swishing sound as they open, then close behind them; Jesse presses the button for the lift, still holding Drew's hand, fingers interlaced. It seems to take forever to get to their floor, walk to their apartment, and close the door behind them. The idea that this is their apartment sends another little thrill through Jesse and he heaves a happy sigh as he double checks the cushions, goes to the bedroom and checks the pillows, runs his fingers over Wicket. Finally, he bends and scoops up Scamp, nuzzles her head.

"Hey, little girl. We're home, did you miss us?"

"Missed you, maybe," Drew says with a snort. "I don't think she even remembers I exist."

"Of course she does," Jesse says, "she's little but she loves big."

"Yeah?" Drew runs his thumb Jesse's cheekbone, curling his fingers under the younger man's jaw and smiling at him.

"Yeah," Jesse whispers and steps back, cradling Scamp in his arms. "I can't play with you now, Scamp. I need you to be a good girl and we'll play later, I promise."

He puts her in her cat cave and stands there for a moment, smoothing her fur. When she purrs, he withdraws his hand and turns to face Drew, mouth dry, and heart pounding. Takes a deep breath and goes to him, sliding his hands around Drew's waist and resting his forehead against Drew's chest.

"Jess, we don't hav ..."

"I want to." Jesse pulls his phone from his pocket and drops it on the coffee table. Drew copies him then waits, a smile playing at the corner of his mouth. Stretching up Jesse kisses the upturned corners, once, twice, three times, sighing when Drew growls and pulls him in for a real kiss. Catches Drew's bottom lip with his teeth, runs his tongue over it. He can feel the beat of Drew's heart against his chest and covers the spot with his hand. Looks up at Drew, shy and unsure. "We should go to the bedroom."

Drew doesn't move, and it takes Jesse a second to realize he's waiting for him. He holds his hand out and when Drew takes it, takes a hesitant step, then straightens his shoulders and leads him to the bedroom. Once there he presses Drew to the edge of the bed, turns, and shuts the door.

Turning back, he toes off his shoes and socks, then kneels. Takes his time to undo Drew's shoelaces, remove his shoes and socks. As he sits, he runs his hands up the length of Drew's legs, denim rough beneath his skin. When he gets to his thighs, he curls his fingers, so he's drawing long scratches through the fabric; smiles when Drew shivers. He moves past the obvious bulge in Drew's jeans, smiles again when Drew groans in frustration. Slips each button out of its button hole and takes Drew's shirt off, being careful not tear it over the plaster cast.

"Move back." He watches Drew inch back on the bed, until his back rests against the headboard. Tugs his tee-shirt over his head and drops it at his feet. Unbuckles his belt and the zipper of his own jeans and steps out of them; takes off his boxers and waits, eyes on the ground, heart beat thudding in his ears.

"Jess?" Drew's voice is gentle, concerned, and Jesse lifts his eyes. He smiles and tilts his head to one side. Drew holds his arms open toward him. "Come here. Please."

Jesse crawls over the mattress until he's kneeling between Drew's thighs, leans forward and kisses him, lets Drew wrap his arms around him. Trembling fingers trace circles around Drew's nipple, close into a light pinch when Drew's tongue licks across his mouth until he opens it and meets it with his own. Explores Drew's mouth, losing himself in the soft sounds he's able to coax out him and the way Drew's skin pebbles into gooseflesh under his touch.

His hand drifts down to Drew's belt buckle and tugs it undone. Makes short work of the button fly and sits back enough to pull the garments off and out of the way. Returns to the safety that is Drew's mouth and kisses him again, easing Drew back on the bed at the same time.

When Drew is finally laying on his back, Jesse sits back on his heels and lets himself just look. He reaches out and takes Drew's glasses off, places them on the bedside table, then runs his fingers along the fingertips on Drew's broken hand again, the way he had earlier. Carefully, he trails his hand over the plaster.

"I hate that you're hurt," he says as he moves on to the skin of Drew's bicep. Rolls the muscle under his fingers. "You're really strong. I feel safe when you hold me."

"Jess..." It's barely a sound, floating on breath.

"I like the sounds you make when I touch you," Jesse continues and drags his fingers over Drew's collar bone and up to his ear. "I like how your skin feels."

Drew moans and slides his hand up Jesse's thigh; brushes his fingers over Jesse's cock.

"Can I touch you darlin'?" he asks, eyes never leaving Jesse's face.

"Yes, but only a little bit. If you touch too much, I ... I won't be able to wait, and I want to."

When Drew pulls him down into a kiss, Jesse refuses give up control. Knows that Drew will take over if he lets him. Part of him wants to let him, the part of him that loves the way Drew strokes and licks and kisses and grinds away everything but pleasure and leaves him shattered and whole all at once. But he wants to give that to Drew this time, not take it. Drew's fingers on his cock are distracting and Jesse moans into the kiss, giving into the feeling for a second then rolling to the side, out of reach, ignoring Drew's protest.

Dipping his head, he nips a line down Drew's throat to his nipple and sucks the nub until it's hard. Drew whimpers and arches into the sensation. Jesse moves to the other nipple, repeating the action until Drew groans in frustration then moves down the smooth skin of his belly, skimming his fingers over jutting hipbones, pressing his thumbs into the flesh below.

"Jess," Drew whines. Jesse looks up; Drew's shoulders are off the bed, chocolate eyes blown wide and almost black with want. He smiles up at him, then leans down to run his tongue down from Drew's navel to the crease of his groin. Nuzzles the skin and breathes in the warm, salty smell. Drew moans. "Jess, oh god, don't tease."

Without warning, Jesse licks the length of Drew's cock, smiling at the rough groan from above him. He rubs the flat of his tongue back and forth over the dampness at the head before closing his mouth around it and sucking gently. Drew hisses and jerks his hips up, fingers of his uninjured hand pulling at Jesse's short hair.

Jesse wriggles back and uses his shoulders to nudge Drew's thighs apart. He runs his tongue over each ball in turn, grazing the skin with his teeth enough to make Drew catch his breath and tighten his muscles. Lifting on to his knees he rubs his thumb down over Drew's balls, over the stretch of skin of his perineum, and back up; smiles at the sound Drew makes. Leans over Drew to reach for the bottle on the bedside table and moans when his hardness rubs against Drew's.

He fumbles the bottle and Drew catches it and sets it on his chest. Closes his hand over Jesse's.

"Relax darlin, you're doing fine," he whispers, and Jesse lets go of a shuddering breath he didn't realize he was holding. When Drew places his hands on his hips, the rough feel of the plaster against his skin sends a tremor through him and he dips his head to kiss and bite at the pulse he can see beating in Drew's throat, until he feels as much as hears the low groan in response.

He squirts cool liquid over his fingers and reaches down. He has never done this, not with the men who picked him up in clubs, not with himself, not with Drew, and he watches Drew's face closely for any sign he's doing something wrong. Something that could hurt. Traces circles around the tight ring, fascinated by the change in Drew's breathing and the way skin and muscle smooth and relax a little more with each circle. Biting his lip, he presses the tip of his finger against it, until he's able to slide it in; concentrating on what he's doing makes it easier to control his own desire, to ignore the urgent heat in his own groin.

Drew wriggles beneath him, rocking down against his hand, and Jesse tries to think about what Drew does to him usually. He crooks his finger a little and feels a smooth lump and when Drew cries out, lifting his hips up hard and fast, knows he's found that spot Drew always finds in him. The one that sends electricity sparking through his body; pleased, he rubs it again.

"Jess, oh God," Drew pants, "feels good. More."

Nodding, Jesse adds a finger and rubs again. This time Drew's reaction sounds like a sob and Jesse closes his eyes, lets himself enjoy the feel and sound of him. Drew's left-hand slips around to dig into the flesh of Jesse's buttock, the fingertips of his right-hand brush over his flank.

"Jess, please I need to feel you," Drew whispers. "Please, darlin', please, I want to feel you inside me."

Swallowing with difficulty and hoping he doesn't look as scared as he feels, Jesses withdraws his fingers, settles back on his heels and flips open the bottle of lube again. Spreads some over himself, eyes fluttering shut as he fights the urge to just keep going to relieve the pressure. When he feels Drew move his hand away, he opens his eyes again and looks down at him.

"Drew..." he can hear the tears that are threatening in his voice.

"It's okay, we don't have to rush, we can try again later," Drew smooths his palm over Jesse's cheek and he leans into the touch. Shakes his head.

"What if I hurt you?" he whispers.

"You won't darlin'," Drew says. "You'll never hurt me, I know that."

214

Reassured, Jesse eases back, guiding himself and rubbing the head of his cock against Drew before pressing in. For a moment there's resistance, then he feels Drew's body relax beneath him and he pushes forward. Stops again, unsure. Drew gives a sharp jerk up and Jesse gasps as he is encased in smooth, tight, heat. The sensation is nothing he has ever experienced and for a moment he doesn't move, just lets his body adjust and his mind try to cope. Drew rolls his hips up again, gentler this time and Jesse moans. It feels so good. All of it. He can smell, taste, and feel Drew all over him. Is this what Drew feels when he's inside Jesse? Groaning and fighting sensory overwhelm, Jesse stretches out along the length of Drew's body, hands curling up around his shoulders and buries his head in the crook of Drew's neck, breath hot and rapid on Drew's skin. Drew. Drew. Drew. He repeats the name over and over, setting a rhythm with it as he begins to move.

Drew lifts his legs and wraps them around Jesse's hips and the moan he makes at the change of angle pulls Jesse from his daze. He lets go of Drew's shoulders and presses up on to his hands. He can feel Drew's cock, hard and leaking, trapped between their bellies. Thrusts forward as hard as he can and is rewarded with a ragged groan from Drew whose hands come to settle either side of his head on the pillow. Jesse places his own on top of them, palm to palm on the left, palm to plaster on the right.

"You feel so good, Drew," he murmurs. "Hot and tight and ..."

Drew cuts him off by turning his head and nipping at Jesse's inner elbow.

"Stop thinking and love me," he orders.

"I do love you," Jesse says. "I love everything. I love how you feel. Inside."

"Oh God," Drew moans, tightening his legs around Jesse's waist.

Jesse knows he can't take much more of this; his senses are close to overload. Taking his weight on one hand, he slides the other between them, so he can stroke Drew's cock in time with his thrusts. At the first touch, Drew flexes his muscles around Jesse and he whimpers, fighting his climax. Pulls back until only the head of his cock is still inside the tight heat, takes a breath and slams back in; he's rewarded with a long, low moan from Drew, his eyes scrunching closed in pleasure. He knows that sound and that look well, knows they mean Drew is close to coming and the thought sends an electric jolt through him, making his balls tighten.

"Drew," he whispers, "I can't hold on. I can't."

In reply, Drew bucks up into Jesse's fist and tightens his muscles around him. Jesse cries out, surging forward, as wave after wave of sensation breaks over him; he couldn't stop the orgasm if he wanted to and oh God, he doesn't want to. He grinds down hard into Drew, hips stuttering, teeth biting through his own bottom lip and drawing beads of blood. From a distance Drew's calling his name and his cock pulses as he comes between them.

Then everything fades to darkness.

When he opens his eyes, his head is resting on Drew's shoulder and Drew is rubbing small circles on his back. He lifts up, reluctant to move and let go of the feeling.

"Welcome back." Drew smiles.

"I ...I.." Jesse stutters, not knowing what to say. He thinks he passed out, maybe, a little. It can't have been for long, he's still inside Drew, and his hand is still wrapped loosely around Drew's softening cock.

"Shhhh, it's okay." Drew kisses him and Jesse can't help the shiver that runs through him.

Gingerly, Jesse withdraws and lays down next to him, head on Drew's bicep, hand on his chest.

"Did I faint?"

"It's okay, you weren't out for long, about a minute maybe," Drew tells him.

"Oh, okay."

"Must have been good," Drew teases and Jesse turns his burning face to hide against Drew's chest.

"Thank you," he whispers against the warm, damp skin beneath his cheek.

"What are you thanking me for, darlin'?"

"Letting me take care of you," Jesse says. "And it *was* good. Really, really good."

"I'm glad," Drew presses a kiss against his head and Jesse stretches up so he can look at him.

"Was ... was ... it okay for you?" he asks, scared of the answer.

Drew smiles.

"Do you remember the very first time you came back here? Not when I asked you out but when we first went to dinner? What you said to me? About how you didn't think you were very good at sex?"

"Mmmhmmm," Jesse mumbles, worry sparking in his eyes.

"You were wrong Jess. You're very good. Very, very good."

"Oh." Then because he's still not sure of himself, "does that mean..."

"Yeah that's what it means."

* * *

Drew closes his eyes and breathes deeply. He wasn't lying, it had been very good. Jesse moves against him, trying to get comfortable and he's filled with a rush of love. He tightens his hold.

"I love you," he whispers. He feels Jesse's smile against his skin and repeats the words.

"I love you too." Jesse draws light circles over Drew's chest. He tenses, and Drew opens his eyes, waiting for whatever comes next. "I never had anyone to love before. Not someone of my own. I have mom and dad but it's different." Drew nods to show he understands what Jesse is trying to say. "You're mine, aren't you Drew?"

"Yeah Jess," he whispers, "I'm yours. And you're mine."

Jesse nestles against him again and he reaches his hand up to stroke Drew's hair.

"I have work to do," Drew says with reluctance, grinning at the mewl of disapproval from by his chest. "I don't really want to either darlin', but it's got to be done."

"Stay here," Jesse pleads.

Drew considers for a moment.

"How about this," he moves Jesse so he can see his face, "what if we clean up and make some tea, and I bring my work back here? I can work while you watch a movie."

"In bed?" Jesse's face lights up. "We could have a picnic."

"Yeah," Drew laughs, "but I have to work too." He leans his forehead against Jesses. "And no Captain Jack."

Jesse pouts.

"Nu uh, you're going to give me a complex if you watch him when we're in bed," Drew says.

"I love you way more than Captain Jack."

"Good, now come on. We're not having picnics or watching movies until we clean up. We're all sticky."

"Well you made us all sticky," Jesse says but Drew can see that under the laughter there's still a need for reassurance. He lands a quick kiss on the end of Jesse's nose.

"Well you made me make us all sticky, darlin', now move that cute butt to the bathroom."

Drew keeps his plaster out of the way as he lets Jesse smooth shower gel over them both before using the hand-held shower to rinse them off. A towel wound around his hips, he kneels on the bathmat, head hung over the tub edge as Jesse washes his hair, fingers gentle and loving as they move through the sweaty tangles. When he stands to dry it off, he feels better than he has all weekend despite the pain in his hand.

Jesse disappears and returns with a clean tee-shirt and sweat pants for Drew, his own already low on his hips.

"Where's your shirt?" Drew asks with a raised eyebrow and is amused when a light blush creeps over Jesse's face.

"I want to be able to feel you against my skin."

Drew slings his arm around Jesse's shoulder.

"Come on, let's make that picnic."

* * *

Drew takes a pill with his tea and eats a sandwich before the pain eases back enough for him to pick up his pen. Jesse chooses *Iron Man* and is chuckling at Tony Stark's wisecracks, hip pressed against Drew's, one hand resting on his thigh. Scamp has ventured down from her cave, shared Jesse's sandwiches despite Drew's best efforts to stop them, and is now curled up on Jesse's feet, eyes squinted shut, purring.

The film still has ten minutes to run when Drew finishes and pushes graded papers and his laptop on to the night table. He pulls Jesse against his chest and settles to watch the last few scenes, feeling contented and drowsy.

As the credits roll, Jesse's hand slips under his t-shirt, rubbing his fingers across the skin of Drew's belly. He hums in pleasure at the sensation, lets his eyes close and feels Jesse's lips on his own. Smiles against the kiss. When the kiss becomes more insistent he opens his eyes.

"Jess," he whispers.

This time Jesse isn't as nervous and lets Drew direct him. Their movements are slow and languid until they're both spent and panting. Drew pulls Jesse in against him, both arms tight around him, cheek on his head.

"Mine," Jesse whispers, voice low and sleepy.

"Yours," Drew answers.

* * *

41

"Jody will bring me home after the staff meeting, okay?" Drew tells Jesse as they reach the pool. He's arranged to meet Jody here, so he could walk with Jesse and at least see him get in the pool.

"Yes, you said that already. Twice." Jesse shoulders the door open, holding it so Drew can go through.

"Want me to pick up pizza?"

Jesse shakes his head.

"It's not Tuesday. I'll make dinner."

"You sure?"

Drew hears the exasperation in Jesse's sigh as he follows him into the changing room.

"Yes, I'm sure."

He sits down on the bench while Jesse pulls off his sweat pants, folds them and puts them in his back pack. A frown flits across his features and his tongue appears in the corner of his mouth.

"Jess?"

"I can't decide." Jesse shoves his things in a free locker.

"On Pizza? We can have pizza if you w..."

"No," Jesse shakes his head and Drew can hear the exasperation again. "Pizza is for Tuesday night. Or weekends."

"Then what can't you decide on, darlin'?"

"On what I like better."

It's Monday morning and he hasn't had nearly enough coffee to deal with Jesse being cryptic.

"What?"

"If I like it better when you top, or I do," Jesse says and slips his goggles over his head to hang around his neck.

Oh God. Thankfully the only other people in the changing room are under the shower and can't hear them. Drew glances around them, then leans forward and risks a quick kiss on Jesse's lips.

"You're a dork," he says, steering Jesse out toward the pool. "And you need a filter."

"Oh," Jesse looks confused. "It's just I ..."

"Jess, you don't have to choose, you can like both."

Jesse stops walking and looks at him.

"Really?"

Oh. My. God.

"Yes, really. It's called switching and the swimming pool isn't the place to be talking about it, Jesse." Aside from any number of people who could overhear, it's giving Drew ideas that are not welcome an hour before school.

"Do you like both?"

Drew closes his eyes and groans.

"With you, I do, now can you please just get in the pool, so I can go and wait for Jody outside?"

"Okay," Jesse smiles, "I love you."

"I love you too, you dork. I'll see you tonight."

He watches as Jesse gets in the water, waves to him, then goes to wait for Jody. At the door he turns around just in time to see Jesse kick off and begin his steady crawl down the lane.

* * *

"Tell me, Nigel," Drew says through gritted teeth, "what the hell were you doing inviting him in the first place?"

The Assistant Principal looks toward Barry Reynolds, sees there is no help forthcoming, and puffs his chest out.

"David has done what was required of him under the terms of the court order and deserves a second chance ..."

"David was drunk so I'm not entirely sure he has done what was asked of him and a second chance to what? Beat me up again? Insult my partner?"

"Do I need to remind you, Drew, that you threw the punch?" Chisolm retorts. Drew holds his hand up and a little thrill of satisfaction runs through him when the man drops his eyes.

"No, you don't. I'm well aware of it, believe me. And you were well aware I was taking Jesse with me on Friday night and that David had no place being there."

"Well that is something that I think requires discussion too," Chisolm says, tone oily with contempt. Drew narrows his eyes and waits. "This young man you are having this relationship with, is he even competent to give consent?"

"That's enough, Nigel," Reynolds snaps, bringing his hand down hard on his desktop. Drew is on his feet, leaning over the Assistant Principal, sweat beading his forehead as rage courses through him.

"I'm going to pretend you did not fucking say that," he growls.

"Drew, I'll handle this. Go to class ..." Barry begins.

"He's twenty-seven years old and is a damned sight more competent ..."

"Drew, please don't make me ask you to take the day off," Barry steps around the edge of his desk. The Hawaiian shirt and shorts have been replaced by a navy suit and tie that he has already tugged loose. "Go to class."

Swallowing the string of expletives he wants to fling at Nigel Chisolm, Drew gives a curt nod, picks up his bag, and stalks from the room, door slamming behind him. There's a flurry of activity from the office staff as he makes his way out to the corridor. Maggie, Barry's secretary offers him a small smile but he's too angry to return it and is half way down the corridor when catches up with him.

"So, what happened?" she asked.

"Chisolm proved he's a prick," Drew snaps. He glances at his watch, they still have fifteen minutes until home room begins. "I need coffee."

"Come on," Jody says, snapping her bright orange suspenders. "I've got what you need in my office."

* * *

"Well you know the guy's a moron," she says when Drew finishes explaining. She hands him his coffee.

"That was beyond moronic, Jody. I laid charges against that guy and he asked him back here for the staff barbeque? What the fuck for? So he could finish what he started?"

"Hey, I'm on your side remember." Jody holds her hands up in surrender.

Drew sighs and nods, pinches the bridge of his nose, then runs his hand through his hair. It's loose on his shoulders this morning instead of in his trademark ponytail and he's aware of how long it is. It had just been too hard to deal with one handed earlier and he wonders if the time has come to go short.

"I know, I'm sorry. I just can't believe he did that. Or said that." He looks at the clock on Jody's wall and blanches. "Shit, I'm going to be late to home room, I have to go."

Hefting his bag on his shoulder, he gulps his coffee.

"No, take it with you. Just bring the cup back later. It's my favorite."

Drew's at his desk before he looks down at the mug and sees it has Captain Jack on it. Scowling, he sets it in the tray on the corner of his desk to return later. Honestly, what does that guy have that a high school English teacher doesn't?

* * *

Drew is taking a pill with a glass of water and turning the kitchen light off when his cell phone rings. He glances at the screen, sees the words *Unknown Number* and lets it go to voicemail. If it's important, they'll leave a message. He flicks the light off and goes to the bedroom.

Jesse is sitting up in bed with Scamp on his lap and looks up when Drew comes in.

"Your phone rang."

One of the many things Drew now labels "Jesse speak" is his tendency to state a fact rather than ask questions. "Your phone rang" rather than "who was calling at ten o'clock at night?" or "someone was at the door" rather than "who was there?" And best of all "spaghetti is your favorite" instead of "would you like spaghetti?" These situations, Drew and Martin have surmised, are ones in which Jesse is not really seeking new information. He knows it's socially accepted to ask these things, but since he already knows someone was on the phone or at the door and that Drew will tell him who it was – and since spaghetti is his favorite it's obvious, to Jesse at least, that he wants it – he feels no need to pose a question. These scenarios are different to those that will give him new information. Questions like "do you think you'll love me for a long time?" or "how do you like to be touched?" or "do you like switching?"

Drew takes his glasses off and puts them on the night table. He glances at the phone screen; no messages.

"It was probably a telemarketer or a wrong number." He swings his legs on to the bed. Jesse nods and scratches Scamp's belly, gives her tail a gentle tug.

"Is your hand sore?" he asks.

"A little, but not as bad as it was," he's not lying this time, "and I took a pill."

Drew waits while Jesse runs his hand over Wicket's head, then turns the lamp off; holds his arm open so Jesse can cuddle in. He hears Scamp get up and make her way to the pillow.

"I need a haircut," he says.

"Not short though. Just a little bit."

"If you have your way I'm going to look like Rapunzel."

There's a small giggle in the dark.

"That would be cool. Especially like Disney's Rapunzel and you could have a lizard. We have some at the shop."

"We are not getting a lizard. You and Scamp are quite enough for me." Drew rubs a lazy hand over Jesse's back. "I promise I'll just get a trim."

"Good."

Silence settles over them, broken only by the steady sound of Scamp purring.

"I decided," Jesse's voice makes Drew jump. He had been dozing off, just sinking into sleep.

"Huh?"

"I decided what I like better."

Drew closes his eyes and fights the urge to laugh. Jesse is like a terrier when he gets hold of an idea. He just won't let it go, but Drew knows this is serious for him so bites his tongue and bumps Jesse's hip with his own.

"I like bottoming best but sometimes I want to top."

Drew smiles into the darkness.

"That's good Jess, because I think that I like topping better but sometimes I want to bottom."

Jesse shifts, lifting his head, then Drew feels warm breath on his cheek, followed by a kiss.

"But tonight, I want to just cuddle," Jesse whispers as he lays back down.

"Works for me, darlin'."

Within seconds both are sound asleep.

* * *

42

Jesse hands Mr Greenwold a carton of fish food from the top of the cupboard and backs down off the step ladder. Marcus is out in the store, leaning on the counter and avoiding doing any work as usual. He's lazy and he's scared of nearly all the animals, including the hamsters, but at least having him means Jesse gets to take some time off now. That he can sometimes have Saturdays off, even if it does mean he has to spend Monday mornings cleaning the store and settling the animals down.

"When does Drew's cast come off?" Mr Greenwold asks as they start labelling the pots of granules. Mr Greenwold sets both ticketing guns to the right price and hands one to Jesse.

"Next Friday. It's his birthday."

"Yes, you told me. Have you decided what to get him yet?"

Jesse sighs. The question of Drew's birthday present has been driving him crazy for weeks. He's never had to buy anything for anyone before except Mom and Dad and Mr Greenwold. Mom and Dad always help him buy their presents and one of them helps him with Mr Greenwold, but usually he has some idea what to get them. Jesse has no idea what he's supposed to get a boyfriend. Drew never takes his Key of Erebor pendant off, not even in the shower, but Jesse doesn't know if he can get him more jewelry or not. Clothes are boring, and he doesn't really like things like games and Lego the way Jesse does, so that's no good either. They have all the movies and music they like, and he doesn't like cooking.

"No, not yet," he says.

Marcus appears in the doorway, eyes like saucers.

"There's someone asking for you Jesse," he says in a surprised voice. "A woman."

Jesse rolls his eyes; he might be the one who is ... challenged... but you'd think it was Marcus some days.

"I have friends who are women, Marcus," he says. He turns toward Mr Greenwold. "It's Jody, she's going to help me find Drew a present. Can I go to lunch?"

Mr Greenwold flaps a hand at him.

"Go on and get. Take your time," he says. "Marcus here can help with the pricing."

Marcus's face suggests he is as enthusiastic about that idea as he is about cleaning out the rat cages. Jesse hands him his ticketing gun, thanks Mr Greenwold, and gets his jacket. Checks his pockets for his wallet, phone, and mini Wicket.

"Hi Jesse," Jody says, hugging him tight. "How are you?"

"I'm good Jody, how are you?" Jody's wearing a knee length pinafore dress over long stripy socks and Doc Martens. There are pictures of the bright yellow Pokémon, Pikachu, on the dress and Jesse grins. "Pika, Pika."

"You got that right, now let's get a sandwich and then go shopping."

Linking her arm through his, she lets him lead her out to the street. Two stores down is a deli and they stop and buy sandwiches and water. Jody waits while Jesse checks the number of things in his sandwich, discarding the lettuce leaf to get the numbers right.

"Not a rabbit food fan huh?" she asks. When he looks confused, she adds "you know, rabbits eat lettuce, so rabbit food."

"Drew always make me eat it. He makes me throw out a cheese slice, but I like cheese better than lettuce."

"Damned right. Don't worry your secret is safe with me. So, do you have anything in mind?"

Jesse blushes.

"Sort of but I don't know if it's possible." He sits down on a bench, waits for her to sit next to him, and fishes in his pocket for his cell phone, thumbs the screen open, and finds the web browser icon. Taps it. An image fills the screen and he tilts it toward Jody.

"T S Eliot, Old Possum's Book of Practical Cats? That's a brilliant idea, Jesse, what made you think of that?"

He takes a bite of his sandwich, chews while he thinks.

"I googled books about cats," he admits, "and I saw someone said that this one is famous and that its poems. That they're..." he scrolls the page on his phone up until words appear, "w.... whi....m..si..ca..l?"

Glances at Jody hopefully. She nods and rubs his shoulder.

"Good work, Jesse. Whimsical. It means kind of sweet and funny and silly."

Jesse brightens.

"Do you think he'll like that?"

Jody puts her sandwich on the bench between them and gets her own phone out. Taps on the screen while she speaks.

"I think he'll love it and if you give me a minute, I'll just see if we can...." Jody's voice trails off as she studies the screen then smiles, tips it toward Jesse but he shakes his head. It's too small and the glare of the white background hurts his eyes.

"There's an early print edition up on eBay for not much more than the pulp paperback. I have an account, it would be here by Monday."

Jesse nods.

"Would he like that? An early, what did you call it?"

"Early print edition. Yeah, he'd like that."

"Can you get it and tell me how much?"

Jody taps the screen several times, then looks up triumphant.

"Done. Twenty-five dollars with postage and packaging."

"Can I give you cash?" Jesse asks.

"Sure can. Now that takes care of the public present, what are you going to give him as a private present?"

Confused, Jesse stares at her, sandwich forgotten. What on earth does she mean by a private present? Jody's eyes light up and she scoots closer to him, pats his knee.

"What's something you would like to give him that's just for him to see, nobody else. Maybe he'll unwrap it at home. In the bedroom."

Jesse frowns. It was hard enough thinking of the book about the cats and now Jody wants him to find another one for Drew to unwrap at home. She giggles and bumps his shoulder.

"Maybe instead of paper, it's under your clothes?"

Jesse blinks, face blank. Jody takes his hand and pulls him to his feet.

"Come on, let's go do some real shopping."

* * *

Jesse doesn't know where to look. There's underwear and books and DVDs ... and ... *things* everywhere in this shop. Things that look like ... like... he tugs on Jody's sleeve.

"Jody, why are we here?"

"It's okay buddy, my friend Tina is going to take care of everything." She studies him for a moment with a grin. "Don't worry about the toys and things, we're not here for that. You've never been in a sex shop before?"

Jesse shakes his head. Some of the ... toys... he's seen online in videos, but he's never actually seen close up. He wonders if Drew would like one but doesn't have the courage to ask Jody. Wonders how he would ask Drew, if Drew knows how to use them. If he likes them. Just being in here is making him feel ... weird.

A tall, slender girl with long pink hair, a ring in her lip, and long fluttery lashes, appears and hugs Jody.

"Tina," Jody says, "you remember my friend Drew, the teacher?"

"The one with the whole cute professor thing going on? Glasses? Ponytail?"

"That's Drew. Well it's his birthday next Friday and this is his boyfriend, Jesse, and we are here to find him something suitable to wear. Something that might make a nice little birthday surprise."

"I'm giving him a book about cats." Jesse steals a furtive glance at Tina and the lashes that look like they are made from Scamp's fur.

"Very cool, very cool. I like cats," Tina says, then turns back to Jody. "What are we thinking?"

"I'm thinking simple, classic, not feminine – don't think bows and frills quite do it for Drew somehow."

Something in Jesse's head seems to whir and click and he tugs on Jody's sleeve again.

"He likes my overalls."

"What?"

"My overalls. He likes them. When I wear them, he gets really um ...?" Jesse scratches his head searching for the right word, "Excited? Is that the right word?"

He sees an amused look pass between the two women and puts his hand in his pocket to find mini-Wicket.

"Excited is exactly the right word, Jesse," Jody reassures him.

"And I think I have exactly what you need," Tina says and beckons them to follow her to the counter.

* * *

Drew stretches his legs out in front of him on the bed and yawns. Rests his head against the head board and groans; it's been a long week. Thank God class is out in ten days. In the kitchen, Jesse is putting macaroni cheese on a plate because neither of them feels like going out, not even to *The Library*. Instead they're going to binge watch *Arrow* on Netflix and ...no he refuses to use the word chill. Not when that damned *Torchwood* guy is on Arrow as well.

"Did you and Jody have fun today?" he calls, reaching for the chopstick on the night table and sliding it down inside the plaster on his arm. Next Friday cannot get here fast enough in Drew's opinion. It looks as though he'll avoid surgery, at least for now, and he's grateful for that. He is. But oh god, he thinks as he tries to get at the itch on the underside of his wrist with the chopstick, twisting his wrist in an effort to make contact with the stick, he wants this damned thing off.

"You're not supposed to move your hand like that." Jesse puts the tray down and climbs on the bed next to him.

"It itches."

"The doctor said you could hurt it more and have to go to hospital if you twist it like that."

"I know what the doctor said, and he doesn't have to live with the damned itching."

Jesse holds a glass of wine out to Drew and waits. Drew sighs and takes the glass.

"I don't want you to go to hospital," Jesse says, not moving.

"I know, neither do I. I'm sorry, I'm just grouchy." Drew sips his wine and repeats his earlier question. "You have fun with Jody?"

He knows they went shopping for a birthday present for him and he's not sure if he should worry or be pleased. Especially when he sees Jesse's face: his cheeks are scarlet, eyes darting around the room.

"Jess? What did you do?" Worried. He's definitely going to go with worried.

"Uh nothing. It's a surprise. A secret and I can't tell you until your birthday." Jesse reaches for his plate and Drew relaxes. Drew purses his lips and thinks for a moment; Jesse isn't good with secrets so that is most likely what is bothering him. Except, Drew reminds himself, he'd been with Jody and Jody can be trouble when it comes to birthday presents. One year she had given him a chocolate dildo. Which would have been fine had he not opened it in front of his parents.

Before he can say anything, his phone rings making them both jump. It's another *Unknown Number* and he swears at the screen before thumbing the mute button.

"That's the third one today," he says. "You have any?"

Jesse shakes his head. Drew has been getting several calls a day from unknown numbers that leave no message even though they go through to voice mail each time. Over the past three days they've started happening to Jesse as well.

"I'll call the cell company in the morning and get them to sort it out," Drew says and picks up his plate, then puts it down and grabs the chopstick again. "Damn it. God I can't wait for next Friday."

Without a word, Jesse turns the television on.

* * *

43

Jesse stares at his reflection. The fabric is soft, really soft, and it feels nice against his skin; he wonders if Drew will like it. He hopes Jody was right when she said he would ... the shower turns off and Jesse scrambles to grab his good black jeans off the bed. Pulls them on and is tucking in his white shirt when Drew appears, naked, hair dripping on to the towel hung over his shoulders.

"Wow," Drew says looking him over from head to toe.

Jesse blushes and hunts for his shoes. Jody said he doesn't need to wear his suit, but he needs to look good since his clothes are the wrapping paper for Drew's surprise. Drew likes it when he dresses up, Jesse knows, and if his surprise makes Drew as happy as Jody seems to think it will, then he, Jesse, will be happy. Besides, the fabric feels really nice against his skin.

"How does your hand feel?" he asks, trying to think about something else. "Your phone rang."

"Yeah?" Drew is hunting in his drawer for clean underwear and socks. He picks up his phone, finds his glasses and puts them on, reads the screen and sighs. "Unknown again. I think I'm going to have to change my number."

Jesse jerks his head up, worry creeping across his face.

"It's okay." Drew smiles at him in the mirror. "I must be on someone's database and they want to sell me something."

Jesse sits on the bed, clutching Wicket to his chest and watches Drew dress. He's s worried about Drew's hand. The doctor said the bones are fragile now and if he hurts it again he'll need surgery.

"I can hear you thinking, Jess." Drew buttons his own shirt, leaving it out over his jeans. When he sits on the bed to put his socks on, Jesse leans his head on his shoulder.

"Is your hand okay?" he asks again.

"My hand is just fine," Drew puts his arm around his shoulders, "I'll prove it later."

Jesse let's Drew kiss him, fingers curling into Wicket's fur as the fabric around his hips shifts. He breaks the kiss and rests his head on Drew's shoulder again.

"Stop worrying," Drew says in his ear and he nods. He'll try. "Come on let's go."

* * *

On Sunday they're going to Drew's parents for a family birthday lunch and Drew's mom has even invited Jesse's parents to join them, something Jesse is excited about. All his favorite people will be there except Jody so they're having dinner with her tonight. She's already waiting at the door of the restaurant when they arrive and Jesse waves to her from the car window while Drew parks. She's wearing a bright red dress with high heels and a headband with cat ears and reminds Jesse of Minnie Mouse.

There's a bag at Jody's feet and Jesse knows the presents he chose for Drew are inside with Jody's. He takes Drew's hand when he holds it out and blushes when Jody wolf whistles at them

"Holy shit, look at you two. You look like you should be on Vogue or something." She hands the bag to Jesse to carry, then wiggles in between them, linking her arms through theirs.

"You look like Minnie Mouse," Jesse says and when Drew laughs, protests, "I like Minnie Mouse. She's cute."

"Yeah, don't be hating on Minnie," Jody says.

The waitress shows them to their table and tells them she'll be back in just a moment for their drink orders. There's a bottle of champagne in the fridge at home for later, Jesse saw Drew put it in there. A shiver runs up his back thinking about later and when Drew raises an eyebrow, Jesse shakes his head to tell him it's nothing.

"How does it feel having your hand back?" Jody asks after the waitress leaves with the wine order.

"Fucking fantastic." Drew winks at Jesse. "I could finally wash my hair properly."

"And pee without complaining about using the wrong hand," Jesse adds making Jody cackle with laughter.

"Uh thanks for sharing, Jess," Drew says scratching an eyebrow with one finger and looking uncomfortable.

"Well it's true, you did. I thought you were going to ask me to hold it, you got so bad."

"Filter darlin'," Drew says tapping Jesse's foot with his own but smiling so Jesse knows he's not upset. "There's chicken stuffed with brie, Jess. You'd like that."

"What are you having?"

"I think that's what I'm having. It has potato and salad with it"

"Will you ask them to do my salad in a dish?" Jesse's keeps his voice down; this restaurant is fancier than the ones they usually go to, fancier even than the one

Drew took him to on their first date, and he's not used to having someone else with them.

"In a dish. With the right number of things in it. Don't worry sweetheart, I've got it covered."

The waitress arrives with a bottle of wine, pours it, and leaves again to let them make their choices.

"What are you going to have, Jody?" Jesse asks.

"I'm thinking of the rabbit," she says, and Jesse can't help the sound that escapes him. Jody looks at him, bewildered. "No?"

"The store mascot is a rabbit," Drew explains, reaching out to rub Jesse's hand.

"Called Sniffles," Jesse adds.

"Pork belly it is." Jody gulps her wine. Jesse gives her a grateful smile and she winks back.

* * *

The waitress clears away the dishes and Drew leans back in his chair with a smile. The food was as good as Bronny had said it would be, Jody has been as funny as she always is, and Jesse ... Drew's not had so much to drink that he can't drive but he's had sufficient that words like adorable are the first he thinks of. Jesse seems happy tonight and a happy Jesse means a playful Jesse and a playful Jesse is Drew's favorite thing in the world he's decided. He reaches over and squeezes Jesse's hand, grateful to no longer be trapped in the hateful plaster, even if he does have a support brace at home that the orthopedic surgeon has assured him he's going to use.

"What does a guy have to do around here to get birthday presents?" he asks. Jody looks at Jesse who is all but bouncing in his seat and nods. She signals the waitress and reaches under the table for the bag of gifts. Just as she's about to reach into it, Drew's phone chimes and he groans.

"Oh, for God's sake," he mutters looking at the screen.

"Drew?" Jesse's hand, holding his wine glass, stops in midair.

"Not again?" Jody asks. "You're going to have to answer it, so you can get off their data base."

"I tried answering it a few days ago but they must have hung up just as I did it because it went dead."

Jody frowns.

"Well then you're going to have to change your number."

Drew agrees. It's a pain in the proverbial though; he'll have to let all his contacts know, change all his official documents, learn a new number. He concedes that it doesn't look like he's going to have any choice.

Just as he's about to voice his thoughts on anonymous marketers who harass cell phone owners, the waitress returns. She's carrying a dish with a small, double layer chocolate cake with candles around the edge and the words Happy Birthday Drew written on the frosting. The other diners join the waitress and Jody in singing *Happy Birthday*; Jesse looks disconcerted by the noise but hums the tune, pressed in close against Drew's side. When it's over, Drew blows out the candles while everyone cheers, and the waitress sets the cake on the table with a smile.

"Thank you," he says and steals a kiss from Jesse, hoping nobody notices or makes a scene.

"If you two are done with the smooching, I have gifts," Jody says, shaking the bag in Drew's direction. He slides a dish of cake to her and hands one to Jesse; is surprised when it's ignored.

Jody hands him a red envelope, his name written on the front in her careful, block, hand. He slides his thumb under the flap and pulls out a glossy black card that informs him in gold script that he's being wished a very happy birthday. When he opens it, there are tickets inside to the musical *Cats* being performed upstate. It's one of his favorite shows and he's been meaning to try to take Jesse to see it for ages.

"Hey thanks Jodes, these are great," he leans over the table to kiss her cheek. "Jess, this is a great show. It's all about cats, you'll love it."

"It's based on a book of poems by T S Eliot," Jody says, eyes dancing and Drew is surprised to see Jesse's face light up with the smile that always undoes him.

"Really?" he asks, eyes jumping from Jody to Drew and back again. He holds his hand out for the bag. He brings out a small, soft package first and hands it to Drew.

"This is from Scamp," he says in a solemn voice. Drew rolls his eyes.

"Dork." He unwraps the gift. It's a soft, black scarf for winter. "I won't catch cold this winter, with this. I'll be sure to thank her when we get home."

Jesse reaches into the bag again and brings out the other gift.

"This is from me," he says softly.

Drew peels back the tape on the edges of the paper and turns the small book over in his hands. It's an older book, an early print run by the look of things, and in near perfect condition. On the front cover a line of cats is making their way up the center toward the words T S Eliot, Old Possum's Book of Practical Cats. Drew turns to Jesse in surprise.

"Did you choose this?"

Jesse nods.

"Yes. I chose it and Jody helped me buy it off eBay."

"He already had it in mind when we met up last week," Jody says, licking frosting off the tines of her fork. "Which gave me the idea for the tickets, but I didn't tell him."

"Really? You didn't know?" he asks Jesse. Jesse blushes and ducks his head and Drew pulls him into a hug.

"I wanted to get you a book about cats and this one said it was poems and someone said they're whimsical," Jesse says, glancing toward Jody who, Drew notices, nods and smiles. "That means they're sweet and funny and silly, right?"

"Yes, it does," Drew says. "And so are you."

"Oh gross," Jody says making a gagging sound, "could you two keep it for later? At home? When I don't have to be reminded of my single status."

"You should get a cat," Jesse tells her when he's swallowed his mouthful of cake. "We have lots of kittens at work at the moment."

"Exactly what I need," Jody retorts, "to become the local crazy cat lady as well as a librarian. I don't think so. Do you have any cute guys who sell cats?"

"Well there's me, but you're a girl." Jesse digs his fork into his cakes again.

"And *you're* taken," Drew interjects.

"That only leaves Mr Greenwold and he's married. Or Marcus and ...ew....no," Jesse shudders.

"Guess I'll just have to spend the night alone with Big Lou then," Jody says, smirking at Drew who shakes his head.

"Who's Big Lou?" Jesse asks.

"Her teddy bear," Drew tells him and raises his hand for the check.

* * *

Drew hugs Jody goodbye at the door.

"Thank you," he says after kissing her cheek, "that was a great evening."

"It's not over," she says, eyes dancing.

"Huh?"

"Oh, you'll see." She turns to hug Jesse. "You guys have a great time on Sunday and bring back cake. Your mom makes the best birthday cake. Stupid system needing reloading."

Jody can't join them on Sunday because the school library system needs updating and reloading and the best time to do that is Sunday with no kids in the library and few of them logged in online from home. As head librarian, Jody needs to be there to oversee the procedure.

Drew assures her he will, and they watch while she gets in her car and pulls away before doing the same.

* * *

44

Dim yellow light fills the apartment when Drew flicks the switch. Shuts the door behind them and flicks the lock before hanging his jacket up. Pulls Jesse to his chest before he can escape to play with Scamp.

"I got champagne for tonight," he says against Jesse's temple. "Would you like some?"

"Yes please."

Drew kisses the back of Jesse's neck making him shiver, then lets him go. As predicted he goes straight to the cat cave and murmurs something to Scamp and scratches her ears; then, to Drew's surprise he goes to sit on the couch and kicks off his shoes. Leans forward to take off his socks, ball them together, and tuck them into his shoes.

The champagne cork comes free with a loud pop and Drew grabs a flute to catch the overflowing foam. He fills the glasses, snags the bottle with the other hand, takes them to the coffee table, and sits down. Jesse smiles at him, looking up from beneath his lashes, biting his lip. Drew leans forward and covers his mouth with his own, licks across Jesse's bottom lip until he responds with a quiet moan and opens his mouth. Eventually Jesse breaks the kiss and leans back a little.

"I have another present for you," he says.

Surprised, Drew picks up his glass and sips the champagne.

"Okay, when do I get it?'

"Now."

"Oh," Drew looks around in confusion. 'Where is it?"

"Here," Jesse says. "To find it, you have to unwrap me."

"Unwrap *you*?"

Jesse nods and bites his lip again and for the first time, Drew notices he's trembling.

"Jess?"

Jesse leans forward to kiss him again, takes Drew's hand and places it on the buttons of his shirt. Okay, Drew thinks, unwrapping it is. He takes his time unbuttoning the shirt and slips it off Jesse's shoulders; trails a line of open mouthed kisses the length of Jesse's jaw to his ear, then down to his ear. Nips the lobe as he unbuckles Jesse's belt and flicks the button on his jeans. There's a soft, metallic hiss as he pulls the zipper tab down.

Kisses his way back to Jesse's mouth and claims it with force as he slips his hand down the back of black jeans ... until his fingers brush something soft and silky, something that isn't the cotton of Jesse's usual boxers. He pulls back from the kiss and looks down, but in the dim light, with the way Jesse is seated, he can't see anything.

"Stand up," he orders.

Jesse stands. Drew reaches out and tugs the jeans down until they drop to the ground. Jesse steps out of them and waits. Drew's breath catches in his throat and his eyes widen.

The briefs are the palest pink and made of very fine, soft-as-butter, lace. A plain boxer brief style, held together with pale pink satin laces, threaded through satin eyelets. Simple lace panels at the front and back. Drew swallows with difficulty and adjusts his glasses.

"For me?" he asks.

Jesse nods.

"You wore those," Drew says, "for me?"

Jesse nods again; Drew hears his breath catch.

"Can I ... can I touch?" Drew asks.

"Yes," Jesse says.

Running his fingers over the fabric, touching nothing else, a quiet moan escapes him.

"For me? Just me?" he asks again in wonderment.

"Yes," Jesse says. "Do you like them?"

Drew looks up at him for a moment, hands resting on Jesse's buttocks, the lace soft beneath his palms. Pulls him forward and rests his head against Jesse's belly. Breathes in deeply.

"Jody thought you would like them," Jesse says, and Drew can hear the apprehension, but he still can't find his own voice, is still too overwhelmed. He's not surprised to hear they were Jody's idea; she probably knows Drew better than he knows himself. "Drew?"

Drew stands, just misses knocking over the champagne glasses in the process, and yanks Jesse into his arms; presses his mouth against Jesse's, tracing his tongue around the outline of it, chasing the taste of champagne. Trembling arms slide up around his neck, and he tightens his grip on the lace and lifts; eyes locked on Jesse's, he slips his hands under his thighs, moving them up so they wrap around his hips.

"Yes," he says, the sound low and feral in his throat. "Yes, I like them."

Sucking and kissing at Jesse's throat, Drew carries him to the bedroom and lays him on the bed. He steps back and takes in the sight before him, eyes tracing a path from tousled hair to wide golden eyes, down to the swollen mouth still damp from being kissed. A light scattering of dark chestnut hair runs from Jesse's torso, down his belly, to disappear under the lace.

The lace. Drew closes his eyes and takes a deep breath, opens them again. Pink so pale it could be white against the light coffee of Jesse's skin, lace stretching hip to hip, silky soft against his fingertips. Jesse, though, is anything but soft and when Drew brushes his hand over the front lace panel, his hips jerk up and he moans. Dropping to his knees, Drew mouths him through the lace, working his tongue through the gaps in the pattern to skin, leaving the fabric soaked and Jesse whimpering. He stands, tearing at buttons and zippers, dropping clothes, not caring where they fall. Crawls up Jesse, straddling his hips, leans forward, and laces his fingers through Jesse's.

"You," he says, rocking his hips forward, rubbing their cocks together through the pink silk, "are the most amazing man I have ever known, Jesse."

Jesse's eyes darken, and he unwinds their fingers and runs his hands up Drew's chest. Drew covers his hands with his own, moves them until Jesse is rubbing his nipples; his hips echo the circles Jesse is drawing with his thumbs. The lace is maddening against his skin; the silky barrier between him and Jesse creating a friction makes it hard to think of anything else.

"You," he says, bearing down again, "are so beautiful."

He's never thought of another man as beautiful before but it's the only word that applies to Jesse. To those eyes. That smile. *Oh God, that smile.*

Jesse shifts, working his legs free, raising them and locking tight around Drew's waist, heels digging into above his ass. Drew lets go of a shaky breath.

"You," he says, grinding against Jesse until he hears him whine, "make me want you so much."

He leans down and takes Jesse's mouth in a rough, hard kiss, then pulls back, pushing up on his hands. Pain slithers through his right wrist, and up his arm but he ignores it, looking down the lengths of their bodies. The tip of Jesse's cock is visible beneath the top of the pink briefs, shiny with pre-come. He groans and rubs himself harder against the lace, against Jesse.

Jesse's hands move from Drew's chest to his hips and his fingers dig in, hard enough to make Drew grunt a curse despite himself.

"I," he pants, "want to see you."

Jesse's eyes flutter shut as his hips roll up.

"Drew," he warns.

Desire breaks over Drew in waves and his movements speed up. Jesse is close, Drew can hear it in his breathing, see it in the twisting of his mouth, the color in his cheeks and the way he gives himself over to it is even more exciting than the feel of the lace.

"Drew," Jesse says again, louder this time, urgent. "Drew."

His hips thrust up, and Drew watches as come pools on Jesse's skin.

"Oh God, Jesse," he breathes, "oh God...oh God …"

Sensation zings down his spine, draws his balls up, and he's coming, hips jerking, fingers tightening in the sheets until he's sure he's going to shred them. The lace between them is wet, skin sticky and slicked with sweat, breath hot and heavy. Unwilling to move yet, Drew rests his head against Jesse's, trying to catch his breath. He feels Jesse's hand in his hair.

"You kept your glasses on," Jesse says in his ear. It breaks the spell and Drew rolls away to lay on his back, runs his tongue over his lower lip, still panting. "Happy birthday."

"Thank you," he replies. Jesse stirs and stands up. "Where are you going?"

"To get a cloth."

He watches Jesse disappear and takes a deep breath. When he shuts his eyes, the image of Jesse standing before him in pink lace floats behind his lids and his cock twitches in vain. Not going to happen, he thinks, not after that. That was mind blowing.

"What are you smiling about?" Jesse's voice drags him from his thoughts and he opens his eyes. The lace briefs are gone – in the laundry hamper he imagines – and Jesse is holding a tray on which are the champagne glasses, the bottle, and a damp cloth.

"Thirsty darlin'?"

Jesse nods, eyes shy and avoiding contact with Drew's. He sits up against the headboard and takes the cloth being offered; wipes himself up with it and lobs it toward the door. Puts his glasses on the night table. Jesse climbs on the bed, holding his champagne out to him and he takes it. Drew is amused when Jesse ducks his head and won't look at him. His hand is stretched out toward Wicket, fingers rubbing over his fur.

"Did you like them?"

"What do you think?" Drew replies, resting his hand on Jesse's thigh. Jesse hums and nods.

"Do you like them better than my overalls?"

"They're different. I like them both." Drew tilts his head to look at Jesse's face. "What about you? Did you like wearing them?"

There's silence as Jesse thinks the question over.

"Yes, they felt nice" he says. Drew watches as he drinks some champagne. "Jody took me to see her friend Tina …"

Drew coughs.

"Tina with pink hair? And a ring in her lip?"

"Uh huh."

He's going to kill her.

"Did you, uh, go to Tina's shop?"

Jesse's face turns a startling shade of red and he gulps another mouthful of champagne. Oh yes, he's definitely going to kill Jody. She took him to Tina's sex shop. What the hell? Of course, if she hadn't there wouldn't be any pink lace but ... what the hell?

"There was lot of underwear and movies in the shop," Jesse says, "and um stuff."

Drew nods and rubs his eyes. Yet another subject they've never broached.

"Do you know what that stuff is, Jess?"

"Kind of," Jesse says finally. "I've seen some in ... in videos."

Startled, Drew considers this; it had never occurred to him that Jesse would have seen porn, although he supposes it shouldn't surprise him. He loves video. Jesse is still speaking.

"I've never used one. Have you?"

It's Drew's turn to blush.

"Yeah, once or twice."

"Oh." Jesse fidgets as he finishes his drink. "Why?"

Why? Drew's not sure how to answer that.

"Well because they can be fun and exciting. With the right person. A bit like your -um - present tonight was."

"Oh."

"We could try one together if you want to," Drew says. He puts his empty glass on the side table. Takes Jesse's and sets it next to it.

"I don't know," Jesse says, and Drew reaches out and turns his face, so he can see Jesse's eyes.

"Jess, we don't have to." He smiles. "We never have to do anything you don't want to do."

Jesse tucks his head under Drew's chin and wraps his arms around Drew's body.

"There's something I would like to do though," Drew says as he eases them both down into the bed. "Maybe we could get you some more of that underwear. We don't have to go into a shop, we can look online."

He feels Jesse's cheek heat up against his skin as he nods.

"I'd like that."

"Good, so would I." Drew brushes a kiss over Jesse's head. "I had a wonderful birthday thank you Jess."

"You're welcome," Jesse whispers.

When Scamp jumps on the bed they're both asleep.

* * *

45

Jesse opens his eyes and groans. It feels as though there's fire in his throat and his eyes are going pop out of his head. He sneezes three times in quick succession, then sits up rubbing his eyes. Marcus came to work with a cold on Monday, sneezed on every surface in the store, and once in Jesse's face, before Mr Greenwold had sighed and sent him home. Obviously, he's caught Marcus's summer cold.

He sneezes again and Drew stirs; he rolls over and opens his eyes.

"My throat hurts," Jesse says.

Drew stretches his arm up and places his palm on Jesse's forehead.

"You're a bit warm but I don't think you've got a fever."

Jesse turns his head away and sneezes to the side.

"I think I've got Marcus's stupid cold."

"Why don't you stay home?" Drew swings his legs out of bed and stretches. "I can phone Mr Greenwold before I leave for work."

In nearly eight years Jesse has taken only three sick days and he knows there wouldn't be a problem. But it would mean Mr Greenwold being stuck by himself or with Marcus, if he's back, all day. It's Wednesday and Jesse always cleans the fish tanks on Wednesdays; if Marcus does it, he'll probably kill the fish. Who will take care of Sniffles? Marcus doesn't like letting her out of her cage. He sneezes into his hands and Drew grimaces, grabs the box of tissues and throws them on the bed.

"Well, no swimming today, my friend. I'll bring you some tea and aspirin, then I'm taking a shower."

Drew leans forward as if he's going to kiss him, then changes his mind and ruffles his hair instead.

"Want Wicket?"

Jesse nods and regrets it immediately. His head feels heavy and hot. Drew tucks the toy under the covers and Jesse closes his eyes; Wicket's fur is cool against his skin.

A few minutes later, Drew reappears with a mug of tea and two aspirin, hands them to Jesse.

"And I've fed Princess Bossy Paws you'll be pleased to know, so you stay there until I get out of the shower and then we'll decide if you're going to work or not."

239

* * *

Jesse swipes at his nose with a balled-up tissue and clears his throat. From the other side of the store, Mr Greenwold looks up and sighs.

"You should go home, Jesse," he says. Rolls his eyes when Jesse shakes his head. "Wednesdays are always quiet."

"I'm okay," he croaks. Shoving the soggy tissue in his pocket he opens Sniffles' cage and cuddles her against his chest, burying his clogged nose in her fur. Kisses the top of her head and puts her down on the counter; she lollops to the end where a bowl of pellets waits. "When is Marcus coming back?"

Mr Greenwold shrugs and shoves a pallet of dog food to one side, muttering under his breath. Jesse goes to help him and suggests it doesn't make much difference whether Marcus is there or not.

"You got that right buddy," the old man wheezes. "But he's better than nothing."

"And at least he won't be annoying me when I clean the fish."

Jesse sneezes, wipes his nose, and goes to collect the trolley he keeps the tank cleaning equipment on. Cleaning the tropical fish is a major activity that they shut early for once every two months for, but cleaning the goldfish is simple. Jesse filled the spare tank last night and the water is up to temperature; he'll transfer the fish, clean and disinfect their tank for parasites, refill it and hopefully by the end of the day he'll be able to put the fish back in.

He's stuffing clean tissues in his pockets when he hears the door buzzer sound followed by Mr Greenwold's voice greeting the customer. Kicking a bag of kitty litter to one side, Jesse goes back into the store, pushing the trolley around the dog collar stand and toward the wall of fish filled tanks. He comes to a halt and blows his nose then picks up the green net. Dips it into the tank and scoops out three gold fish, gently moves them to the other tank.

"Doing a good job with the fishies there," a low voice in his ear makes him jump, "retard."

When Jesse turns around, David is behind him.

Fear crawls down Jesse's spine and the net slips from his fingers into the fish tank. Why would David be here? The big man's hulking form is surrounded by a cloud of alcohol and body odor; he's dressed in a winter coat and jeans despite the heat and sweat drips down his cheeks. His nose is crooked, and Jesse knows it's because of Drew's punch and feels a moment of vicious pleasure at the thought.

"Why are you here?" he asks, gripping the handle of the trolley.

"Oh, I just dropped by to say hello." David steps closer. Jesse leans away. "See how you and Andy Pandy are doing. I've been calling but it keeps going to voice mail."

Jesse shakes his head; he doesn't know what David is talking about, but he doesn't like the way he's saying it. Something in the tone sends a tremor up his back and he wishes Drew was here.

"What's the matter Jesse?" David asks. "It is Jesse, right? Not Jessica."

Jesse takes another step back, still silent.

"Is everything okay, Jesse?" Mr Greenwold asks, coming around the end of the fish food stand. His tone is light and directed at Jesse, but his eyes never leave David.

"Just having a chat." David's smile is cold, and Jesse wants to tell Mr Greenwold to just go back to the counter and call Drew because David is drunk and he's being mean, but he can't make his voice work. "Everything is fine, isn't it Jesse?"

Jesse nods. David moves closer to the wall of fish, leans against the tank of Neon Tetras.

"Please don't lean on the tanks, sir," Mr Greenwold says, frowning.

David gives Greenwold another flat, unfeeling smile. Looks from the store owner to Jesse and back again, before, in one swift moment, he jerks his elbow back against the side of the ancient, glass tank. Jesse's gasp is lost beneath a loud cracking sound as the tank disintegrates, water and fish spilling on to the floor in a rush. Bits of glass stick out of David's sleeve, but he doesn't seem to notice.

"I'm calling the police," Mr Greenwold starts to turn but David moves, much faster than Jesse expected, crushing fish beneath his boot, and grabs his arm.

"I don't think so," he hisses, twisting Greenwold's arm up behind his back. He frog-marches him to the door and kicks the door shut. Orders him to lock it. When he's satisfied the door is locked, he pushes Greenwold toward the counter and turns to look at Jesse. Crooks his finger and beckons him.

"Come here, pretty boy, I want to talk to you." His lips turn up in a sneer.

Taking care to avoid the few fish still flapping in the glass filled puddle of water, Jesse approaches the front of the store.

"What do you want?" he asks. The clock behind the counter shows it's nearly eleven and Jesse knows Drew will be in class; even if he could send him a text he wouldn't see it for another half an hour. David signals him come closer and he obeys. "You'll go to jail."

"Will I just?" David laughs. "Better make it worth it then."

He reaches into his coat and takes out a broad, flat hunting knife; Mr Greenwold slumps back against the counter, pale and breathless. Jesse goes to him, asks if he's okay.

"I'm fine, Jesse. Do you know this ... person?"

Jesse darts a look up at David then back down at his feet.

"He's David," he says. "He's Drew's old boyfriend."

"Little less of the old, thank you pretty boy." David waggles the knife in Jesse's direction. "Give him that chair from behind the counter. Don't say I don't respect my elders."

When Mr Greenwold is seated, Jesse rests a trembling hand on the back of the chair, eyes flicking from the ground to the knife in David's hand. He flinches when David reaches into his coat again but this time he takes out a bottle, half filled with a clear liquid. Spins the lid off, lifts it to his lips and takes a slug. Smacks his lips and belches.

"Now, my pretty little Jesse, let's you and me talk, shall we? Let us talk about Andy Pandy."

Jesse's head jerks up.

"Don't call him that. His name is Drew."

"Oh Jesse, Drew is short for Andrew, just like Andy is," David says as if he's speaking to a child. "Didn't you know that, pretty little Jesse? No, I bet you didn't, retard. So, tell me, how long have you been together?"

Scrubbing his runny nose with the back of his hand, Jesse says nothing. David leans over and taps Mr Greenwold's knee with the flat blade of the knife.

"Come on now, pretty little Jesse. How long?"

"Since February," Jesse whispers.

David nods and takes another swig from the bottle.

"Since February," he says. "He ask you out or you ask him? No, wait, don't tell me. Let me guess. He asked you, didn't he?"

Jesse nods and David nods with him.

"Of course he did. You'd be too scared to ask someone out wouldn't you, retard? Huh? Wouldn't you?" His tone is conversational, as if he's asking Jesse who he thinks might win the next World Series. "You'd be right up Andy Pandy's alley, so to speak, something pretty and vulnerable that he can pet and save and protect. Oh yes you'd be right up his alley."

He leans back and considers Jesse for a moment.

"Except you aren't, are you? He's up yours. You finally got Andy Pandy to do it, didn't you? Was it because you were cherry? Were you cherry, pretty little Jesse? Because I can see Andy Pandy topping for a first timer ..."

"Shut up and don't call him that," Jesse yells, then cringes back, afraid. To his surprise David laughs.

"Oh, our pretty boy has enough of a pair to stand up for his man, does he? Well, well, who would have thought?"

"You're going to go to jail this time. Not...not to the hospital like before, like when you hurt Drew. You're going to go jail."

"Yeah, you wish. I must have really ruined him if he's fucking retards now." David's eyes narrow and he puts his bottle on the counter; he leans forward and runs a finger along Jesse's jaw. "Though I gotta say, you really are a pretty little thing. No wonder he turned top for you. Maybe I should give you a try."

David reaches out and yanks Jesse toward him. The press of his fingers hurts but Jesse refuses to give him the satisfaction of moaning. He can't help gagging though when David's smell fills his nose; it's worse than the mouse cages when they get left too long, worse than anything Jesse has ever smelled. A fetid mix of alcohol and urine and vomit. David runs his tongue up the side of Jesse's face and Jesse gags again at the slimy, rotting feeling of it.

"Leave him alone," Mr Greenwold growls and David kicks back against the leg of the chair.

"Why don't you fucking shut up, old man?" he snarls and turns back to Jesse. Presses against him and Jesse whimpers in fear when he feels the hard outline of David's erection. He tries to wriggle out of his hold and hisses in pain when the fingers around his arm tighten, pinching the skin. David is scrabbling with the button of Jesse's jeans as he humps against him, cursing and muttering.

There's a tap on the door behind David and when Jesse looks over his shoulder, it's Mrs Jones with her two schnauzers. He calls for help, hopes she'll understand and David lets go. Jesse doesn't see the backhand slap, simply reels away, catching himself against the counter. She taps again and strains to see what is happening on their side. David goes to the door, and holds his fist up against the glass, extends his middle finger.

"Fuck off bitch," he snarls, and she stumbles back. He barks out a laugh, then turns to Jesse and Greenwold. Takes a mouthful from the bottle and puts it back down. Mr Greenwold's face is red and perspiration has soaked big dark circles over his shirt; the air is thick with the acidic smell of sweat and the swampy smell of the broken fish tank. Jesse is really worried now that it means he's having a heart attack like his Grandpa did. He asks him if he's okay and Mr Greenwold pats his hand and gives him a weak smile.

"I'm fine, Jesse, don't worry about me."

"Aw isn't that sweet?" David sneers and leans toward Jesse, "Andy Pandy know you're being friendly with the boss? Oh, don't look so worried, I'm just fooling with you, Jesse. I know you only have eyes for your big, bwave Andy Pandy. Son of a bitch broke my nose. Think I might just have to break something of his."

He palms himself through his jeans, then reaches for Jesse who jerks back out of reach, stumbling against the counter. The movement startles Sniffles who runs the length of the countertop, knocking the gin bottle over the edge. It shatters, and the acrid smell of gin fills the store. Fury fills David's face and roaring, he lunges for the animal, trapping it by its back legs and holding it up in the air. Sniffles struggles, trying to kick and twist free; Jesse moves to take her, but David leans out of reach, a sly smile surfacing.

"Don't hurt her," Jesse pleads, tears in his eyes. "Please, please don't hurt her."

"This your bun bun, Jesse?" David asks. "Bun bun got a name?"

"Sniffles," Jesse whimpers reaching a tentative hand toward the rabbit. David steps back and holds her up higher. Jesse can see she's terrified, eyes wide and nose twitching.

"Aw, Sniffles, isn't that a cute name for your little wabbit?" With a sharp jerk, he whips his knife hand up, sinking it into the soft belly of the rabbit and with a swift downward movement, disembowels it. Jesse shrieks, a high-pitched, agony filled sound, as blood sprays across his face and over Mr Greenwold.

"No!" he sobs when David drops the still twitching body on the floor. Forgetting the knife and David, he bends and scoops the lifeless form up, cradling it. "Sniffles, no, no, no."

From what seems a long way away, he hears Mr Greenwold cursing and David laughing. Then there's pounding and muffled shouts from outside. Jesse looks up and through his tears can see two police officers with Mrs Jones through the door. David follows his gaze and when he turns toward the commotion, a growl rumbles up from Mr Greenwold and he tackles him. Together they fall against the door and the knife goes flying.

Jesse hunches over Sniffles, as if he can protect her one more time, and the door explodes in on them.

* * *

46

Drew's sophomore English class still has twenty minutes to run when the door swings open, revealing Barry Reynolds. His face is pale as he asks Drew to join him in the hall.

"Drew, I've just had a call from the police. There's been a problem at the pet store Jesse works at. They've been held up."

Terror steals Drew's breath, and he grabs the principal's shoulders.

"Jess?" he asks.

"From what I gather, he's okay, but they need you there now. I'll take you. Ellen has a free afternoon and she'll take over your kids; Jack is coming over to finish this class."

Drew isn't listening. All he can think of is Jesse. What does okay mean? Is he hurt? Scared? Damn it why didn't he make him stay home today? Jack Lawson arrives, claps him on the shoulder, and Drew follows Reynolds down the corridor, not daring to think about what might be waiting for him at the pet store.

* * *

The street has been cordoned off and two police officers refuse to let them through. Drew tries to push past and fails, is beginning to panic when Reynolds remembers the name of the officer who called him and gives it to the man in front of him. Holding his finger up – one minute – the officer speaks into his device telling the man in the store who he has with him. He gets a swift response and lifts the tape.

Unable to control his fear any longer, Drew runs to the store, stops on the pavement, eyes wide. The glass panes in the door are smashed, the wooden frame is buckled and splintered. A police officer steps over it and speaks to him.

"Mr Oliver? Come with me please." Drew follows him through the mess. He looks around, searching for Jesse, takes in the overturned trolley, broken fish tank, and the mess of glass, pebbles and dead fish on the floor. A broken moan rises from his throat, when he sees blood on the floor and counter. *Oh God, where's Jesse?* The police officer takes his elbow and leads him around the blood and glass toward the back room.

Mr Greenwold is sitting, a blanket around his shoulders, while an ambulance attendant takes his blood pressure. The man is pale, his breathing shallow, shirt soaked in sweat and blood. Behind him, to Drew's relief, is Jesse. Wrapped in a blanket, covered in blood, he's rocking back and forth. Tears drip from his face. Greenwold looks up, then over his shoulder at Jesse. Drew shakes off the officer's hand and rushes to him, falling onto his knees. Jesse stares at Drew, eyes blank, face pale. Then his eyes clear and his chest begins to hitch.

"Drew," he sobs and falls against him, slender body shuddering.

Drew wraps his arms around him, not caring about the blood and mess, just holding him as tight as he can, grateful for the solid feel of him in his arms.

"I'm here, Jess, it's okay, you're okay, I'm here." He looks up at the ambulance attendant and asks if he's hurt.

"No, the blood isn't his," the attendant says, "it's from the rabbit."

"Sniffles," Jesse sobs against his shoulder. "He killed Sniffles. Drew, he killed Sniffles. He killed her with a knife because she knocked over the bottle, Drew. Drew, David killed Sniffles."

Disbelief washes over Drew and he freezes.

"What? Jess, what did you say?"

"David. It was David. He killed her with a knife because she knocked the bottle over."

"Shhhh, I'm here, Jess. It's okay, I'm here. You're safe now." Drew says drawing Jesse in tighter. Over his shoulder he searches for the police officer. "Do you have the guy who did this? Was it David? Did he do this?"

Jesse makes a high keening sound and his fingers dig into David's ribs at the mention of David's name. The office consults a note pad, then nods.

"Yes, we have a David O'Henry in custody. I believe you were involved with Mr O'Henry previously. Is that correct?"

"Yes, he's my ex," Drew says.

"It would appear that Mr O'Henry was drunk, possibly under the influence of narcotics..."

"He has drug and alcohol issues," Drew interrupts, "he's done time in rehab."

"He came in around eleven, broke a fish tank and harassed the owner, Mr Greenwold, and your uh friend ..."

"My boyfriend," Drew corrects. The officer squirms and clears his throat.

"Uh yes, well he made them lock the store and threatened them with a knife. Evidently, he wanted details of your relationship with uh," he consults his notes, "Mr Peterson. He was drinking gin from a bottle and had placed it on the counter and the rabbit knocked it off." The officer pauses.

"Drew," Mr Greenwold's voice sounds tired and strained but something in the tone makes Drew turn. "He tried to touch Jesse .... He was going to..."

His voice breaks and Drew closes his eyes against the horror of what he knows the man must be saying. Looks up the police officer who nods, then turns back to Jesse, pulling him in closer.

"He killed Sniffles," Jesse repeats, face, hot and wet, buried against Drew's neck. Drew rubs his back and asks the officer how they knew to come to the shop.

"A customer tried to come in and Mr O'Henry verbally abused her and sent her away. She alerted us."

* * *

It's another hour before the police let them leave. Jesse's sobs have tapered to quiet whimpers but he's still rocking and clinging to Drew. Barry Reynolds, who has been waiting in the crowd, says he'll drive them home. The officer in charge tells them they'll be in touch and Drew, finally, is able to bundle Jesse into the car, murmuring soothing noises as Barry drives.

* * *

Barry helps him get Jesse upstairs and waits while Drew unlocks the door, then reminds him if he needs anything to just call before leaving. Drew locks the door behind him and nudges Jesse toward the bathroom. Jesse's movements are wooden, he doesn't bother checking the cushions.

"Come on sweetheart, let's get you cleaned up," Drew says softly.

He turns the shower on and undresses Jesse with swift, gentle movements, throwing the blood-stained clothes at the door to be put in the trash later. When he tries to move Jesse into the shower, he refuses to let go and eventually Drew undresses and climbs in with him. After the water has run over them both for a few minutes, he soaps Jesse all over, taking care to get rid of any spots of blood he sees. Picks up a washcloth and washes away snot and tears from Jesse's face. Washes his hair and turns the water off. Drew gets out first and finds towels, wraps one around Jesse and takes him to the bedroom. Finds his pajamas and helps him into them, then finds himself some shorts and a tee-shirt. He picks up Wicket.

"Why don't you get into bed with Wicket and I'll make some tea and I need to phone a few people," he says.

"Don't ...don't ... leave me here," Jesse cries, panic rushing into his face and throws himself in Drew's arms.

"It's okay, it's okay, I'm not going to go anywhere, I won't leave you Jess, it's okay."

Finally, he takes him with him, clutching Wicket with both arms, to the kitchen and puts the kettle on. While it boils, he begins to make phone calls.

* * *

Erin leans down, and kisses Jesse goodbye then hugs Drew.

"I'll come over tomorrow, okay honey?" she says. Jesse just looks at her, eyes round and wounded. She raises a hand to her mouth and Drew hugs her again, knows this must be hard for her. "Try and get some sleep."

"Drew," Ray is saying, "if you need to call us, don't hesitate. Don't worry about the time."

"I promise," Drew says, grateful to them both for their calm.

"Are you sure you don't want to stay with us for tonight?" Erin asks but they've already discussed this, and Jesse says he wants to be here, with Scamp who is currently curled in a ball on his lap.

Drew goes to stand, and Jesse whimpers and grabs his hand.

"Don't get up," Ray waves his hand at him, "we know the way."

At the door, Ray repeats the order to call for any reason, then he's pulling it shut and silence settles on them. Drew feels sorry for them but is relieved they've gone. He's managed to put his own parents off for now with a promise he'll call in the morning. For now, though, he wants to get Jesse into bed and hopefully to sleep.

Even with Drew holding him, and Wicket held against his chest, Jesse is still rocking. His stare keeps going blank and if Drew tries to move away, he begins to cry. Erin has left him some tranquilizers and Drew is beginning to think he'll have to use one.

"Jess, why don't we get into bed?" he suggests, carding his fingers through Jesse's hair. "We can put a movie on and if you want we can have a picnic."

"Are you coming too?" Jesse asks.

"Of course I am." Drew gets him to his feet and across the room.

It takes him a while to get the bed sorted and a movie on while Jesse stands, trembling, staring at his feet. Drew pulls the covers back and presses Jesse down onto the mattress, then climbs in next to him. Immediately Jesse is curled against his side, knees drawn to his chest, still rocking.

"I'm here, Jess. I'm not going to let anything hurt you. I'm here."

David, on the other hand, he wants to hurt. He wants to hurt him a lot.

* * *

Drew wakes in the early hours of the morning to a high whining sound. Jesse is thrashing in his sleep, tears on his cheeks, crying out. When Drew tries to shake him out of it, he screams and jerks away. Drew follows, trying to draw him into his arms. The sheets are soaking wet, cold and clammy, and Drew throws the blankets back revealing Jesse tucked into a tight ball, pajamas and bedding sodden.

Wide awake now, Drew finds his glasses, gets up and goes around to the other side. Succeeds at last in waking Jesse and getting him upright, heart tightening when Jesse's eyes, wide and startled, dart around the room in fear.

"Jess, it's okay, it was just a nightmare. You've wet the bed," he says trying to stay calm as he takes Jesse to the bathroom, grabbing his cellphone as they go. "I'm going to run you a bath, then I'll change the sheets."

When he lets go to turn the faucet on, Jesse begins to rock and moan, calming only when Drew holds him again. One arm around Jesse's waist, Drew puts his phone on the floor by the side of the tub, adjusts the temperature of the water and waits for it to be deep enough then peels the soiled pajamas off Jesse and drops them in the hand basin. Jesse doesn't move or speak.

"Jess, you can get in now," Drew says but Jesse just blinks and still doesn't move. "Jess, come on, you need to get in before the water gets cold."

Still nothing. Sighing, Drew lifts Jesse leg and maneuvers it into the water. Repeats on the other side and tries to step back. Jesse's reaction is instant. And loud.

"Okay, okay, shhhhhh, Jesse, it's okay."

With a sigh, and not bothering to remove his own pajamas, Drew gets in the tub behind Jesse and sits down, pulling him down with him. After half an hour, although Drew has managed to coax him to lay against his chest, he realizes Jesse isn't responding. He's just rocking and trembling, sending ripples through the cooling water.

He gropes on the floor until he finds his phone, finds Ray's number and taps it. After three rings he hears Ray's voice.

"I think I need help."

* * *

47

It takes twenty minutes to get them both dry and into clean clothes, hampered by Jesse's refusal to let him move away. Another ten to calm him down after unlocking the door to leave it ajar for Ray and Erin. Finally sinking onto the couch and pulling Jesse against his side just to have him scramble onto his lap, Wicket wedged between them, head pressed against Drew's chest. Drew looks at his watch and sees it's not even eight o'clock and he's already exhausted.

"Jess, you're safe," Drew murmurs into his hair, rubbing his arms to try and calm the shaking. There's no reply.

They're still sitting like that when a tap on the door makes Jesse whine and press against him. Ray's head appears around the door and Drew beckons them in. Erin rushes to them and tries to pull Jesse into her arms but he refuses, tightening his hold on Drew. Pain and sorrow flicker over her face and Drew wishes he could say something to make it easier for her.

"He won't let me go." He strokes Jesse's hair.

"How long has he been like this?" Ray asks, passing a hand over his face. His eyes are bloodshot and there are heavy bags beneath them. Neither he nor Erin appear to have slept much; Drew can relate.

"He woke me up about two hours ago with a nightmare, kicking and crying. He wet the bed, so I got him up and into the bath, but I had to get in with him."

Erin has managed to capture one of Jesse's hands in her own, but he still won't look at her. A tear slides down her cheek.

"He hasn't let me go since," Drew says.

"Jesse," Ray crouches next to them, "son, can you hear me? I need you to talk to me Jesse."

Nothing.

"Honey, please, you're scaring us." Erin tries. "You need to talk to us."

Jesse's eyes slide to look at his mother and then away again. He doesn't move except to draw his knees in tighter. Scamp lands on the back of the sofa and meows.

"Erin, I'm really sorry to ask but could you feed her. I haven't been able to."

"Of course," Erin sniffs and wipes her face. "Can I get you some coffee?"

Drew agrees coffee sounds good and gives her directions to Scamp's food. When she returns, she's carrying a tray with coffee for the three of them and apple juice for Jesse. She tries without success to get him to hold the glass; gives Drew a desperate look and he takes it, holds it to Jesse's mouth but gets no reaction.

"You need to drink something Jess." He presses the cup against Jesse's lips. After a moment, he dips his head and sips. "Thank you, darlin'. Look, your mom and dad are here, can you sit up?"

Jesse doesn't answer, just lets his head drop back against Drew's chest.

"Sorry," he says with a sigh. Erin shakes her head and hands him his coffee. He takes a sip, rests his cheek on Jesse's head. "Has he ever been like this before?"

"He used to withdraw when he was little, before we got a handle on the autism and the dyslexia," Ray says. He rubs his eyes. "I can't remember the last time he withdrew as an adult. Not even when you two had that fight."

"When Ray's father died," Erin says. Ray looks at her. "Not like this, but he withdrew for about a day."

"What did you do?"

"Just waited it out," Erin says, filling her coffee cup again. "There wasn't much else to do."

Drew drinks his coffee. He doesn't know what to say or to do. Has never felt so helpless. Silence fills the room; Drew notices Jesse's breathing begins to even out and he lets himself think perhaps things are calming down. The thought has barely formed when his cell phone rings and Jesse jumps, crying out and cowering against Drew.

Drew fumbles with the phone, trying to calm Jesse at the same time; Erin tries to help but Jesse pushes her hands away, keening and kicking at her.

"It's my mom, could you answer it?" Drew asks, pushing the phone into her hands and grappling with the upset man in his arms. "Jesse, please, come on, calm down."

He's barely aware of Erin explaining what's happening as he tries, with little success, to soothe Jesse. If this is going to happen every time there's a noise, it's going to be a long day.

He's calm when Erin hangs up. Drew's parents are on their way she tells them and sets about opening drapes and tidying the room. She goes to the bathroom and comes back with towels and Jesse's wet pajamas, bundles them into the washing machine, ignoring Drew's protest to leave everything.

"I was thinking," Drew says, "of maybe calling Martin Sutton. He's the doctor I've been seeing to help me understand Jesse," he glances from Ray to Erin, embarrassed. "If that's okay with you."

"I don't know, Drew," Erin begins to say. "Some doctor we don't even know?"

"I know him Erin, Jesse knows him," Drew points out.

"That's not the point, Drew..."

"I think you should," Ray interrupts. "It's worth a try."

"Ray, we don't even know this man," Erin protests, "and I know Drew means well but let's face it, it's because of Drew Jesse's like th..."

"Erin, that's enough," Ray snaps. "Drew didn't do this. He's not responsible for what that man did and there is nothing he could have done to stop it. Not that any of it is important anyway; the only thing that matters now is helping our son. And if this Doctor Sutton can help, I think we should try."

Erin's mouth trembles and Drew asks her to come and sit next to him. He takes her hand and places it on Jesse's back, covers it with his own.

"You're right, Erin. If it wasn't for me, this wouldn't have happened. But you have to believe me when I say I love him because I do," he says. She shuts her eyes, sighs, and hands him his phone.

He taps the screen and pulls up Martin Sutton's number.

* * *

Jesse is asleep when Drew's parents arrive, his breathing even, hand curled in a loose fist on Drew's shoulder. He stirs when they knock on the door but doesn't wake and Drew wonders again if the worst has passed but doesn't let himself hope. His mother leans down and kisses him, strokes a finger over Jesse's cheek, sadness darkening her eyes when he flinches at the touch. She goes to Erin and puts her arms around her; asks her if she's okay. Peter and Ray lean against the mantle, talking in low voices.

Drew moves, trying to find a more comfortable position. His right hand, trapped behind Jesse, aches and his bladder protests the weight resting on it; it occurs to him he should probably get Jesse to a bathroom as well.

"Ray," he calls, trying to not wake Jesse, "could you give me a hand?"

"What is it, Drew?"

He's aware all the eyes in the room are on him and reminds himself now is not the time for embarrassment.

"I, uh, really need to pee," he says, "and I'm probably not the only one."

Ray nods.

"Okay, how are we going to do this?"

"I think him first," Drew says, "and he seemed to respond before when you spoke to him. If you can help me wake him and get him moving, I can take care of the rest. Then if you can take him while I ...you know..."

"Yeah, okay," Ray comes over to them, followed by Peter, "come on then."

"Jess," strokes Jesse's face, "come on sweetheart, wake up. Jess? Can you wake up for me please?"

"Jesse," Ray says, his voice louder and more authoritative, "you need to wake up, son. Come on, pee time for boys." Drew raises an eyebrow and Ray shrugs. "Always worked when he was toilet training."

It works now too; Jesse pushes off from Drew's chest and rubs his eyes. Stares around the room without expression until he gets back to Drew.

"Drew," he whispers.

"Yeah, darlin', come on, I'll take you to the bathroom," Drew says, fighting a lump in his throat as he eases Jesse to his feet. Holding his hand, he leads him to the bathroom, and when he's done, helps him wash his hands. Ray and Peter are waiting on the other side when he opens the door.

"Jess go with your dad, I'll be right ou ..."

Jesse's head whips around, eyes wide and distressed. He moans and Drew looks to Ray for help. Ray takes Jesse in a firm hold and pulls him toward the couch. Jesse resists and Peter takes the other side. Together they get Jesse him to move, moaning and struggling, as Drew shuts the door and uses the toilet.

When he comes out, Jesse is huddled in the corner of the couch with Wicket, rocking again. Steeling himself against the sight, Drew goes to the kitchen and gets some water, then hugs his parents. Thanks his father for helping with Jesse. Takes a deep breath and goes to the couch, sits next to Jesse, lifting his arm up to let him slide against him. Offers him some water and is pleased when he takes a sip.

He leans back against the couch, feeling tired and strung out. A knock at the door makes Jesse jerk upright, breath coming in short, rapid gasps.

"That will be Martin." Drew rubs Jesse's shoulders as he coaxes him to settle back down. "It's okay, Jess. You know everyone here, you're safe." He looks up as his dad lets the doctor in. "Hey Martin, how are you?"

"Well, I'm going to say I'm doing better than you are right now," Martin says from the doorway.

"Got that right. Mom, Dad, Ray, Erin, this is Doctor Martin Sutton. He's a specialist in autism and intellectual disabilities," Drew says.

"And a friend." Martin shakes hands. He crosses to the couch, pinches the crease in his beige slacks and sits down. "Hey Jesse, how are you today?"

Jesse looks up at Drew in silence, then turns his head back into his chest. Drew shrugs.

"Sorry."

"No need." Martin shakes his head. "How long has he been like this?"

Drew recounts the morning's events and Erin repeats the information about Jesse's previous episodes.

"And are you able to tell me what set this off?"

Oh God, how can he tell him about yesterday with Jesse here? How in the hell will Jesse react if he hears David's name or what he did? Looking around in panic, he doesn't know how to begin and is relieved when Ray clears his throat and speaks.

"I think Drew's worried about Jesse hearing that," he says. "If you come over to the kitchen, I can tell you what I know."

"Thank you," Drew mouths to him, and pulls Jesse tighter against his chest. A wave of anger toward David threatens to engulf him and he pushes it down. Wishes again he'd made Jesse stay home because of his cold and kisses his head. "It's okay Jess, I'm not going to let anyone hurt you, I promise."

* * *

Martin Sutton leans back against the counter and looks at the two couples in front of him. One worried about a son who has had so many chances denied him and the other worried about a son who has had every chance. Both worried their sons may not recover from whatever the events are that have taken place.

Ray speaks in a low voice, starting with the fight at the barbeque. When Martin interrupts and says he knows about that, Ray jumps to the pet store, glancing over his shoulder from time to time to look at his son.

"I am so sorry," Martin says when Ray finishes speaking. "I hope they throw the book at that son of a bitch. These boys don't need that kind of crap, they have enough to deal with."

He doesn't miss the look of surprise in Erin's eyes at the use of the word 'boys' or the gratitude in Sarah's and makes a decision. Drew can either thank him or kick his ass later, for now Martin suspects it might just be what is needed.

"I met Drew and Jesse about six months ago," he says, "about six weeks or so after they started dating. And do you know what I noticed about them then?"

His question is met with silence and he nods toward the living room; they all turn to follow his gaze. Drew has brought Jesse back on to his lap, both arms around him, cheek resting against short hair; his lips are moving as he whispers reassurances and rocks the younger man gently.

"That is what I noticed." He nods toward the pair. "I don't know many couples who are as suited for one another as those two. I'm damned if I know why, but they seem to fit perfectly."

He smiles, watching Drew stroke Jesse's cheek and settle him in better. Turns to the group of parents.

"I know," he continues, "that this is hard for you Erin. You've spent your life with a child who has been locked out of everything and you've needed to protect him. And Sue? Your son has the world at his feet and could achieve anything. You both want to protect your children, and I understand that. Everyone does, but you're forgetting one thing. This isn't about what *you* want, it's about them. You have got to stop focusing on what makes them different and start looking at what they share."

He looks around the four faces staring at him. Waits.

"Doctor Sutton ..." Peter begins but Martin holds his hand up.

"Martin, please."

"Martin. I think I can speak for all of us when I say you're right, we are worried about their safety. It's all very well to tell us to ignore the differences but those differences are part of what caused this situation, we all know that – no, let me finish – but you're right, what they share is more important. And we'll do whatever we can to help. The rest ...well we'll deal with the rest as we get to it."

Ray murmurs his agreement. Martin looks to Sue and Erin, sees Sue make up her mind and put her arm around Jesse's mother.

"Jesse is family now, we'll do whatever has to be done to get him through this. To get them both through this."

Erin turns her head against her shoulder and a muffled sob escapes.

"What do we do?" Ray asks.

"Let's go figure it out."

* * *

Jesse's mom sits in one of the armchairs; she looks as though she's been crying, and Drew feels another surge of pity for the woman. He notices his mom sits on the arm of the chair and holds her hand. Dad and Ray are back at the mantle. Martin sits back next to Drew and Jesse and smiles at him.

"Okay, this is called disassociation. Jesse has decided the world is too hard to deal with and has disassociated himself from it," Martin explains. "It's not uncommon in people on the autism spectrum and it has varying levels of severity. At one end are those cases where subjects don't communicate, they stim constantly, and are unable to live independent lives. At the other end are those people who ..."

"Are like Jesse," Drew says, and Martin agrees. "So, what do we do?"

"Well, the fact that Jesse hasn't had many of these episodes, and those that he has had have been short, is a good sign. The fact that he appears to not have completely disassociated is also a good sign."

"What do you mean he hasn't completely disassociated?" Drew asks. Martin puts his hand on Jesse's leg, and when he cringes into Drew's hold, Martin chuckles, not unkindly.

"That's what I mean. He hasn't disassociated from you, Drew. So hopefully that means we will be able to help you convince him to come back and join the world."

Drew thinks this over for a moment. Takes a deep breath and lets it out.

"He woke up with a cold yesterday, I wanted him to stay home," he says, fighting tears. "I should have made him."

Erin clears her throat.

"I was wrong before, Drew, this isn't your fault. Jesse can make his own decisions, he chose to go to work, and you couldn't know what was going to happen. Nobody could."

"Which brings me to my next point." Martin leans forward. "I don't think Jesse's state has been brought on entirely by what happened yesterday."

Confused, Drew looks around the room – sees the confusion he's feeling on everyone's faces - and back to Martin.

"Jesse's had a big year," Martin says, and Drew can see he's picking his words with care. "He's met someone and fallen in love, moved in with them, he's had a sexual awakening, he's established his full autonomy as an adult from his parents. That's a lot for anybody but for someone in Jesse's world, it's massive. It's a lot of physical and emotional stimulation that he's not used to. That he hasn't withdrawn already is probably a miracle, so it's hardly surprising yesterday tipped him over."

Drew is aware of the heat in face – discussing his personal life with Jesse in front of both their parents is uncomfortable, no matter how he feels about him.

"What do we do?" he asks.

"Well since in the past, he's come back by himself I suggest we try and wait it out. I'll get my secretary to reschedule my patients for today and stay here to keep an eye on things."

"What happens if he doesn't ..." Drew falters, "if that doesn't work?"

"Then we'll have to hospitalize him," Martin says. Drew slumps back against the couch. The thought of Jesse in hospital makes him feel ill. If he ever lays eyes on David again...he pushes the thought away.

"Well," Sue stands up, "Erin, how about we see what the boys have in the kitchen and do a supermarket run. I have it on good authority you make a killer meat loaf." She waves at Ray and Peter. "Maybe you two could turn the mattress on the boys' bed so at least they can sleep there later. We can sort out getting it cleaned later."

Drew flashes his mother a grateful smile; her practical no-nonsense attitude might have driven him mad as a teenager but he's happy to see it now.

* * *

The afternoon drags and fades into evening, marked by Jesse dozing fitfully, then jerking awake to sit and rock, compulsively stroking Wicket's fur. He allows Drew to take him to the bathroom or to press juice and water to his lips but won't eat and still won't respond to questions, flinches if anyone but Drew touches him. When Drew needs to use the bathroom, needs to shower, Martin, Ray and Peter hold him, reassure him until Drew returns.

Right now, he's dozing again, the blanket his mother has draped over the two of them pulled up over his shoulders. Scamp has crawled beneath the blanket and curled up on his lap, Drew can hear her purring and see the movement of Jesse's fingers opening and closing in her fur.

"He loves that little cat," Erin remarks over the top of a mug of tea and Drew agrees.

"At least some of that will be his need to touch soft things," Martin says. "It's a form of stimming."

"He does it with my hair too sometimes," Drew adds in an absent voice, pushing his glasses up and fighting a yawn. Smiles when his mom and Erin giggle at the comment. "And when we went to the farm for his birthday you should have seen him with the animals. Especially the big ass dog they have."

Jesse stirs and mumbles something against Drew, making everyone sit up; he hasn't spoken in hours.

"Jess? What did you say? Jess?" he asks. From the corner of his eye he sees Martin is paying attention. "Sweetheart?"

"George," Jesse mumbles, his voice thick with sleep before settling again.

Drew stares down at his face, at the long lashes against the pale skin of his cheeks and bites his lip. He turns to Martin.

"I think I have an idea."

* * *

48

Drew rubs his eyes and takes a sip from his water bottle. Jesse has slumped against him, head on his shoulder, and Drew adjusts the seat belt digging into his neck. Smiles at the snuffling sound Jesse makes before soft snoring resumes. He snags Wicket from where he's fallen between them and the front seats of Ray's SUV and tucks him back under Jesse's arm.

"Okay back there, Drew?" Ray asks.

"Yeah, we're good. Sleeping Beauty is still out like a light."

"Good," Erin says. "Who knows, maybe when he wakes up, he'll be ... feeling better."

Drew doubts it but agrees with her anyway.

As soon as he mentioned his idea to Martin, the doctor agreed, passing Drew his phone to make the phone call and explaining the plan to others. The Johnston Farm phone rang four times before Frank Johnston answered, his tone softening when he heard who was calling. Drew explained the situation as best he can and is astounded when the farmer interrupts him.

"You want to bring him up here and see if the animals bring him out, Drew? He sure did love Hazel."

"Well actually I was thinking of George, and I know it's short notice, but yeah that's exactly what I want. We'll pay for a privat ..."

"No, you won't," Frank said. "You just bring Jesse here and we'll see if we can get that little spark he has when he's around animals to warm him back up, okay?"

"Thank you, thank you," Drew had said, voice heavy with unshed tears. "We'll drive up in the morning, so we should be there around ten I suppose."

"Don't you worry about it, we'll see you when we see you."

He had hung up and relayed the news to the room. Ray and Erin immediately volunteered as drivers and when Martin suggested they book a couple of nights in Alberton, Drew's parents took care of the accommodation.

"Just doing our bit to help," Peter said as he hung up and put his credit card away.

There was no change in Jesse when they woke this morning but getting him up and in the shower was easier than Drew had anticipated. After thirty seconds of agony over Ray and Erin's presence, he'd decided to hell with it, and climbed in with him, figuring it resolved more than one problem in short order. Erin tried without success to get Jesse to eat but Drew had better luck getting him to drink some milk and half a bottle of water. The rest of the bottle sits, untouched, on the seat next to him.

Getting him out of the apartment and into the car was the biggest obstacle. At first, he refused to step through the door and it wasn't until Ray had stepped forward and scolded him, visibly fighting guilt and tears as he did so, that Jesse folded in on himself, allowing Drew to get him in the lift and eventually out the front door. Drew had had to physically force him into the car and put his seat belt on him, before pulling him as close as the seat belt would allow and heaving a sigh of relief.

He looks at his watch. Nearly ten thirty; another ten minutes and they'll be there. Please, let this work Drew thinks, shifting so he can see Jesse's face. He hates this. The idea of losing Jesse fills Drew with dread but this... Having him there and somehow lost, disconnected from him, this is torture. Knowing the man he loves is in there and won't, or can't, come out is killing him. Barry Reynolds was very understanding and promised to apologize to Drew's classes on his behalf; Mr Greenwold had been, Drew is sure, close to tears as he told Drew to take all the time Jesse needs. Jody made him promise he would give Jesse her love, even if he didn't understand it yet, and said yes of course she would take care of Scamp. They are all being fantastic and it's breaking Drew's heart.

"Jess, you are so loved," he whispers against Jesse's head. "Please come back."

He's aware of Ray's gaze in the rear vision mirror and of Erin leaning back to rest her hand on his knee and is grateful to them both. They could have decided to simply take Jesse home with them, after all they still hold power of attorney and Drew has no legal rights. This has to be as bad for them as it is for him, probably worse given that Jesse has attached himself to Drew. He sighs and leans against the window, watching for the sign for the farm.

* * *

Ray brings the car to a halt in the turnaround where a couple of months earlier Jesse had stood, looking at Drew with equal parts excitement and worry as they waited for Mr Johnston. Now that they're here, Drew thinks he understands that feeling. Hopeful this will be the key, terrified it won't be. He takes a deep breath and shakes Jesse's shoulder.

"Wake up, Jess, we're here." He get only a soft grunt in reply. "Jesse, wake up. If you wake up, you can ride Hazel."

From the front seat comes the sound of Erin catching her breath but Drew has no time to explain that they are going to do whatever it takes and if that means tying Jesse on that damned horse, that's what they'll do. He counts to ten and tries waking Jesse again.

"Jess, you need to wake up. We're at the farm. Mr Johnston and Brenda have got Hazel and George ready for us."

This time Jesse stirs and lifts his head. Peers around the car with sleep heavy eyes and tries to snuggle back against Drew. Unfortunately for Jesse, Drew is a step ahead and unclicks both seat belts. Reaches for the door handle.

"Ray can you be ready?" he asks, and Jesse lifts his head again, slight frown flitting over his face. "Jesse, we're going to get out of the car and go see Hazel and George, okay? You remember Hazel?"

Ray opens the door behind him and Drew backs out, bringing Jesse with him. The minute they are out, Jesse wraps his arms around Drew and buries his head in his neck. Drew squeezes the back of his neck and murmurs something indistinct to him. When he looks up he sees Frank Johnston approaching, looking just as he had the first time he met.

"Hey Jesse, Mr Johnston is here, he's wearing his overalls," Drew says, then lowers his head to whisper in Jesse's ear. "You have overalls too Jesse. Remember how much I like them?"

"Drew, Jesse," the farmer's face falls as he takes in Jesse's state, "it's good to see you again."

Drew holds his hand out.

"Mr Johnston, this is Ray and Erin Peterson, Jesse's parents."

"Please call me Frank," he shakes hands with the Petersons and looks at Drew, "you too, Drew."

Frank rubs the back of his neck and makes a face.

"How is he today? Any better? No? Ah, Drew I'm so sorry. Thank you for the email last night telling us what happened. Brenda's just beside herself."

Drew looks around.

"Where is Brenda? Feeding the chickens?"

"She had to take George to the vet for his booster shot but she should be back soon," Frank tells them. "Why don't we take Jesse and his folks over to the stable and see Hazel? See if that helps at all."

Drew slides his hands around so they're on Jesse's chest and gives him a gentle push back, then wraps an arm around his waist to propel him forward. He's disappointed when Jesse bows his head and looks at his feet; reminds himself they've just arrived, this could take time. If it works at all. Erin falls in on the other side of Jesse and hands him Wicket, curling his fingers around the arm of the toy until he has a grip. If Frank Johnston is surprised or shocked by the object, they see no sign of it. Ray moves behind them, ready to catch Jesse if anything goes wrong.

When they get inside, Drew remembers the cat, Pumpkin, and looks up. He spots him on a rafter and nudges Jesse to show him, but Jesse still doesn't lift his head.

Frank stops in front of Hazel's stall and takes the halter off the door. Holds it out toward Jesse.

"Do you remember how to do this Jesse? Can you put these on Hazel for me?" When he gets no reaction, he continues. "No matter, I can show you again. Lots of people forget."

He opens the door and clucks to the mare, smooths his hand over her nose and slides the halter on. Leads her out. Hazel follows him out to the sunlight.

"Come on Jesse," he says, "let's show your mom and dad how good you are with horses."

They join Frank outside and Erin hangs back; Drew can see the horse makes her nervous. Still holding Jesse around the waist, he moves him closer to the animal and slides his free arm around her neck. She turns her head and snorts a breath in their direction.

"I think Hazel remembers you," Drew says.

As if to confirm that of course she remembers him, Hazel gives a soft whinny and bobs her head twice. Without a word, Jesse rests his hand on her muzzle, then leans his head against her neck. Drew hears Erin stifle a sob and a rustle he assumes is Ray putting his arm around her. He tightens his own around Jesse.

"Jess, *please* can you come back," he whispers to him. "I miss you darlin'."

Jesse doesn't answer but turns his head so he's looking at Drew and for a moment, Drew gets a brief glimpse of him in his eyes. There's movement behind him Frank suggests to Ray and Erin that they might like to come and have coffee. Erin hesitates, picks up Wicket from where Jesse has dropped him, then follows the men back through the stable, their voices fading into the distance.

"We can take the horses for a ride when you come back," Drew says, unaware he's crying. "Please, Jess. Please."

They stand, the three of them, letting the sun warm them.

* * *

Drew doesn't know how long they've been there when he hears a vehicle pull up, followed by the sound of car doors opening and shutting. A bark echoes across the yard and Hazel whickers and stomps a hoof. Jesse looks up and Drew catches his breath when he sees the flicker of a smile.

"Did you hear him, Jess? Shall we go see him?"

His heart is pounding so hard, he's sure Hazel can feel it, and his fingers tighten in the coarse hair of her mane.

* * *

The tunnel Jesse is in is filled with the smell of Hazel. He loves the smell of all animals. Dogs. Cats. Rab...no he can't think that word. He can't. If he thinks that word, it will hurt. And the tunnel will collapse and... Drew, he loves the smell of Drew. He loves that even more than the smell of animals because Drew loves him and he loves Drew but he's so scared. So scared that if he comes out of the tunnel something Very Bad will happen. To Drew and there will be blood and it will hurt.

At the other end of the tunnel there's a familiar sound. A bark. It's a long way away, but Jesse thinks he knows who it belongs to. He thinks it belongs to a dog. A very big dog. A dog he knows.

He looks up. Drew is at the end of the tunnel. Hears him say something. About the dog. The big dog. He knows that dog. He knows him.

"George," Jesse whispers.

* * *

Forcing himself to stay calm, Drew takes Jesse's hand and takes a step toward the stable. He half expects Jesse to resist and when he doesn't, tells himself not to get too excited. Hand in hand they make their way through the stable and Drew thinks, but isn't sure, he sees Jesse's eyes flick toward the roof. Unwilling to risk the progress they've made he says nothing.

Jesse's parents are seated at one of the picnic tables and Drew can see Frank introducing them to Brenda. George sits to attention at Frank's feet, watching them approach, and Drew can see the fear on Erin's face. He understands; George is even bigger than he remembers, and it must be daunting for her to think the massive dog might lead her son out of this nightmare.

Jesse's fingers twitch in his hand and Drew glances down at them. *Please let this work. Oh, please let this work.* When they're near he raises his finger to his lips to forestall any questions, smiles at Brenda who is unable to hide her shock and tugs Jesse down to the ground with him. He lifts the hand clasped in his own and forms a fist with it, the way he'd watched Jesse do with Tommy, and then moves it toward George. Waits. After a couple of seconds, he inches their hands closer. George blinks, leans forward, and swipes his tongue the length of Jesse's face. Erin gasps and moves forward but Ray grabs her hand and pulls her back.

* * *

The tunnel fills with the warm, comforting smell of dog. Of George. Somewhere behind that smell, Jesse hears voices. His mom's and his dad's. Drew's voice. Drew's hand on his. A soft, warm feeling at the tips of his fingers. Something rough and wet sweeps across his face and the tunnel begins to collapse around him.

* * *

For a moment the air is electric, as they all wait. Then Jesse throws himself on the oversized creature, buries his face in the long fur, and begins to cry.

* * *

Drew stumbles back and sits down with a thud, teeth clicking together over the tip of his tongue. He lets go of the breath he wasn't aware he was holding and looks up at Erin and Ray in relief. They're clinging to each other, in tears; Brenda puts her arms around Erin and pats her shoulder, tears on her own cheeks. Even Frank Johnston is wiping his eyes with an oversized handkerchief.

Okay, Drew thinks, okay we've made some progress, we're not home yet. Not yet. Taking a deep breath, he crawls forward through the grass and puts a tentative hand on Jesse's shoulder, wincing when he feels him stiffen. Jesse turns and wraps his arms around his neck.

"I was so scared, I was so scared. He killed her, he used a knife and she squealed and there was so much blood, Drew and I was so scared. He wouldn't stop touching me, trying to do things to me and I was so scared he would ... would... hurt me or Mr Greenwold and then he would come and get you and hurt you and she *squealed*," he sobs.

"It's okay, it's okay," Drew runs his hand up and down his back. "It's over, Jess, it's over."

"What if he comes back and hurts you? I couldn't take care of her and he hurt her Drew, she squealed, and I couldn't take care of her and what if they don't put him in jail and he hurts you and I can't take care of you."

Drew can hear Erin sobbing and Ray and Brenda trying to calm her down. Knows how terrible, how heartbreaking, this must be for her but ignores her anyway and edges back from Jesse to cradle his wet face in his hands.

"He's going to jail, Jess, I promise. He can't hurt me or you or anyone again. I promise. It's over. I promise you're safe." Jesse's eyes are searching his face and he drops his hands to pull him against his chest. "Jess, I promise. It's over. You don't have to be scared. He can't hurt you."

* * *

Drew slides the key into the lock of the hotel room and stands back to let Jesse and his parents go in. Erin and Ray's room is next door, but Drew doesn't have the heart to make them leave the two of them alone yet. It's been a rough few days for everyone. He slips his arm around Jesse's shoulder as he pulls the door shut behind them. Motions for them to sit down as he throws his jacket on the bed.

"How are you feeling, honey?" Erin asks Jesse.

"I'm okay, mom." He sets Wicket on the night table and runs his fingers over his head. Seeing him reminds Drew of what he had done before leaving home and he picks his jacket back up and pats the pocket. Pulls out Jesse's keychain, complete with keys, and holds it out to him with a smile. Jesse takes it and hugs him. "Thank you."

"You're welcome, Jess," Drew whispers and strokes his cheek. He dips his head and brushes his lips over Jesse's, conscious of Ray and Erin watching but unable to stop himself. Rests their foreheads together and closes his eyes.

"Are you boys hungry or are you still full of grilled chicken?" Erin asks.

Brenda and Frank had insisted they have lunch with them; Ray and Frank grilled the chicken and Erin helped Brenda with the salads while Drew held Jesse who sat blinking as though he'd just woken up from a long sleep, which Drew supposes he has. Now and then tears broke through and he would grip Drew's hand or wind his fingers in George's fur, but he gave hesitant answers to questions about what he wanted to eat and reassured his mother he felt fine. Even ate some chicken and a bread roll. The purple circles beneath his eyes, testimony to his nightmare crowded sleep of the past two nights, were impossible to ignore and eventually promising the Johnstons they'd return tomorrow, they'd left.

Jesse says he's not hungry right now, just thirsty and Erin gets him a bottle of water from the mini bar. He drinks most of it in one mouthful, belches, and covers his mouth with his hand.

"Sorry." The smile that follows is faint and tired, but Drew will take it.

"Why don't I go get our bags?" Ray says. "I don't know about anyone else, but I could use a shower and then maybe a beer and some room service. What do you think?"

"I'll give you a hand," Drew offers but Ray shakes his head.

"Actually, I think you should just kick back for a bit Drew," he says. "Jesse how about you come and help me get the bags from the car?"

Drew sees Jesse's eyes widen and shakes his head.

"I don't think that's such a great idea," he starts to say. Ray holds his hand up to silence him.

"Jesse, I'd like you to come with me to get the bags from the car. It won't take us long and Drew will be right here when we get back."

"Ray, I..."

"Jesse," Erin's tone is firm and clear, "go with Dad and get the bags. Drew and I will wait here. I promise we won't go anywhere."

Jesse's lower lip quivers, bloodshot eyes filling with tears. Again. Drew hates it but he thinks he knows what Erin and Ray are doing so he kisses Jesse's cheek.

"I promise I'll be right here when you get back. And then we'll have some juice and find a movie to watch, okay?"

"Right here?" Jesse asks.

"Right here."

Ray takes his elbow and ushers him to the door; Drew forces himself to smile when Jesse looks back in panic.

"See? Not moving. It's okay Jess, you can go."

The door swings shut behind him and Drew drags his fingers through his hair with a sigh.

"Jesus," he whispers.

"He has to know he can let you out of his sight," Erin says. "I know it's hard, but if you don't make him do it now, it will only be harder later."

"Okay, yeah, that makes sense." Drew sinks on to the edge of the bed and covers his face with his hands. He can't remember the last time he felt so tired or so empty.

"Drew?" Erin's voice is gentle, and he looks up to answer her but when he opens his mouth to speak, can't. With no warning he's crying, low harsh sobs that he can't hold back or control. She sits down, puts her arms around him, hands cool on the back of his neck. "Oh honey, it's okay. The worst is over, you can let it out now."

He clings to her shivering and crying, giving in to the shock and the fear that's been riding in the back of his mind since Barry Reynolds pulled him from his classroom. Erin lets him cry, rubbing small circles over his back as if he was a child; comforting him the way, Drew realizes, she would have comforted Jesse. Before Drew came on the scene. He adds guilt to his shock and fear.

"I'm so sorry, Erin. It's my fault. None of this would have happened if it wasn't for me." He curls his fingers into the back of her blouse. "I love him, Erin, so much and I would never, ever ..."

"Drew, I know you love him. You'd have to be blind to miss how you feel about him, how you feel about each other." She brushes his hair away from his eyes, tucks a strand behind one ear. Smiles. "No wonder he likes to use your hair for stimming, you must use a great conditioner." Drew laughs despite himself and she pulls a tissue from her purse on the ground, mops his face with it. "Drew this wasn't your fault. I know I said it was, but I upset and that's not an excuse but it's all I have. This is not your fault, okay?"

Drew swallows, squeezes his eyes shut against another wave of tears, and shrugs.

"Listen to me, Drew. Martin was right, if it hadn't been this it would have been something else. Sooner or later this was going to happen, and it was always going to be hard. But he's going to be okay, Drew, and so are you. And now you know what to do so if it happens again, you'll be prepared."

Drew takes her hand and gives her a watery smile.

"Does it get easier?"

"No," she shakes her head and looks sad, "it doesn't. But you've got this. You'll be okay. You'll both be okay."

"I hate that this happened to him," he says, swiping at the fresh tears that threaten to overflow.

"I know you do but all you can do is keep moving forward. And we're all going to help you do that."

The door swings open, cutting off Drew's reply and Ray and Jesse drop the bags on the floor. When Jesse sees Drew's face, he lets go of his back pack and runs to him.

"You're crying. Are you okay?"

Drew hugs him, breathing in Jesse's scent as deeply as he can. Thinks about brushing off the tears and decides he can't lie to him.

"You weren't the only one who was scared, Jess, but I'm okay now. It's over now."

Over Jesse's shoulder, he sees Erin and Ray slip out the door.

* * *

Jesse is stretched out on his side, one hand tucked under his cheek, studying Drew. They're both still dressed, bare feet entwined. On the night table on Drew's side is the bottle of beer he's opened and they've both had a mouthful from. Jesse runs the fingers of his free hand through Drew's hair and tries to smile.

"I'm sorry about Sniffles, Jess," Drew whispers and Jesse shuts his eyes, unable to stop the flood of tears.

"He hurt her so bad," he tells Drew, "and I couldn't stop him."

"I know darlin' but it wasn't your fault. You did your best. Nobody could have done better."

"It was my job to take care of her and I couldn't save her."

"Shhh, Jess, it wasn't your fault. You did take care of her, everyone knows that. You did nothing wrong." He traces the line of Jesse's jaw, brushing the tears away as he goes.

Jesse takes a deep breath and lets it go, puts his hand on Drew's chest; he looks up, eyes dark and filled with pain.

"I can't take care of you, Drew. I couldn't take care of Sniffles and I can't take care of you."

He lets Drew pull him closer until his cheek is rubbing against the stubble on Drew's chin.

"Jesse, you took care of Sniffles and you take care of me. All the time. Nobody has ever taken better care of me."

Jesse shakes his head. Doesn't believe him.

"Jess every time you make me grilled cheese sandwiches, that's taking care of me. When you make me change the sheets on our bed, that's taking care of me. When you tell me I have to stop working and watch movies or silly old Captain Jack with you, that's taking care of me." He puts a finger under Jesse's chin and when Jesse tilts his head up, dips down and kisses him. "When we make love, you take care of me. But mostly you take care of me by letting me love you and loving me back."

Jesse frowns; he doesn't understand that.

"You make me be a better man. You make me want to be a better man. And that is how you take care of me."

"But..."

"No darlin', there's no but. You do take care of me, all the time, every day."

"I'm scared," Jesse says, ducking his head under Drew's chin again.

"I know, Jess, it's okay. I won't let anything hurt you, I promise. I love you."

"I love you too," Jesse whispers.

* * *

49

Late Sunday afternoon, Drew waves goodbye to Ray and Erin, shuts the door and surveys the room. His mom and Jody have tidied the apartment while they were away. Laundry has been washed, dried, and put away. The living room has been vacuumed and dusted, the cushions were all lined up in the correct order when they walked in and are now stacked on the floor at the end of the couch. A message on his desk tells Drew his parents have replaced the mattress and included a rubber sheet as future proofing; he decides Jesse doesn't need to know about that.

Jesse and Scamp are on the sofa, nose to nose, Scamp purring and Jesse whispering to her about how beautiful she is. Drew drops down next to them and closes his eyes for a moment.

"I'm sorry I woke you up in the night," Jesse says. Both nights in Alberton had been punctuated with nightmares, last night ended in a prolonged bout of crying that eventually brought Erin in from their room.

"You have nothing to be sorry for." Drew scratches Scamp's head. "It's not your fault. Hey, I think my mom left a lasagna in the fridge."

Jesse nods, still not looking at him. Drew sighs.

"Jess, what's wrong?" He stops scratching Scamp's head and starts stroking Jesse's instead. "Are you scared? We don't have to stay here if you don't want to. We can go to your mom and dads."

Jesse puts Scamp on the couch next to him and picks at his thumbnail.

"I don't want to go to Mom and Dad's, I want to stay here."

"Then what is it sweetheart? Tell me, so I can help."

Jesse's head bows even lower and his voice is so quiet, Drew leans in to hear him.

"I wet the bed," he says. "The other night."

Drew sighs in relief. Is that all? He's embarrassed because he remembers wetting the bed?

"Come here." He pulls Jesse around so he's straddling him, ignoring the shiver of want that runs through him at the feel of him on his lap. "You don't have to be embarrassed about that. It's just one of those things that happen."

"Little kids wet their bed. I'm not a little kid."

"Nobody thinks you are. Something really bad happened to you, and everything just sort of shut down for a bit. It doesn't mean you're a kid."

"What if it happens again?"

Drew takes his glasses off and rubs his eyes, trying to figure out what to say and how to say it.

"I'm sure it won't happen again but if it does, well, it does. That's what washing machines are for. It's not the end of the world, Jess." A thought occurs to him and he frowns. "Is that why you haven't been drinking? Jess, you can't do that, you'll make yourself sick."

"But ..."

"But nothing. If it worries you that much, just make sure you go to the bathroom before we turn the light out." He kisses Jesse's forehead. "I'm not worried at all. I'm sure it won't happen again. Okay?"

"Okay," Jesse leans in against him. "Can we have the lasagna now? I'm hungry."

Laughing, Drew pushes him back of his lap.

"Yeah, we can have it now. Shall we watch a movie while we eat? It's summer vacation so I don't have school tomorrow."

He glances at Jesse and puts a hand out to steady himself against the counter when he sees the first full open smile he's seen since he left Jesse at work on Wednesday.

"You'll be home all day?"

"Yup. All day. Every day for the next month. You'll be sick of me by lunchtime."

Jesse shakes his head and scrubs at his eyes with the heel of his hand.

"No. I won't. Can we go swimming in the morning?"

Drew laughs.

"What else would we do on a Monday morning?" He puts the plates of lasagna in the microwave and hits the buttons. "So, what do you want to watch?"

"Can we read instead?" Jesse asks, pouring Drew a glass of wine.

"Yeah of course," Drew frowns at the wine glass, then gives Jesse a pointed stare. "If you're not having wine, I better see a glass of juice being poured."

Jesse opens his mouth to protest, snaps it shut again and gets a small glass out of the cupboard. While he gets the apple juice from the fridge, Drew replaces the tumbler with a larger one. Smiles when Jesse stops and stares at it, protest in his eyes.

"Jess, you need to drink. I'll read you anything you like. I'll even watch Captain Jerk with you if you want. But you have to drink."

"Captain Jack, not Captain Jerk. Fine." He fills the glass halfway, looks at Drew who folds his arms and waits, sighs and fills the glass the rest of the way. "Can we read the book I got you for your birthday? The poems about the cats."

Drew picks up his plate and steals a kiss.

"Yeah, we can read the poems about the cats."

* * *

Jesse frowns. He needs to change Scamp's litter box and he can't because the litter container is empty. Glances over his shoulder at Drew, stretched out on the sofa reading a book; not the cat poems book, another book, one that Jesse isn't interested in. Too many big words on too many pages. He looks back at the litter box and empty container, unsure of what to do. Usually he brings home kitty litter from work, but he hasn't been at work since Wednesday and he's not sure how he feels about going back yet. What if there's still blood everywhere? He shuts his eyes and makes himself think of French fries and ice-cream and kissing Drew and playing with Scamp. Shoves his hand in his pocket to touch his key chain. Maybe they could go to the supermarket and get some; they don't have the right brand, but he needs to change the litter box today.

He goes to the couch and sits down, lifting Drew's feet and putting them in his lap.

"I can hear you thinking, darlin'."

"No, you can't," Jesse replies only half paying attention. A minute later he jumps when Drew digs his toes into his thigh. Drew is looking at him over the top of his book, only his hair and glasses visible above the pages. "We need kitty litter."

Drew puts the book on the floor and holds his arms open. Jesse hesitates then stretches out along his body, head on his chest.

"Okay, kitty litter's no big deal. I'm sure Mr Greenwold would love to see you."

Drew's drawing circles on Jesse's back with his thumb and it feels nice; it makes it easy to ignore the kitty litter.

"I...I don't know," he says.

"I can go and get some and you can wait for me here if you like," Drew offers.

No, Jesse doesn't want to do that. He knows Drew will come back, that he'll be okay, but he had a nightmare last night that he couldn't find him. He wants to be able to see him today.

"I could get some from the supermarket."

"They don't have the right brand, she won't like it."

Drew sighs.

"Jess I don't think Scamp really cares what she pees in, okay?"

Jesse glares at him and Drew snickers.

"Okay, okay. What do you want to do? Come with me or stay home?"

"I'll come with you."

"Excellent, I have a feeling we might be getting ice-cream on the way home."

"Cheesecake."

"Ice-cream."

270

"Okay," Jesse concedes. "Chocolate."

"Chocolate it is."

* * *

Drew parks at the top of the street and sits for a moment, running his hands around the wheel.

"You sure?" he asks Jesse.

Lip quivering, Jesse shakes his head. No, not at all. But he takes a deep breath and gets out of the car. Drew follows and hand in hand they walk toward the store. Everyone knows Jesse in this street, they're all used to seeing him with Drew now, and some of the store owners come out to hug him. Ask him how he's feeling. Touched, Drew watches as Jesse tries to stay calm as he answers, grip on Drew's hand getting tighter with each person.

As they approach the store front, Drew slips his arm around Jesse and kisses the side of his head.

"You're doing good darlin'," he murmurs.

The doors are open as usual, but the framing is new, and the glass is shiny and clear. Feels Jesse tense at his side. Jesse stops in front of the canary cage, pushed up against the window.

"Idiot," he mutters and begins to turn the cage around. "He's got the door facing out. People can open it and the canaries will all fly away. You have to put them against the door."

"Hey, what are you doing?" Marcus appears from the depths of the store, arms flapping as he yells at Jesse. When he sees who it is he stops, lowers his arms. "Oh. It's you. You don't look sick." He half turns and calls out toward the back of the store. "Mr Greenwold, it's Jesse. He doesn't look sick to me."

Drew decides he agrees with Jesse; Marcus is an idiot. He presses Jesse forward, into the shop. As they cross the threshold, Mr Greenwold appears, smile creasing his features when he sees Jesse.

"Jesse," he pulls him into a hug, "how are you feeling buddy?"

"I'm okay," Jesse mumbles and Drew follows his gaze. He's staring at the counter. It's been cleared of everything but the register and a few pamphlets for local vets. There's no cat nip mice. No bowl of doggie treats for regular customers. No dish of rabbit pellets. He tightens his hold on Jesse's waist. "How are *you* Mr Greenwold?"

"You're a good boy, Jesse." Mr Greenwold pats his shoulder. "I'm fine, thank you. It's so good to see you. I've been worried about you. And this one," he jerks his head toward Marcus who is pushing a broom around the fish food stand, "he's driving me crazy."

"He had the canary cage around the wrong way," Jesse says. Drew grins when the old man rolls his eyes. "We need some kitty litter for Scamp."

"Of course, let's get you some of that," Mr Greenwold says and bustles down the aisle to the bags of litter. "I think you better take two and you best take a catnip mouse for her too."

Drew reaches for his wallet but Mr Greenwold closes his hand over his and shakes his head.

"No need. Jesse has more than earned a few bags of kitty litter over the years." He turns to Jesse, who is still shooting sidelong glances at the counter, and places his hands on his shoulders. "You take the time you need to feel better, okay? You don't have to worry about a thing."

"Thank you Mr Greenwold," he says, picking up the bags of litter. Drew takes one from him and takes his hand. "Scamp will like the mouse."

* * *

He's able to hold on to the tears until they're in the car, then he turns and buries his face in Drew's shirt, so nobody can see him. When he's done, Drew drives them home.

They don't stop for ice-cream.

* * *

"Hi Martin." Drew leans against the counter, eyes on the bathroom door. The shower turns on and he hears Jesse step under the water; he doesn't have much time.

"Drew, how are things? How's our boy doing?"

Drew sighs and pinches his nose.

"Not so good, Doc. I was wondering if you could maybe call in at some point."

"Of course. I'm finishing here in about an hour and I've got nothing planned for tonight. I could swing by if you like. What's up?"

"I'd really appreciate it. I just ... I'd like you to take a look at him. He's not really sleeping and when he does he has nightmares. We called into the pet store today and well, he's been upset on and off since then. I know it's going to take time but, I don't know ..." his voice tapers off and he scratches the back of his neck. Now that he has Martin on the phone, he feels a bit silly; maybe he's overreacting.

"Is he eating?"

"Not as much as usual but yeah he's eating. Getting him to drink is a bigger issue because he's so worried he'll wet the bed again."

"Anything else?"

"He hasn't talked about what David did ... tried to do ... to him," Drew says, cocking his head toward the bathroom. The water's still running.

"What about sex?"

Drew stares at his phone, then puts it back to his ear.

"Uh, beg pardon?"

"Sex. You know, the fun stuff nobody wants to talk about, but everyone wants to do."

"Well uh no, we haven't. I don't want to him to feel he ... um, why is that even relevant?"

"Best sleeping pill I know of but aside from that, I'm just trying to get a clear picture of how he's coping. Is he going to be okay if I call in?"

Drew ponders this for a second. In the bathroom, the water stops running.

"Yeah, I'll tell him you're coming. Thanks."

"No problem, Drew. I'll see you around six thirty."

Jesse appears in the bathroom doorway, a towel around his hips, his chest damp.

"You were on the phone," he says. Drew knows the phone worries him now; the police confirmed on Wednesday evening that it had been David calling them both on the unlisted number and Jesse jumps whenever he hears a chime.

"Yeah I was. Martin is going to come over on his way home," he says, eyes straying to the towel and for a second, he's tempted to cross the room and test Martin's sleeping pill theory.

"Why?" Jesse asks, and he dismisses the thought.

"Because he's our friend and he came over on Thursday and he'd like to know you're okay." Now he does go over and kisses Jesse on the mouth. "Go get dressed, you don't want your cold back."

Jesse is almost to the bedroom when he stops and turns around.

"You're not my mom. I don't need your rules." His voice is shy, as if he's not sure if he's allowed to play anymore.

"I'll phone your mom if you're not careful," Drew says. "Go get dressed you dork."

* * *

A bottle of red wine is open on the coffee table next to three glasses and a carton of apple juice when Martin arrives. Drew offers him a glass and asks him to sit down.

Jesse accepts a small glass and as usual sits on the floor, his back to Drew's legs. The familiarity is comforting and Drew hopes it's a sign that things are starting to ease up in the wonderful confusion that is Jesse's mind.

"How's your wrist, Drew?" Martin asks, taking him by surprise.

"Not bad actually. I've only had to use the brace a couple of times, so hopefully I got lucky."

"Well, be careful you don't go overusing it and give yourself an RSI." Martin smirks and Drew rolls his eyes but the insinuation goes over Jesse's head. "What about you Jesse, how are you feeling?"

"I'm okay," Jesse says and sips his wine. He rests his head on Drew's knee and Drew runs his fingers through the short spiky hair. It bothers him the way Jesse keeps saying he's okay. What does okay even mean? He's giving serious consideration to banning it in his classrooms next semester.

"Drew said you've been having some nightmares," Martin says. Jesse shrugs.

"Yeah."

"Can you tell me what you dream about?"

"I don't want to," Jesse whispers.

Martin sips his wine and slides down so he's on the floor facing Jesse. Crosses his legs.

"I understand that, Jesse, but maybe if you tell me a little about what your dreams are I can help make them go away," he says. Jesse looks from him to Drew and then down at his glass. Drew feels like he's just kicked a puppy and wishes he hadn't called Martin. "Drew's worried about you, Jesse. It would help him if you let me help you."

Jesse snaps his head up and looks at Martin, eyes wide and worried.

"It was frightening for Drew as well," Martin says, "and one way you can help him not be frightened anymore is if you let me help you."

Drew spreads his legs and wraps them around Jesse as if he's hugging him and continues to stroke his hair. Jesse's fingers dig into the flesh of his calf.

"I keep dreaming that David is in here and that he ... he hurts Scamp and ... Drew. With his knife. One night I dreamed that when I got into bed, Sn ... Sniffles was in my bed. Only she was like," he gulps a mouthful of wine, "like after he did it."

Drew feels sick. No wonder he hasn't been sleeping.

"One ...once... I dreamed it was Drew and that he did it to him not ... not ... Sniffles and then he said he was going to do it to me." His chest starts to hitch, and Drew can hear the panic in his voice. He's willing to bet that's the dream that caused the wet sheets. Leans down and pulls Jesse up onto the armchair with him and wraps his arms around him.

"Shhhh, that's enough now. It's okay sweetheart. We're safe. It's okay."

"Jesse," Martin says, "you know dreams aren't real, don't you? Good man, that's what I thought. They're just how your brain deals with what happened to you. They're normal even if they're frightening. What do you do when you have one?"

"I hold Wicket and I make myself think of things I like. Things that are nice."

"Like what?"

"Like chocolate cake. Or Scamp. Or when Drew reads to me." He looks down at his fingers and Drew is surprised to see he's blushing. "Sometimes I think about Drew kissing me."

Martin laughs.

"That's a very good strategy, Jesse. Do you wake Drew up?"

"I try not to, I don't want to worry him."

"Jess..." Drew protests but Martin cuts him off.

"Jesse are you scared of waking Drew up because you remember what David was trying to do to you before he hurt Sniffles?"

Jesse's head drops but he's silent.

"Jesse, you did nothing wrong. Not then and not now, okay? I understand you don't want to wake him up, but I want you to promise that if you're really scared you will, okay?"

Jesse looks doubtful.

"There's nothing wrong with being scared Jesse and if you can go back to sleep just by thinking about chocolate cake or about Scamp, that's great. But if that's not working I want you to wake Drew up and if thinking about kissing him helps, try actually kissing him."

What the hell? Drew stares at Martin who, to his infuriation, is ignoring him.

"Jesse, sex is a good thing when two people love each other like you and Drew do. You don't have to be ashamed or embarrassed, so I want you to try and replace the scared feeling with a good feeling, so you can go back to sleep okay?" Jesse nods and Martin smiles. "Good. If it doesn't work, we can try something else. Okay? Okay. Now, Drew also said you're not drinking very much."

Jesse hides his face against Drew but says nothing.

"He told me why Jesse," Martin says gently, "and we all understand why you're worried. If it was me, I think I would be worried about it too. But Jesse, look at me," he waits until Jesse peers around at him, "you only wet the bed because you were so frightened by your dream that your body couldn't wake up. That's one time in lots and lots and lots of years that your body has been able to wake you up. You didn't wet the bed because you don't know to go to the bathroom but because your body got stuck in the scared part of your dream. Do you understand what I'm saying?"

"I think so," Jesse says.

"It hasn't been stuck again has it? No. So what I want you to do is I want you to make sure you drink properly during the day and at about nine o'clock you can stop drinking if you're worried. Make sure you go to the bathroom before you go to bed and if you and Drew have sex," he quirks an eyebrow when a small snigger escapes Jesse, "yes sex is funny, Jesse, and if you do, then I want you to go to the bathroom after. That way you know that even if you get scared in a dream, your body won't get stuck again. Okay?"

Jesse nods and sits up a little. Slides his arm around Drew's neck.

"Jess, can you tell us what upset you at the store today?" Drew asks and Jesse flinches. "Was it just the memory?"

He shakes his head.

"No," he whispers. "I ... I could see it. The blood. Sniffles' blood. And ... and... I could..."

"Okay, you don't have to tell us any more Jesse," Martin interrupts. "That's called a flashback and it probably happened because it's the first time you've gone back. Hopefully it won't happen again, but I want you to tell Drew if it does okay?"

"Why?"

"Because sometimes when people have flashbacks they need to come and see someone like me to help make them stop."

Jesse mulls this over and nods.

"Good. How are you feeling now?"

Drew braces for okay and is surprised when Jesse says 'better' instead.

"That's great, one step at time okay?" Martin says, accepting another glass of wine. "What do you guys have planned for tomorrow?"

"Swimming," Drew says, "and ice-cream."

"Ice-cream?" Martin raises an eyebrow.

"We were supposed to have ice-cream today, but it didn't quite happen."

"Drew's on summer vacation so we can swim lots and have lots of ice-cream all day," Jesse says, nestling against Drew's shoulder.

"Well," Martin says, "that's what summer vacation is for. Swimming and ice-cream."

"And lots of sex," Jesse says, ducking his head down as Drew chokes on his wine.

"*Jess!*" he splutters over the sound of Martin's laughter.

* * *

Martin declines an invite to stay and eat with them; shakes Drew's hand at the door before turning to Jesse and holding his hand out to him.

"Jesse, do you trust me?" he asks.

"I ... I think so."

"That will have to do, I guess," Martin says, still holding his hand. "What happened to you is horrible but you're strong. Much stronger than the man who did this to you. So when I say you are going to be just fine, I want you to believe me."

Jesse's cheeks flame red and he stares at his feet, rubbing his neck. Amused, Drew rubs his back, grateful to the doctor.

"Good night, guys. Thanks for the wine."

They watch until the lift doors close and go back inside.

* * *

Drew leans on the counter, sipping wine, while Jesse makes grilled cheese sandwiches for them both. Enjoys the view when Jesse bends to look for something in the fridge; smiles when he stands up with a triumphant cry, brandishing an onion and a tomato.

"Onion or tomato or both?" Jesse asks.

"Both? Want me to chop them?" He's treated to the same glare Jesse had given him earlier on the subject of kitty litter. "Okay, okay, just offering."

"I chop them when you have school work," Jesse says as he peels the onion, "I can chop them tonight."

Within a few minutes the onion and tomato are chopped and laid next to slices of cheese. Drew comes around the end of the counter and leans his chin on Jesse's shoulder as he drops the buttered bread into the heated pan, layers them with cheese, onion, tomato, and more bread. Drew holds the plates up for him while he serves, watches while he pours himself a half glass of apple juice and kisses his cheek. A half glass without prompting is a win in his book.

Scamp jumps up on next to Jesse and for the next ten minutes Drew battles the two of them, trying to stop Jesse from feeding most of his sandwich to her.

"I'm sure grilled cheese and onion sandwiches are not a good idea for cats," he says, rolling his eyes as Scamp licks crumbs from her paws. "And I'm pretty damned sure they don't like tomatoes."

"Shows what you know," Jesse retorts feeding her a last piece of crust. "Scamp loves tomatoes."

"If you say so." He smacks Jesse's hand when he tries to pinch a piece of Drew's sandwich. "No, you can't feed her mine as well. She's had enough."

He puts his plate on the coffee table and picks up his wine. Looks at his watch and falls back on the sofa.

"It's only eight o'clock. What do you want to do now?" he asks. Jesse shrugs, scratching Scamps ears as she noses the empty plates looking for more morsels of cheese. "Movie? Captain Jerk?"

"You're a jerk," Jesse pokes his tongue out. "Not tonight."

"Read? I've got a new book I think you'll like." Drew has been dying to read Neil Gaiman to Jesse, is sure he'd like him, that it wouldn't be too hard for him to follow.

"No," Jesse says in a wistful voice, shaking his head.

Drew frowns, bemused. He thought, after Martin's visit, Jesse might be a little more relaxed but now he's not so sure.

"Well, what do you want to do then?" He takes a mouthful of wine.

Jesse reaches out and winds a strand of Drew's hair around his finger, a half smile playing on his mouth as he does so. Locks his eyes on Drew's and gives the strand a gentle tug and bites his lower lip.

"Oh." Understanding creeps up on Drew and he smiles. He tilts his head and leans in to kiss him; Jesse's other hand skims over his shirt and around his waist. Sighing into the kiss, Drew closes his eyes and lets his tongue dance over Jesse's lip until he opens his mouth and meets it with his own. When the kiss breaks, he stands and holds his hand out. Jesse takes it and leans his head against him as they go to the bedroom.

Drew shuts the door and peels his tee-shirt off; tosses it in the corner. Jesse is perched on the bed, brow furrowed, chewing his lip.

"Jess?"

"When ... when David was in the store, he kept asking me things about us. And he kept trying to touch me. I ...I know he wanted to hurt me, to do things to me."

Drew shuts his eyes and sits down next to him. Takes his hand and runs his thumb over the back of it.

"But I think he wanted to do it because everyone thinks I'm beautiful." There's no conceit or arrogance in his words, just acceptance and Drew squeezes his hand and tells him he is beautiful. "I don't think he likes that you have something beautiful and he doesn't, so he wanted to hurt it. Like ...like he did with Sniffles."

Jesse is talking about spite and jealousy without realizing it and Drew doesn't know what to say.

"When I used to go to those clubs and people ... men ... would take me home, they always said I was beautiful too but when they found out I wasn't normal they wanted to hurt me too. You're the only one who never did that. Nobody ever took care of me like you do, Drew. Not in sex and not in anything else."

"I'll always take care of you Jess," Drew says desperate to not lose his battle with the tears that are threatening, "in anything you need."

"I know," Jesse says. "That's why you took me to see George isn't it?"

Drew nods, unable to speak.

"I couldn't get out of the place in my head by myself because I was too scared that something would happen to you because I can't take care of you. But I knew George could take care of both of us."

Drew gives in and tears drip onto their joined hands; Jesse wipes them away.

"It's okay, Drew. I know I can't take care of you if someone tries to hurt you. I don't know how, and things get muddled in my head and I don't know how to think. But I can love you anyway and I can make you grilled cheese sandwiches."

"Yes, Jesse, you can."

"Good. I'm glad." Jesse turns to face him and brushes at Drew's tears with his fingers. "In my nightmare, sometimes the police officers don't come and he ... hurts ... me and then you don't want me anymore."

"I'll never not want you," Drew's voice is a faint whisper, fighting for breath. No wonder he wanted to hide from the world, he's been dreaming of being raped and discarded. If Drew ever gets his hands on David ... the thought is cut off when Jesse's smile surfaces, radiant and sunny.

"Can you take care of me tonight, Drew? I don't want to have that nightmare anymore."

Drew cups his cheek in one hand and brushes his lips over Jesse's. Tries to keep the kiss light and soft but Jesse has other ideas. He flicks his tongue around Jesse's mouth, exploring and tasting and it's both familiar and new. Eases him back on to the bed and moves his mouth down over his chin to his throat. Runs his tongue over his Adam's Apple to kiss the hollow at its base.

Jesse's hands pull at him until he's resting between his legs, kissing as much skin as he can lay his mouth on and tugging at the well-worn *Star Wars* tee-shirt Jesse's wearing. He moves his legs so he's straddling him and lifts him up, so he can yank the shirt over his head. When it's on the floor, he takes his glasses off and puts them on the night table; gets the lube bottle from the drawer and drops it on the bed.

He looks down at Jesse and smiles, runs his fingers down Jesse's chest, through the dark curls of hair, and scratches his nails over his nipples. Moaning, Jesse rolls his hips up to meet Drew's and Drew bites his own lip when he feels how hard he is. He stands, ignoring the whine of protest, and undoes Jesse's jeans, pulls them off and discards them. Takes off his own shorts and kicks them to the side.

When Jesse wriggles up the bed, Drew follows, on his knees. Smooths his hands up Jesse's inner thighs, over the crease where they meet his body, and across his chest. Knows the trembling isn't just from desire; there's fear as well. Continues the trajectory along Jesse's shoulders, down his arms, to his hands. Brings one hand toward him and curls Jesse's fingers around his own erection. Hisses when his hips jerk forward as if he has no control over them. And if Jesse strokes beneath his balls like that again, he won't have; he edges back out of reach.

He pours lube on his fingers and reaches down to massage, easing a finger inside and when Jesse moans, bends down and takes the head of his cock in his mouth. Jesse's fingers pull on his hair and he shivers; that feels good. Adds a second finger, rubs both over the small bundle of nerves he finds without difficulty, and is rewarded with a spurt of saltiness on his tongue and a short, sharp cry from Jesse. More tugging on his hair but it's desperate now, wanting him to pull off and there's an audible pop when he does so.

Head thrown back, eyes closed, and panting, Jesse is beautiful; Drew pinches the base of his own cock for a moment to retain control. He pours more lube over his fingers and slicks himself with care. Strokes over Jesse's prostate one more time, provoking a shuddering cry and Jesse widens his legs.

"Drew, now, I need you now," he says between gasps.

Drew takes his time, pushing in with care, not wanting to cause any pain, even minor. Not tonight, not when Jesse needs to feel loved and protected. Pleasure ripples through him and he takes as much weight on his elbows as he can, pressing his lips to Jesse's ear.

"I'll always take care of you Jess," he whispers, "and I'll always love you."

Jesse rests his legs over Drew's thighs, digs his fingers into his back and rolls up again. Surrounded by tight heat, Drew can't help but move; driven by want. Grits his teeth and rocks forward as deeply as he can before pulling back almost all the way. Matches his thrusts to Jesse's breathing and pleas for more.

When he slides his hand between them, Jesse clenches his muscles and Drew groans loudly enough that for a split second he worries about the neighbors. Then decides he does not care, this feels too good. Rubs the pad of his thumb over the damp head of Jesse's cock; strokes down to the base, back up with smooth, firm movements.

"Feels ... good," Jesse pants and the naked lust Drew can hear sends a shudder through him. Tightens his fist, squeezing Jesse until he hears him moan.

"Jesse, can't hold on much more," he whispers and moves his hips in a figure eight that drags a whimper from Jesse and he tightens beneath him. His eyes widen, and his breath comes in long, rapid bursts.

"Drew, I ...I.... Drew...I'm going to ..." he stammers and then his hips are jerking up and he sinks his teeth into Drew's shoulder as he comes, twisting and thrashing.

Without letting go, Drew gives in to the need to thrust hard, face turned against Jesse's skin as he moves closer to the edge. Jesse moves his knees back toward his chest and the slight change in position is all he needs. Orgasm rushes him, and he tips over the edge, repeating Jesse's name; it seems to go on forever.

Jesse's arms wrap around his back and pull him closer; his cock twitches and he shudders one last time. Lifts and dots gentle kisses over Jesse's face.

"Okay?" he asks finally.

Jesse brushes Drew's hair back off his face and nods.

He pulls out with care and rolls on to his back and Jesse drapes himself over his chest, resting his chin on Drew's bicep so he can look at him. Drew knows they need to clean up and get under the covers, but it can wait for now. For now, he just wants to lay there and feel Jesse's weight on him, smell him on him, have his taste on his tongue. Just wants to feel happy for now.

* * *

Jesse spreads his fingers wide over Drew's chest. Drew's heart is pounding, and Jesses closes his eyes and lets himself feel it under his hand. When he opens them, Drew is looking at him with a small smile.

"Hey, you," he whispers, and Jesse stretches up to kiss him.

"Hey," he says when the kiss breaks.

"I missed you."

"I'm sorry."

Drew shakes his head still smiling.

"It's okay."

Jesse asks if he wants his glasses, but Drew says no, he's fine, so Jesse snuggles up as close as he can. Drew is warm and it's comforting even if his skin is damp. More than damp in some places.

"I should go back to work," he says. Going to the store today was hard; worse, it was frightening. It seemed like everywhere he looked, what had happened was overlaid. Like a double exposure on a photograph and when you ended up with two images. There was the clean, tidy, comfort of *Greenwold's Pets*, familiar even with a new door and the tidy counter and over the top, like a transparency were the events of last week; everywhere Jesse looked he saw it. Blood, water, crushed fish, broken glass, Sniffles. He shudders at the thought. But beneath it all is the knowledge that his job, even if some people think it's ordinary, is important. Not just to him but to Mr Greenwold and to the animals. On a more unconscious level, one he's not really aware of, it's part of what makes him who he is, it's where he met Drew, and it's impossible to imagine life without it.

"You sure you feel up to it darlin'?" Drew is scratching his nails the length of Jesse's back; it feels nice, kind of satisfying and sexy. He shrugs.

"I don't know but Marcus is an idiot and Mr Greenwold is getting old."

Drew huffs a laugh against Jesse's head.

"Why don't you wait until next week?"

Jesse props himself up on one elbow and asks why.

"I don't think it would do you any harm to have a few days off, Jess, and besides, I'm on vacation – we can spend some time together."

Jesse thinks about this, screwing his face up in concentration.

"Go swimming and have ice-cream?"

"If you want."

"Can we go to the zoo?"

"Yes," Drew laughs, "God, I haven't been to the zoo in years."

"Can we have a picnic?"

"Better, we can take a picnic to the zoo and have ice-cream after. How would that work?"

"What about sex?" Jesse asks, eyes glimmering with mischief.

"At the zoo?"

Jesse pounces on him, tickling and giggling.

"No, not at the zoo. Here."

"Oh," Drew grans his hands and holding them away from his skin, "well if you insist, here would be a better spot, I suppose."

"You're a dork."

Drew lets go of Jesse's hands and reaches up to cup his face.

"So are you, but I love you anyway. And yes, we can have lots of sex here. We can stay in bed all day and make love if you want."

Jesse's face flushes at the idea of spending entire day in bed with Drew and he covers the hand on his cheek with his own. Dips down and kisses Drew, drawing his bottom lip in between his teeth. Bites just hard enough to make Drew jump. Licks at the same spot and smiles when Drew shivers. Drew's hand slides down his back to his hip and Jesse presses against him.

"Again?" Drew asks. "Already?"

Jesse nods and kisses him.

* * *

50

Jesse slumps in the passenger seat and rubs his eyes. He's tired; he'd had three nightmares last night and the last one had been nasty; it had taken an hour of Drew reading to him before he was able to fall asleep again. Swimming helped but he still isn't sure if he wants to go to work.

"You know, you don't have to go in today," Drew says, leaning on the steering wheel.

"Yes, I do," Jesse picks at his jeans, "Mr Greenwold needs me. We need to do the monthly orders and Marcus gets them muddled up."

The truth is he would much rather go home and spend the day with Drew. Maybe they could spend it in bed again, like they did on Friday. That had been fun. But it's not fair to Mr Greenwold to keep getting paid when he's not there, no matter what anybody says.

"Want me to pick you up tonight?"

"No," he says. "I'll take the bus. I always take the bus on Mondays."

"It's okay," Drew starts the car up, "I'm on vacation, I can pick you up."

Jesse shifts in his seat so he can look at him. He's in an old tee-shirt and shorts, his damp hair loose and curling over his collar; normally it would be in a ponytail for work and he'd be in slacks and a shirt, sometimes even a tie.

"I like it when you have your hair like that," Jesse says, tugging on the ends.

Drew snorts and rolls his eyes.

"Nifty subject change," he says.

Jesse stares out the window, watching the traffic, before taking a deep breath.

"I'm not a little kid; I'm not scared."

"Okay darlin'," Drew says and there's something sad in his voice that bothers Jesse, but he doesn't know why, "get the bus since it's Monday. Can I meet you at your stop, at least?"

Jesse nods and when Drew has finished parking the car, he leans over and kisses him, rests his smooth cheek against Drew's rough, unshaven one for a minute.

"I love you," he whispers.

* * *

At eight thirty Jesse rolls the canary cage out to the sidewalk and waves hi to Gary from the deli. He makes sure it's turned the right way, so nobody can open it and let the birds out. Stops on his way back inside, to run a hand down the new framing on the door; it needs to be painted still.

At ten o'clock Marcus says he can't clean the rabbits out because they bite. Jesse rolls his eyes and snaps that he'll do it. He's emptying soiled straw into a bag, trying to not think about Sniffles, when Marcus tells him it took him an hour to clean the blood off the counter. Mr Greenwold sends Marcus to the supermarket with a list of things they don't need and the instruction to take his damned time.

Jesse goes to restock the dog food and Mr Greenwold cleans the rabbits.

At eleven thirty Jesse takes a deep breath and gets the trolley of tank cleaning supplies. While he was away, there was a delivery of new aquarium plants and Marcus forgot to treat them before placing them in the tanks – *of course*, thinks Jesse. Now there are three tanks full of white snails for Jesse to deal with. Muttering under his breath, he pushes the trolley toward the back of the store.

Mouth dry and heart pounding, he's trying to think of seeing Drew later and walking home together from the bus. Maybe they'll get an ice-cream from the man on the corner if he's there. Just as he's losing himself in the thought of chocolate ice-cream and holding Drew's hand, a customer backs into the shelf of aquarium pebbles, sending the bags in every direction with a crash. Someone walks on one of them and they crunch underfoot.

Lost in his terror, Jesse backs away, a low whine rising from his throat.

At eleven forty-five, Mr Greenwold picks up the phone.

* * *

Drew doesn't go straight home after dropping Jesse at work. It's been a long time since he had a day to himself even though Jesse works most Saturdays. Those days are usually spent either doing something for school, running errands, or catching up with family; today he has the luxury to do anything he wants. What he wants is coffee from his favorite café and a walk down by the duck pond at the local park. Most Sundays they come here, usually with Jody, to feed the ducks and it feels strange to be alone. Strange but nice; he needs some time to think.

Barry Reynolds has been chasing him for a response about the Department Head role and wants an answer. To his surprise, Drew's unsure if he wants to accept it. It's a great opportunity, especially at only thirty-five, but lately he's been thinking about doing something different. Maybe picking up some extra college credits and specializing in teaching kids like Jesse. When he finishes his coffee, he tosses the cup in the nearest bin and decides to go home and do some research into it.

The apartment feels empty without Jesse in it. Of the two of them, Jesse is the tidier and more organized. He makes sure laundry is done and that the apartment doesn't look like a combat zone when the cleaning lady comes. He's also quieter and more reserved than Drew. Yet he fills the apartment in a way that Drew only notices now that he's here without him. Smiling he looks around, spots Scamp curled up on top of her cat cave and goes to scratch her ears.

"What did we do before he came along?" he asks. She flicks her ear and stretches as if to say *"you're welcome, if it wasn't for me..."*

Leaving her to snooze in the sun, he turns his laptop on and pulls up Google. He's engrossed in what's available – or to be honest, not available - in schools for students with Jesse's challenges, when his cell phone rings and he picks it up without looking away from the screen.

"Hello?"

"Drew? It's Max Greenwold here, I think you need to come and get Jesse."

* * *

It takes fifteen minutes to drive to the store and another five to find a parking spot. Thumbing the remote lock as he goes, Drew runs toward the store, dodging walkers and shoppers as he tries not to panic.

Marcus is standing in the doorway, watching someone measure one of the dog kennels and Drew ducks around him, panting and flushed. Greenwold turns to greet him from behind the counter where he's filling out stock forms.

"Drew, I'm sorry," he says. "He's out back."

"What happened?"

Drew scrapes his hair back off his face as Greenwold explains and follows him to the door leading to the backroom. Remembers the day he came to pick up the cat tree and he'd asked Jesse on a date. Asks himself, not for the first time, if this the result of that?

Jesse is sitting at the table, a cup in front him, rocking. He looks up when Drew approaches and looks surprised.

"Jess? You okay?" Drew asks; he can feel the blood rushing through his veins. The hand he stretches out toward Jesse is trembling.

"I don't think so," Jesse says taking the hand and holding it against his cheek.

"Can you tell me what's wrong?"

Jesse eyes are bewildered and sad, when he shakes his head.

"Why don't we go home?"

"Okay, I think that would be a good idea." He stands, picks up his backpack and walks over to Mr Greenwold, still in the doorway. "I'm sorry."

"You can try again in a day or two, Jesse," the old man says, sadness etched on his face. He claps Jesse on the shoulder as he passes, looks at Drew. "Let me know how he is."

Drew guides Jesse out the door, nodding at Greenwold as he passes.

* * *

The tears Drew expects don't come. Jesse is listless but calm in the car as they start to drive and after two blocks asks if they can get ice-cream. Worried and desperate to help, Drew agrees. They go to *Swenson's Ice Cream*, by the park and for the second time in one morning, Drew is seated in the sun watching ducks mill around searching for crumbs.

"What happened?" he asks finally. Jesse's eyes cloud and he licks at the chocolate ice-cream oozing down the side of his cone without answering.

"Was it like last week? When you could still see everything?" Drew wonders if he should phone Martin or Ray; he doesn't want to worry anyone if he can avoid it. But if they're about to visit what Jesse calls The Tunnel, Drew thinks it would be better to get help sooner rather than later.

"No," Jesse say, then with a small smile he adds, "and it wasn't like when I'm in the tunnel."

"Then what was it, Jess?"

"It was a bit like when there's a storm and I can feel it in my skin. Everything just felt tight and fuzzy." He thinks for a minute. Drew takes his hand, hating how miserable he looks. "Like when there's lots of thunder but only there wasn't any."

"But you don't feel like going away? Hiding in the tunnel?"

"No," Jesse says and finished his ice-cream. He breaks the cone in pieces and scatters them for the ducks. "Not at the moment."

Not at the moment. That will have to do, Drew supposes. He doesn't want the last of his cone and offers it to Jesse who takes it, lapping at the sides with enthusiasm.

"You'd live on ice-cream if we let you," Drew muses.

"With French fries."

"Oh God, that's revolting." Drew makes a face. "So, what do you want to do Jess? Do you want to go back tomorrow or give it another week?"

Jesse feeds the second cone to the ducks and shoves his hands in his pockets. Leans his head on Drew's shoulder.

"I don't know."

* * *

51

On Martin's advice, Jesse returns to work three days a week. Mondays, Wednesdays, and Fridays he works from nine until three. Drew drops him after swimming and he takes the bus home. The idea, Martin tells them, is to give Jesse time to finish processing what happened and be able to see the store as a safe place again.

After two weeks, Drew isn't sure it's working. Jesse's nightmares are always bad after a day at work and he's stimming more than Drew has seen. At night he clings to Drew, whimpering if Drew needs to get up to the bathroom or turns over. They don't make love on the nights Jesse has been at work, and when they do make love, he's eager to please Drew but hesitant to relax.

The bus pulls up at the stop and Drew remains seated, letting Jesse get off and come toward him. His shoulders are hunched, he's dragging his backpack; he looks like a small boy, tired after a day at school. A small, broken boy. Drew's heart aches at the sight and he wishes he knew what to do.

"How was work?" he asks, standing up and accepting a hug and a peck on the cheek.

"It was okay."

That's been Jesse's standard reply for two weeks and Drew doesn't like it any better now than he did a month ago when this nightmare started. He longs for the days when Jesse would come home and tell him about lizards and mice and puppies. And rabbits.

Once home, Jesse goes through his routines. Hangs up his jacket and backpack, checks the cushions and pillow slips, curls up in the corner of the sofa with Wicket on his lap and Scamp nosing over his shoulder.

"You want to watch something?" Drew asks.

Jesse shakes his head.

"Can we read?"

For the past week, they've been reading *The Wizard of Oz*. Or rather Jesse has been, his finger beneath the words as he sounds each one out, prompted and encouraged by Drew. It usually takes him an hour to get through a page or two, at which point Drew stops him and they do something else. Reading it was Jesse's idea and he's dogged in his perseverance.

Drew gets the book from by their bed and is about to sit down when there's a knock on the door. When he opens it, he finds Lisa Macey, the prosecutor in charge of David's case checking her phone while she waits.

"Mr Oliver, good afternoon." She looks over his shoulder at Jesse. "Mr Peterson, how are you?"

"Ms Macey, can we help you?" Drew asks. Her presence is unnerving. The last time he had spoken with her, David's lawyer was trying to negotiate another stay in rehab over and it had seemed to Drew that she wanted to agree.

"Could I come in?"

Drew sighs and steps to one side. Jesse has pulled his knees up to his chest, his arms wrapped around them; Drew sits next to him and tries to reassure him. Signals to the lawyer to take a seat.

"I was in the neighborhood and ..."

"I doubt that," Drew says. "Has something happened?"

"David has decided to plead guilty."

Jesse's hand creeps over Drew's thigh and he huddles against him.

"What does that mean?" he asks.

"It means that he isn't fighting us anymore, Mr Peterson."

"Can you call me Jesse?" Jesse asks and Drew smiles to himself. "Does that mean he's going to jail?"

"Well," Macey says, leaning forward so she's speaking directly to Jesse, "I can't promise that, it's not my decision ..."

Drew snorts and glares at her. This is it, this is where she tells them he's going to get away with it. Just like last time. Only this time there's more than broken bones to heal and he's damned if he's going to let it just happen. Lisa Macey holds his gaze without flinching and continues.

"I have recommended a maximum sentence which in this case, given the threat of rape to someone who is incapacitated, the holdup itself, and the aggression and violence, is five years." Drew's surprise must show on his face because she gives an embarrassed grin. "It's unlikely he'll get that but I'm hoping we'll get at least half plus rehab. He'd be out in a year if he behaves but it's a start."

"Drew?" Jesse asks, tugging at his shirt.

"They're going to ask the judge to send David to jail, darlin'."

"Good," Jesse sits up straight but doesn't let go of Drew's shirt.

"We go before the judge on Thursday and we've been assigned Judge Landis. Landis isn't the hardest guy out there but he's reasonable. And he does listen to victims." She looks from Drew to Jesse. "If he hears from them."

"What are you saying?" Drew asks but he thinks he knows damned well what she's saying.

"If Jesse were to read out a Victim Impact Statement, I think that would..."

"No," Drew says, "that's not going to happen."

"Drew?" Jesse asks again.

"Look Mr Oliver, I understand ..."

"No, you don't. A Victim Impact Statement means he would have to see him again and that *isn't* going to happen."

"Mr Oliver, we can lodge a statement from Jesse that will be put in front of the court, but it would be so much more powerful if he read it ..."

"No. You are not using his ... challenges... to score points."

"You would rather he did a couple of months in rehab and walked? Again?"

"*Drew!*"

Drew and Lisa turn to look at him.

"Stop talking about me like I'm not here," Jesse says, and Drew sees the anger flash in his eyes. "*Explain* it to me."

"Jesse," Lisa says, crouching in front of him, "if you come to court on Thursday and tell the judge what David did to you and what has happened since then, we can probably send him to jail for quite a while."

"I still don't understand," Jesse's eyes flick from one to the other. Back again.

"They want you to tell the judge about what happened and about going in the tunnel and your nightmares," Drew says, voice icy.

"Do I have to see him?"

"Jesse, you're ..."

"Yes, I'm sorry, Jesse you would have to. And I'm so sorry, but it's the best chance we have."

* * *

"No."

Drew pours himself a glass of scotch and leans against the kitchen counter. The thought of Jesse having to face David fills him with dread. Even if it goes the way Macey says it might, the risk of it pushing Jesse back into his own head, into The Tunnel is too high.

"I want to do it," Jesse says, and Drew can hear the stubborn tone that is usually reserved for another round of Mario Karts even though it's after midnight or ice-cream instead of vegetables.

"Jesse, they can do it without you. Mr Greenwold can present a statement. We can write one from you that can go in the file..."

"But it won't be as good," Jesse insists.

"It will be fine."

"No, it won't, it won't be fine. It won't ever be fine if he doesn't go to jail."

"Darlin', I understand, really, I do," Drew says, "but I don't want him anywhere near you again. I don't want him getting in your head again."

"Drew, I..."

"No, Jesse, you're not doing it."

He stalks to the bedroom, slams it behind him, and runs his hand over his face. A part of him knows he's being unreasonable but the thought of Jesse disappearing from him again stamps out all rational thought. The door opens, and he senses Jesse in the doorway.

"It's not your decision," Jesse says. "I'm not a kid. I'm not stupid. I'm not retarded."

"Jess..."

Warm hands are slid around his waist and he smiles when he feels Jesse's head against his back.

"Drew, you always say I'm a man. A real man, even though my brain doesn't work properly."

Drew squeezes his eyes shut, fighting fatigue and fear. Jesse continues.

"I'm scared of him, *really* scared of him, Drew. And when I shut my eyes, he's always there. I don't want him to be there and I don't want him to hurt anyone else. I don't want him to hurt you."

Drew covers Jesse's hands with his own, leans his head back on Jesse's shoulder.

"What if seeing him scares you so much, you get lost in The Tunnel again, Jess?" he asks, unable to lift his voice above a whisper.

"You know how to find me."

* * *

52

Max Greenwold takes his seat, folding the piece of paper he's being reading from and slipping it in his pocket. He leans forward and squeezes Jesse's shoulder. Lisa Macey stands and addresses Judge Landis.

"Your Honor, we have one last Victim Impact Statement from Jesse Peterson."

The Judge looks at the gathered group and nods. Drew nudges Jesse.

"You ready?"

Jesse swallows, adjusts his tie, and stands up.

* * *

Looking out at the court room is scarier than Jesse thought it would be. Lisa has told him what would happen but now that it's real, it's different. His parents are next to Drew and his mom has moved over into Jesse's seat now that he's up here. Sue and Peter have come for the day and are sitting next to Ray. Jody is behind Drew, with Mr Greenwold and next to her are Drew's sister Sarah and his niece Mandy. Mandy raises a clenched fist and grins at him.

"Hello," Jesse says to the judge then remembers he's not supposed to say that, "oh sorry."

A small smile flickers over the judge's face and he signals to Jesse to continue.

"I ... I'm a bit nervous," he says.

He has spent the last two days writing his statement, agonizing over the words and refusing to let Drew help him or see what he's written. Jesse focuses on Drew now though, his grey suit, his hair pulled back into a ponytail, his chocolate brown eyes behind his glasses. Drew mouths 'I love you' and Jesse rubs his palms down his suit jacket.

"My name is Jesse Peterson and I'm twenty-seven years old. I work for Mr Greenwold in the pet store. I like animals. I've worked there for nearly eight years. My..." his voice falters, and he takes a deep breath, "my boyfriend is Drew. Andrew Oliver. He's a school teacher. I love him a lot."

He pauses and looks at Drew, smiles. Drew smiles back.

"I have some problems. I'm dyslexic and when I was little they said I was autistic," he turns to look at the judge, "I have some other things too, but I don't think they're important." When the judge nods, he continues. "I'm ... uh... I am eye dee which most people think means I'm retarded but Drew says it just means I don't learn things the way other people do. That I'm a man anyway."

The court room is silent, and it makes Jesse nervous. He's worried the judge might stop listening now that he knows. His mom has gone as white as vanilla ice-cream and Drew is putting his arm around her.

"When Drew and I started being together, you know, like boyfriends, he told me about David. But he didn't tell me all of it until when we were going to the barbeque and then he told me about David hurting him. At the barbeque, David was really mean, and he called me names and he called Drew names and Drew hit him," Jesse turns to the judge again, "but he only did it because he was protecting me, and he broke his hand and I don't want him to be in trouble, okay?"

The judge waves his hand for Jesse to continue.

"When ...when David came into the store, he smelled really bad. Like he hadn't showered and had drunk too much beer. He broke a fish tank and killed the fish. He was um rubbing himself on me like he wanted to um ... have sex ...and he kept trying to touch me ... touch my ... penis ... um.... and then," he looks down at his shaking hands and takes a deep breath, "then he hurt Sniffles. Sniffles was the rabbit we had at the store. I looked after her and she was really tame, and all the little kids liked playing with her."

He can't help it, thinking about Sniffles always make him cry, and he swipes his arm over his face.

"She squealed. It must have really hurt her because rabbits only squeal when they're really hurt or really scared. It was horrible. I tried to stop him, and I tried to help her, but I couldn't. And she died."

Lisa asks if she can approach with a tissue and when the judge agrees, she hands him one and the glass of water at the same time.

"After what David did, I got really scared and sometimes when that happens I get lost in my head. It's like being in a tunnel and not being able to come out; you can hear things from a long way away, but you can't talk to people. It's really warm and really safe in there. Drew knew how to get me out though and he looked after me." Jesse stops and looks at David, fighting the fear that makes him want to drop his eyes. "But he couldn't make it better. I have nightmares. In my nightmares, you hurt Sniffles all the time and sometimes you hurt me and worst of all you try to hurt Drew. You keep trying and I can't stop you. I thought if I went back to work I would be okay, that it might help me feel better because I like my job. But we have a new door and new tanks. And no Sniffles. Because of you. And when there are loud noises it makes me jump and want to hide. The pet store is Mr Greenwold's and it ... it was mine, but you came, and you broke it and now it's not mine anymore. You broke it. Just because I love Drew and he loves me."

David shows no emotion. Jesse looks from him to the group of people in the seats behind him. His mom and Drew's mom are both crying, and Mandy is clinging to her mother. Dad and Peter both look as though they've heard really bad news, like when his grandpa died. Worst of all are the tears on Drew's cheeks.

"You broke it," Jesse continues, "but you still didn't win. Because I still love Drew and he still loves me. And I think that's what you were really trying to break but you didn't. You didn't win. You should go to jail because you hurt Drew and you killed Sniffles and you broke up Mr Greenwold's store but even if you don't, you still don't win. Because you can't stop him loving me." Wiping his face, he turns to face the judge. "I don't have anything else to say, is that okay?"

"Yes, Jesse that's okay," the judge says, "and can I just thank you for the courage you have shown by being here today and sharing that with us. May I also say, that Mr Oliver, Drew, is right, you *are* a real man. A better man than many in this room."

* * *

Three years. Eighteen months without parole.

Drew's fingers, laced through Jesse's, tighten and he shuts his eyes. He's not naïve enough to think everything has been fixed but it's a start. He presses a kiss to the side of Jesse's head.

"I'm so proud of you," he says.

David turns to look at them and Drew squares his shoulders, resists the urge to spit on the man. For one horrifying second he thinks David is going to speak, then he shrugs and follows the bailiff from the room. His dad leans in front of Ray and pats Drew's knee.

"Thank God," he says. "Now, let's go get something to eat."

Drew turns to Jesse.

"Hungry?" he asks.

"Little bit."

Mandy wraps her arms around Jesse's neck.

"You rocked, Jesse. I wish I had met Sniffles."

Jesse twists around and gives her a watery smile.

"Me too."

Mandy turns to Drew. "You rock too Uncle Drew. But only by association."

Drew laughs for what feels like the first time in forever and it feels good.

* * *

Dinner is nice. His mom hovers a bit, checking his plate, and raising an eyebrow when he asks for a third beer; she and Drew don't think he sees the look they exchange but he does. When Jesse comes back from the bathroom, his dad is talking to Drew and he sighs. He sits down next to Sue and asks her how Hairy Harry is.

"He doesn't like this heat much. I'm taking him to the groomer tomorrow, so hopefully that will help."

They talk about Harry until Drew joins them, slipping his arm around Jesse's shoulders.

"Mom, I think Dad's ready to head home."

Jesse puts his head on Drew's shoulder and closes his eyes. It's warm in the restaurant and Drew smells nice; Jesse lets himself drift off listening to the sound of voices washing over him.

"Hey, sleepy head," Drew is stroking his cheek with a finger. He rubs his eyes and sits up. "Want to go home?"

"Yeah. Scamp must be hungry."

Jesse watches his dad and Drew's dad tell Drew to sit down and be quiet, then argue over paying the bill. Accepts hugs and praise from everyone and lets Drew bundle him into the car. They're almost home when he looks down and frowns.

"Where's my tie?" he asks, peering, cross-eyed at the open throat of his shirt which he's pulled out from his body. Drew chuckles and tells him to check his jacket pocket. He pulls the missing tie out and scratches his head. "How did that get in there?"

"Dork," Drew says, pulling into the first spot he finds in their street.

"You're a dork," Jesse retorts through a yawn.

* * *

Jesse hangs his suit up, scratches Wickets head, and sits back against the head board, stretching his legs out in front of him. Pushes the blankets back and sighs. It's been a long day; people kept asking him how he feels now that it's over. How does he tell them he doesn't know? He's not sure how he feels.

A sound makes him look up; Drew is leaning in the doorway watching him.

"What?" he asks.

"I can hear you thinking," Drew says coming over to the bed, puts his glasses on the night table. Jesse pokes his tongue at him, snuggles in when Drew sits down and holds his arm open for him. "It's over."

"How do you know?" Jesse asks and Drew's face drops; he runs his fingers along his jawline. "Why do you look sad?"

Drew sighs.

"Because when I met you, you wouldn't have asked that question," Drew says. "Jess, he's going to jail, and he can't hurt you anymore. Now, we can work on you being happy again."

Jesse thinks about that. He's not *unhappy*, not when he's with Drew or playing with Scamp. There are even times he's happy when he's at work. It's just things are different now; before, sometimes people were rude to him, sometimes they bullied him a bit. Sometimes they were mean. Killing something he loved just because he loved it wasn't mean though, it was ... wicked is the only word he can think of. Worse than even the worst villains in the stories he reads with Drew because those ones aren't real and what David did was real. It feels to Jesse as though his head gets stuck on it sometimes, especially when he goes to work. The feeling of seeing two photographs overlaid isn't as strong but Sniffles' absence bothers him, and it doesn't feel like he can tell people. She was a rabbit, he can see in everyone's eyes; everyone except Drew.

"I'm happy when I'm with you," he says.

"Yeah?"

"Yeah." Jesse tilts his head to accept a kiss.

"That's good, darlin', I'm glad."

This time Jesse reaches up to kiss Drew; lets it deepen into something more, something warmer. Slides down in the bed, bringing Drew with him and for the next few minutes that's all they do. Lay there, chest to chest, kissing. Kisses shift from gentle to hard and back again; tongues exploring and tasting. Jesse winds his fingers in Drew's hair, gives a gentle pull and gets a quiet moan in return.

Drew breaks the kiss and leans on one elbow looking down at him, tracing his thumb over Jesse's face. Whispers that he loves him. Jesse ducks his head and kisses the hollow at the base of Drew's throat, hands smoothing over his body, sliding under the elastic of Drew's pajama pants. Drew helps him take the garment off, then returns to kissing him, chasing his tongue with his own while he eases Jesse's boxer shorts off.

Drew rolls onto his back, pulling Jesse with him. Jesse reaches between them to stroke him; firm, gentle movements that Drew rocks up and into, breath catching each time he lifts his hips up. Drew fumbles in the drawer and finds the bottle of lube. Hold it up for Jesse. Jesse says nothing, just sits back on his heels, biting his lower lip, still stroking Drew's cock.

He takes the bottle and flicks the lid open, dribbles liquid over his fingers. Hesitates.

"I love you," Drew says again, eyes locked on Jesse's face.

Jesse strokes two fingers down Drew, down over his balls, over the skin of his perineum, pushes them past the resistance and curls them.

"Jess," Drew murmurs, hips stuttering up. Still stroking him with one hand, Jesse continues to rub the smooth, silk walls of muscle, scissoring his fingers so they relax. Drew's hands are on his hips, fingers digging in, leaving small purple marks on the skin. "More."

Jesse adds a third finger. When Drew closes his eyes, tipping his head back and moaning, Jesse shivers.

"Please touch me," he whispers. Drew opens his eyes and obeys; smearing pearlescent drops of precome the length of Jesse's aching cock and making him whimper. They match rhythms, hands moving up and down in time with each other; Jesse's fingers providing counter rhythm.

Jesse can't decide what to do so Drew decides for him, wrapping his legs around Jesse's waist and pulling him down so the tip of his cock is nudging the fingers that are stilling circling inside him. When he withdraws his fingers, Drew's moan fades to a whine and he lifts his pelvis up, chasing the lost sensation.

Panting, Jesse pushes in, taking his time. Drew matches his movements to his, rolling up into Jesse's hand and back down on to him. His skin is soft and velvety beneath Jesse's fingers; his nipples are hard peaks and his breath comes in sharp gasps.

"Jesse, don't stop," he tells him, letting go of Jesse's hips and running one hand up Jesse's belly, over his chest, flicking at his nipple. The other hand soothes over the round of Jesse's buttock, kneading and rubbing. "Don't stop, darlin', I'm so close."

His words ricochet through Jesse, sending a shudder through him and he surges forward with a groan, tightening his fist.

"That's it, Jess, that's it," Drew pants, "like that."

Jesse shuts his eyes and gives himself over to the sensations around him. Thrusts into Drew as hard as he can. *Oh God, that feels good.* So good. Drew tightens around him and Jesse knows it won't take much more.

"Jesse, oh Jesus, Jesse," Drew's voice is low and rough and then he's bowing his back, come spilling over Jesse's fingers.

Jesse leans down to kiss him; groans at the hands that press against his head, holding him there while Drew continues to rock against him.

"It's okay, you can let go, Jess," Drew says when he can breathe again. "Come for me, sweetheart. Please."

Jesse curls his hands around Drew's shoulders and thrusts against once, twice, three times.

"Oh God Drew," he gasps, "now, now, now, now, *now.*"

When at last the pounding in his head recedes and he opens his eyes, Drew is looking up him; a gentle smile playing on his lips.

"I love you." Jesse's voice breaks as he dips head to kiss him again.

"Shhhh, it's okay, I love you too," Drew pulls him down against his chest, "I love you too."

* * *

53

Drew reaches back and pulls the elastic from his ponytail, letting his hair fall on shoulders and rakes his fingers through it. Swipes his palm over his face. As usual, since being on vacation he's stopped shaving and let his beard grow in. Jesse, who is as obsessive about shaving as he is about the direction the couch cushions go in, is equal parts fascinated and disapproving of the facial hair. Earlier this morning, at the swimming pool, Drew had had to distract him from pursuing a discussion on what the beard feels like when Drew goes down on him. The conversation had been about as comfortable as this one is shaping up to be. He looks at Ray over the table and searches for the right words.

"You know the last time we had a conversation even remotely like this one, I nearly lost him," he says. Ray purses his lips and nods in agreement.

"I know, but this isn't about how you treat him, it's about his wellbeing."

"He might not see it that way."

Ray asked him after the sentencing to meet him for coffee today, Monday, while Jesse is at work. He wants to talk about what to do. About Jesse. Right now, though, Drew thinks he looks frustrated; he resists the urge to smile, he's seen that look on Ray's son's face many times.

"Drew, we both know that there are limits to Jesse's independence. That there are some things he isn't ever going to be able to make informed or rational or even independent decisions about. Call it processing or understanding or whatever you like, he just doesn't see some things the way they need to be seen."

"Yes, but ..."

"There is no but. You signed on for this, spent most of the past damned year telling anyone and everyone how much you love him and that you're in this for the long haul. Well, son, it's put up or shut up time."

Stung, Drew sips his coffee. He's not sure where Ray wants to go with this conversation about what to do with Jesse and right now he's not sure he wants to know. Ray rubs a hand over his face, scratching at the stubble on his chin.

"I'm sorry, that was unfair. I know you're doing everything you can to take care of him. But I think we both know, he's not settling back in at the store. How are the nightmares?"

Running his finger around the rim of his cup, Drew fights the urge to lie.

"About the same. No worse, but no better," he looks up at Ray, "though Martin says it may take a little while."

"Yes, I imagine it will. Drew, I really don't want you to take this the wrong way, but I need you to think hard about what is right for Jesse at the moment ..."

Drew holds his hand up.

"Look, if you're asking me to walk away, I can't do that. I won't do that. I don't believe it would be the best thing for him."

To his surprise, Ray rocks back in his chair and laughs. It's a rich, genuine sound and Drew waits, one eyebrow lifted, to find out what's so funny.

"Trust me when I say I would no more try and separate you two, than I would stick my head in a lion's mouth. That wasn't what I meant. I think Jesse needs a complete change. A new start I guess."

"Leave the store? It would break his heart."

"There are other stores. In other towns. I know I'm being real unfair asking you and his mother would hate him moving further away but ..."

"But it might be the best thing for him," Drew finishes. Ray's mouth thins into a humorless smile and he agrees. "I've been wondering that myself. And to be honest, I've been thinking about a change of direction myself. Maybe picking up some college credits to teach dyslexic and autistic students, maybe looking at some schools who run dedicated programs for that kind of thing, rather than a bigger school like Central. My concern is I don't want to do the wrong thing and make things worse for Jess."

"Look, I understand, none of us do."

"Ray, when Jess withdrew ...disassociated ... I felt like part of me was missing. And I know how that sounds, I teach poetry for God's sake, trust me I know how it sounds," he huffs a small laugh, staring at his fingers, "but I don't want him to go through that again."

Ray pushes the sugar bowl around the table before speaking again.

"I think if we don't do something soon, that's exactly what will happen. He's running on empty and most of it is because he wants to please you. No, I'm not blaming you but that's how it is, and you have to accept that. Drew, I know you don't want to risk upsetting him like you did the last time, but this is different. And well if he does get upset, just like last time, he'll come around." It's Ray's turn to chuckle. "Your friend Jody is right, you two are sort of nauseating with your mutual admiration thing going on."

"Whatever," Drew says with a smirk. "Okay how are we going to do this?"

"Hey, you're the fancy educated teacher, you tell me."

Drew knows Ray isn't mocking him or trying to hand off responsibility, neither of them knows what to do next. For several minutes they sit in silence, thinking. Drew's phone chime and he glances at it; it's just a marketing email from the hotel in Alberton and he drops the phone back on the table. Then picks it back up.

"Ray, what are you doing on Wednesday?"

"Plumbing," Ray says without missing a beat, "why?"

"I think I might take a drive while Jess is at work and I could use some company." When Ray looks confused, Drew taps on his phone for a moment, and spins it to show him.

"Really? You think that's possible?"

Drew shrugs.

"No idea, but it's worth asking."

* * *

54

"Magical Mister Mittens and Fleas," Jesse sings with a giggle, settling back on the bed with his glass of champagne.

Mister Mittens and Fleas? What the hell? Drew laughs.

"Mister Mistofles, you dork," he says.

"'S what I said," Jesse sips his drink and hiccups.

"Uh huh, you've had enough," Drew takes the glass and sets it on the night table.

They drove up to the city after Jesse finished work earlier and used the tickets Jody gave Drew for his birthday. Jesse was enchanted by the show, loving the makeup and costumes, singing and babbling with excitement about possible cosplay during the walk back to the hotel Drew had booked for the night. The Marriott isn't the fanciest hotel in town, but Jesse appears to love it as much as he did the show, standing on the balcony with Drew, sipping icy champagne and humming *Memory*.

The glass Drew has just taken is Jesse's third. As amusing as the younger man's tipsy state is, Drew doesn't want to risk a hangover tomorrow. Thinking about the next day brings a twinge of guilt that Drew pushes down; he's not going to think about that now. Instead, he crawls up the bed to the headboard and wraps an arm around Jesse's shoulders; rests his cheek on his head.

"Did you have fun?" he asks even though he knows the answer. This is the happiest he has seen Jesse in a long time; there are still black smudges beneath his eyes from broken sleep and he still has flashbacks and nightmares, but he hasn't reached for Wicket once since they got back to the hotel room.

"Yes," Jesse hiccups again, "I wish we could see it again."

Drew makes a noncommittal sound into Jesse's hair, he knows where there is going. Takes his glasses off and puts them next to the champagne glass. All afternoon Jesse has been trying to get him to tell him what they're doing tomorrow and as expected he asks again.

"I told you, it's a surprise," Drew say, nuzzling Jesse's neck.

"I don't like surprises."

"Uh huh, of course you don't," Drew flicks his tongue under Jesse's ear. Jesse tries to twist around to look at him, but Drew holds him in place. "You'll find out tomorrow, okay?"

"Fine," Jesse succeeds in wriggling around. "Can I have my drink back?"

"Nope."

"Why not?"

Drew laughs at the pout.

"Because I have a better idea," he says, leaning forward to kiss him. Jesse's hand is cool against his cheek; it sends a shiver down Drew's spine.

"I'm glad you shaved it off," he says.

"I'm glad you had a good time." Drew smiles and kisses him again, pulls him down on to the bed and slips his hand up the back of Jesse's shirt.

Slow, lazy kisses that taste of champagne soon give way to more urgent ones, filled with heat and need. Drew takes his time undressing Jesse, stroking him, and getting him ready before finally rocking forward, eyes open so he can watch his face. As usual, Jesse's hands are everywhere, wanting to touch and caress and scratch and, when he comes, fingers dig into Drew's hips until there are small purple bruises marking the skin.

"I love you," Drew whispers as he gives into his own orgasm.

* * *

"Come on sleepy head, time to get up."

Drew shakes Jesse again and the head of spiky hair disappears under a pillow. He sniggers and lifts the pillow off.

"Good try, come on you need to get up. We have to go."

"I don't want to be awake," Jesse grumbles. Normally he's the first awake but, Drew concedes, normally he hasn't been to a stage show, drunk three glasses of champagne, and then made love twice. Also, there had been no nightmares and Drew had wanted him to sleep as long as possible, but now, they need to go.

"Well tough. You can sleep in the car. Come on, we have to go."

He looks at his watch; seven thirty. He'd told the Johnstons they'd be there before ten which means they needed to leave ten minutes ago. Jesse sits up and rubs his eyes, accepts a glass of apple juice and drinks it in one mouthful, covering his mouth with the back of his hand when he belches.

"Charming," Drew says. "Shower. Now."

"You're so mean to me."

Jesse reaches for Wicket and rests his chin on the toy, pouting.

"That's not what you said last night, darlin'," Drew yanks the covers back as he kisses him, "now go shower."

While Jesse showers, Drew sends a message to the Johnstons to let them know they're behind schedule. It's impossible to ignore the guilt this morning. It's been two weeks since he and Ray visited Alberton and even though he knows they're doing the right thing, Drew is worried. Regardless of Ray's reassurances, this could blow up in their faces and if it does, it isn't going to be pretty. They've spoken to Max Greenwold – Ray organizing another coffee meeting while Jesse was at work – and he'd agreed this was for the best, but Drew had felt terrible watching the old man struggle with his emotions.

"He's a good kid," Greenwold had said blowing his nose into an oversized blue handkerchief, "and I'm glad he found you Drew. Place just won't be the same without him though."

The shower turns off and Drew rubs his eyes; oh God, this better go right, he thinks.

"I'm hungry," Jesse announces from the bathroom doorway where he's drying off.

"We'll get something to eat on the way."

"Pizza?"

"For breakfast? Nice try. Bagels."

"Donuts," Jesse pulls on his boxers.

"Fine, donuts. Now hurry up."

Grinning, Jess puts his jeans on.

"You love me," he says.

"Mmmmmm."

* * *

Jesse falls asleep as soon as he finishes his second blueberry donut, head lolling against the car window, soft snores filling the car. Drew lets him sleep and turns the radio down, runs through the plan in his mind. They'll go to the farm and talk with the Johnstons about their offer and if that doesn't end in Drew having to coax Jesse out of a tantrum – he refuses to consider anything worse – they'll meet Karen Rodgers, the realtor, in Alberton. If, following that meeting, Drew is still in once piece and Jesse is still speaking to him, they're spending the night in their usual hotel. It's a lot of ifs and the acid burning the back of Drew's throat isn't just a result of bad takeout coffee.

As they approach the road the farm is on, he shakes him, slowing down and hugging the side of the road so he can be sure he's awake. Rubbing his eyes with the heels of his hands, Jesse peers around him. Frowns, then recognition sparks in his eyes.

"We're going to the farm," he says. "Aren't we, Drew? We're going to the farm."

"Yeah, we're going to the farm."

"Will I be able to ride Hazel?"

"Yes, you'll be able to ride Hazel. And George."

"Don't be a dork. George is a dog."

"And you're the dork," Drew retorts.

"Yeah but you love me."

"Maybe," Drew says, glancing at Jesse, heart dropping when he sees uncertainty on his face. "See? You're a dork. Of course I love you."

Jesse relaxes as they drive down the driveway to the parking turnaround. There are already half a dozen cars parked but Jesse is reaching for his seatbelt already. As much as he is reticent around unknown people, the promise of riding Hazel is a big incentive.

Drew comes around the end of the car and takes Jesse's hand.

"Let's go find Brenda."

* * *

54

"You look so much better than the last time I saw you," Brenda tells Jesse. He blushes and ducks his head, not wanting to think about that.

"I feel better." He reaches down to scratch George's huge head with his free hand. Drew squeezes his other hand and smiles but something about the smile looks strange, almost unsure. "Can we go and see Hazel?"

"You sure can," Brenda says, "Mr Johnston is in the stable and I know he'll be pleased to see you."

Brenda gives Drew a funny look as they pass in front of her; it reminds Jesse of when his mom and Drew are about to say he, Jesse, has had enough to eat or enough beer. He resists the urge to roll his eyes and mention that he's twenty-seven. Instead he lets Drew lead them to the stable, passing Pumpkin on the way.

"Hey Pumpkin," Jesse calls. Drew smiles. "What?"

"Nothing. Just thinking how much bigger than Scamp, Pumpkin is."

"That's because he's a farm cat. He might even be part Maine Coone."

Drew snorts and tells him he'll take his word for it.

Mr Johnston is waiting at Hazel's stall for them and raises a hand in greeting.

"Boys, good to see you." He gives them both a rough hug and holds Jesse at arm's length. "It sure is good to see you back to normal."

Blushing, Jesse asks if he can put Hazel's halter on and Mr Johnston holds it out to him. Hand smoothing over her muzzle he eases the halter on the mare and leads her out into the sun. Dallas, the grandma's horse, is already there and saddled. As he reaches for the saddle, Mr Johnston stops him.

"In a minute, Jesse," he says and looks at Drew. "Why don't you two sit over there, Drew?"

Disquiet coils in Jesse's belly. Why does he have to sit over there with Drew? He wants to ride Hazel.

"Jesse," Drew takes his hand and pulls him onto the bench next to him. "I need to talk to you. And I want you to listen very carefully. And...and...not get upset, okay?"

"O-okay." The disquiet is blooming into something more, something bigger.

"I've been offered a job at the Alberton Senior High," Drew says.

"You have a job." Jesse frowns when Drew's smile looks sad.

"Well this is a better job."

"But it's too far away to come here to work. It's like two hours drive and it's further than your mom and dad's place."

"I know," Drew says, "I'd have to move here if I take it."

Panic bursts, sharp and acidic in Jesse's chest, rises up the back of his throat, into his nose and eyes.

"What about Scamp?" Tears are already threatening. "What about *me*?"

Something flashes in Drew's eyes and then he's being pulled into his arms.

"Oh darlin', no, I'm sorry that's not what I meant. You and Scamp would come with me. Jess, I'd never leave you."

Jesse draws back, breathless and confused.

"I don't understand. What about my job?"

Drew takes a deep breath.

"Jesse, your dad and Mr Greenwold and I are all worried about you. You're still having nightmares and flashbacks; you're not sleeping well, you're not drinking properly still. Don't look at me like that, I know you're not." He takes a breath. "Anyway, we had a talk and we think maybe you need a change. You need to be somewhere you're not constantly reminded about what happened."

Jesse scratches his head. It feels as if it's going to explode. They've been talking about him? Why would they do that?

"Jess, we don't think you're stupid or that you can't make up your own mind. We know you can, I promise we do. It's just that we've been really worried about you, darlin', and I promise the final decision is yours. If you really don't want to do this, that's fine too. I can go back to my old job at Central and you can keep working with Mr Greenwold."

It's the last bit that catches Jesse's attention.

"What about my job? I don't think there's a bus route to the store from Alberton."

Mr Johnston chuckles and joins them.

"Jesse, if you decide you do want to move up here to Alberton, well I've been looking for someone to help around here for some time," he says.

Jesse looks around him and bites his lip.

"Work here?"

"You're better with animals than just about anyone I've ever met, you're strong, and I have it on good authority you're a hard worker."

Jesse looks from one face to the other, still confused. Rubs his eyes.

"Can I ride Hazel now?"

Drew pinches his nose, just under where his glasses sit and nods.

"May I come with you?"

"You don't like horse riding," Jesse says.

"No, but I like you. Please, Jess?"

Jesse nods. He's not angry with Drew – or with anyone – he's just confused. They want him to come to Alberton and work here? Won't the nightmares and the flashy things just be the same? It's not like they happen every day. Just ... most days.

Mr Johnston helps them on to the horses and reminds Jesse to stay on the marked trail. He can hear Drew cursing softly under his breath as they begin moving and Jesse can't help smiling.

When they're half way around the trek, Jesse asks if they can stop and just sit a while. Drew agrees and slides off Dallas with a loud sigh of relief. Still holding the reins, they sit on the grass; the horses chewing grass is the only sound they hear.

"It's not fair," Jesse says after a moment.

"What isn't Jess?"

"Everything was good. It was perfect. And then he broke it and now it's ...not good."

"Oh, darlin', everything is fine and if you don't want to do this, it's perfectly fine."

Jesse shakes his head.

"No, it's not. He's everywhere, even though he's in jail, he's everywhere. He broke *everything*, and I can't fix it. I want to fix it, I want to feel right again but I just can't."

He smacks his palms against his head.

"It's because I'm broken and now everything else is too."

Drew's fingers close around his wrists, pulling his hands away from his head.

"No, that's not true. Martin and I think that this isn't just about ... David. You've had a busy year. You met someone and fell in love and that's a big deal. And you moved out of your apartment. And you made new friends. And," Drew clears his throat, "you were attacked. That's a lot for anyone. Jess, I just want to find a way to help you feel better, okay? This is just an idea and if you don't want to do it, we don't have to."

Sighing, Jesse rests his chin on his knees, wrapping his arms around his legs. Drew's hand settles in the small of his back; warm, it feels like home.

"You said that falling in love was a big deal," he says finally.

"Yes."

"Was it big for you?"

He turns to look at Drew who cups his face and places a gentle kiss on his mouth.

"The biggest ever," he says.

"I don't like it when you talk about me when I'm not there, like I'm a child."

"I know, Jess, and I swear that isn't why we did it. We just wanted to help."

Jesse nods. He thinks he understands; he still doesn't like it, but he *thinks* he understands. Stands up and takes Hazel's reins.

"Let's go back."

* * *

When Jesse hands the reins back to Mr Johnston and says he would like to work with him, the farmer gives him a quick hug, then hands the reins back.

"You can start right now. They'll need a good brush both of them and you know where the saddles go. Then we'll have some fried chicken."

Relief washes over Drew, leaving him dizzy, and he sits down for a minute. Frank Johnston sits next to him and grins.

"That bad huh?"

"You have no idea," he says, combing his fingers through his hair.

"Well, seems to me the worst is over now," Frank nods toward Jesse who has put away the saddles and is brushing the horses; contentment in his eyes.

"Thank you," Drew says, "for everything."

* * *

55

He parks the car in front of a small bungalow. There's a woman leaning against a For Sale sign in the front yard, and she waves when Drew gets out of the car.

"Who's that?" Jesse asks.

"Come and find out," Drew pulls him toward the house. "Jesse, this Karen Rodgers. Karen, this is Jesse."

"Hello, Jesse, I've heard a lot about you," the woman says. She's tall and slim with grey hair and kind blue eyes.

"I haven't heard anything about you," Jesse replies and Drew bumps his with his shoulder, mutters 'filter' to him.

"Could I take him through?" Drew asks. Karen nods; the house is open.

Empty, the house smells as though it's been shut up for a while and Drew explains it's been on the market for some time. There's a large kitchen and dining room. This latter opens into a large living room with bay windows out over the back yard. Down the hall are three bedrooms and a bathroom; off the master bedroom is a second, smaller bathroom. They go back to the kitchen and Drew leads them out the back door.

The gardens are overgrown and all but gone. Although someone obviously mows the lawn it hasn't been recently. There's a garage and at the back of it, Drew says, is a small work shed.

"It needs some work," Drew sits on the back step, "but nothing structural. Mostly just paint and stuff."

"Okay," Jesse says.

"Do you think Scamp would like it here?"

Jesse frowns.

"But it's for sale, not for rent. How would we buy it?"

"Well," Drew licks his lips, "I have some savings and we would have to use the money from your apartment. We'd need to get a mortgage, but it wouldn't be a big one and between us we'd be able to handle it."

"Oh." Jesse falls quiet again. Runs his finger along the mossy edge of the step. "Uh my dad would have to sign with me. The bank said he had to when I bought my apartment. Because of the you know..."

"Not necessarily," Drew says and puts his hand in his pocket. When he pulls it out he's holding a plain silver ring between his thumb and forefinger. "If we're married, he won't have to."

He watches Jesse's face. It shifts from confusion to wonderment, back to confusion again.

"Are we ... getting married?" he stammers, still looking at the ring.

"I would like that, Jess, but it's up to you. All of it is up to you."

Waiting for Jesse to answer is killing him. It's worse than worrying about whether he'd understand what they'd been doing. Jesse runs his finger over the ring, as if it might burn or bite.

"Jess?"

Jesse turns to look at him, face solemn and serious, and nods.

* * *

56

"*Jesse!*" Mandy squeals and throws her arms around his neck.

"Hey, I'm the actual uncle here," Drew says taking her parents' coats and holding his hand out for hers.

"Yeah but he's cuter," she retorts. Linking her arm through Jesse's she demands he give her a tour of the house. They've been here two weeks, school started a week ago, and this open house lunch on an autumn Sunday afternoon had seemed a good idea at the time. Now Drew is not so sure. At least one thing is good: Jesse looks better. The nightmares aren't gone but they're bearable and there have been no flashbacks since they got here. He hangs the coats up watching them disappear down the hallway.

"Mom and Dad can't be far away," Sarah says, kissing his cheek and holding out a dish covered in tinfoil. "Where do you want this? The plate is for you guys, Mandy chose it."

Drew shows her where to put the plate and leans around the front door to see his parents arrive and goes to greet them. Dad is tugging something out of the boot of the SUV; a large grill with a bright blue ribbon tied around it.

"Wow. Really?" Drew is touched, even though he's sure it simply means that now, he can destroy food inside and outside. Yippee. His mother holds up a cooler.

"We even brought the chicken and steak," she says.

"Oh God, you two are awesome." Drew leads them around the back to set the grill up. Ray comes out from the kitchen and shakes hands with Peter and they begin to work together Sue goes inside to hug Erin. Rolling his eyes, just a little, Drew returns indoors too.

A fire blazes in the fireplace even though it's probably not cold enough yet; Jesse had insisted on it. Speaking of whom, where is he? Mandy appears at his elbow.

"He's over there by his mom," she says and at last Drew spots him, hugging Scamp to his chest while he talks, and relaxes. "This place is cool. You have three bedrooms – you could convert one to a nursery."

Drew chokes on his mouthful of wine, spraying Mandy with a fine rain of Merlot.

"Sarah," he calls to his sister, "mind controlling your brat?" He turns back to Mandy. "You better not have said that to Jesse, I do not want to spend tonight explaining why we are not having a nursery."

Mandy giggles, kisses his cheek.

"What fun would that be? You on the other hand..."

He swats her rear and sends her to get soda. Just as he's about to go and sit next to Jesse, there's a knock at the door; when he peers around it, his face lights up.

"Jess," he calls over the growing noise. "Can you come here?"

Jesse passes Scamp to Mandy and steps over legs and feet, a puzzled look on his face. Drew pushes him toward the door.

"I think you should get this one," he says.

Jesse swings the door open and freezes. Frank and Brenda Johnston are on the step, holding what looks like a fur muff. The muff wriggles and lifts its nose to sniff the air. Jesse looks back at Drew who smiles.

"Frank says when she's bigger, she can go to work with you. Might even be able to breed her with George if you like. But *you* have to teach her to not chase Scamp." He scratches the Leonberger puppy's ears. They're warm and soft and he takes Jesse's hand and places it on her head. "And if she eats my shoes or my books, I'm going to be grumpy."

He steps back and waits. After a minute, Jesse turns and throws his arms around Drew's neck. When he leans back, Drew is treated to his favorite thing in the world, the only thing that matters now. Maybe, he thinks, the only thing that has ever mattered.

Jesse's smile.

FIN

Thanks

Writing *Jesse's Smile* was only possible because my amazing family put up with hastily thrown together meals, distracted conversations, and a lot of very late nights.

I need to thank the members of several autism support groups on Facebook for welcoming me in, being so candid with me, and teaching me that the biggest challenge they face is not autism but the attitudes around them. Any errors or inaccuracies are mine, not theirs.

Thank you to my beta readers who came to love Jesse as much as I do and for making sure I didn't let him come to too much harm.

To you, my warmest thanks for adding the final ingredient needed to bring Jesse and Drew to life: a reader

And thank you to Jesse for popping into my head one night and telling me his story - I'm forever grateful.

ARJ

January 14, 2018

* * *

About Angelique R Jurd

Former print journalist, Angelique lives in Auckland, New Zealand. She writes contemporary fiction (M/M romance) and non-fiction and is currently completing a Master of Arts in Media Studies with a thesis on the significance of fan fiction.

Angelique, by her own admission, drinks a lot of coffee and champagne, owns an excessive number of Springsteen albums, has a mild obsession with the TV show *Supernatural*, and is owned by four very bossy cats.

* * *

The San Capistrano Series

Book1: The Beach House
Book 2: Tides of Love
Book 3: Winds of Change

The Mason Jar

Hollywood celebrity, Rian Johns has a habit of leaving a mess behind him. Flamboyant, cocky, and intent on having a good time, after being caught by both the police and the media with his pants quite literally down, his studio sends him to cool off and sober up. He shouldn't be able to get in any trouble on the Oregon Coast.

After the death of his son's mother, Mason Andrews came home to Cliffport to raise him. Owner of a small bar and grill, Mason has spent his time focused on his son and his business. Twelve years later, as he prepares for Jake to leave for college, the very last thing Mason Andrews needs or wants is any kind of trouble.

Rian, it seems, has other plans.

AVAILABLE ON AMAZON

Daisy, Yellow

Just months after breaking up with his boyfriend, Noah Jenkins inherits his grandfather's farm and he decides it's time for a change of scenery. He packs his bags, buys a dog, and moves onto the property. When his Labrador puppy Daisy gets hurt he meets local vet Hunter Ross and life starts to look interesting again.

Hunter Ross has always lived in small, conservative Newton, in rural Illinois. At 39 he's never been in love and never had a lover and may have neglected to tell anyone he's close to that he's gay. It's never been a problem – until Daisy, Yellow and her owner Noah show up.

Is Noah's love enough for Hunter to risk everything? Does Hunter have the strength to make the hardest choices he'll ever make and survive?

AVAILABLE ON AMAZON

Connect with Angelique:

Website: http://angeliquejurd.com
Twitter: http://twitter.com/AngeliqueJurd
Facebook: https://www.facebook.com/AngeliqueRJurdWriter/
Facebook: https://www.facebook.com/groups/CocktailsandDenim/
Instagram: https://www.instagram/angeliquejurd/

Made in United States
North Haven, CT
27 September 2022

24599402R00176